£2.0

KU-278-343

1/23

04327064

HIGHBRIDGE

PHIL REDMOND
HIGHBRIDGE

CENTURY

Published by Century 2016

2 4 6 8 10 9 7 5 3 1

First published in Great Britain in 2016 by
Century
Random House, 20 Vauxhall Bridge Road,
London SW1V 2SA

www.randomhouse.co.uk

Addresses for companies within
The Random House Group Limited can be found at:
www.randomhouse.co.uk

The Random House Group Limited Reg. No. 954009

A CIP catalogue record for this book is available from the British Library

ISBN 9781846059858

The Random House Group Limited supports The Forest Stewardship Council (FSC®), the leading international forest certification organisation. Our books carrying the FSC label are printed on FSC® certified paper. FSC is the only forest certification scheme endorsed by the leading environmental organisations, including Greenpeace. Our paper procurement policy can be found at www.randomhouse.co.uk/environment

Typeset in Ehrhardt MT by Palimpsest Book Production Limited,
Falkirk, Stirlingshire

Printed and bound in Great Britain by
Clays Ltd, St Ives plc

To those who know how long this took and helped it along its way – especially Mrs. R who has had to cope with rediscovering what it's like to have a writer in residence.

Prologue

Like most people, Janey knew she was going to die. But like everyone else she just didn't know when. She never imagined nor expected it to be outside the Co-op.

Like a lot of people she was simply looking forward to a great Friday night out with her sister-in-law and gang of mates, so had stopped at the cash machine. She had just got back to her car and was fumbling for her keys when she felt the shove that sent her one way and her bag and keys the other.

Lying sprawled on the ground she saw the indicators flash, heard the doors unlock, and realised she was being mugged. As the engine started she pushed herself up and leaned over the front of the bonnet holding her hands out, instinctively, perhaps in the vague hope that whoever it was would stop before running her down. But when her eyes locked with the wild, dilated ones peering over the nodding Buddha she kept on the dashboard, she knew there was no hope.

The Peugeot 207's low-profiled front end did what it was designed to do and scooped her up to prevent her being run down. Before the car swerved right to throw her off – where she smashed her skull against the car park wall. This in itself might have been fatal, but the carjacker couldn't know this.

But those wild eyes had seen hers. And her eyes had seen the face that contained them. That was why the car stopped. Then reversed. At speed. To run her over.

Then, just in case, the car jumped forward and crushed any remaining life out of Janey. Then, again, to make sure, reversed. Then leapt forward over what was now nothing more than a lifeless shape. To escape. Swinging out into the High Street and off into the night.

The withdrawal receipt from the cash machine fluttered and blew in the backdraught, coming to rest against the lamppost that illuminated the place where Janey had died. The latest random casualty of the so-called war on drugs.

The receipt was for £45. It was all she had had. Just enough for a night out. Or a night's supply.

Janey never knew her killer. Neither did Buddha. Three years on, nor did anyone else.

1

Coming Home

The trouble with living in a mediocre town is that you end up having to support a mediocre football team. Something might happen every forty years when, somehow, they get to something like the semi-final of a cup competition. Everyone gets excited. Mayors make fatuous speeches about it being an historic day. Then 95 per cent of the fans are disappointed because the ground is too small to hold them all. Then they get whacked and everybody goes back to sleep for another forty years. But at least they tried. Typically British tosh.

Well, it used to be like that until Sky Sports came along. Now you can see Arsenal and Chelsea shirts in every High Street. And even Man U in cities like Newcastle and Liverpool. At one time that would have been like wearing a suicide vest. These days, it's just kids following the telly, isn't it?

It was one of Joey Nolan's recurring themes as he drifted in and out of consciousness, during his weekly journey home. Back to Highbridge. Where once was a rural village with rural villagers with rural mentalities is now a sprawling urbanised place on a map. A collective of urban dwellers. With urban dwellers' mentalities. Home is where the Internet is.

The town owed a lot to its inn, the Lion, still at its centre but once a famed stopover for its game pies. Then the canal came by and after that the railways, which took the pies the length and breadth of Britain and then the four corners of the Empire. In Rawalpindi and Christchurch they knew of Highbridge pies. And in return people came to see for themselves. This tiny village that supplied the Empire with pies. And so the street market that sold the pies grew. To become a thing in itself.

Joey grinned when he recalled this bit of history. How where he lived was because someone, at some time, made a great pie. But everything has to start with one idea, he mused, just as the train crossed the motorway. The latest transport revolution, with the strings of pearls and rubies of commuter traffic stretching into the distance. No time for buying pies or napping in that lot, he thought, starting to stir himself as he knew it was now only a few minutes to where the Romans once paused, as did the Saxons, long before it had become the site for a new town, complete with its own industrial estate built not on any entrepreneurial instinct, like that of the piemakers, but from a post-Second World War recovery plan and managed economy.

Out went rationing and dried bananas and in came nylons and the transistor. Gone was rural deference and knowing one's place, replaced by the promise of a welfare state and the white heat of technology where people never had it so good. Or so everyone thought.

For a decade or two they made white goods, nuclear components and secretive parts for the military. But with old technology. And an increasingly expensive as well as increasingly unwilling workforce. The signs of decline were there but nobody wanted to look. Nylons and fresh veg were gradually squeezed out of the market by tights, bin bags and previously owned DVDs. The pies of Empire are still sold in the supermarket where the cattle market used to be, but now they come in artificial atmosphere packaging, delivered by tailored Euro-lorries from the factory in Kent which is owned by a secretive family from Wisconsin who promised to protect jobs but never said which or where.

The factories were razed. Industrial estates became business or retail parks and every now and then money arrived from various European social funds to build inappropriate leisure facilities in inappropriate places. Rural idyll replaced by political ideal. But there are only so many discount three-piece suites you can buy and only so many hours at the health club when either you don't have a job or spend all your time commuting, thought Joey, watching the metal lattice of the railway bridge glide past the window as the train slowed on its approach to Highbridge Station.

He once asked his dad why it was called Highbridge and was told it was because it was higher than the old road bridge. For years he believed this, until Sister Maria had pointed out that it had been called that in the Domesday Book, long before Robert Stephenson and his dad George gave railways to the world. Amazing what you take off your dad when you're a kid.

Joey stood and stretched his aching six-foot frame, then reached up for his holdall. It wasn't there. What the—? He looked up and down the carriage but half were asleep and the others a thousand miles away, tethered to the Internet or their iPods. Then he saw it. The luminous logo. Passing the window.

He grabbed his coat and went up the carriage in the same direction, hitting the platform just in time to see his oversized sports bag heading up the stairs, across the bridge, over the track and towards the station exit. With the weary commuters and weekenders congealing on the stairs and the train still blocking the route across the tracks, Joey decided to go under them. Over the fence into the overflow car park, down the slope and through the underpass.

As Joey turned into the underpass, a couple of miles away, on the hill overlooking Highbridge, his lifelong friend and brother-in-law, Luke Carlton, was pressing his weather-worn face against the buffer, looking down the scope of a Barrett M82A1 suppressed sniper rifle. 'Where'd Billy get this?' he asked.

'Where'd you think? He's just got back home.'

'God Bless America. God Bless al-Qaeda,' whispered Luke, as he turned the ring on the Leupold scope to bring the fat target in the chippy into sharp focus. Nearly a mile away. One squeeze. No frying tonight.

Just under a mile from Luke, on the other side of the hill, Joey's brother Sean was coddling his suntanned face in thick Egyptian cotton as he emerged from his waterfall shower. As always, Sean took too long in the shower for the environmentalists but he reckoned he'd already put in a life's worth of sacrifice as a child, when he, his brother and sister were allowed just one bath a week and then only after the immersion heater had been on for twenty-five minutes. No more. No less. Regardless of time of year, regardless of the water temperature. Now he enjoyed the luxury, probably indulgence, of having constant hot water, his conscience salved by the fact that the water came from a water butt, was heated by solar, used less than a bath and was more fun for two to share.

That would be part of the theme of his speech tonight. Another after-dinner. He'd talk of those memories. The clichéd tales of waking up to iced-up toilets and curtains frozen to the windows. But as he always said, clichés were only clichés because they were truisms. Like, how do you break the chain that stretches from childhood poverty to adult crime?

Yes, he'd give the tale another outing tonight. How he and his siblings had started in deprivation but by their own endeavours were now doing relatively well. How their friends all took different routes but only a few followed a criminal path, and even then often through circumstance rather than choice. And now, how he is wealthy enough to have constant hot water and a body dryer, despite the angst around global warming competing with that instilled by the Christian Brothers, and how the Venerable Bede, the patron saint of writers, taught him to fight for the things you think are important. The things you cherish. Like your life. On the number 10 bus. A memory that took him to where he didn't want to be. Remembering what had happened to his sister.

It was that same early education in survival that drove Joey, as he came out of the underpass and vaulted the fence into the car park opposite the station exit. He came up behind a parked Audi Q7 and, as he passed, tapped on the window and dropped his shoulder bag on the bonnet, nearly causing his wife Natasha to spill her cappuccino into her lap, but then watch, first puzzled, then with rising alarm as she saw her husband slip into that all too familiar purposeful swagger. Even under the bulk of the CAT insulated twill jacket that masked his fit but slender body shape, she could see him stiffen. Shoulders back, arms at his side, fists clenching and unclenching. Then she saw the spin of his hand. She started up and waited. For trouble. For someone.

Two miles further on, three girls were walking down the appropriately named Hill Street towards the equally appropriately named High Street.

'I'm just saying, he's a psycho.'

'You think everyone's a psycho.'

'Five per cent of people are psychos.'

'You just hate him because he's foreign.'

'Christ, will you two give it a rest.' It was the tall one, Tanya Nolan, Sean's niece, Joey's daughter. The one with the ASOS oversized bucket bag. She was walking between her two friends, Becky, the short one, with the now scuffed Stella McCartney Python tote bag, and Carol, the medium one, with a leather Topshop slouchy holdall. All were in jeans. Parkas pulled tight and arms folded, huddled against the cold. They were all in boots. Tanya and Carol in worker's. Becky in biker's.

'It's five per cent are deviants. Not psychos,' Tanya added as she hit the pedestrian crossing button but didn't stop to wait for green.

'Well, he's a deviant, then,' insisted Carol, following automatically.

'What about hating foreigners? That's deviant,' countered Becky, as she hesitated and looked right, left and right again. But quickly.

'It isn't. Deviancy is when you stray from the norm. Right, Tan?'

Tanya refused to comment. She, like her dad, always seemed to end up playing the role of mediator. And like her dad, sometimes wished other people would sort out their own issues.

'You saying that being racist is the norm?' Becky fired back at Carol.

'No.'

'You just did. You said hating foreigners is normal.'

'I didn't.'

'You did.'

'What am I supposed to do now? Say "didn't"? And then we grab hair and have a catfight?'

'You said—'

But Tanya cut across them. 'Will you stop it? It's like a bad version of some big celebrity reality slag-off.'

Back at the station, two other deviants from the norm were about to collide as Joey's bag came out of the door. The guy carrying it was busy checking back over his shoulder so had no idea that Joey was about to stand in front of him; no idea that Joey was pulling his beanie down to cushion his own forehead, nor any warning that Joey's head was about to hit his own. He went down under the force and a cascade of sincere-sounding apologies from Joey.

'Sorry, mate. Really sorry. You OK?'

This had the desired effect of guiding the slowing onlookers on their way. Especially as Joey knelt down as though to administer further aid. The guy looked far from OK. Groggy. Blood running from his nose.

'Don't move too quickly. Take it easy.' Then, more quietly, 'It's not like on the telly, is it? It really hurt, yeah?' Then quieter as he leaned in. Closer. And flicked the bagman's nose. 'Like that. Looks broken. Hope so anyway.'

Bagman was now starting to look more wary than shocked.

'Yeah. Weren't expecting that, were you? Like I wasn't expecting you to carry me bag off the train for me, you thievin' get. Now go, before I break every other bone in your body.' Joey leaned back, with a cheery smile for the benefit of the last onlookers. 'You'll be OK, mate.'

Bagman hesitated, but saw the cheery smile fade and didn't like what replaced it. He rolled to one side and was already up and running as a jobsworth approached from the station.

'Oi. Did you just go over the fence on the other side?'

'Yep. And?'

'Do you have a ticket?'

'For what? Jumping the fence?'

'Don't get smart with me, lad.'

'OK,' said Joey, handing over the ticket.

'Then why did you jump the fence?'

'Never been one for sitting on them.' Joey turned and walked away towards the car park. He never saw the bag snatcher again. He didn't want to and he didn't care. His body loosened. His smile returned. His mind had already moved on. To Natasha. As she brought the Q7 alongside.

Sean was standing under the body dryer for a last blast of warm air to help dry his hair and beard, looking across to the floor to ceiling mirror. Sandra's right, he thought, we shouldn't have that mirror there. There are other ways of demonstrating success than carrying round a pot belly, even it was all paid for. She preferred jewellery. He liked having a body dryer in his bathroom. The eco-warriors and anti-carbonists would hate it, though. Having an electric heater to save drying yourself with a towel is a bit OTT, he knew. But it was fun.

Perhaps I should include that in the talk tonight, he mused. How the carbonists had started to make everyone feel guilty about switching on anything electrical. And never mind all the talk of asking the Indians and Chinese not to follow the same path to industrialisation that we had trodden, it's hard enough for people like himself, who had had to develop mountaineering skills to traverse from the bedroom he shared with his brother Joe to the kitchen. Every morning. Clothes bundled in his arms he'd go down the wooden banister, then use the skirting boards to shimmy his way along the hallway before swinging on the kitchen door to land on the seat near the cooker. All to avoid having to walk on the glacial surface of the quarry-tiled floors. He'd light the grill to warm up the kitchen while he got washed and dressed at the sink, using the pan of water his mother had boiled before heading off for work as a cleaner at the local Comp where Joe and Janey ended up going.

Those skills were learned because he had passed the old eleven-plus, which meant he had to go to the grammar school across town. Which meant he had to get a bus. Which meant he had to leave the house by 7.30 and be in school at 8.30, while the others fell out of bed to a warmed-up house at 8.30 to walk the 300 yards to the Comp. And they would be home at four, while Sean had to battle his way back across town to get back by five. His parents might not have named him Sue, but they certainly sent him out with a target on his chest. That badge of St Bede on his blazer pocket.

The childhood memory, like all the others, had started to become bittersweet, taking on the rosy tint of lost innocence. A time before responsibility pressed in and grief started to visit. Like every child who wakes up suddenly an adult, he had come to accept that one day he would lose his mum and dad – but not his sister Janey. Even the cat and dog fights he and Joey had had with her were becoming cherished memories. Which was why he was now spending less and less time fretting over trying to persuade the Chinese to buy an extra sweater rather than build another power station, and more and more poncing about, as his brother Joe put it, with after-dinner speeches on the charity circuit. If they couldn't stop people like Janey being killed on their own streets, then what was the point of everything else?

'What was all that about?' Natasha asked as Joey dropped into the car and leaned over to kiss her. She smelt good. She always did.

'Mediocre dickhead in a mediocre town. Product of what our Sean calls the cycle of deprivation.'

She knew better than to take the bait, so pointed the car in the direction of home, via the underpass Joey had just run through. He looked at the graffiti and piss stains and smiled as he let his mind go back to the time he kissed Margi Hewland under there when he was fourteen. That's the thing about kids today, he thought. They never get to learn the shortcuts. No need. No hot pursuit. No door to door. No reading the clues trying to track the gang. Now it was all precision rendezvouses by GPS. Live feeds from their mobiles.

'You have to break the continuum, don't you?' It was Luke's spotter, Matt O'Connor, lying next to him. And, like him, wearing black Gelert packaway waterproofs over his Helly Hansen jacket and jeans. Equally effective in the dark, cheaper and less conspicuous than cammos. Matt rolled to one side, reached down and massaged the scar on his inner thigh. He'd started to notice that the pressure cramps were coming more frequently, a consequence of age. And weight. Although medium build, he'd always been referred to as stocky in youth, then as a bull of a man, but now he was veering towards rounded. One of life's natural sociologists, always quick to find the black humour in life, believing it was naïve to be surprised by anything people do. They are, as he often says, only human, but Matt also believed that every day is a crossroads and it is up to everyone to decide which turning to take next. Some choose a selfish route, others tend towards helping others. Each is a choice. Each comes with its own consequences.

'Take out all the warlords at once,' he continued as he shifted his weight from the scar. 'Otherwise, pop one, another steps up. Slot 'em all. Or, give their women the vote. They'd soon be bogged down putting up shelves and decorating instead of blowing up marketplaces. Democracy. They're going to have it whether they like it or not.'

'Great idea. And end up like us? Not having a clue who or what we are voting for?'

'You never voted.'

'That's not the point.' Luke turned, his tall frame extending a foot or so beyond Matt's boots. He was still trim, almost angelic looking. When he chose to be. More often the angel of death, but the transitions were getting harder as the ageing cracks started to multiply. If Matt was the sociologist, Luke was the philosopher. Which made him one of life's squad leaders, but also deepened the cracks. Understanding why people committed evil did not prevent it. Or excuse them. But it made killing them easier.

'In a democracy, O'Connor, you're supposed to ask. Not sit round carving it up for yourself. The political class we now seem to have are as bad as the herders round their campfires.'

'What did you expect? They'd phone you up or something?'

'Why not?' Luke went back to his scope. 'They've got my mobile. They've got all our mobiles. No point havin' GCHQ, MI6, Echelon or Homeland Bloody Security if they haven't.'

Matt laughed. 'They could just send out a sort of national emergency text, like: Do you, or do you not, agree with nuking Europe. Text one for yes. Or three for no.'

'I vote we focus on tonight's target and sort out the voting system tomorrow.'

Matt rolled back to his spotting scope to see the chippy owner getting into his daily opening routine. 'I know I've put on a few ounces, but he's like a bin bag full of balloons.' Then, without a pause, 'Are we going to slot him?'

'Dunno,' Luke replied and then grinned. 'Do we get to vote on it?'

'Do you care?'

'Gave up caring in Somalia.'

'We weren't supposed to be there, remember. And Janey definitely wasn't there, Luke.'

'But we were. And I was. When it happened.' It was as harsh as it was still raw.

Matt had learned over the past three years that, unlike

his thigh, this was an open wound, but he never gave up trying. 'You couldn't have done anything. It was just one of those crap wrong place, wrong time things.'

Luke knew his friend was right, but it never made it any easier. Why should Janey have been in the wrong place at any time? Just because of pieces of filth like the one in his scope right now. He tightened his finger. One small squeeze. Then he felt Matt's version of the Vulcan nerve pinch on his shoulder.

'He's the bait. Bigger fish to fry.'

Luke hesitated for a moment, but then relaxed his finger. 'Was that an attempt to defuse the moment with humour, Dr O'Connor?'

'Only following orders.'

'I hate democracy.'

'That is the point, mate. It makes it inconvenient for psychos like you.'

The girls were heading along the High Street. In silence, heading for Sanderson's, one of the few remaining independents to survive the supermarket wars, passing the local hoodies loitering with intent outside the Lion. Intent on doing what was always open to question, but typically one detached himself from the pack to stand blocking their path.

Tanya instinctively reached for her phone. Becky and Carol instinctively stepped off the pavement to walk round. The hoodie instinctively turned and watched them, with a power grin. Until he suddenly felt himself knocked sideways. He spun round ready to confront whoever it was but hesitated as he took in the big brown eyes, big lashes and bigger hair as Tanya, apparently busy texting, looked up from her phone, and was right in his face. 'You're in the way.'

Another instinctive reaction, as Hoodie stepped back. Meekly. The ASBO manual didn't tell him how to deal with Barbie on steroids.

'No need to apologise.' Tanya threw the comment and her hair back over her shoulder as she strode away, leaving Hoodie to sidle back to the pack, all of them obviously enjoying his moment of discomfort.

'If anyone's a psycho, it's you,' said Becky as she looked back at the brooding hoodie, kicking out at one sidecrack too far.

Tanya just grinned as she strode on. The young lioness. Her father's daughter. And like Joey, she never realised how much she intimidated people. She was also her mother's daughter and, like Natasha, she never realised that a lot of it was because of the way she looked. Just as she still couldn't accept that she had been in real danger a fortnight before when she was clawing and scratching at some randomer who had tried to snatch not hers, but Becky's bag. And why Joey had gone over the edge.

'Do you know why each generation is taller than the next?' Joey was still musing as Natasha guided the Q7 on to the so-called expressway.

'Am I supposed to say nutrition?'

'You are, but it's communication. Each generation learns how to communicate better so they don't wear their legs out looking for each other.'

'Is that the sort of thing you think about on that train every Friday night?'

'Nah. I have much better things to think about than that.' He reached across and felt for the telltale bump under her thick woollen skirt.

'I don't know why you like these stupid things. They're freezing in this weather.'

'And I don't know why you keep asking. You know I'm damaged. Sexually abused as a kid.'

'Oh, you think being seduced by the woman next door amounted to sex abuse, do you?'

'It'd count now. Just a male fantasy then. But that's it, isn't it. It left me vulnerable. Conditioned. Well, it'd be groomed now. Susceptible to manipulated media images of sexuality.'

'Spent all week looking at pin-ups in the mess room, more like.'

He turned and grinned. 'Exactly. Only that lot can only dream. I've got the real thing.'

She laughed. She always did. Just as she always denied her own looks. Something Joey put down to his mother-in-law, which she would tacitly admit on the rare occasions he could get her to see how she had everything other women paid good money to achieve.

A childhood spent learning to be self-deprecating. A childhood that led to a life of self-criticism. A childhood conditioned by the manipulations of a demanding mother.

Even when she had lived up to the expectations of doing well in her A-levels, her mother had criticised the fact that she only got one A while her friend got three. Because Natasha was brighter. Which she was, but suffered the irony of a proud mother suffocating her by being over-demanding. She had decided not even to try for university, opting instead for one of the new regional colleges of further education, where she studied graphic design. Her mother, being a nurse, had wanted Natasha to do better and become a doctor, although her father, on being told of her plans, was delighted, having always regretted becoming a quantity surveyor rather than an architect. He wanted someone to take up his lost spark of creativity.

Unfortunately, his untimely death from cancer meant he never lived to see her achieve her degree, and was probably also a reason why she took up with Joey. He was strong and supportive when she needed someone to fill the gaping hole in her life. She stayed with him because she got to lean on him, not his reputation. And discovered the man she then fell for. And he had been smitten from the moment she showed any interest.

Joe squeezed her thigh and looked across. Like him, she was buttoned up, head to toe against the cold. But instead of Screwfix work gear, an All Saints Fin jacket masked the heavy, but practical sweater and skirt, creating an almost androgynous shape. Only the waves of perfume and hair suggesting what may lie beneath. The deep brown hair she had passed on to Tanya, but because of which, she was always threatening to cut it short. The eyes. Also brown, but always bright, sharp and mischievous that pointed to her Irish ancestry. As did her tongue. Never short of an opinion on anything and everything, but usually correct, and an ability to talk to anyone, about anything, which was probably one of the main things Joey admired about her. He preferred to keep his opinions to himself and couldn't see the point of small talk, accepting that if it were not for Tasha, their social life would be extremely limited.

This train of thought looped back to his mother-in-law. 'How's your mum been this week?' he turned and asked.

Natasha gave a weak, sad smile. 'OK. Just OK. Sometimes she's as bright as she always was. Then . . .' She gave a sad shrug. 'But it's only going to get worse. And I'm still learning to go with the flow, as the doctors said. Correcting her all the time only makes things worse.'

'They sure she's losing it? My mum's always been scatty. And she's nursing people with dementia.'

That started to bring the smile back to Natasha's face, helped by Joey reaching across and stroking the back of her neck. 'I love you, you know. Especially for coping when I'm not here to share the load.'

She didn't reply. She didn't really want appreciation.

She wanted him home. But she didn't want to tell him that. They had made the decision for the future. So she just reached up and held his hand in acknowledgement.

This was something else her mother had drummed into her. Almost contrary to the self-deprecation. Independence. An independence that made her more than a mental match. He could quite easily have ended up on the wrong side of the law, if she hadn't been there to drag him back and keep at him to finish his electrical qualifications. She earned enough working at the local newspaper to allow him time to go on the training courses, until it was bought by a national group and things were rationalised. Which meant she was out of a job, but fortunately just when Joey started bringing in cash. She did the books during the first pregnancy, with Tanya, and had done so ever since, with a bit of coaching from her brother-in-law Sean. That developed into doing the design work for the garden centre promotional literature, which in turn led to a few other small contracts and from that she started selling cards and wall prints on Etsy.

Joey was still looking at her with all this running through his mind. Brains and beauty. It didn't get much better. She could easily have won the last Rose Queen title, before it was hounded off the social calendar by the townies, just as much as his sister-in-law Sandra, Sean's wife, but Tasha never had any interest. Unlike Sandra, who still thought she held the title, which she did in a way, so appeared to dress the part. Joey sometimes thought it would be nice if Tasha dressed more girlie, but always ended up smiling. If she put herself out more she wouldn't do this for him. He ran his fingers over the armoured cloth that disguised the suspender clasp again, causing her to glance across with a knowing, wicked grin. She could turn it on when she wanted to. But only for them.

'You'll have to control yourself tonight, though. Tanya's having a gathering.'

Joey groaned. 'What happened to wanting her freedom and individuality? And staying out later than I say she can?'

'Something to do with them all wanting to protect Becky from some bloke who's been pestering her.'

'Oh great, not only babysitting but we're likely to have a bunch of blokes round on the sniff.'

'Think it's a bit heavier than that. And anyway, thought you always wanted to know where she was.'

'I can know without having her in the house on a Friday night. They must have figured that out by now. Alex and Ross go to their mates. Lucy goes to ballet. Tanya thinks she's sneaking off to the pub without me knowing. That's what Friday nights are about. It's taken quite a bit of logistics to get that organised.'

'Calm down. Another few hours won't kill you. And as far as the kids are concerned we don't do sex. Urrghhhh. Gross.'

Joey smiled. Another of life's great truisms. And,

unfortunately, more and more so as the kids got older. Kids really are life's natural contraceptives.

Breaking the chain. Yes, that would be the theme for tonight, Sean thought as he reached for his dress shirt. How we need to break the cycle of deprivation that leads people into petty crime and anti-social behaviour, that in turn condemns them to a life of missed opportunity and social prejudice. Once branded, how do you redeem yourself?

Yes, he'd talk about his own life, and perhaps that of his siblings. How they had come from the wrong side of town but had taken different paths. Both he and his younger brother Joe had passed the old eleven-plus and while he thrived at St Bede's, Joe didn't. Despite what Joe said about not hacking the academic bit, long disproved by breezing through his electrical qualifications, the truth, as Sean had included in his Best Man's speech at Joey's wedding, was that he dropped out because he was a randy sod and didn't fancy turning gay.

His sister Janey on the other hand, he had found out later in life, had pre-empted any such decisions by deliberately failing the eleven-plus so she wouldn't be separated from her friends. All of whom she stayed in touch with and all of whom turned up at the funeral. Who was really the brightest of them all?

Yes, Sean thought, his own life story, from college-pud, uni-geek and accountant to hippy garden centre owner has always gone down well at the charity dinners, especially since his sister Janey's senseless death. Tonight was about yet another anti-drugs initiative. How many had he been to? Better detection. Better prevention. Better education. Better medical help. Better counselling. He'd given up counting, but the emerging pattern was obvious. Whatever people tried, it didn't seem to work. Usually because of two things. Short-term thinking and independent action. Not thinking far enough ahead, and therefore not providing adequate funding, and trying to work in isolation. But there was never one reason for people getting into difficulties, so how could there be one solution?

Tonight, it was Stepping Stones. Or 'stepping on stoneheads', as Joe called it, but in reality a charity that wanted to give ex-offenders somewhere to go. Where they could get help with their particular problems and avoid slipping back into the drug culture. Not to find an immediate answer, but to be guided towards people who might have one. Sean got it. Give them a stepping stone. A place they can gather their thoughts and get themselves together. To work out what to do next and not, as brother Joe was quick to point out, where to get their next score.

Sean knew that his brother was playing back popular sentiment, and within it a fundamental truth – most ex-offenders did reoffend – which was why tonight he would float a new idea. Instead of wasting time constantly trying to raise money, like tonight, to help the charity, so they could go on trying to persuade employers to take on ex-offenders, why not make it a statutory obligation? Part of the rehabilitation ethos of the judicial system. All local authorities must give ex-offenders a job on release. It was simple. If any organisation should have the capacity to handle ex-offenders, it should be the public services. But another great public truth stood in the way. Would any politician have the guts to do it? Probably not. Sean zipped up his trousers and fastened the waistband. Tighter than last time. When it came to diet, he too was a recidivist.

'You have to break from tradition, see, Luke. Tradition encourages traditional thinking that leads to risk aversion and then inertia.' Matt was also still musing as he prepared to slip out on the daily coffee run. The one operational luxury they permitted themselves.

'And this is more of you trying to manage my PTSD and steer me away from my particular problem, and grief, is it? Engage me in the more general scenario relating to the global drugs trade?'

'Yep. But it's not just drugs, is it? It's like all crime. Or conflict. Or corruption. Like when we went over to Basra. Round 'em up. Explain that there's a better way to make a buck than turning over the neighbours. And if, or when, they didn't embrace democracy, hand out a good smacking. If we do it over there, why don't we do it here?'

'Which, I think, is why we are here,' Luke said. 'How far do you reckon that is?'

Matt brought the spotting scope up to his eye. 'Twelve

hundred. Downhill. No wind. Back soon.' He pulled off his waterproofs and slid out of the hide.

The Barrett is generally considered an anti-material weapon with an effective range of 1800 metres but a maximum range of around 6800 metres, although at that distance it was more for harassment than accuracy. At 1800 metres its job was to stop vehicles by punching a hole in an engine block. But that took a bit of time as the fluids leaked and the engine seized. Unless you got lucky and took out a steering rod or ball joint. Every sniper knew that the best way to stop a vehicle was to kill the driver. For that Luke would have preferred an Accuracy International L115A3, but at 1200 metres a No. 1 Sniper, like Luke, could use the Barrett to kill the fat lump he now had centred in his scope. It did not have to be a precise head shot and he could also do it with much less remorse than he had when shooting at the Taliban. At least, he thought, they were fighting for something they believed in, no matter what you made of it, but as far as Luke was concerned, the guy running the chippy was nothing. A parasite feeding on the community. A canker or cancer to be taken out. Maybe not tonight. As tonight was about the explosive force the Barrett could deliver. The shock and awe of blowing things apart. One night, though. Soon. Perhaps tomorrow.

'His face, though.' Carol was scanning the pizza across the self-service till. 'He probably thought it was Buffy Croft, the Hoodie Slayer or something.'

Becky laughed, then reverted to default anxiety. 'But, what if he'd been like that loser with the knife the other week, Tan?'

'As if. That 'tard was Barry Lupton's little brother. He probably hasn't even got hairs between his legs yet.'

'Probably about all he's got down there,' said Carol. 'We can't have this one.' She was reading the ingredients on the pizza box. 'The chicken's reconstituted.'

'How do you know?' asked Becky, taking the box from her.

'It says "made from" not "made with". If it's "from" that means it's mushed up bits pressed into a shape. If it's "with" it means whole pieces.' She headed off into the shelving maze.

Becky waited for her to disappear between Meals and Soups before she turned back to Tanya. 'What do you really think? About Huz?'

'Do you really want to know?'

'I'm asking.'

'I know, but do you really want to know the answer? Or do you just want reassurance that Carol's got one of her things going about him? Did you put this Cookie Dough in?'

'You sound just like my mum.'

'Did you?'

'Er, yeah. Sorry. It's just that . . .'

'What, missing your Pharaoh and need some comfort food?'

'I'll put it back.'

'No way. It means I can keep my Cookies 'n' Cream.'

'You didn't answer my question.'

'You didn't answer mine.'

'You sure you really want to know?'

'Well, yeah.'

'OK. He's creepy.'

Tanya was right. It wasn't exactly the response Becky was hoping for.

'Is she in all night then?' Joey finally asked, as the Q7 came across the old Victorian swing bridge into Highbridge. He had been sitting brooding, trying to figure out how to salvage something of his planned evening. He'd been thinking it through since Wednesday when she told him both the boys were going to be going on sleepovers. With Lucy out at ballet, for the first time in God only knew when they would have the house to themselves for most of the evening. They usually only had an hour by the time they got back from the station, before he had to start his regular Friday night taxi collection service. Stay by the corner. Don't speak. Just drive. He knew the drill.

'Don't know. She just said that she and Carol were trying to keep Becky occupied and away from some bloke.' Natasha leaned over and squeezed his thigh. 'But thanks for the flowers.'

'Why, though?'

'Because yellow roses are my favourite. And because I love the way you love me.'

Joey looked across and she had that wicked grin again. 'And I love the way you love me too, but why is Tanya keeping Becky under house arrest?'

'She'll tell me tomorrow.'

Joey gave an exaggerated exhale of breath. Fed up. 'My daughter's sabotaging my homecoming and you haven't even got the inside track to gossip about. Should have agreed to go out with the lads over to—' But he was interrupted by a sharp blow to his right biceps as Natasha's left arm lashed out, just as he spotted something, or someone, on the side of the road. 'Pull over. Just for a sec.'

'What for?'

As soon as she stopped he was out of the car and moving towards the Costa. Natasha turned to see Joey hand-clutching and shoulder-hugging Matt who was now carrying a couple of to-go's and a panini bag.

'How's it going?' Joey asked.

Matt glanced across at the car and waved to Natasha as he spoke.

'Does she, er, know anything?'

Joe just looked at him. Get real.

Matt nodded. 'Friggin' freezing up there in the wind, but we've got the fatty's POLO down to the minute. We know more about him than Tesco do on his Club Card.'

'Er, what's his POLO?' Joey asked, once again bewildered by jargon.

'Pattern of Life Operations. Another yankism,' Matt explained.

'You positive it's happening?' Joey asked.

'Positive,' Matt confirmed. 'He slips the gear in with the fish and chips. Just have to know the right combo to ask for.'

'What? Fish and chips with salt, vinegar and throw in a bit of crack?'

'It's slightly more subtle than that. But, basically, yeah. Cod is coke. Has a "C". Haddock has a "H". For smack.' Then in answer to Joey's puzzled look, 'Yeah. Smack. Heroin.'

'What would I get if I asked for jellied eels?'

'Funny looks. You been down sarf too long,' Matt replied.

'Tell me about it,' Joey replied with a giveaway glance at the Q7. An obvious raw nerve. 'But how's it work?'

'Like all scams.' Matt grinned. 'Dead simple when you figure it out. They have their own currency.'

'What?'

'Druggie meets the banker round the corner. Druggie hands over cash. Banker hands back note. Any note. Fiver, tenner, whatever, right? Druggie then gets back same note with a C or H or whatever on it.' He held out his arms. Simple. Then chuckled again. 'But not J. And they couldn't do cockles either. 'Cos that'd have to be C too.'

'Could be an E, though,' Joe offered. 'For eels.'

Matt nodded, taking the point. 'Or E for Ecstasy, I

suppose. Anyhow, druggie then takes marked note in to Fatty, say, one with a C. "Cod and chips" he asks for, but Fatso waits until he sees the C note. Recognises a real customer and gives him a special.'

'Neat. But how does he pass over the goods without others seeing him?' Joey asked.

'We haven't got that next link in the chain. But we will,' he added with a grin as he directed Joey's eyes to the Q7. 'Haven't you got things to do?'

Joey glanced back at the waiting car. Like Natasha earlier, he could see a familiar look and read familiar body language. Even at 20 yards. 'Er, yeah. I'll catch you tomorrow.'

Sean was looking for his cufflinks. He wore them so infrequently he never remembered where he put them. And he couldn't ask Sandra because she would remind him of the fact. Sod it, he thought, and as usual folded back the cuffs. He spent a fortune on Sandra's jewellery but never bothered much himself. He liked watches, though. She had bought him a gold Longines out of their first year's dividend from the garden centre, but he got so fed up taking it off every time he had to roll his sleeves up properly that it stayed in the drawer for five years. Then one Christmas she surprised him with a Jaeger-Lecoultre Polo. It was, he had discovered, originally designed in 1931 for actually playing polo. As such, the watch could slide and be swivelled in its case to show only the steel back and protect it from stray mallet attacks. It now very rarely left his wrist, and the back plate displayed both the scars of history and the practicality of the design.

It was something Sean had come to appreciate more as his wealth grew. That the things often seen as the symbols of wealth usually started life with a very practical purpose. True, there was very little demand for playing polo in Highbridge, but the watch survived the rigours of potting conifers, even if the straps didn't.

'I need a new strap for my watch,' he called out to Sandra.

'Right now?'

'Next time you're in having your jewellery serviced.' Then his mind changed tack. How ridiculous was all this? How ridiculous is life. From peeling icy curtains from frosted windows to living in a six-bedroomed house with constant hot water, and wanting a new strap for a watch that was worth more than a few months' pay for most of his staff, simply because he was too sentimental to take it off.

Sandra emerged from the dressing room looking, as she always did, as though she'd stepped off a fashion shoot but immediately picked up his now pensive mood. 'C'mon. You know why you got into all this anti-drugs stuff. Although I don't know why you bother. Dressing up for dinner isn't going to change much. But if we are, do you have to wear that suit?'

Sean turned to look at himself in the mirror. Automatically

sucking in his stomach. 'What? This is my favourite suit.'

'Which is why it's worn out. Too small and . . .' – she playfully prodded him in the stomach – 'ten years old. Wear the blue Gieves and Hawkes.'

Sean let out a resigned sigh. He knew she was right, so turned back towards his wardrobe. 'OK. I give in. On the suit. But as for tonight, everything starts with someone thinking they can do it better.'

'And that's you, is it?' she asked, smoothing down the lines of the Anglomania Taxa dress. She'd also put on a few pounds since she bought it.

'Someone has to try,' Sean replied but wanted to move on. It was a recurring conversation. 'Er. . . But if I'm changing, what happened to the red dress you showed me earlier?'

'Too low.'

'That's why I like it.'

'But not for a bunch of do-goody druggie-huggers. Or having Rupert Bronks from the Golf Club's nose in my cleavage all night. I'll feel better in this.'

'Then why ask my opinion?'

'See if you can make the right choice. And if you still fancy me.'

'You're still here, aren't you?'

'And God only knows why. Do this up for me then.'

He crossed to help her fasten her bracelet but held her hand for a moment. 'The cost of that could fund this whole drug rehabilitation programme for three years, you know.'

'And we didn't work for twenty years to give it away. Now come on, we're late.'

'What's with the we . . . ?'

'And don't go on about your mountaineering skills being honed by deprivation, again. Hard times are affecting everyone at the moment.'

'Says the woman in the megabucks bracelet.'

'And the guy with the Lecoultre watch? A lecture on poverty would sound rich, coming from you.'

Sean laughed at the barbed pun. 'Good one, that. But we worked for it.'

'Exactly. We didn't get here by shoving stuff up our noses, sponging, or mugging other people. We worked bloody hard. And God knows, some days I feel like part of a persecuted minority. Doomed to solve all political issues by paying more and more taxes. Don't we do enough, spending it to keep the economy going? Mind you, I know that's not going to get any sympathy votes, is it? Just as I know you'll want to recount your adventures from the most deprived council estate in the world. But stick to what happened to Jane. And what we need to do to stop it. Cut the liberal tolerance crap and get them into jobs. OK. Let's go.'

There. She'd done it again. Found the nutshell. It was what attracted him to her in the first place. Just after her breasts. And her legs. And her sense of independence.

He had met Sandra while auditing an engineering factory. While he was employed by an independent firm of accountants and was there on a four-week assignment, she worked through an agency and was on a six-month maternity cover. To Sean, out of the two of them, she seemed to have the better idea. She basically worked for herself and could come and go and dress as she liked, which often hardened opinions and various other male body parts. Although he also moved from company to company he still had to conform to the sombre suit and sensible shoes dress code of his almost Dickensian accountancy practice.

Everything about her used to fascinate him. He was captivated by everything from the works of art she would often dangle from a swinging crossed leg to the speed she pounded away at what was probably one of the last old-fashioned electric typewriters. Then there were the looks on his colleagues' faces when he told them how much she earned for preferring not to have a proper job and the fact that, as a temp, he could chat her up without risking a sanction for fraternising with the clients. However, it was only when it was time to wrap up and move on that he realised he wanted more than the office banter. That coincided with a small retirement party for one of the older secretaries and that led from one thing to another and one room to another until he and Sandra found themselves well and truly caught beyond fraternising.

While Sean moved to another job, Sandra simply never went back, continuing to see him until the inevitable consequence. He fell in love with her and out of love with being an auditor. It was not long before they had moved in together, into a dingy flat above a dingy shop, and despite Sandra's ability to see things coming and his ability to add up, it wasn't long before one and one made three and what would become known as Noah was on his way.

That wouldn't have been so bad if it had not been for the night when Sean was so depressed and tired with all the travelling and sleepless nights that he found himself almost hitting Sandra when she insisted he got up and looked after their increasingly noisy second child, Megan. It was the lowest point in their relationship but the starting point of their future strength as Sandra took him once again to find the nutshell: life should be better than this. They should stop living as everyone expected them to live; stop trying to meet or feel guilty about not meeting the so-called standards that everyone else set. Sandra, with her own previous nomadic lifestyle, gave Sean both the confidence and support to decide to live his life for himself not for what his father, mother, teachers or employers expected of him.

They agreed it was daft paying dead money in rent, or even accepting the life sentence of a mortgage as, after working out how much it cost them both simply to go to work, they figured out they could live on less, bought a motorhome and decided to travel the world. They could live, work and eat wherever and whenever they wanted. So they did.

Yes, that was why she was still here. He'd be lost without her. He followed her out, grinning.

So how does he pass the gear over? Luke was wondering as he watched Fatchops go back and forth preparing for the night's business. Same routine. Fresh white warehouse coat: fryers on; warmers on; check the wrappings; stock up drinks cabinets; float in till; shouts at the part-timers to get the food on the go, and then the bit that Luke always found curious. Fatchops would meticulously wipe down all the surfaces. Here was a bin bag of balloons, dealing drugs in a chippy, but with an obsession with cleanliness.

They'd been watching him for about two weeks now and he never varied. The first thing he did when opening up and the last thing he did when closing. Wipe down every surface. He never left it to anyone else. It was his job. His pride and joy.

Luke's train of thought was interrupted by the vibration of his phone. He looked. Matt was on the path on his way to the hide. A moment or two later he slid in and handed a latte and panini to Luke. Luke nodded thanks and then nodded towards the Barrett. 'Do you think Fatso's ambition, when he was growing up tending chickens or goats or sheep or whatever his family did back in the Albanian mountains, was always to run a chippy in a crappy northern British town?'

'Probably lay on a hill not unlike this one and longed

for it,' Matt replied, as he rolled over to reposition the spotting scope.

'Yeah, like I always wanted to run a hamburger stall in Rhyl.'

Matt had now refocused the scope. 'He does take a pride in his work though, doesn't he?'

'Yeah, but he didn't get that scar down the side of his face because he missed a grease spot somewhere. Saw a few of those in Kosovo, which is just across the border from where Mr Sheen there was daydreaming about having his own chippy.'

'So what was that about. Back there.'

'Oh, just asking what Luke was up to over the weekend.' Joey replied, then quickly added, 'He wants me to look at the electrics up at the cottage.'

'How long's he staying then?' Natasha asked.

'How'd you mean?' Joey tensed, having known this moment would come.

'Luke never usually hangs around this long. Comes back for the anniversary then goes.'

'Yeah. Don't know. It's been three years now. Perhaps he's getting over it?' Joey offered, hoping it would satisfy her curiosity.

'Have you? She was your sister,' she asked.

Joey didn't answer. He knew he didn't have to. It was more of a statement. But also a question he had continually avoided. Who felt the loss more? The brother or the husband? When the husband is the best friend of the brother.

Natasha knew the inner conflict. Just as she had her own. The wife and sister-in-law. Yet they had been through it so often before. Let it go. But how did you do that? She knew Joey had been trying. Luke had. They all had. But now she sensed something else was going on.

'Just seems odd. Him and Matt both here?' She tried to make it casual.

'I think they're between jobs. And Matt just tagged along.' Joey did sound casual but he was making it up as he went, knowing he would have to stick as close to the truth as he could otherwise she would sense something was wrong. She had always been as good as his mum for knowing when he was lying. 'I, er, don't really know. Think they've been working together. Since they were all made redundant in the cutbacks.'

'Doing what?'

'Do you fancy going to the Palace, if the house is occupied?'

'Sure. Or we could go gatecrash your Sean's do.'

'What's he doing tonight? Strategy, selling or syringes?'

'Stepping Stones.'

'Those stone heads again. Have they got something on him? Or hacked naked pictures of Sandra, or something?'

'You know why. He's trying to do something. He's got a social conscience.'

Joey bristled at the implication that he didn't seem to

care as much as his brother. He was doing something. But something he wanted to keep away from her. 'I've got a social conscience. And we won't solve the drug problem by turning out in penguin suits and having raffles at the Golf Club.'

It was a bit too forceful. Natasha looked across. But he was staring out the window, chewing on his lip. What's he up to? she wondered, but knew now was not the time. Instead: 'It's at Treetops.'

'Then the Palace it is.' He reached over and felt for the bump.

She put her own hand on his and glanced across. What was going on in that head tonight? She had learned to give him about an hour after he came off the train. Whether it was the journey itself or the week away, but apart from the sex, which she looked forward to as much as him, he was always fixated on something. Whether they were acting as good role models for the kids? Was the separation worth the material returns? Whether society had its priorities right. How come the town had gone downhill? Should they just take the kids and go on a gap year? She knew tonight's brooding was all connected with the third anniversary of Janey's death and, like Luke's guilt, his own anxieties about being away so much. Especially after Tanya being threatened with a knife the week before last.

And when he came home he tried to cram everything into the weekend, but then became too tired to really enjoy it. He'd always put the hours in, something she admired about him. But at least he used to see the kids passing in the hall every now and then when he was home. The older the kids got, the more independent they became and the less he saw them at the weekend.

'How long do you reckon this London job will go on?'

'Dunno. Another few months. If they don't stop frigging about and adding things. Why?'

'Just wondered how long I'd have to put up with this on a Friday night?' She pushed his hand on to the suspender clasp.

'You're stuck with them, I'm afraid. As long as you're married to me.'

'I could end it that easy, could I?'

'Yep. But it'd be over then anyway.' She looked across at him. 'Because if you ever left me, you'd be dead.'

'Why don't I doubt that?'

'Because you know me. Where I come from. And how much I adore you.'

And she did. Ever since the day he had pulled her out of the snow. It'd taken a couple of years to finally get together but she had known from that day. 'Do you remember that day down in Bottom Edge?'

'When I saved your life?'

'I was only stuck in the snow.'

'You could have frozen to death.'

'It's a five-minute walk back to the High Street.'

'Not in heels. Anyway, how could I forget? Why?'

'Just remembering. I did get stuck with you, didn't I?' At last the smile came back to his face.

'What do you think the white coat's all about?' asked Luke watching Fatchops buttoning up the warehouse coat.

'Obviously to give the place a bit of class,' Matt replied, before switching track. 'You can tell a lot from a good scar, can't you?' Almost instinctively, he reached and rubbed his own scar before adding, 'Initiation rite, perhaps?'

'Initiation rites are supposed to be secret. Which is why the Yakuza wear suits to hide their tattoos.'

'They do that Yacobutsomething-or-other though, don't they?'

'Yubitsume.'

'Yeah, chopping off bits of their little fingers so everyone knows when they've screwed up,' Matt replied. 'I reckon Fatty's mates done him for something.'

'I was thinking it being some form of accident,' Luke said.

'Nah. Too boring that. Gotta be some form of ritual thing. They like their feuds over there. Remember that tale that squad in Cyprus told us about their tour in Serbia? About the fella who had kept an old wood saw in his house for fifty years waiting for the collapse of Communism. So he could use it to saw the head off the bloke who had used it to saw his own dad's head off? Fifty years. Guess Balloon Boy got off light then, if that scar's some sort of feud thing.'

'If,' Luke said. Matt nodded, conceding the point. Or perhaps not, Luke continued the thought. The real scars are mental. Seen a few of those, even my own. Still, no matter what brought that and what it has or hasn't done to you, mate, even if you did or didn't deserve it, you shouldn't be doing what you're doing now.

To Luke, it was as simple as that. Now. There had been a time when he had tried to rationalise and understand what made people turn to crime or killing or terrorism. Before he met Janey he knew he was on some form of destructive path that he couldn't alter. It seemed that life had dealt him a particular hand. A poor one. He couldn't change his circumstances, no matter what they said in school. He knew at an early age he was already tagged and bagged. Factory fodder. Except that there weren't any. So what do you do then? What countless people had had to do in the past. Live for the day. Enjoy the moment. And fight. Not for what you want, or even need. But just to stand still. Upright. Whether that was walking the streets or leaning against a bar. Always someone wanting to prove they were bigger, harder, tougher than you. They had all come through it. But he had felt trapped by it. Until Janey. And even that had been a fight.

It was like a classic teen movie. It wasn't Janey's dad he had to get permission from, but her brother. His best mate. Joey. Perhaps that was why Janey had been attracted to him. Living, not with Joey, but under his protection. Anyone who went near her was quickly frightened off. Big brother was always watching. Until Joey's fourth child's, Lucy's, christening and Janey had kept on and on at him to dance. She wanted to have fun. Enjoy life and she wanted him to do the same.

She told him she had always enjoyed him coming to the house. Ended up longing for it and then, without Joey realising it, engineering it. You could get Luke to help. You could ask Luke. Luke wouldn't mind. And he didn't. Whatever it was. She was the first person who saw just him. Not a label. He was neither a tearaway nor a hooligan. Just a nice guy looking for someone to love him. And she did. She told Joey before she told him. She then gave him a reason for living. A belief that he could after all, like Joey with Natasha, change things. They could change things. And have a great life together.

Four years of being an item, three years of marriage and then she was snatched away. Senseless. Painful. Agonising. And the reason for living was replaced by a reason for killing.

After that, he'd finally decided that life, as his dad had always told him, just wasn't fair. Now, it was just good guys and bad guys. And bad guys were the ones who made life unfair. He'd also recognised that he'd always known this. Even at school. Then it was your mates against the psychos. The older he got the more he realised that there were psychos everywhere, but you couldn't just round up the posse and sort them out in a four o'clock ambush. They were often your bosses so you got sacked for fighting back. That's why he'd joined the army. See the world. Get a trade. Meet and sort out more bullies.

And, after Janey, he'd given up the rationalising. While those behind the gunsight provided the motivation for what he did, those in front of it gave the outlet for his frustrations. They got what they deserved. Nor did he any longer deny that he had found a home. A camaraderie he had not had since the old gang at school. With Janey he sometimes wished the trade he'd been given was something a bit more useful. Like fixing cars or plumbing. But afterwards he accepted that there didn't seem to be much call for No. 1 Snipers down the Job Centre. But he didn't care. Not the army's fault. He knew what he was getting into and now acknowledged that he actually enjoyed it. The covert positioning. Scoping. Picking the shot. The evac while avoiding detection. He also acknowledged that it was a deliberate choice. Being able to operate at distance. Know and pick his own targets. So he hadn't had some of the trauma he's seen in others who have gone through both sides of the friendly fire scenarios. On the other hand, he knew he had been desensitised to the obvious product of his job: killing. Now he had no compunction, worry or anxiety about taking out anyone he thought deserved it. Like this fat so-and-so in his reticule.

'All right then. If it wasn't some homeland feud. What about the riots?' Matt asked.

'What?'

'I'm just trying to come down to your rather mundane take on life. So, if it was just an accident, perhaps it was during the 2011 riots, when he got it . . .' Matt hesitated for a second or two to build up the expectation. 'He got it . . . On a smashed shop window when he was nicking some trainers.'

Luke started to laugh. 'What? Does he look like he's ever gone looking for trainers?'

'Just a thought,' Matt replied.

'And we could lie here all night dreaming up daft ideas but in the end he's still what he is.'

'A thievin' drug dealer?'

'Which is probably all the explanation you need. The druggies like their knives too.'

Finally Matt seemed to concede the boring point, as Luke went back to wondering, once more, why life was like this.

'Why do we have to do this anyway?' It was Becky, moaning again as she threw the Sanderson's bag on to the central reservation and set the oven to warm up while unwrapping the pizzas.

'Why can't we just get a takeaway?'

'Because it's healthier,' Tanya responded.

'And,' added Carol, 'we know which takeaway you would want to go to.'

'No I wouldn't.'

'Yes you would.'

'Enough,' Tanya cut across again, throwing the ice-cream tubs to Becky. 'Freezer. Carol, plates. And why does he hang out at that place anyway? It's horrible. That fat fella who looks like he's eaten all the pies.'

'Oh God, yeah. And in that creepy doctor's coat he wears. What's that about?' Carol gave an exaggerated shudder at some obscure thought. Although she didn't share it, the others exchanged a look of not knowing exactly what she thought, but assumed it was from one of the freaky downloads she would later try and get them to watch.

'He's his uncle or something,' Becky offered. 'He's letting him stay there for a while.'

'Why, though?' asked Carol.

'Dunno.'

'You don't seem to know much about this great love of yours.'

'It's . . . It's something to do with his parents not liking his lifestyle.'

'What? Like going out with white girls?'

'You're being racist again.'

'No I'm not. You read about it all the time. They want them to marry their own. Me dad's just as bad about wanting to know the ins and outs of everything and everyone I go out with.'

'Tell me about,' Tanya added as she started to chop the now washed salad.

'At least he'll be glad you're at home tonight.'

'It's Friday night, Carol.'

'Oh yeah.' She and Tanya exchanged a grin and then another exaggerated shudder at the thought of parental sex.

'What?' asked Becky.

Tanya exchanged another look with Carol. She is clueless.

'Is that why you find him attractive then, Becks,' Carol asked to get back on subject. 'That you are his forbidden fruit?'

'Well if I am he hasn't had a bite, yet.'

'But you're thinking about it?'

'No, well . . . No.'

Tanya dumped the salad on the table. 'Anyone want dressing?'

'Are we allowed, Mum?' Carol asked as she went to the fridge, synching her phone with Tanya's wireless speaker on the way.

'It's your figure you're jeopardising, my girl,' Tanya responded in mum mode. 'And not that playlist you had at Jules's party last month. It's all old people like Take That and I'm not quite my mum yet.'

'She's into old people, aren't you, Becks?' Carol grinned.

'Oh My God. Will you stop? You're obsessed.'

'You're the one obsessed with the Pharaoh.'

'And will you stop calling Husani that? He just happens to be Egyptian. And he's about twenty-six.'

'That's older than Mr Hibbert in History and you wouldn't go out with him.'

'Mr Hibbert wouldn't buy me a Chloé bag.'

Tanya laughed. She couldn't help it. 'It's one of Bobby McBain's fakes. You can get one for about twenty quid at the end of market day.'

'Mr H. wouldn't even buy me one of those,' Becky protested. Lamely.

'No, because at twenty-five he's not sniffing round a sixteen-year-old schoolie either, is he?' asked Carol.

'What's wrong with him giving me things?'

'It's what he thinks he's paying for.'

'I don't know why you two are so down on him.'

Tanya started slicing the first pizza. 'I told you. He's creepy.'

'Why, why do you say that?'

'It's the way he looks at you.'

'You mean, never stops looking at you,' added Carol.

Becky turned to Tanya. 'Like you never get that everywhere you go?'

'He's different, Becks. The others try sly looks, but he's, he's . . .'

'Blatant?' offered Carol.

'Even more than that. Like, you know, he's just constantly sizing us up.'

'What? Don't treat me like a sex object!' Becky shot back defiantly.

'I can't quite explain it, but he's like the dog when we're eating.'

'Yeah,' Carol agreed. 'And that's what makes him creepy.'

'How, how can you say that? You've never spoken to him.'

'We don't need to. We don't like him, OK?' Carol shot back at Becky, patience finally strained.

Becky turned and headed out of the kitchen, slamming the door behind her. Carol turned to Tanya, anxious, but Tanya carried on switching pizzas in the microwave. 'She's left her fake Chloé.'

Carol looked across to where Becky had indeed dumped her bag, and relaxed.

'Don't kill yourself, Cags,' Tanya said, as she dug out the pizza cutter and designated Carol as slicer. 'She needs to hear it.'

'I know, but I think we made the same mistake my dad always does.'

'Unsuitable boyfriend syndrome?'

'Yes, Mum. Any ketchup?'

'Yes, darling. In the fridge. Get it yourself.'

As Carol opened the fridge, Tanya opened Becky's bag and removed the Samsung. She killed it and frisbeed it into the mound of old blankets that covered the dog's bed. With a bit of luck he'd eat it.

*

'You may be right,' Matt conceded.

'I am.' Luke was his usual dogmatic self. 'No matter which way you go at it, it always comes back to the one answer. Unemployment. They never really focus on that in films. Do you remember *Rambo*?'

'Brilliant film. In my top ten. The first one.'

'Yeah, but if they'd only given John Rambo a decent job when he came home . . .'

'They wouldn't have had a movie?' Matt interjected.

'There is that. But it's like the 2011 smash and grab riots. Whenever you see something on the telly about the bad guys terrorising people on council estates . . .'

'Projects, they called them in things like *The Wire*.'

'Thanks. But are you still trying to defuse any potential build-up of psychotic stress-related blame tendencies?

'Is it working?'

'No,' Luke replied. 'I'm not blaming anyone. Except those clowns on TV who are quick to blame the cops. And the politicians. They haven't got a clue. Never have had, especially as most of them didn't come from the estates.'

Matt just nodded. He knew where Luke would go next. He'd heard it all before. There was no point debating, because he agreed with it. It was the reason he was lying on a freezing hill beside his mate. A reason the politicos would never understand. Because they were definitely a world apart.

They blamed their predecessors and drugs and failing education and, well, almost anything and everything they could crap on about, except the one thing they could do nothing about. Jobs. What happens to 30,000 people when their main source of income, their employment, just ups sticks and walks away?

Luke was definitely on a similar track, as he panned the Barrett to look down over what was laughingly called Meadow View. It used to be called Butler Fields after some long-forgotten councillor but became known locally as Butcher's Field when things started to fall apart in the 1980s. Luke adjusted the focus on the scope to take in the empty concrete slabs where the industrial park used to be.

'What've you seen?' Matt asked, suddenly alert.

'Nothing. Just history.' Luke panned back on target. Noting again the array of domes clustered on the corner by the alley. All-round view. Way over the top for the average chippy. His mind went back to the consequences of the global tides of change that send manufacturing overseas. The local factories are closed, dismantled and shipped overseas too. More shipwreck than train wreck, but they still should have seen it coming. The companies sail away leaving their workforce behind. Marooned. Marooned on concrete islands once built as so-called new towns of opportunities and amenities. Sometimes referred to as overspill estates as they socially cleansed the inner cities to get rid of the Victorian slums or Second World War bomb damage. When the Council did more damage than Hitler, as his mum and dad often said.

'Do you think politics is war by other means?' he asked Matt.

'You what?'

'Never mind.' He went back inside his head. How

many times had he heard that one about the Council doing more damage than anyone while he was growing and fighting for his life on the walkways and underpasses of Butcher's Fields? He saw it coming. At thirteen. When he opted out and left school. Voluntarily excluded himself. They didn't like that. But back then they didn't really give a toss. Well, no one carved themselves a nice little earner and gold-plated pension pot by caring or siding with the people.

It was also another reason why he joined the army. They liked that. Get him off their statistics on to someone else's. Hopefully one of the casualties. But something the politicos always forget. People. Punters. Voters. They don't just read the papers. They live, breathe and create the stories that go in them. Politicians read about life. Real people live it. They also do another very dangerous thing. Well, some of them do. They read books. No wonder the first thing any puffed-up dictator does when they try to grab power is stop people reading. These days it's cutting off the Internet, but it's the same trick. Stop people getting ideas.

'You think too much, Luke. Always been your trouble, mate,' Matt said, puncturing the thought bubble Luke, as Matt had often pointed out, always retreated into. 'There's nothing you can do about the shifts in global capitalism mate, so why bother yourself?'

'What? Get pissed or get something from the likes of that fat bastard down there?'

'No. But you could spend a bit more time trying to fill that bloody black hole left behind by losing Janey.'

Luke turned ready to have another go, but saw Matt was waiting for an outburst. It had been a deliberate shot. Bang on target. You see. People. They get ideas. Uncomfortable ideas. Right ideas.

'You should have stayed at that seminary, Father O'Connor. Priesthood lost out when you decided to join our band of homicidal maniacs.'

'Better than ending up a kiddy fiddler.'

'Welcome, Mr Joe. And Mrs Nolan. You well tonight?'

'All the better for seeing you, Lin.'

'Yes. Those Chinese people in London. Not real thing. Usual?'

'Yep. You know me. No imagination.'

'You just have excellent taste. Be right back.'

Joey flopped into the seat. The adrenalin from the station now subsiding.

'You didn't answer my question,' Natasha said as she picked up the menu.

He didn't need a reminder about which question. He knew when he changed the subject in the car, just as he knew she wouldn't let it pass. But at least it had given him a bit more time to think. 'They're doing private security work.'

'What? Group 4 or something?'

'Don't think they're nursemaidin' prisoners back and

forth to court, or sitting as cocky watchmen outside some factory somewhere.'

'They're mercenaries?'

'Close Quarter Operatives, they call it.'

'Where?' she asked, but Joey just stared back at her. Don't ask.

'What? You'd have to, or they'd have to shoot me if you tell me?'

'I don't know. All I know is that they left the army, well, got their P45s in the last round of cuts. Apparently Matt was one of the ones who had to finish his medical rehab before they binned him. Bit like those old movies isn't it, where they patch people up and get them fit so they can hang them.'

It was Natasha's turn to just sit and stare. And wait. She wasn't going to let him drift off this time. 'So what do you do when all you know how to do is kill people?' Joey asked. Eventually.

'Oh for God's sake, Joe. Don't be so dramatic.'

'I'm not. That's what Luke said to me. They had a look around at life outside the services and decided it wasn't for them. So went back out and signed up with one of the security firms offering close quarter protection. Four times their army pay.'

Natasha nodded now. She seemed to get it. 'And I suppose with what happened to Janey . . .'

'Exactly. What has he got to come back for? Not sure why Matt's in it, though.'

'You're joking, aren't you? He's (a), a lazy sod so where and how's he going to get a decent job. And (b), he's a basket case.'

Joey had to concede with a slight nod. Typical. She had always had them all sussed, which is why he'd been constantly walking on eggshells since agreeing to bankroll Luke. It was true that he had come back to see his mum. But he had carefully never said why they had stayed.

'So, they would shoot people if necessary?'

'What?'

'Your mates. As, what did you call them, Close Quarter Operatives?'

'Er, yeah, they provide close quarter protection as Private Security Operatives.'

'Mercenary bodyguards, in other words.'

'If you like.'

'And they'd shoot people.'

'If necessary.'

'And who decides when it's necessary?'

'Er, whoever pays them, I suppose.' Which was suddenly a very uncomfortable thought. He hadn't reasoned it through before, but if he was bankrolling Luke, that probably meant it would be his call as to whether they killed the fat fella in the chip shop. Shit.

2

Catch-Up

Joey was at the kitchen window with his thumb hovering over the send icon, watching the dog tripping the passive detectors on the garden lights as he went on his morning bladder patrol. Every week he meant to turn down the sensitivity, but every week something else took precedence. It was usually something like replacing the wattle fence panels, now just visible in the spill from the path lights, not whether he would be asked to pass a death sentence on some fat bloke in the chippy. The microwave pinged. He turned and as he did his thumb stroked send and the progress bar started to fill. U R NOT ACTUALLY DOING HIM R U? was on its way. Unstoppable. Damn.

He walked across, took out his World's Best Dad mug with the warmed milk and put it under the built-in coffee maker. Part of the Saturday morning routine. He'd get an hour or two to himself before taking the boys to swimming and football practice, while Natasha got those few hours in bed after a week of school runs. He was always still too wired and tired to lie in. Especially today. Especially now. He looked at the green text bubble on the screen. It was the one thing he hated about the iPhone. The send icon being too close to the keyboard layout for work-thickened thumbs like his.

He'd had a fitful night pondering that text message. Even the sight of Natasha unclasping her stockings had done little to lift his sense of anxiety which, thankfully, she put down to Tanya's counselling session with Becky getting in the way of their usual Friday night routine. He took his pre-brewed, pre-frothed coffee back to the window. He used to spend these quiet hours catching up on the local newspapers, until the kids bought him an iPad for his birthday, just like their Uncle Sean's. It had been Lucy's idea, mainly because she wanted to play Angry Birds but then became one herself when she realised he would take it to London every Monday. That's how he now kept up to date with the local news and saved a fortune on newspapers. Sean was always going on about how daft the newspapers were for giving away their stuff online. Like him offering free compost to everyone, and then chuckling when he said, as he always did, not much difference really. Then again, Sean had said those wattle panels would last about ten years when he and Joey had put them up. Had they had the house ten years already?

Must have, he thought. Lucy's nearly eleven and Nat was pregnant when we moved in.

As the dog came back with a much more relaxed swagger, Joey opened the door and felt the sharp edge of the cold. He wondered if Luke was up on the hill now. I should have thought it through. What else would Luke and Matt do? He kept telling me. That's what they were trained for. Was Fatchops already a dead man walking?

'Hey up. Side alley.' Matt was refocusing the spotter scope.

Luke directed the Barrett's scope on to the alley. Two young girls were being let out of the reinforced side door at the back. It was difficult to make out who was helping them in the gloomy morning light. Could be male or female. 'What do you reckon?' he asked Matt.

'Someone up to something they shouldn't be.'

'That your professional opinion, Sherlock?'

'Yep, but someone else's mission.' Luke responded and eased the Barrett back on to the chippy. Which was still in darkness. 'No target.'

'I'm only here, you know.'

'Old habits.'

Matt nodded. As he kept the spotting scope on the young girls. Just in case. He could already feel his heart rate increasing along with the pulse below his scar, indicating that his anxiety level was rising. Slow it down. Just another reminder. Stay on mission. Push it back, he told himself as he watched the girls until they reached the end of the alley, took a cautious look out and then scurried off away from the chippy. Away from the target. Old habits, indeed. But the anxiety diminished. The old memory dealt with. Controlled. As he put the scope back on the chippy, he grinned. 'I'd never have hacked it as a priest.'

'What?'

'Old habits. Monks. Priests. You rabbitin' on before.'

'Have you thought of donating your brain to science?'

'Nope. Nor could I have dedicated my life to celibacy.'

'You'd have found some young nun to look after your needs. Locked in a conspiracy of guilt and silence. But great sex every Saturday night.'

Matt rolled on to his back again and grinned. 'Sunday afternoon more like. State of grace after eleven o'clock Mass.'

'See. You've got the mind for it,' Luke replied, as he scanned the street outside the chippy. Just for something to do. Until he came to rest on the AMG Mercedes SL500 they'd seen arrive in the early hours. 'What do you reckon that's doing round here?'

Matt immediately rolled back to his own scope. 'Courier?' he suggested. 'But defo someone else up to something they shouldn't be. Won't get one of those on the Mobility Allowance. No wheelchair access.'

Luke panned back to the chippy, just as Fatchops came from the back with another man, both just visible in the blue light from the bug zapper. They hovered in the doorway. 'Door.'

'Looks family.' Luke was watching Fatchops unlock the shop door and then go into the now almost obligatory male gripped wrist and body hug parting. He then relocked the door and went back through the shop as his visitor headed down the street, head bowed in the typical religious pose of a serial texter. Towards the Mercedes. Opening it and starting up without fumbling for keys.

'Keyless entry and quick getaway. Invented for the bad guys those things,' Matt said, as he watched the car speed away. 'What d'you reckon? Asian or East African?'

'Does it matter?'

'Nah. That's the beauty of globalisation. No one cares who kills who.'

Sean tapped the code into the garden centre alarm system, then stood back to let Glynnis enter. She was always there before him. Often there after him. He watched her wander off towards the café, pulling her coat tighter against the cold. Within half an hour she would have the café open and ready to start serving the first breakfast of the day. His. One of the perks of owning the place was every day having a Full Welsh, as Glynnis insisted it be called, as he skimmed through the news headlines on his iPad before going through the previous day's takings, or sorted out any changes to the coming day's work patterns. Today it was the switch from Halloween to Christmas and he'd been pondering on where best to place the Singing Santa Gnomes.

He knew they'd be a winner because Sandra hated them. She'd almost kicked the sample over the fence when it started singing 'We Wish You a Merry Christmas' as she arrived home from her tennis lesson. Fortunately she was better at tennis than football so she'd sliced her shot, and Santa had only gone into the box hedging. Still singing. A testament to its build quality. He'd wondered about putting that on the display sign, 'Will Keep Singing If Kicked', but decided he'd probably end up with too many warranty claims.

As he settled in to the corner table he used as his early morning office, Glynnis arrived with the Welsh. Fried egg, two Red Dragon sausages, bacon, beans, fried tomato, Welsh black pudding, one piece of brown toast, to show willing, a glass of orange juice and a pot of tea. 'Where do you think I should put the Santa Gnomes, Glynnis?'

'Anywhere except in here.' She went back towards the kitchen with a just perceptible shake of her head. Then stopped. 'But I'll have the nodding polar bears.'

'I was going to put them in the entrance as a come-on.'

'That's daft. If they're at the door they've already come. You need to get them in here and spend some money. My mark-up's better than out there.' She straightened a chair, went a few more steps and stopped again. 'You doing that Santa Shed thing again this year?'

'You mean the Grotto?'

Another slight shake of the head. 'Well, if you are doing it, you should put a Christmas garden outside. It could be where he grows sprouts and cranberry and has free-range turkeys. All the Christmas food. Like where he has his allotment.' She turned and left with a parting shot over her shoulder. 'Everyone knows it's a shed.'

Sean watched her go. Late forties, single. Not unattractive even though she never seemed to be bothered about her appearance. She always looked like she ran her fingers through her hair every morning and seemed to have only seven different outfits. All a combination of black trousers with black tops. It was as though she was in a constant state of mourning. She lived alone. No family. And didn't appear to have any other life except work. Sean suspected there had been some tragedy in her past and had tried several times over the years to tease it out of her, but she never responded, always changing the subject. He'd long since stopped being surprised by her. The only thing that still amazed him was why she was like she was. She was the best employee he had, yet she couldn't read or write.

He assumed that was why she didn't mix. It was an avoidance strategy. The less she mixed with people, the less chance of being forced into a situation where she would be found out. She didn't speak much, but whenever she did it meant something. Like the Santa Shed. She was right. And the garden idea was great.

He switched to email and sent a note to himself. REMEMBER SANTA SHED + GARDEN + TURKEYS. He then turned back to dissecting the black pudding. He'd put the Singing Santas near the tools. Like the old Big Mouth Billy Bass singing fish, it'll be the guys who will go for the laughs.

Joey looked at his phone again. Nothing. Radio silence, he thought. He hoped. He raised his mug to drain the coffee, but nearly dropped it as a pair of arms came round his waist. Jesu. It was Natasha.

'You OK?'

He turned and put his arms round her, went to kiss her but she turned away. 'You stink of coffee.'

'You're not usually up.'

'You're not usually so preoccupied. What's wrong?'

'Nothing. Everything's fine.' He pulled away. Immediately confirming that it wasn't. 'Want a tea?'

'Rather have an answer.'

He could already see the corner he was being boxed towards. 'Just missed our weekly catch-up last night because, you know, Tanya and her counselling session.'

She looked at him, now with his back to her, in only boxers and T-shirt, his strong legs and shaped back still trim enough to suit the fitted tee. He'd always been sensitive about sex with the kids in the house, but she could see the tension in his shoulders. 'It's something else, Joe.'

It was. She saw the shoulders drop.

'It's not. Everything's fine,' he lied. But she was silent. Still. Waiting. He was already in the corner. He tried a feint. 'Well, if it's anything. It's about Benno.'

'Benno? Why? What's wrong with him?'

He sensed the slight gap he could spin through. 'I can't remember leaving his envelope.' Joey raised his phone. 'Been trying to get in touch.'

It seemed to work. Benno was the guy he worked with down in London. 'You shouldn't be doing that, Joe,' she said as she headed for the toaster. 'If the tax catch up with him you'll get it too.'

Joey shook his head. 'It's a gift. On top of what he gets off the job. I'm just helping out a mate because he watches my back down there. But I must be getting old to forget leaving his envelope.'

'Or too tired.' She smiled, turning back for the expected riposte and defence of his hunter-gatherer virility, but instead caught the pensive look on his face. 'What?'

The look was quickly replaced with one of attempted reassurance. 'Nothing.'

'C'mon Nolan. How long we been together?' She broadened her grin as she pulled him towards her, hooking a leg behind his. 'You still in a state over last night?'

Another opening. 'Well . . . Mother Teresa and her gang do tend to dampen the mood.' He nodded at the yellow roses as the toaster donged to tell them it was ejecting the toast. It always made Joey smile.

'You sure it was just that? And not the money again?'

Another of their recurring topics. Was travelling to London worth the money? It was good. Daft, even. Even after paying out for the train and digs, he was still pulling in three times what he could locally. Provided he didn't get sucked into the card school and avoided the traditional and so-called swift one on the way back after work or any other overheads. He couldn't believe how so many of them just blew what they were earning. Might as well stay at home on the crap jobs and go home to the missus every night. He looked across at Natasha. She was wearing the red silk dressing gown and matching strappy nightie he had bought for Valentine's Night. As she buttered the toast every movement accentuated her shape. 'Nobody butters the toast like you, do you know that?'

'No one else wears this sort of thing to butter toast, I know that?'

He knew it was a weekend gesture as her preferred choice was passion-killing winceyette floral pyjamas. Perhaps that was it. The others didn't have a missus like his so they enjoyed living the life down there. Or perhaps they did and it was him who was being daft. 'I couldn't make the sort of money I do now up here. Not enough oligarchs or sheiks trying to outdo each other. The bloke we're doing this house for, well knocking all three into one.' Joey shook his head. 'The stuff he has installed then ripped out when he goes somewhere and sees something he likes better. He's changed the M&E spec three times.

Ivantmoreofich we call him. Now he's discovered he's the only one in the street not to have a three-floor basement. So he's got them digging out another floor. They're insane.'

'They're running away. They don't like their own country so they spend most of their time flying round the world looking for something better. It's not about money, Joe. It never is.' She offered the toast and squeezed his hand as she said it. And the big brown eyes said everything else. We made the decision.

'I know. But, well, I just need a bit more time. Get finished on this job and we'll have enough to last about six months, I reckon.'

She leaned up and kissed him. 'You sure? Is it the right decision?' I hate you being away, but . . .'

'You like Friday nights too?' The impish grin was back on his face.

'We can still have all that. But we agreed for you to do it until you had at least a year's worth of work.'

'Stop.' He put his arm round her shoulders as he leaned against the granite worktop next to her. 'It's the right decision. I'm coming back. I don't want to miss the kids growing up just so we can have a self-loading singing toaster.'

He didn't have to mention that it was also a result of the recent scare over Tanya with a knife and that he would never be able to cope if something did actually happen to her when he was away. He knew what it was like to be the brother. Had seen how it chewed up Luke as the husband. No matter what sort of world-weary faces they had put on over Janey. What would it be like as the father? Instead of mentioning this, he simply tightened his squeeze on Natasha's shoulders.

She grinned and pushed her body more into his. 'It does match the food mixer, though.'

'It does. And it makes us smile.'

'Especially if we can still have our Friday nights.'

She pulled herself round, into his chest, never appreciating that her hair nearly suffocated him every time she did this. But he thought it would be a nice way to go.

'We've got a couple of hours before you have to go and get the boys.'

'What about the girls?'

'They won't surface until at least the shops open.' She reached up and kissed him quickly. 'But brush your teeth first.'

She turned and headed out the door, he ditched the coffee down the sink then turned to follow but saw her quickly return with a frustrated grin on her face as Tanya came hurrying into the kitchen, still in a hooded jersey sleep shirt, and across to the dog basket. 'Move, Roscoe.'

Joey looked at Natasha, who was now trying to suppress a giggle, then back at Tanya. 'What are you doing?'

'Becky's phone.' She waved it as she went across to switch the kettle on while flicking through the phone and apparently deleting text messages.

'Should you be doing that?' asked Joey.

'Should you two be walking round in your undies with the house full of my friends?'

It was a more pertinent point. Joey turned to Natasha, now really struggling to contain herself. She grabbed his arm and dragged him to the door as Tanya curled her lip and threw a parting shot. 'And remember. There's only a stud and plaster wall between you and us.'

Out in the hall Joey turned to Natasha. What now? She just giggled again and dragged him upstairs, towards the spare room. At the far end of the landing. No, Joey thought, life is not all about money.

'It just takes one.' It was Matt, breaking open a fruit breakfast bar from the Vestey Army Ration Pack they had brought with them. 'One bad apple. The whole barrel's toast. Toasted apples, I suppose. Do you want the porridge?'

Luke took another sweep along the street. All quiet. He glanced at his watch. It would be another half-hour before the van that dropped off the spuds and stuff. Every day. 10.30, give or take a minute or so. They had been eyeballing Fatchops for three weeks now. Clocking his lifestyle POLO. His timings. His habits. And he had them. Most people do and they don't even know it. How they get up in the morning. Which ball or breast they scratch first. Which curtain they open first. Whether it's tea or coffee. Whether they get dressed and eat, or eat and dress. Whether they pick up a newspaper before breakfast, or on their way out. Once you have it clocked it's just a question of waiting for all the other stuff to fall into place. Whether the postman, milkman or paper lad delivers on time. Is early or late. Too early and they might knock the routine. Too late and they discover the body and it all kicks off too early. He rolled to face Matt.

'Yep. Creature of habit. We all are. Even your toasted apples. Clock their habits. And here we are. Same brekkie every morning.'

'Not much choice in these things,' Matt countered. 'But doubt anyone'll slot us if we opt for the Chicken Masala before sun up. And if these packs weren't so bloody expensive I'd probably just live on them at home. Always had a ten-man box in me dad's shed. Before he popped his clogs. Just in case. Got a new one every summer and me and the old fella would scoff the old one when we went fishing. Especially after me mum went and he didn't have anyone nagging him.'

Luke looked across and saw the watery eye and the habitual rub of his scar. He was not as hard as he tried to make out, so decided to move the conversation on. 'I thought you told me not to worry about the shifts in global capitalism.'

'It's not global capitalism I fret about, mate.' Matt sniffed, pulling himself out of his memories. 'It's the greedy gets in the union suits who have worked out they can bring the country to a standstill by stopping the overnight deliveries. Imagine if Fatty down there didn't get his regular supply of spuds?'

'People could be healthier?'

'It's not his spuds that's killing people. Otherwise we wouldn't be up here freezing our nuts off.'

'You reckon a ten-day box is enough, do you?'

'Yeah. Two days of posturing. Two days to mobilise the troops to step in. If necessary. Two more of huffing and puffing. Two days for some sort of deal to be made. Two days to get back to normal.'

'Still a bit tight.'

'Nah. You're forgetting the panic buying. Shops'll know before anyone that a strike's on its way. They'll overstock because they know the public are stupid. Whack a couple of pence on here and there. Get rid of everything in the panic buying running up to the strike. Big boost to profits. Then, lay off all the casuals for a week. Saving on wages. Only ones who lose, as usual, are the ones in the front line. Not the suits. It'll be the bloody delivery drivers. But hasn't that always been the way?'

Luke looked across at Matt finishing off the breakfast bar. He never ceased to amaze. 'This the sort of thing you think about when we go dark?' he asked.

'I'm always dark me mate.'

'True. But is it?'

'Actually, it's usually only when I'm lying frozen in a tank track for fourteen hours trying not to be seen by some goatherd with his standard issue AK-47 and pondering on what service I am actually doing for our beloved country, while some dickhead with a company

72

credit card is swanning round the country trying to get paternity leave or something for his members. Things do tend to come into focus then. Until the sun goes down. And we take off again. And I know why I chose what I do. Did. Just wish they'd be a bit more grateful. That's all.'

'Part of the deal though, isn't it. Keep them safe in their beds?' Luke asked.

'Oh yeah. So they can get their legs over and have more kids so they can get more paternity leave. All coming into focus now. Democracy.'

'Never have so many been so lucky because of so few?'

'You got that off the bog wall in Helmand.'

'I did.'

'How long d'you reckon? Before we pop Fatty?'

'As soon as we find out how he's passing the stuff over.'

Tanya heard the creak of the ceiling boards as she finished cleaning up Becky's phone. She let a slight sigh escape as she shook her head. Typical. They sneak along to the guest room, forgetting it's above the kitchen. She brushed Becky's phone across the butter, tossed it over to Roscoe who initially eyed it with suspicion until his nose, then tongue, registered the butter. As he licked away Tanya reached for her own phone, then smiled at a message. T'HOUSE? 9-ISH? It was the local name for the pub now known as the Sandstone Box. Originally called T'House at Cross it was a 500-year-old former coaching inn that marked the eastern approach to the town. It was built in sandstone blocks that matched the cross opposite its front door, the monument to the old Abbey that once stood on the site.

In the late 1990s old Jim Mulligan, whose family had owned T'House for three generations, finally decided he had had enough trying to scrape by as an independent and sold out to the brewery. Five hundred years of history was immediately absorbed by the marketing machine and turned into yet another themed outlet, the new name aimed at the transitional youth market. Somewhere 'between the sandpit and thinking out of the box', the Planning Committee was told. They didn't really care so long as old Jim got a decent price for his service to the community and the community itself got to keep their pub, with real ale and a bronze, not cheap brass, plaque on the wall outlining the site's heritage.

Everybody seemed happy, especially in refusing to call it by its daft new name. It was, is, and always will be T'House. If you didn't know that, you weren't local. And there was some value in knowing that. Especially as Billy and Shirley McGuire, who now ran it, interpreted the brewery's transitional youth policy as any local over sixteen, as Billy and Shirley knew who they were and knew their families would appreciate knowing where they were.

Which was exactly where Tanya would be tonight.

However, MIGHT B, was all she texted back as she heard a hollow thump from overhead and decided it was time to go back to bed, trying to blank any images of parental sex.

*

Even Sandra, who could talk the leg off a chair, had not got far with Glynnis, telling Sean that the only thing she found out was that Glynnis had moved into the area about twenty years ago. So whatever it was had happened before that. The only other thing Sandra suspected was that Glynnis had 'a thing' for Sean. Initially, like the rest of the staff, she thought it was a crush, but it became more than that. Not romantic, more protective. She would do anything for him. And only the three of them knew why. She had become dependent on him.

Sandra had suggested they try and get her to learn to read and write, but Sean said he had tried when he found out but she reacted so badly that he had to work hard not only to stop her moving on, but also to convince Glynnis that her secret was safe with him. Which is why he had really laid down the law with Sandra, and even then only told her when she was getting a bit too pointed in asking him what the attraction was with Glynnis. Since then, and to his great delight, she had been true to her word and had even helped work out strategies to protect Glynnis.

It was Sandra who suggested they always had a junior member of staff working with her to keep all the paper-work up to date, as it was Sandra's idea to present the menu in pictures, an idea picked up when they had been to Japan during their travelling years. It was supposed to be for letting kids pick their own meals, for which it had been a great success, but it was really to allow Glynnis to put up the Specials Board. And in this she had blossomed to become both photographer and graphic artist as she herself took the pictures when they changed the menu, then imported them to the graphics package, manipulated the menu style and printed out the new versions. Even words like Menu, Starters, Mains, Puddings, Service, VAT and everything else that creeps on to menus she recognised by the font design and word shapes rather than the cluster of letters.

Sean was reflecting on this as he finished the last bit of Red Dragon, then wiped the runny remnants of egg, beans and tomato sauce from his plate with a piece of toast. Something Sandra wouldn't let him do at home. It was another of life's great mysteries still to be solved, why no one had yet been able to bottle that extraordinary culinary mix that remains after a runny egg breakfast. Probably linked to individual preferences, Sean thought as he got up to go. One person's amount of egg against another's beans and sauce. These are the things that make us unique. As a species we tolerate conformity but we desire individuality. It is also what makes us survive. What makes someone at some time, somewhere, decide that enough is enough and go after change.

It was, Sean thought as he headed off, like his brother Joey's dog Roscoe, for the daily toilet patrol, what allows people like Glynnis to slip through the education and social net. Non-conformers who are either tolerated because of a uniform understanding of difference or, more likely, dismissed for not conforming. You can be tolerated outside the system if you don't make trouble for the system. That was what Glynnis had opted for. Something had set her apart from the herd but if she didn't make trouble, the herd would leave her alone. But what a waste of human potential. What a waste of a life.

As he ticked the inspection sheet on his way out of the toilets he realised he was back on the same theme he had finished up talking about the night before, after his tales of boyhood mountaineering: wasted potential. His idea for local councils to take on recidivists had gone down, as expected, like the proverbial lead balloon, although, Sean smiled, at least he had left them with the question: how do local towns face the challenge, perhaps curse, of modern life and find local solutions to their local problems when everyone seems to be focused on national targets and benchmarks?

He had talked about the issue of teenage unemployment being, as he thought, high on the list as a root cause of all the town's social problems. Boredom. Teenagers bored with nothing to do or look forward to, but with an almost irrepressible energy and need to explore the world around them. That was what they were genetically programmed to do. If they can't do it legitimately, then they will find other ways. Like the drugs problem the town was currently facing. Why had it got so bad in recent years? And why did he always finish his breakfast with these sort of thoughts? Better get on and get Santa's Garden on the go.

It was such a good idea he would tell Byron that it was Sandra's. Byron had a real soft spot for Sandra. Well, so did most men of a certain age who still recalled her time as Rose Queen, but Byron was also one for his own ideas. Sean had appointed him as Manager of Rock 'n' Shrub not for his people skills but because he was as straight as a die and a stickler for detail, process and procedures. Every bulb, cutting and bag of peat would always be meticulously documented and every timecard stamped, checked and kept up to date. He was, as everyone said, anal.

It always made Sean smile. The five-foot illiterate café manager and the six-foot-five anal-retentive garden centre manager working alongside each other. If only he could blend them and split them down the middle. But as he couldn't, he knew it wouldn't be a good idea to tell Byron that the Santa Garden was Glynnis's idea. Glynnis would understand. So would Sandra. She'd lost count of how many good ideas she had supposedly had, as well as the amount of times, as a consequence, Byron had told her she should be running the place, not Sean. He picked up his plate and took it over to the counter and shouted thanks to Glynnis as he went off in search of Byron, nodding to the wannabe Mohican haircut who was talking to the Coy Carp, as he did every morning. Where would life be without its dysfunctionals? Sean mused, as he spotted Byron heading into the Salvage Barn.

Joey deliberately and noisily scuffed his feet as he went past Tanya's room, not wanting anyone else to wander out after bumping into Carol on his way out of the guest room earlier. He went down the stairs two at a time, staying on the edges so they wouldn't creak, heading for his North Face All Terrain jacket hanging on the rack near the garage door. As he pulled it on he took a look at his phone. Nothing. He tapped in the code to unlock the garage and just as he opened the door he nearly jumped out of his skin.

'Morning, Mr Nolan.' It was Becky, halfway down the stairs on her way to the kitchen in search of her phone, with that similar knowing but slightly embarrassed smile Carol had upstairs. She was also, like Carol, only half dressed in a tight tank and boxer-type shorts. He had once asked Tanya if she paraded round her friends' houses like that, but was, he thought, given a backhanded compliment by being told no, only in their house. There were no adolescent predators and he was, well, her dad. Which obviously meant Alex and Ross were still babies and he was no threat, but equally was a constant source of embarrassment. A role in which he appeared to be excelling this morning. He grinned, as he always did, when he turned the key in his pride and joy. The boys hated it and usually refused to go out in it. But this morning they would have no choice if they wanted to get a lift a home. He pressed the fob to open the garage door and checked the phone again. Still nothing.

The Mark 2, 3.8 Jag was politically incorrect in every way, according to all the family, except one. It was part of Britain's past and future. It was part of the manufacturing heritage that had built the country, a symbol of its past loss, while emphasising the need for recycling. At least that is how Joey defended it during the family dinner arguments. But in reality he just loved it. It had been built ten years before he was born but he could actually fix it if anything went wrong, unlike the Q7, which required a man with a white coat and a laptop. He also loved it because he had taken it in exchange for the outstanding account on the golf club job, when Rupert Bronks had run out of cash, or so he said. Unlike Sean, Joey was a bit wary of Rupert. Under the country squire act there was some form of scrap merchant, in all ways. Something in that 2 second 7 second thing: 2 seconds to decide if you like someone or not, 7 seconds to confirm. Rupert was about 3.5. Meaning Joey was still not convinced.

He turned into the car park opposite the Michael Greeves Memorial Playing Fields, named after a young lad who had collapsed and died during a school football match ten years earlier. Something to do with his heart. He'd just got taken on at Stoke and was destined for big things, so they said. Tragic. But every year at the town festival they held a football tournament named after him. His dad used to come and give out the cup, but stopped about two years ago, saying it was getting harder to take the longer it went on. So much for time being the great healer.

Suppose that's part of the reason I took up the offer from Luke, Joey thought as he wandered over to the touchline. There's enough ways for parents to lose their kids without scum like him in the chippy. He had wanted to drive past it on the way but had resisted, taking Luke's advice not to be seen anywhere near Fatchops and a CCTV camera at any time. Especially in what Luke called, disrespectfully, his bucket of bolts. Joey glanced down at his phone. Nothing. He glanced up at the hill dominating the town. Nothing. He went over to the touchline. Half-time. No score.

'There's Joey in his pride and joy.' Matt had him in the spotting scope. 'Talk about conspicuous.'

'He's not supposed to be trying to hide anything.' Luke stayed on target, watching the chippy.

'True.'

'And here comes the spud man to give us our daily spuds.'

Matt moved his scope back to the chippy. Luke glanced

at his watch. 10.30. Every time. Give or take a few minutes. The van pulled up in the side alley. As usual. Monitored on the CCTV. The steel side door opened immediately. As usual. Fatchops was out organising things. As usual. Lots of waving arms, but never actually lifting a finger. As usual. Until the end. The smallest box was always his. Wouldn't break any sweat. As usual. Take the box from the front seat. Sign the chit. Dismissive waves. Van away. Fatchops back inside. Barred and bolted. Everything as usual. But not quite.

As the van driver came back from the front of the van he slipped or tripped or stumbled, but even before he did Fatchops moved with a speed they had never even imagined he was capable of thinking about, never mind achieving. He had the box in his hands before the driver knew he was falling. Which he probably wouldn't have done if Fatchops hadn't kicked him in the knee, following up with a hefty toe poke to his back.

'Do you reckon that counts as negative customer feed-back?' Matt asked.

'Hmmm. Beats phoning a helpline.' Luke shifted the Barrett to put the scope on the driver. 'He looks terrified.'

'So would I be, delivering to a customer like Fatty.'

'That's it, isn't it? Who's working for who here?'

'The answer to that is probably in that box.'

Luke nodded and went back on Fatchops, refocusing the scope on to the box, now locked tightly under a fat right arm. He just had time to make out some of the lettering before the box and arm and owner disappeared behind the steel door. 'Something . . . t – i – c?' Luke asked Matt.

'Is that something, then t – i – c? Could be attic?'

That'd be something, something t – i – c. Just three letters at the end.' He tapped the scope. 'Like, Op-tic? Drama-tic?'

'Mas-tic? Fantas-tic? Could be anything. Could be just any old box he picked up to use.'

True, thought Luke. He glanced at his watch again. 10.41. Time to go and catch up with Joey. And figure out how to get eyes on that box.

'Why's it all sticky?' It was Becky, still busy trying to clean her phone with the remnants of a tissue previously used during some emotional tragedy in the distant past.

'I told you. Roscoe was guarding it for you,' Tanya replied, as she scooped up the train tickets from under the bullet-, terrorist-, drunk- or irate-passenger-proof protective barrier that kept the station staff safe, and headed for the platform, careful to avoid Carol's eye – she was trying to focus on Twitter, desperate not to smile.

'Urgg. It's disgusting. He's disgusting.'

'You should be used to sloppy dogs slobbering all over you.'

'Don't start again. OK? I hate dogs. Why'd he do that anyway?'

Carol was unable to resist joining in. 'He was probably guarding it in case Pharaoh texted. And he'd have barked if he did.' Carol threw a conspiratorial look to Tanya. 'He always texts, doesn't he?'

Becky shook her head, deflated. 'Not last night.'

'That's it, then,' Tanya said quickly. 'Must be over.'

'You wish.'

'I do, yeah. He's bad news, Becks. Have I mentioned that?'

'Only as often as he usually texts her,' Carol added.

'That's why he gave me this one. He said it would always work.'

Carol shook her head. 'You're hopeless, do you know that?'

But Becky was more focused on Tanya. 'Don't give me that look, Tan. You don't know what it's like to be in a proper relationship.'

'Neither do you. Relationships are not just about someone having a flash Mercedes or giving you a real designer handbag. And don't you think giving you a phone is, well, creepy?'

'Why? He likes giving me things. What's creepy about that?'

'It's what he thinks he's getting in return. What he's paying for.'

'Like what?'

Tanya held back for a moment. Was Becky being deliberately obtuse? Or just stupid? 'He is twenty-five, isn't he?' she finally asked.

'Urghhhh.' Whether she was being obtuse or stupid,

she was now getting annoyed. She bit her lip for a moment but then said. 'And?'

'And,' Tanya repeated. 'Why's he sniffing round a fifteen-year-old then?'

'Will you stop? You make him sound like that stupid dog of yours.'

'That's what he's like,' Tanya hit back. Slightly harsher and louder than she intended. But she too was getting annoyed. 'You can practically see him salivating. Like when we give Roscoe a Dentastick. In the Pharaoh's case it's probably more Rent-a-dick.'

Becky went to respond but Tanya was in full flow. 'And you're already in a deep and meaningful relationship.' She gestured to herself and Carol. 'With friends who care about you. It's nothing about him being foreign or even the money, Becks. He's just, well, creepy. But you've heard that a million times too, haven't you. Come on, here's the train.'

Tanya and Carol moved towards the edge of the platform. Becky had one last forlorn look at her phone. Nothing.

Neither was there anything on Joey's phone as he joined the other assorted waterproofed and anoraked dads clustered against the wall of the Community Centre that served as a windbreak and took the edge off the hailstones that were bouncing off their tightly pulled hoods. 'I hated playing in this.' A voice came from along the line.

'I loved it,' a second voice responded, with a deep growly laugh.

'You would,' said a third voice, which brought another growly laugh from number two, but a few nervous titters from the hail-battered hoods as number two, in what looked like an Alexander McQueen leather parka, was Bobby McBain, who was actually number one in the Highbridge villain stakes. His seemingly pebble-dashed face a road map of how he got there. He was generally regarded as OK, if you didn't get too close to him. Or antagonise him. Which was about to happen, because Joey knew that growl.

'You loved it because the Ref couldn't see you doing everyone else,' voice number three added. This brought instant silence as every eyeball swivelled towards Bobby, now leaning forward to look up the line.

'You talking to me?'

Hearing the classic challenge, voice number three pulled his hoodie forward and leaned back, making it harder for Bobby to see him. 'If I was, I'd have whistled first. Like you do for any animal.' It was Joey.

The line of assorted dads collectively reached for their assorted phones to check the time or texts, collectively realising they must have assorted things to do elsewhere. Most headed back to the touchline, preferring the skin-lacerating hail than anything that might follow as Bobby weighed up his challenger, now nonchalantly looking at his phone too.

'You looking up your doctor's number?'

Joey ignored him.

'Hey, gobby, I'm talking to you.'

Joey waited a moment, then pulled down his hoodie to reveal the huge grin on his face. A crack also appeared in the pebble-dashed face. 'I might have known it'd be a headcase like you, Nolan.'

The two men closed the gap and wrist-gripped, but didn't hug. Old acquaintances. Not friends.

'You still scrounging for work in London?' Bobby asked, with more than a ring of disdain as he fell back against the wall.

'You still scrounging and scamming back here?' Joey asked as he turned back to watch the boys trying their best to play while hunched up and shivering against the hail.

'Doing me best with the hand life dealt me.'

'Still a victim of circumstance then?'

Bobby shrugged with a wider grin. 'Like you'll be filling in your VAT and tax returns as diligently as the vicar.'

'He probably doesn't need one.'

'True. He gets everything he wants off everyone else. And you know what, Saint Joe, I bet I pay more tax than anyone else in this town.'

Joey looked across to see that Bobby was also staring out across the field to where some older boys were playing. He was now pensive. This was not just banter. 'Go on then. Enlighten me.'

'VAT. Fuel duty. Stealth taxes. Every pound I spend the government gets 20p, doesn't it. Every time you tank up your car, ker-ching, they take their cut.'

'You shouldn't have such an expensive lifestyle, Bobby.'

'You mean my ex shouldn't. She's unbelievable.'

'You still paying, then?'

'Too right. Got me by the plums, she has. Every six months she threatens to go to court to get – get this – proper maintenance. She knows she gets more than any court would give her. Just as she knows she gets it because I can't go in there and declare all me earnings.'

Joey nodded. He knew that too. Everyone did. Just as everyone knew how Bobby got his cash. Any way he could. And as Tanya, Becky and Carol knew, nearly everyone in Highbridge had a fake designer logo courtesy of Bobby.

'Sounds like you're about to have that six-month chat, then?'

It was Bobby's turn to nod. Then another nod towards the football pitches. 'Got the lad for the weekend, but the wicked witch says we'll have a chat when I drop him back tomorrow.' Another growly laugh. 'You know the daft thing, Joe? I could have her topped for five hundred.'

'You what?'

'Yeah. Could get it done for less than fifty by some of the smack street brigade, but for five hundred? Job well done. And it'd all be over. Imagine that. I've told her, too. But she just laughs. She knows me too well. I mean, what would it do to the boy. Plenty of other reasons to top people. Plenty of people willing to do it too. But, I suppose it's a bit over the top for a bit of alimony.'

'Suppose it is.' It was all Joey could manage to say as their attention was caught by the noise of many whistles sounding across the different pitches. He glanced at his watch, too early to finish. Seems odd to have a foul on every pitch at the same time, he thought, as he looked across to see something even more odd. Both referees and various helpers and coaches were shepherding the teams off the pitches. No one seemed to need a second coaxing as the mad scramble began to get to the changing rooms, piles of bags and cars before the hailstones took the skin off the players' bones. What was going on?

The answer came when Alex, Joey's fourteen-year-old son, came trudging over. He looked every inch a potential Premier League prima donna although now tinged slightly blue with cold. Behind him came his bag carrier in the form of his twelve-year-old brother Ross.

'Cameron Gordon went to retrieve the ball from the bushes and found a dead body.'

'And they wouldn't let us go and see it,' complained Ross.

Joey exchanged a concerned glance with Bobby, who just shrugged. 'Another smackhead sniffs the dust?'

Joey gave him a do-you-have-to look, with a glance at the boys. Bobby just gave another shrug and then turned to Alex. 'Better tell your old man what's been going on while he's been away earning enough to buy those Nike Mercurials for you.'

He held out his hand to Joey for a fist bump and moved off. They could already hear the emergency sirens on their way.

Joey headed for the Jag, wondering what Bobby was alluding to but not getting much time to dwell on it as the boys were already moaning about the Jag and how long the heater took to warm up.

'Can we go with Noah, instead, Dad?'

Joey turned to look where Alex was pointing. It was a two-year-old VW Golf and Noah was seventeen. A couple of years ahead of Alex as school sports hero and Joey's brother Sean's eldest. 'I'm sure Noah has got other things to do than run you two back to the house.'

'I'll ask him,' said Alex, as he dashed between the cars that were slowly starting to dissipate. 'Bring the bags, Ross.'

Joey turned to see his younger son, still carrying his puppy fat but dragging the sports bags out of the car, as Noah was giving an OK signal.

'You're twelve now, Ross. You don't have to do everything he does, you know.'

'No, but your job's to be understanding, Dad. He'll just give me a right hard time later.'

True, thought Joey, as he scooped up the boys' sports bags and walked Ross over to join his brother and cousin. 'You sure you're OK with this, Noah?'

'Yeah Uncle Joe, no worries. We might stop off at Maccy D's on the way back.'

'OK.' He took out a £20 note and handed it to Noah. 'Thanks, and tell your dad I'll call him later about lunch tomorrow.'

'Er, you could text him yourself.' It was Alex, now busy bluetoothing his phone to the car's radio, which burst into life as Noah pulled away.

Joey watched them go. What would he have given for such a car when he was seventeen, something else he would soon be facing as Tanya counted down the months. That's a few more grand I'll have to find, he thought as he made his way back to the Jag, stopping to let Bobby McBain's gas-guzzling but tax-delivering Range Rover Autobiography pass with a flash of its headlights. Black on black.

'Can't help himself, can he?'

Joey turned to see Chief Superintendent Hilary Jardine standing behind him, in uniform but holding a golf umbrella as a shield against the hail, a wry smile on her face. 'Never could resist flashing the cash, could he?'

It was a reference back to their shared youth. When they had all been at the Comp together. She held out the umbrella so he could join her. Whereas many would baulk at being so close to a police officer, Joey accepted the offer without hesitation and saw that although the years had left a few lines around her eyes, she was still recognisable as the fit hockey player they used to lust after, and still stood and sounded like the head girl that terrified them. Well, most of them.

'You here because of that?' Joey asked as he nodded over to where the police and paramedic vehicles were congregating.

She nodded. Then the smile faded. 'Young lad.'

'Druggie?' He was close enough to feel the warmth of her breath.

'We don't know yet. Probably.'

'Sounds a bit matter-of-fact, Hilary. Common event, is it?'

'Better to say not uncommon.'

'Oh yeah?'

'Yeah. Like fights in the Lion.'

Joey let out a sigh. 'Bit below your pay grade, isn't it?'

She nodded. 'But spotting patterns isn't.'

'Like?'

'Like, we're getting too many of these tragedies.' She nodded over to the congregated vehicles where a forensic tent was being set up and the area cordoned off. 'And like,' she continued, but turned to face him. Close enough to indicate that she felt safe with Joey. Close enough to betray a past intimacy.

'. . . you seeing more of Luke Carlton. Like Matt

O'Connor being home at the same time. Bit like the old gang. Fighting at the weekends. And then I see you and McBain in a huddle?'

Joey didn't respond. He just stared at her and waited. But she was giving nothing back.

Eventually he smiled. 'You used to do that as head girl, you know.'

'Do what?'

'Widen those big hazel eyes. Pretending you knew more than you did, until someone told you what you needed to know.'

She turned away, slightly embarrassed but amused by his recollection of their past. But the professionalism returned quickly. 'And is there anything I need to know?'

'You asking officially, or as a friend?'

'Can I say, both?'

Joey nodded. Then, 'But there isn't much to know.' He turned away and looked at the now emptying car park as the last of the frozen footballers were being rescued. 'You probably know that Luke has been brilliant at holding me together after what happened to Janey.'

'I do, and I don't know how often I can say it, but we are still trying to find . . .'

Joey waved it away. 'He's also been good at making me accept the shit happens thing. Christ, some of the things he's told me. Or, like that.' He nodded across to the now officially designated crime scene. 'But, that fight. It started in the Co-op car park where some, some . . . idiot was pissing against the wall where Janey died. Not just that. But it was the anniversary. Did you know that?'

She shook her head. Then waited for him to continue.

'Anyway, Luke had put some flowers there earlier. And . . .' Joey didn't have to finish. She nodded, now getting it.

'It spilt over into the Lion?' she asked.

Joey nodded. 'It was just verbals in the car park, but when we went in the pub later he was there. Few mates. Started sounding off about why we shouldn't be inter- vening overseas. Creating psychos like Luke coming back. And, well, he just lost it. I was actually fighting to stop Luke killing the guy more than anything else. So, if you came to warn me about it, Hilary, it's done.' He turned and leaned forward to make eye contact. 'We've got a lid on it. OK?'

She stood, considering it for a moment or two. 'And Matt being back is no more than a coincidence, is it?'

Joey shrugged. 'They do happen, you know.'

She nodded. Considered it for a moment before saying, 'OK. But keep the lid on, eh?'

She touched his arm briefly. 'Please'. Then she headed off to her assembled troops. She still had it, Joey thought as he flopped into the Jag. He watched her stride across the playing fields, remembering how her chest bounced and her hockey skirt flounced as she ran rings round the others on those same pitches. Christ, he thought, with a last look back. Coincidences? How come one of my school-mates is the top cop and another is the top gangster who tells me it'll only cost five hundred quid to have someone topped? Properly.

Luke, now wearing a Berghaus Ulvetanna parka, was half a mile away from the hide before he switched on his phone. It vibrated as soon as he did. Damn. Same old security issue. What was the point of them going dark to make sure the cell data couldn't put them close to the hide if Joey sent stupid texts like that. Right then, though, his immediate concern was the weather. If it kept up like this nothing would happen this weekend, Luke thought as he saw Joey heading up the road towards him.

'You know, most of the people we take down is not because of surveillance, but because they can't help broadcasting what they are doing.' He waved his phone at Joey.

'I know, I know. I didn't mean to send it but . . . Sorry.'

'OK. So, who am I supposed to be "doing" then?'

'What?'

Luke waved the phone again. 'It's deleted off here, as I hope it is off yours?' He saw Joey nod. Apologetically again. 'And although I very much doubt our chums at GCHQ have us tagged, if it ever comes to someone wanting to take a peek at our data, who am I supposed to be "doing"?'

Joey looked at a loss. But Luke turned to the cottage. 'Well, as the cops have a log of our anti-social behaviour the other week, I suggest we need to have a reason why we are in each other's pockets at the moment.'

Joey finally nodded. Then added, 'Hilary Jardine cornered me earlier.'

Luke returned a vindicated, but wary, look. 'What's she guessing?'

'Just thinks we are up to something. Because Matt's back. And I was talking to Bobby McBain.'

Luke's expression changed to one of amusement. 'Typical. Too busy looking for the conspiracy that they miss the obvious. It's true, you know.'

'What is?' Joey asked as he followed Luke up the cottage path.

'Hide in plain sight. Can't see what you don't know you're looking for.'

Joey twisted that round in his head and thought he got it, as Luke carried on.

'All the more reason we need to have ourselves covered. Got to be something to do with the electrics on this place. What do you reckon?'

'Er, yeah, but . . .'

'What's the usual way you get done in your game, Joe?'

'Some prick undercuts me.'

'Exactly. So, if I give you the estimate I've just had from that guy on the industrial estate to rewire this place,

we . . .' it was emphasised, 'We . . . could "do him",
couldn't we?'

'Er, yeah, I suppose . . .'

'And that look and sound of your voice makes me
think you are uncomfortable with such, what, unethical
practice? Which is exactly what your text meant to me.
Oh, Luke, surely you couldn't "do that" to a fellow
tradesman?'

Joey nodded. He used to run with Luke and Matt. He
could handle the clowns on any building site. Or stand
up to guys like Bobby McBain, or that skag bag on the
train, but when he brushed up against Luke and his world
he always felt like some gawky kid.

Luke recognised the look. 'It's OK, mate. Our game's
about mindset. It takes years to get into it. Then you
never lose it. Someone's always watching.'

Joey nodded, then turned to the cottage. 'You really
got a quote for the electrics?'

Luke nodded in return as he opened the front door.
'Promised Janey I'd do a bit every time I came home.
Just want to finish it now.'

'Why? It must, well it must do your head coming back
all the time?'

Luke gave a wry smile. 'My head's well done in, Joe.
And what else am I supposed to do? Move on? That's what
Matt's always banging on about. Get on with my life? She
was it, Joe. Besides, what else would I do with the cash?
Put it in a zero-rate savings account? Or spend it? On

what?' He didn't wait for an answer. There wasn't one. He just headed for the cottage door. 'Do you want a coffee, while you give me a quote to undercut the other fella?'

'Is it Colombian?'

'Most of the good stuff is.'

As Joey followed Luke into the living room, straight off the street, as all good artisan cottagers used to do, he saw nothing much had happened since Luke had hacked back to the brickwork and exposed the floor boarding. The old rubber-sheathed cables hung from the exposed first-floor joists.

The kitchen was the only room in the house that not only looked like part of a house, but was actually fully fitted and fully working, as Luke demonstrated by taking a couple of clean mugs from the Neff dishwasher that was colour co-ordinated with the combination oven, hob and microwave.

Joey was already compiling a mental estimate. He couldn't help it. 'Do you want sockets in each corner. Lights switched from either side?'

'Whatever. So long as it's cheaper than that.' Luke offered him the estimate he had stuck behind a fridge magnet on a brand new Smeg fridge. He then went over to rinse out the cafetiere, tapping the head of a nodding Buddha on the windowsill as he did. A Buddha that matched the one Janey had on her dashboard. It had gone when they eventually found her car. Something that added to Luke's sense of loss. Sense of violation.

They had bought them on a trip to Thailand, after she flew out to meet him on a 72. All that way for three days together before he was deployed again. He thought it was precious at the time. For three days they lived the dream. Then it became priceless. Three weeks later she was dead. Crushed with her own car by some druggie looking for the next score.

After all this time. After all the verbiage he had spent and wasted, the questions were still always there. Especially at night. Lurking in the dark. Refusing to be dislodged by the cold light of day. Why? The question. The one he and everyone else kept coming back to. Why did it happen? And why her? Why did she go out that night? Why didn't someone help? Why didn't the police catch him? Why, why, why? And the biggest why always came back to why wasn't he there to protect her? Why was he even in Afghanistan supporting the Yanks? What was that all about, anyway? What's changed? He knew it was irrational. Shit happens. None of it made any sense. It never would.

'You still do that?' Joey asked, having noticed Luke tap the Buddha.

'Yeah,' Luke smiled. 'We used to say if Buddha was laughing, so were we. Been everywhere with me, this fella. This, and her voicemail on my real phone. Which is backed up to a USB in my lock-up. She was so excited about this kitchen, Joe. We'd just been on a two-week search and destroy. The Yanks lost a couple of guys and that voicemail . . . The sound of her being so happy . . . Better than all the debriefs and shrink stuff. Makes you realise . . . Well, did at the time. Thought I was doing it to protect, what, our way of life? Keep her safe . . . Then she gets killed back here.'

Luke turned and handed Joey his coffee. 'There you go. One dose of Colombian. We drink this drug. And another killed Janey. One farmer may have provided both. What do we make of that then, eh?'

The following day, the question still hung over Joey as he pulled the Q7 into the Old Mill car park, stopping right by the restaurant door so Natasha and the kids didn't have to fight the driving wind and rain. Another druggies' den that had been socialised and formalised over time but at its heart was one of history's greatest killers, alcohol.

'Don't start, Dad,' Tanya said as she slowly, delicately, started to climb out of the back seat.

'Start what?' Joey asked, looking at her in the rear-view mirror.

'Your sermon about drinking. It's all over your face.'

'Don't have to. Looks like you've got the hangover that proves my point.' Tanya just threw him another teenage lip curl of death. 'At least I'm here, aren't I?' It was her parting shot and, as if to illustrate the point, she slammed the door and then swung her bag at her two annoying brothers, while protectively escorting her younger sister towards the restaurant door.

Joey turned back to a grinning Natasha. 'Aye, at least she is. Heavy night up at T'House was it?'

'Heavy date more like.'

'Not surprised after what she was nearly wearing when she went out. Or is that a typical dad-like comment?'

'Yes. Especially thinking about what you'd have me wearing, given your own way.'

'Ah – and you were, are, someone's daughter?'

Natasha grinned and leaned over to kiss him. 'And remember whose daughter she is. If she goes off the rails it's . . .'

But he'd been through this one before. 'No. It's your fault. You seduced me, remember. Laid a trap for me with that see-through chiffony blouse . . .'

'It was not see-through. That was the wind, but if that's what makes your memories better. So don't go on about it over lunch and don't get your Sean started.'

Joey followed her look to see Sean's Mercedes 500S indicating to turn into the car park. 'But ask him when he's delivering those panels for the back fence.' She jumped out and hurried in against the rain to join the kids.

Joey moved the Q7 to park up and let Sean stop by the door. As he walked back Sandra was already out trying to shield her hair from the wind, as she dashed inside followed by the new teenage queen, daughter Megan.

'Why couldn't I have come with Noah?' Megan was back on another familiar item.

'You know why,' Sandra responded.

But Megan pointed at Joey. 'Uncle Joe lets Alex and Ross go with him.'

As Sandra guided Megan towards the door she smiled back at Joey, but remained focused on Megan. 'Uncle Joe allows a lot of things that your father and I don't agree with. So for the last time: you are not travelling in your brother's car until he has done twelve months on the road without killing himself. Especially in weather like this.'

'She off on one today then?' Joey asked Sean as he made his way back from the car.

'My fault. Jumping ahead of myself again, with an idea for sprucing up the restaurant – sorry, café – at the garden centre.'

'Oh. Fence panels.'

'What?'

'Nat told me not to forget to mention them.'

'Right.' The two brothers hugged and stepped under the entrance porch out of the rain.

'And we're not to talk about alcohol being a drug and all that,' Joey added with a laugh.

'It's cannabis this week.'

'What, like Disability Week or something?'

Sean laughed, then took a quick look through the glass door as though he didn't want Sandra to hear him. 'I'm hosting a CAD event next week.' Then, in answer to Joey's quizzical look, 'County Against Drugs, CAD. It's a private–public anti-drugs partnership and they've got some new idea about showing people what cannabis plants look like. So if they spot any growing where they shouldn't . . .'

'They'll suddenly lose all fears of being kneecapped by the local druggies and turn in their neighbours, will they?'

'No. But we've got to start by educating people.'

'You should start by doing something more useful. More direct.'

'Like what? Beating them up in the Lion car park, perhaps?'

Joey held up an apologetic hand. But then added, 'Although it would be cheaper.'

Sean gave a slightly nervous glance at the door. 'You're sounding like Sandra now.'

Joey grinned. 'Go on then. How much is this spot the pot plant campaign going to cost? Couple of grand? For a few weeks? A few posters, leaflets, talks and visits to schools and then on to something like "get your three, oh no, five a day"? And when they want to waste more of our cash they change it to seven a day?'

'I get it. But most of it has been raised through private donations.'

'Still a waste of money. They'll never solve anything like that. The druggies, Sean,' he nodded inside to make the point, 'are like the brewers. They're out there 24/7. To fight it you have to meet it with a similar level of resource. And commitment.'

'Which is exactly why we need things like the CAD Partnership. To backfill. Plug the gaps in awareness.'

'It's not awareness you need to worry about, Sean. It's taking away the opportunities. And those who will exploit those opportunities. And other people.'

Megan came out of the door. 'Come on Dad, or Mum will make me have that salad thingy.'

'On our way.' He then turned back to Joey. 'Sandra hates me spending money on these things, but,' he shrugged. 'It'd only go on a necklace or something. And, well, this might help. A bit. So, why not?' He let the question hang in the air before following Megan back inside.

Joey waited for a moment and looked out at the hill dominating the skyline. Why not, indeed. It was his money that was funding Luke and Matt while they waited for their opportunity. It was money he was hiding from Natasha. And how long would he have to keep that up? Luke had told him that it definitely wouldn't be this weekend. They wanted the right opportunity. At least three settled days so that the wind and rain wouldn't compromise what they were doing. They wanted a few good clear nights. The weather forecast was crap for the whole of next week. Fatchops might be a dead man walking, but he might just see another weekend. The thing is though, thought Joey, as he went inside to join the now traditional family Sunday lunch, can I hold it together for another week?

3

First Contact

By the time Joey settled into his seat on the Monday 5.36, he knew his daughter had become the target for some young buck's raging hormones; her mate Becky was being stalked by some foreign bloke; his brother Sean was as idealistic as ever; there'd been three drug-related deaths in the past six months; Fatchops was still alive, and he still hadn't fixed that fence panel. Just another typical weekend at home really. He took a quick glance round the carriage. The usual weekly nomadic tribe of mixed gender and skills heading off as latter-day hunter-gatherers to the richer pastures, or jungle, of London. He nodded to one or two he had shared the journey but nothing more with over the past year or so and flicked open his iPad to catch up on the news. It wasn't long before his mind drifted away from the irrelevant world of sports headlines, political adultery and celebrity trivia.

105

Would Luke stick with the agreement simply to scare off Fatchops, or would he take it further? Joey just couldn't call it any more. When they were young bucks cruising the streets he'd seen what he thought was a killer look in Luke's eyes many times. When the adrenalin was pumping and he was itching for a fight. Yet, over the past few weekends he'd seen glimpses of something else. But as Joey had told Hilary Jardine, it was Luke who had been acting as the calming influence on him. Until that night at the Co-op and the Lion. That was when it changed, Joey thought. That was when the look in his eyes had changed. He'd heard about the thousand-yard stare. About guys having it after battle. Becoming detached from the reality of war. But Luke now seemed far from detached. It was almost the opposite. Luke was totally engaged. On a mission. And that, Joey reasoned, probably proved he was detached from reality.

He automatically reached for his phone but knew he couldn't contact Luke. He'd have to wait while everything took its course. He'd have to wait for the updates. Instead he scrolled to Natasha's number. Another weekly ritual. ON TRAIN. MISSING YOU. SPEAK 2NIGHT. LXXJ He then went back to the iPad and opened the latest revision to the electrical layout he'd downloaded the night before. The steam shower had been doubled in size, the spa had got bigger, again, and now Ivantmoreofich wanted the mood lighting in the pool to be co-ordinated with the cinema, and a separate ring main installed in the kitchen to run at

110 V so he could bring over appliances direct from the US. That, plus the mark-up on the transformers would go a long way to buying a car for Tanya. Keep it coming. Live the dream, mate. And let Benno scavenge at the weekends.

His concentration was broken as the train cruised through Stafford, momentarily projecting an image on to the reflective black of the windows. Another hour for the sun. Instead of refocusing on the drawings, his mind went back to Fatchops. From somewhere on the hill that dominated the town, Luke and Matt would be watching, waiting for that one static moment. When the conditions were just right to take the shot. Or take him out? Christ. The usual nagging question. How did he get involved? Well, he knew that. The typical pub chat about something needing to be done. And Luke saying he knew how to do it.

Joey glanced down the compartment. There were several guys about his and Luke's age. City warriors suited and booted with their laptops out and smartphones at the ready. Most slightly overweight. Some with the polished and honed look that only comes from the controlled conditions of the gym culture. They could probably run a marathon and bench press double their own weight but how many could sleep for ten days on the hill overlooking the town? How many would he want to be standing next to him on a Saturday night, or on the site in London, protecting his back? He reflected again on the ironies, perhaps cruelties of life that determined who and what you became almost as soon as you were born. We all start from different places but the rules of the game never change. Learn to blend in and survive.

He knew he could no more hold his own in whatever corridors of power, meeting rooms or conferences the suited brigade were heading off to face, just as he doubted he could survive something like Iraq or Afghanistan, as Luke appeared to have done. But then again, Joey thought, one of life's biggest ironies was that Luke probably wouldn't last five minutes on a United Nations building site. A bit like a cop being thrown into prison. Without the authority of greater firepower, he'd soon become an Equal Opportunities or Health and Safety casualty. That was something Joey was determined never to become. Which was how the catch-up conversation had turned to why, in all walks of life, someone usually needed to give someone a good slapping. When you couldn't turn to, or rely on, the so-called forces of law and order or the rules and regs that governed life. When Health and Safety could stop you climbing a ladder, but offered no guidance on what to do when you were shoved into a room by three guys demanding a commission on everything you earned or they'd kill you, your wife and kids and dog. Or when everyone knew who the druggies were but kept saying they had to have proof.

That was the common bond, from battlefield to playing field. When natural justice had to take second place to bureaucratic process. That was what had pushed them over the line. Especially when it came too close to Joey's own front door. When it put Tanya in danger. That's how he had got involved. When Tanya, like Janey before her, had found herself fighting off some knife-wielding druggie. When Luke asked if it was time to act. Would he like him to sort it out? It was one simple word. Yes. That was it. That was how it all started. That one word. And what he was keeping from Natasha.

His phone vibrated just as the train hurtled into the Kilsby Tunnel, the twin vibrations causing Joey to jump. He looked at the text. Natasha's reply. YOU 2. MORE EACH WEEK. MUST TALK TONIGHT. LXXT. Must talk? He looked at the time. 6.15. Too early for the school run, he thought. Guess I didn't hide things too well after all. He went to reply but whilst the tunnel was one of the engineering wonders built by Robert Stephenson on the London–Birmingham line in the mid-nineteenth century, with the gradients, bends and railway bed still able to facilitate today's inter-city flyers, Stephenson never envisaged mobile phone signals. Joey stared at the No Service icon. At least it would give him time to think.

'He's up to something, Sean. I know your Joey. And his mate Luke. He's always been trouble. He was only back five minutes and he and Joey were in the police station.'

Sean was trying to keep up with this trail of feminine intuition as he dried off after his morning waterfall shower. He was going in late, to give Sandra a lift. 'Is all this coming from seeing Joey talking to Luke in Sanderson's car park the other day?'

'It was the way they were talking.'

'Which was?'

'The way the kids do when they don't want us to know what they're up to.'

'Right.'

'Is that it?'

'Yes. I could throw you a "so what", if you like? But what's really going on here is displacement.'

'Enlighten me.' Sandra stood, with her old Armani trouser suit in one hand while she held in her stomach and looked in the mirror wall that lined their dressing room. If the Anglomania had been a bit tight, what was this going to be like after a couple of years?

'That.'

'What?'

'You having to go in and see the VAT man. So you think you have to squeeze into your old business suit. That's what's getting to you.'

Sandra let her stomach go. He was right. 'You want me to look the part, don't you?'

'You do in whatever you wear. Anywhere. Any time. And,' he added, slightly wearily, 'we do own the place. You can wear what you like.'

'I know. But I also know,' she added, pulling her stomach in again, 'I want to look the part.'

Sean put his arm round her waist and pecked her neck.

'I love every bit of you. Every inch means a special memory.'

'That's the trouble. Too many memories. And I've always hated this wall of mirror.'

Sean didn't want to remind her that she designed the dressing area, so tried more displacement theory. 'I don't know why you don't just buy yourself a new suit. I'm sure no one would notice you've gone from size 12 to size 12.5 or whatever size you've ballooned to over the past fifteen years or so. What time's he coming?'

'Nine. And that's another thing. It's not a him. It's a "Miss". Bound to be some size 8 stick insect.'

'What time will you be free, then?'

'Fancy taking me to lunch?'

'In that old suit? Not anywhere public, but er, I was wondering if you'd fancy dropping in to something at lunchtime.' He saw that she had picked up his hesitancy, although, fortunately, a mark on the Armani sleeve had her full attention so he tried to make it sound as casual as he could. 'You know, I'm letting the anti-drugs partnership use the demonstration area to show people what cannabis plants actually look like.'

A lick and dab at the sleeve. 'Why?'

'So they know what they are looking for. And can spot the decoys. We're going to put the real ones in among a few others like tomatoes or lupins. And a few more exotic varieties like Cleome or Castor Bean. To see if people can actually spot the real thing.'

111

Having salvaged the Armani sleeve, Sandra had moved to the shoe museum, as Sean called her racks of shoes, so he felt confident enough to continue.

'There's a great tale of an old couple in Bradford who bought what they thought was just a nice little plant from a car boot sale. A few years of TLC and they had a lovely bush outside their window. And armed cops demanding to know why they were growing cannabis in their garden.'

'Don't tell me. They got sent to prison, or something?'

'Not this time. Genuine mistake. But they got their bush confiscated.'

'And I suppose while you're donating our premises, staff and no doubt lunch, everyone else there will be being paid by the taxes we also pay?'

Sean sighed. She'd found the co-ordinated shoes so he now had at least 25 per cent of her attention.

'It's a public–private partnership. You know. Business in the Community and all that?'

'Where was the public bit of the partnership when we needed planning permission to turn that muddy field into a car park?'

Sean thought about replying along the lines of water under the bridge but saw that Sandra was about to try on the trousers. 'Spending our taxes saying no, Sean.' One leg. 'That's where they were. And why are they having this session today?' Other leg. 'The Council and police are supposed to be being paid because they know what they are doing.' She was delaying trying the zip.

Sean wondered if he should make his escape as Sandra rattled on, building up the momentum to try the zip. 'Like, perhaps, anti-drugs people knowing what the drugs they are anti-about actually look like?'

Her mood suddenly changed. Lifted. The zip had closed easily. 'I don't mind writing cheques to good causes, Sean, but a free lunch for people who should know what they're doing comes way down the list, for me. Sorry.'

'You sure you didn't vote UKIP?'

She ignored the gibe, as she twisted and turned in front of the mirror wall and held in the slight bulge above the waistband. 'I'll keep the jacket on.'

'So, it's safe to give your seat to someone else, then?'

Sandra nodded. 'I think I'll give this one a miss.' But I'll check out the lupins in Mum's garden, when I drop in there later. She often talks about how people should be allowed cannabis for pain relief.'

'That's just to save the surgery's drug budget.'

'If it makes sense and saves money?'

'Your mum's a receptionist, Sandra, not one of the medics.'

The look was all Sean needed to know that it was time to drop the subject or go. He was already dressed in his Barbour Countrywear shirt and moleskins, which he felt gave the right image at the garden centre, as well as the fact they were comfortable. He reached over for the Gieves and Hawkes suit and shirt that was hanging in a suit carrier, which in turn was hanging on the towel rail radiator. This was for lunchtime and, as Sandra had said, looked better than his favourite. But Sandra wasn't finished yet.

'But . . . that's part of the issue, isn't it? You're always saying most crime comes from social deprivation not criminal genes, so isn't the drugs issue a social issue as much as a medical one? Why don't we just let anyone who wants to do what that old couple in Bradford did, do it?'

'Grow their own?'

'For their own personal and private use. Then you handing out free lunches might be worth doing.'

'Bit radical coming from you. Thought you were in Joey's camp. Shoot druggies on sight?'

'If they are dealing and wrecking other people's lives.'

'I might just suggest that over lunch. Especially the shooting bit.' She shot him another sarcastic look, then turned back to the shoe racks. He stepped forward to nuzzle her neck before heading for the door, but she turned and pointed a Manolo Blahnik left foot at him.

'I bet that's what Joey and Luke are up to.'

'What? Growing or shooting? And I think your L.K. Bennett flats should be about right for the VAT Goddess.'

But Sandra was too focused to joust. 'They're growing stuff in that old cottage of Luke's.'

'Our Joe? No way.'

'OK. But he could be putting in the electrics for all the hydroponics and growing lights. Well? Couldn't he?'

Sean was about to say it was ridiculous, but there was that intuition thing. Joey and Luke had looked a bit odd in the supermarket car park the day before. And that business at the Lion. And, he had to concede, Joey often walked too close to the line.

'Joey won't be doing the drugs bit, Sean.' She'd read his mind. 'But you know what he's like. Anything to help a mate. Ask him what's going on. There's something.'

Sean nodded. He knew they'd be up to something. But drugs? No. Joey wouldn't do that.

By the time Natasha heard the shower pump signal that their elder son Alex had finally dragged himself out of bed, Joey's train was just passing the Roundhouse on its final glide down into Euston and he knew he might have something else to tell her tonight. He had almost made the decision to go back. Almost. When at that moment his phone vibrated. OUTSIDE. USUAL SPOT. It was from Benno. Waiting in Drummond Street just across the road from the side entrance in Melton Street. From there they would be on site in what had become known as the Billionaire's Bunkers within a matter of minutes.

Joey left the train and the travelling herd behind, turning right instead of left as he came off the platform ramp, and strode out through the loading bay to see Benno sitting in the old ambulance he used as a travelling workshop. He had long ago given up driving a white van mainly because he was fed up having it broken into overnight, despite fortifying it to a level Luke and his team wouldn't have objected to in Helmand, but mainly because even the traffic wardens who were paid per ticket usually ignored the ambulance. According to Benno. However, according to Joey, although Benno looked the part, especially in his dark overalls, hi-viz vest and the two old paramedic jackets he had hanging behind the seats, he usually remained untroubled because he had a face anyone would think twice about aggravating. In comparison, Bobby McBain's pebble-dashed features looked like an ad for Botox.

Benno was around five foot three of sinew and scars with a face that not only looked like the proverbial bag of spanners but looked like it had been formed by being hit with one. Which, in a way, it had been. When, thirty or so years before, he fell from a scaffolding, right on to his own bag of tools. He had told Joey he couldn't remember much about it except waking up to discover that as well as not being paid while he was off work, his then employers said he wasn't covered by any insurance because the accident had been his own fault. He had used the scaffolding, rather than the provided ladder, to take a shortcut to get from one floor to another. Everyone did it. In the time before Health and Safety became a religion and ladders were deemed instruments of the devil.

He was philosophical about it, as cases like his were now part of the chanted creed, just as he was philosophical about hitching the site fuel bowser to the back of his van one night. If they wouldn't give it to him. he'd take his own compensation. Everyone did that. In many ways it was a much fairer system. Everyone took what they thought they were owed, instead of some bean counter or computer calculating what some tax table said they could have. It was the face and the philosophy that had watched his back the past couple of years.

As Joey got closer to the ambulance he could see Benno in that all too familiar slightly bent forward position, staring at his lap. For most it would be taken as the BlackBerry Prayer position and he was checking his phone. With Benno it meant he was busy manufacturing one of his foul-smelling rollies. Sure enough, as Joey pulled open the door he had to clear the seat by scooping up the old Oxo tin that contained Benno's Rizlas and baccy.

'Do you have to light up every time I arrive?'

'Do you have to arrive every time I light up?' Evidence of which was slowly being dragged along Benno's bottom lip.

'How old is this thing?' asked Joey as he dropped the tin between the seats and wound down the window.

'Older than me.'

'Antique, then?'

'Probably. Me ma gave me that for me snap when I started out. You can get two rounds of cheese and pickle, a pasty, apple and a biscuit in there. As she did. Every day. I ended up hating cheese and pickle.' Having lit up, Benno started the ambulance and moved off, the rollie dangling from the corner of his mouth.

If you put Benno in a line-up with Luke and Matt and asked people to vote out the mercenary, tiny Benno would win hands down. He was, in a way. Like Joey, he was going from job to job, away from home and family, following the money. Which was how they'd met. Working on a hotel refurb in Luton. Then being asked by the builder to do some work on his own house in Borehamwood. From there one of his rich mates had asked them to work for him and before long they had formed an informal partnership, moving from one bling merchant to another. The houses and jobs getting bigger and more lucrative. Joey – well, Natasha – took care of all the paperwork and Benno pulled on a network of contacts they had built up over the past few years. Even as Benno exhaled and filled the cab with another cancer-inducing cloud of pollutants, he was someone else Joey would always want on his shoulder when things got tricky. As they seemed to be doing more often these days. That was why it was so hard making the decision to go back home. What would Benno do without him?

'Then what was up with Dad over the weekend?' Tanya asked, making herself a cup of coffee in her Starbucks to go mug. 'I mean, I know he does the Neanderthal thing because he thinks he has to, but he was a bit excessive on Saturday night.'

'How do you expect him to react after what nearly happened to you the other week?'

Tanya let out a long sigh. Not this again. 'Oh come on,

Mum. I nearly got killed like Aunty Janey? Really? She got jumped from behind by some mugger and run over.'

'That lad had a knife out at you, you said.'

'Yeah. And, like, right outside the garage with a million CCTV cameras. Not in the empty car park of the Co-op.'

'He had a knife, Tanya. And if he was crazy enough to do it outside the garage, then he was crazy enough to stab you.'

That point, along with her mother's obvious anxiety, was enough to at least make Tanya hesitate. 'OK. But he didn't, did he?'

'No. thank God.'

Which was enough to allow Tanya to swing back into gear. 'He was crapping himself more than we were. Well, except for Becky. And what would you have wanted me to do anyway, Mum? Let him rape me or make me go down on him, or something? Without a fight?'

'He was probably only after money,' Natasha replied quickly. She didn't want to contemplate anything else.

'Yeah. Exactly. And when I told him he wasn't getting any he backed off. Went looking for someone he could intimidate. Don't make yourself the victim. Isn't that what you and Dad have always said?'

'And which is why your father is probably being over-protective.'

'OK. I get that. Just as he has to get the fact that he can't be away all week and then come home and come over all heavy handed at the weekend.'

Even though she agreed with her daughter, and it was what had got her up so early, Natasha didn't want to get into family politics when she still had to get Lucy and the boys out the door. 'Can we talk about it tonight?'

'Sure, no big deal. Do you want a coffee to go?'

'Please. But how was Becky after not hearing from her Egyptian prince?'

'Don't let her hear you say that, Mum.' Tanya laughed. 'His name's Husani.'

'OK. I'm still getting used to every second person in town being an immigrant.'

'That is so racist.'

'It's not. It's a fact. Well, perhaps an exaggeration. But you know what I mean anyway. So how's Becky after not seeing Humani?'

'Husani. He still hadn't phoned her up to last night. After we cleared her phone he was probably giving her the silent treatment back, thinking that she had blanked him all Friday and Saturday. So, she's still devastated.' Tanya put the back of her hand to her forehead for the melodramatic effect. Then: 'God knows how Dad'd react if I came home with one of Hus's friends.'

'Actually, he'd be OK. Provided you weren't showing as much as you were on Saturday night. You can do short or low cut. But not both.'

'You mean Dad doesn't like me dressing the way he'd like to see you dressed?'

'I'd never be able to dress the way your father would like. And that's the point. He is your father. You're his daughter. And he knows there's too many blokes like him out there.'

'Which blokes are like Dad?' It was a bleary-eyed Ross heading for the cereal cupboard.

'None you know,' replied Natasha to prevent any potential Monday morning conflict. She picked up her phone and saw the text from Joey. OK. I'LL CALL WHEN FINISHED.LXXJ. But then noticed the time. 7.45. 'Any signs of your brother, or Lucy, Ross?'

'Someone's in the bathroom, which I guess won't be Alex.

Pass us the milk.'

'I hope you're not talking to me,' his mother replied.

''Course not. Her.'

'And who's "her"?'

Ross picked up the motherly tone, let out a huge symbolic sigh and trundled over to the fridge. Natasha headed for the door in search of the feet-draggers, but stopped as she passed Tanya. 'Tell Becky to be careful, though. Racist or not. I don't like the way they treat their women.'

'Point's already been made.'

As Natasha left, Tanya instantly replaced Sky News with *Friends*, while Ross unscrewed the top of the milk carton and tipped almost as much on to the table as landed in his cereal bowl.

'Look at the mess you're making, moron.' Tanya moved quickly to scoop up a sponge to wipe it up.

'I don't buy these big cartons, do I?'

As Tanya tried to work round Ross, and his namesake on screen was about to deliver his punch line, *Friends* was replaced by the planner and a nanosecond or two of Ross's favourite programmes until he settled on *Embarrassing Operation*.

'Don't move whatever you do,' Tanya growled.

He raised his bowl so she could wipe underneath. Then increased the volume on the TV. She reached over and turned it down. He turned it up. She snatched the remote and hit the standby button. He looked at her for a moment. She looked back, waiting for what he'd try next. It came.

'You're hormonal.'

'What?'

'You got a new boyfriend?'

'What?'

'It's not time of the month, so . . . ?' He let it hang with a shrug. Then: 'That what Dad was giving you a hard time about? You putting it out for this new bloke?'

'You're watching too much MTV.' With that she turned to go, but stopped. 'And how do you know when it's "time of the month"?'

'Apart from you being a right pain. Every four weeks or so, isn't it? Two of our ten-day timetables. It's week two. And I've seen the wrappings in the bin.' He gave another shrug and then grabbed the remote and turned the TV back on. 'I don't tweet about it or anything, though.'

'Thanks. You're such a comfort.'

'Is it him that's like Dad, then? This bloke?'

'Eat your breakfast. Like a good little boy.' She put the emphasis on little, but as she swept out the room she wondered if she'd been as grown up at his age.

And while Natasha was on the school run, Matt had left Luke in the hide and was on the scenic route home. Past Fatchops's chippy. Everything looked as it always did. Shuttered, barred and bolted, like almost every other shop along the High Street. Sign of the times, Matt thought as he ambled along. Almost. But no one else had so much CCTV and closed shackle hardened steel padlocks on their shutters. Supposedly bolt-cutter proof, they also had the highest insurance rating. Seemed a bit excessive to protect a few spuds and mushy peas, Matt thought as he went past, turning up the side alley where they had seen young girls being let out of the yard behind the chippy.

What were these characters actually up to? Matt pondered again as he felt the pulse in his leg quicken. Another reminder. Stay on mission, he thought as he carried on walking. Aware that someone would be watching the CCTV monitors, he was careful not to be too obvious while taking another long look at the steel door that must have opened into the yard. Double keyholes. One top. One bottom. Typical. No matter where they went they found similar scenarios. The bad guys thinking in fortress mode. Determined to keep everyone out, they concentrated on defending one entrance, forgetting that it also meant there was only one way out. Rats in a trap.

He hesitated just past the door, reached for his phone and adopted the BlackBerry Prayer position. He moved his thumbs but never touched the keypad. After a moment the phone screen lit. *⌡ſ₢% Random characters. It could be a pocket dial. But it meant Luke had been watching from the hill. It would mean nothing to anyone else. Especially to those who later might want to construct an incriminating timeline.

As Matt wandered on his way, Luke eased away from the spotting scope and ran over things again. They now knew what the chippy gang were up to. How they distributed. How they would try and escape. All we need now, Luke told himself, is how they are getting the stuff in and out.

Then he began to wonder if that mattered. The next link was the delivery guy. Follow him. Find the next real link. But, he thought, better to bring them to us. He put the scope back on to the side door to the chippy. He knew Fatchops would be out later to take the regular delivery. Luke's money was still on the delivery guy. Especially the way he had seen Fatchops react when the driver had dropped the box.

Perhaps we'll get a bit more when Matt does his return trip, Luke was thinking, when his train of thought was broken by something obscuring the scope. He looked up to see a stray Sanderson's shopping bag snagged on the gorse bush just in front of the hide. Before he could reach out to move it, it billowed and was lifted away on a passing swirl of wind. Luke watched it fly higher and higher, then dip and dive over the town as it was carried on the wind to land serendipitously who knew where, another symbol of the transient, disposable society that had both created and condemned towns like Highbridge to an uncertain future. Economies built on passing fashion rather than heritage. It also reminded Luke of the days he, Joey and their crowd used to come up to the top of the hill and set fire to the paper potato sacks they nicked from Sanderson's, when it was still a proper greengrocer's. Long before the Chinese lantern craze, if the wind was in the same direction as today, they would watch the sacks float towards the town, betting on how far they would travel. Until one came down in the cornfield behind T'House. And set the whole field alight.

Brilliant to watch, but leaving a long-lasting regret when they discovered it was the final nail in the coffin of Holt's Farm. The lost corn was the difference between between survival and bankruptcy. They had not spoken about it much, either then nor recently, but he and Joey had learned one of their first big lessons about consequences, and they still felt some form of obligation to their old community. Hard to express, but it was there. He put the scope on where that cornfield had been – now, of course, covered in housing – and wondered how much old farmer Holt lost, how much he'd sold up for and how much whoever bought it made from selling it for houses. And would it still be full of crops or cows instead of houses if they hadn't set that paper sack on fire? Or, his thought continued, if they had used plastic sacks instead.

He allowed himself a nostalgic sigh as he turned the scope back to the chippy. And then he made the connection. Plastic bags. Ends in t-i-c. Plastic. The chippy used plastic bags to put stuff in. But they would need more than one box. What came in a box? He focused the scope on to the chippy counter and panned along. Then. There it was. Best place to hide anything is in plain sight. Plastic forks. That's how they did it. It was the forks. Now they had it all. As soon as the weather settled, it would begin.

'But why bother? That's what I don't understand.'

'You're not going to give me a hard time about the free lunch too, are you, Glynnis?' Sean asked, as he came into the demonstration area still fastening his tie while shouting thanks to young Ben, their online wizard with a sensible haircut, now scurrying away with the cart he had used to bring in the chairs.

'It's your money so you can waste it any way you like, Sean,' Glynnis responded, more focused on straightening up the back row of chairs. 'If people want to grow drugs and kill themselves, then why stop 'em? It'd save us all money in the end. All that policing and hospital bills when they OD or whatever they do. And you'd sell a lot more compost.'

'Have you been speaking to Sandra?'

'Why? She saying how daft you are too? Although Byron seems to be enjoying himself at your expense.'

Sean followed her eye line to see Byron coming in with Gill Hawkess, the Project Co-ordinator of Working Together Today, or WTT as she referred to it. She was, as usual, perfectly coiffured and manicured, the flowing coat giving glimpses of her figure-sculpting but strictly business suit. Byron had a schoolboy's entranced grin on his face, as he pushed a plant trolley full of Gill's promotional material. Sean couldn't quite remember exactly what WTT actually was, beyond the fact that he knew they were some regional organisation that helped facilitate community action. Gill was always talking about the quest to train community organisers, which Sean found a difficult concept to grasp as he felt people were either organisers or not. Still, a lot of people in council and police circles must think that Gill and WTT were wonderful, as they kept giving her money to facilitate things, which, in itself, seemed to prove something, although Sean was still struggling to understand what.

'Surprised you know how one of them works, Byron.' Glynnis nodded towards the trolley, pressing on before

Byron could reply. 'Like a cup of tea?' That one was aimed at Gill.

'Oh, only if it's not too much trouble.' Gill flashed a professional smile that was supposed to convey how approachable she was. It merely bounced off Glynnis.

'Not for me it's not. And it's his money we're throwing away, isn't it. You can have a biscuit too if you like.' She turned to Byron. 'You can get your own.'

With that she wandered off to the café, leaving Byron to control his obvious irritation. He knew she was deliberately baiting him. As she always did when Sean was around.

'I'll, er . . . leave you two to it, then. Nice to have met you, Miss Hawkess,' he said.

Gill flashed another smile. One of charmed gratitude. 'Thanks for the help bringing them in.' As Byron left, Gill turned to Sean and dropped the smile. 'She's a bit of a character.'

It was a statement that didn't need a response, issued while she unpacked her portable pull-up banners. One about the CAD partnership: County Against Drugs. One about the local partnership. One about WTT. Of course.

Sean looked at the local banner. HAD: Highbridge Against Drugs. She caught his eye. 'Good, isn't it? HAD – following the CAD line. Each town across the county will have one.'

Sean looked at it again. 'Does that mean Barnfield will be BAD? Sandwalk will be SAD and Templeton a bit TAD?'

There was a moment's hesitation and uncertainty before another smile. This one of amused tolerance. 'That's the point about doing a pilot. Canvass views and opinions.'

Sean nodded but continued to stare at the poster. Gill's smile slipped again. She sensed there was something else. 'And?'

'Oh, er, I was just wondering, Highbridge Against Drugs, well, whether it looks a bit like a poster for a referendum? That there could be an opposition view. Highbridge For Drugs? Vote Yes or No?'

The smile of tolerance was replaced with one of polite bemusement. It was an adaptable weapon. 'Not really. We are all against drugs, aren't we?'

'Er, yes.'

He didn't get the chance to develop the argument as he saw that Gill was again reaching into her quiver of smiles. This time it was welcoming, as her attention had turned to something over his shoulder. He turned to see that she was now heading, hand outstretched, teeth flashing, to greet one of her benefactors, Chief Inspector Hilary Jardine.

As they went into a full networking exchange, Glynnis returned with two teas on a tray. And a plate of biscuits. 'I figured out what WTT means.'

'Go on,'

'Witches' Tittle Tattle.' With a nod at Gill and Hilary, Glynnis went off chuckling at her own joke.

Sean looked at the two women. One perhaps tittle-tattling, the other, he knew, more used to trials and trib-ulations. As Gill was busy searching her smartphone for something obviously important to pass on, Sean raised a teacup to Hilary, who glanced at Gill then raised her eyebrows and grinned in return. Obviously not one of the faithful. But all part of the job.

What was not part of any job, at least as far as Joey was concerned, was people taking advantage. As he was now witnessing outside the container that served as the mess room on site. The Italians were walking out grumbling, while the Chinese were lining up to pay. It was theoret-ically known as the Workforce Weekly Lottery Ticket, for which everyone was supposed to contribute £10. No one ever saw a ticket, nor doubted that tickets were ever bought. But Gustav, Ivantmoreofich's East European project manager, or all-round enforcer as the other site managers referred to him, sat at his table every Monday collecting the contributions for the kitty. From everyone. Except Joey and Benno.

'Hey Joseph,' Gustav called.

Joey ignored him, going to the tea table to make a brew.

'Joseph? Why do we have this conversation every week? You the only one not paying.'

'Then as I say every week, Gus, I'm the one missing out on the chance, aren't I.'

'And what about your friend. Doesn't he deserve the opportunity?'

Joey was going to ignore him again when he saw Gustav was deliberately looking out the window, up towards the third-floor scaffolding. He went to the door and looked up, and his heart sank. His back stiffened and his hands started to clench and unclench, as he saw Benno obviously cornered by two of Gustav's known associates.

Joey turned back to Gustav. 'Going to have a nasty fall, is he? If I don't pay up?'

Gustav just shrugged. Then gestured out across the site. 'These places can be very dangerous. Yes? But you buy ticket. Good luck comes.'

Joey looked up at Benno, holding a half-metre length of rebar and ready to try and give as good as he would get, but Joey knew that, whilst he had the heart, the years would let him down.

'So you reckon it's the forks then?' Matt asked.

'Got to be,' Luke answered. 'He's been in and done his usual Mr Sheen act. Everywhere spotless.'

'Make even RSM Bronson smile, that would.' Matt grinned. 'Squeaky clean and free of any traces. Of anything, yeah?'

Luke nodded, slipping back to the Barrett as Matt continued, now convinced by Luke's logic. 'Which is why he puts a new box of forks in there every night. It's not just out with the old evidence but in with the new supply.'

Luke refocused the scope on the box. It was all so

obvious. Now. When someone passed over a marked note, Fatchops gave them a wrap. But his wrap contained a plastic fork wrapped in cellophane, inside of which were the drugs. Neat.

'What do you reckon?' Matt then asked. 'If Fatty doesn't take the bait, we go after the delivery driver? Weather's looking good for it, right?'

'Right,' Luke agreed as through the scope he picked up Fatchops bringing in a bucket of fish from the back. He put the Barrett right in the middle of his chest as he watched him start to batter the fish. The .50 cal round would blow him apart. Shock and awe. He held his breath and counted. At this range, the bullet would take around one and a half seconds. But it would only take a second for a stray head to bob in and out of the reticle. They needed five. The five seconds it would take someone coming in from the front or the back door to reach the counter. Five seconds when Fatchops would be standing still and no one else was likely to step into the shot.

Five seconds was a long time in a busy chippy so Luke knew they were unlikely to get that clear a shot until the mid-evening lull. Like the changing of the tide. When all the people coming home from work had been fed and just before the pub exodus began. Then, with luck, Fatchops would once more be battering the fish. Luke started breathing again. And let Fatchops continue to do the same.

'Do you think she ever stops to take a breath?' Hilary Jardine asked Sean, as she nodded towards Gill Hawkess.

'Nose breather. Like the Aborigines. Circular breathing. In the nose, out the digee. Hum-da-hara-hum-da-hara.

'Done a bit with your didgeridoo, have you, Sean?'

It was the sort of risqué remark that never ceased to amaze Sean, coming, as it did, from the lips of Chief Superintendent Jardine. He was never sure whether she meant it or just had the knack of triggering something in his own brain. He knew there was gossip about her and Joey once, even though everyone said she was out of his league. Middle class. Posh. But then, they said Natasha was out of his league too. Joey and Hilary had always denied it, but everyone knew they had something going. Whatever it was, it was short-lived as she surprised everyone by leaving before her A-levels, refused to go to university and joined the police. She was head girl. She was supposed to become a doctor like her father. But she had moved to Manchester and become a copper.

No one could ever quite read Hilary. Especially when she had that mischievous glint in her eye. As she had now, while they stood waiting for the Chair of the County Council to arrive to anoint the initiative and probably drone on about the increasing importance of public–private partnerships in an age of austerity.

Sean took a look around. The usual shirt and tie brigade scoffing his sandwiches and tea. The Chair of the Town Council, Harold Peagram, was present. One-time carpet king on the High Street, now retired and enjoying restoring classic tractors. He had probably only turned out because the Chair of the County Council was coming. At the moment he was swapping stories with the Secretary of the Round Table, Jason Charles and the guy who ran the tyre outfit behind the railway station, whose name Sean could never quite remember. Brenda Hodgson from Pets Parlour was talking to Samir Khan who now ran the Trading Post, the only real local shop for local people left on the High Street he kept telling everyone, deliberately ignoring the fact that he had only arrived five years earlier.

The current Head of the Comp, Julia Erskine was there, as was the Vicar, Deborah Joynston, known as Dilby after her TV counterpart, talking to Lady Winifred Garstang, or Winnie to the locals. Pushing ninety, now a bit unsure on her feet but still sharp as a razor. She seemed to have been around for ever and been on every committee, and had been a governor on the Comp while Sean was still there. Her title came from her deceased husband, who had been knighted for services to a military charity. Although neither talked about it, he was something of a war hero with the RAF and they had lost two sons to military action during the slow dismantling of the British Empire. The only clue left was the commemorative plaque in the porch of the parish church, a porch paid for by Sir Dennis and Lady Garstang.

All this was something of an irony as while Winnie

was very happy to chat to Dilby she had refused to set foot in the church since her arrival. It wasn't that she didn't agree that women should be ordained, but it was ridiculous that any woman would devote herself to the idea that God could have been a man. Men worshipping men was one thing. She could tolerate that. Women did that too. But to see another woman worshipping at the altar of what was nothing more than the creation of a serial adulterer and wife Killing King was too much. Now that Dennis had passed away she had no one else to pacify.

Hilary's grin had widened as she looked across at Gill Harkess, in full networking mode, offering her card to the Director of Public Health.

'She's certainly one of a tribe. Still, I suppose we need them. Get between us and the people we need to reach. Just a pity we seem to spend more time talking to them than doing the day job.' She paused for a moment, then asked, 'But what about you, Sean? Why are you doing this?'

'You're the third woman to ask me that today,' Sean said.

'Oh dear. And?'

'And . . . You probably know the answer, Hilary.'

'The Nolan equivalent of the Armalite and the ballot box?'

Sean turned, genuinely surprised. And irritated by the inference.

'Sorry,' Hilary said. 'Too long in counter-terrorism,

perhaps. But you favour politics over, I'm guessing, Joey's and Luke's desire for direct action?'

Sean's irritation was turning to anger. 'God, Hilary. Talk about two and two make five. If Joey and Luke wanted to take "direct action", as you term it, do you think they would have waited three years?'

She went to respond, but Sean could feel his blood pressure rising. 'No, hang on. And this . . .' He waved his arm round. 'Well, what? My sister gets killed by druggies, so I want to try and do something about the growing problems? Doesn't take much police work to figure that one out, does it?'

Hilary was starting to feel uncomfortable. But Sean kept going. 'So what's the issue here? I don't know what Joey's up to, if anything, but if I don't support this sort of thing, who will?'

'I'm sorry, Sean. I never really meant anything. It's just . . .' She looked and sounded full of regret. 'OK. Sorry. You heard what happened in the park at the weekend?'

Sean started to nose-breathe. Calming down. 'Noah gave me chapter, verse and every social media posting.' His anger was now displaced by curiosity.

'Oh, I put my foot in it with Joey too,' Hilary explained. 'Grilling him about what his friend Luke Carlton is doing home.'

'And?'

'Two and two make five. Anyway,' she added, 'keep on

doing what you are doing. We do need and appreciate it.' She offered a weak, almost apologetic smile as she moved away.

Sean watched her go, recognising that it must be difficult policing a community of old friends, but wondering as much about his own reaction as hers. Joey and Luke both had bad reps. He accepted that. And she was, when all was said and done, a copper. But why did it cause him to react so forcefully?

Joey was still looking up at Benno, cornered on the edge of the scaffolding. Remembering the fall he had had in the past, he turned back to Gustav. 'OK. Call off the dogs and I'll sort something out.'

He stepped back from the window, boiled up the kettle and started making a fresh pot of tea.

Gustav weighed Joey up and down. He was still not sure how to read him. Most would have buckled a long time ago.

'It's only ten pounds, Joseph. Not a lot. I offer you five. And you still refuse? What is the point?'

'That is the point, Gus. It doesn't sound much, but from one hundred blokes?'

'Ah, you jealous?'

'No. I just think you're a parasite.'

Gustav laughed. 'We don't have to get married.' Then his voice became more threatening. 'Just help out your friend.'

Joey nodded. He could see he didn't have much choice, dug into his pockets, pulling out a few coins. He counted them before putting them on the table. 'Two pound forty. All I got on me. Until tomorrow.'

Gustav looked, gave a smirk of derision, then turned to the window and gestured for the others to let Benno go. 'That will be twenty pounds tomorrow. For you both. This I keep as interest.'

Joey glanced out to see that Benno was now safe and coming down the scaffold, before picking up the teapot and then suddenly kicking the edge of the table so it rammed into Gustav's stomach. Then he reached over and pulled his head down hard on the table. Holding it there, with the teapot hovering just above, he leaned over him.

'Listen, you. I don't care what you and the others do. But I'm telling you now, once and for all. I'm not inter-ested. And neither is Benno. And if you get any ideas of coming after us again . . .'

He poured the tea across Gustav's neck, causing him to yell in pain. Joey held him down for a moment or two before letting him pull his head up.

'You're right, these are dangerous places.'

'I kill you.'

'You can try. But first, you'd better get that under a cold tap. Or get to a hospital.'

Gustav shoved the table aside as he made for the door, pushing a surprised Benno out of his way.

'What's going on?' Benno asked.

'Tea?' Joey said, offering up the teapot.

Benno looked out to see Gustav being bundled into a car. 'Looks like he's off to A&E.'

Joey glanced up at the clock. 'Let's hope the waiting time's still around four hours, then. We'll be away by then.'

'And what about tomorrow? You know he'll be back.'

'I do,' Joey replied, calmly pouring the tea. 'And as James Bond said, Benno: tomorrow is another day.'

4

Certainty

The buzz had already gone round the site. Joey had put Gustav in hospital. It both enhanced his reputation and increased the chance of retaliation. It was now also one of the key factors Joey was considering while trying to make up his mind about going back home, while, at the same time, figuring out how best to run the 110 V ring main Ivantmoreofich wanted.

He wondered if it would make it easier if he told Benno he could keep all the stuff they had stashed. Or reclaimed, according to Benno. The idea had been that they would use it for refurbs instead of buying new, and they had around £10,000 worth in a lock-up in Camden. If I let him have that, Joey thought, it would give him a bit of a head start. Or would it? Would it only help ease Joey's conscience? Initially Benno had been the one who had taken Joey under his wing and found the work, but recently his age had been catching up with him and, as the incident with Gustav had demonstrated, Joey was now his minder.

Sean was still pondering on what had triggered his anger with Hilary Jardine earlier. He knew everything had been heightened when his niece Tanya was threatened and he had spent a lot of time after that, like Luke, talking Joey out of going hunting with his baseball bat. But it was deeper than that. The attack had tapped into something else. Something deeper.

A growing desire to try to do something to make things happen. He was getting more and more fed up listening to everyone complaining about why things never got done. Whether it was emptying the bins, fixing the street lights or clearing out the druggies from the park. It was always the way. Why can't the Council do something?

He was never quite sure what had initially fired him up, but knew it had started with the fight over planning permission. All he and Sandra had wanted to do was expand the business, create more jobs and sort out the parking issues with the neighbours. He couldn't understand why, when the local paper's letters pages were constantly full of people moaning about his customers parking on the grass verges, the planners took such an intransigent line. The muddy field, as Sandra constantly referred to it, had suddenly become an important wet meadow, which just happened to be right opposite one of the local councillors' houses.

At first Sean had taken the line that that was just local gossip until Sandra came home from tennis one day to tell him that Dorothy Mathis, whoever she was, had confirmed that it was indeed the Executive Member for Tourism and Business who lived directly opposite that muddy field. Not only that, but after googling it on her phone while changing ends, Sandra had galvanised Wendy, who apparently ran what was regarded as the militant wing of the Mums 'n' Tots Club at the community centre, to organise an online petition while Nicky, who knew the mother of Arthur Young, the local newshound, soon got him on the case. Within a week a perplexed and bemused councillor was in the local paper sweeping aside any misunderstandings or objections to the excellent plan to resolve a long-standing community issue while helping a local business to thrive. That was, after all, why he was elected, the quotes said.

While it all worked out well in the end and Sean made a point of throwing a Christmas party for the Mums 'n' Tots militant brigade, he, like many others, was left wondering why it always seemed to be like that. Why was the community always fighting the Council? A lot of it could be put down to the fact that the Council had to do what was for the good of the many over the needs of the few, but Sean sensed it was deeper than that. He'd sensed it as soon as he and Sandra had come home from their global wanderings. Having experienced the 'why not?' atmosphere of the greater global emerging economies, even in parts of the USA where 'why not?' still trumped 'why?', he had found the restrictive, rule-driven, jobsworth psychology of Britain oppressive.

Had it got worse while they were away? But thinking back he had concluded that there were now more rules because there were now more things to do in life, and therefore to regulate. If you didn't have anything to do you didn't need a rulebook. It was a legacy of the aristocratic feudal system that the country had still not quite shaken off. Everyone, as far as officialdom was concerned, was still expected to know their place. That was the trouble with politics. Before they were elected, candidates wanted to be representatives. Once elected, they became leaders. And leaders expected people to, well, follow. Follow their lead. Be told what to do. Didn't they?

And to do that they needed a way to control things. Rules. Regs. And the police. Was that what Hilary was querying? Why was he stepping out of his place? Not leaving things to them to sort out. All this was going through his head as he heard the Chairman of the Council thank him for his support and hospitality and ask him to come forward and say a few words.

'Thank, you Mr Chairman,' Sean began. 'It's a pleasure to do whatever I can to help our local community.' He turned back to the assembled community representatives in front of him only to focus on Glynnis apparently chasing Arthur Young away from the food with a shake of her head as she started to quietly clear the buffet.

That was it. No more. She was protecting her profit margin. His eye caught Hilary Jardine's and he saw she was smiling at him. A supportive smile that would have made Gill Hawkess proud. It was the old friend again. Not the rule enforcer.

He returned the smile, and then heard himself say, 'This is the bit I always like. When I find out what I am going to say.'

'Run it past me again.' Luke was trying to absorb one of Matt's latest ideas.

'The average smoker costs the NHS about thirty or forty grand over their lifetime, especially at the end when they're coughing their guts up. OK?'

'So you tell me,' Luke responded. 'And this is one for the list, is it?'

Matt nodded. 'One hundred and one things to do with a sacked sniper.' He had started compiling the list when they had heard that they, like many others, were being 'released to pursue their careers elsewhere', as some suit had told them at the debriefing. Funnily enough, as Joey had told Benno, they had not found many jobs advertised for their skill sets once they were out of the services.

'I haven't started ranking them yet. Just, you know, brainstormin' the ideas and that. But I think stopping smokers beats shooting badgers and foxes.'

Luke conceded the point with a nod. 'It certainly takes things up a level or two.'

'OK,' Matt continued. 'So how much does a bullet cost?'

'What calibre?'

'It's supposed to be theoretical, Luke. But, OK, let's say we'd use a standard H&K PSG1. So, 7.62, right?'

'About three dollars a box or something. Or what was that gear we used on the last job?'

'Er, Tulammo. Yeah. Around 25 cents that Canadian guy said. OK, bulk buy. We'd probably get 'em for less than 15p.'

'So, your argument is, we just shoot smokers and instead of the thirty grand it costs to treat them, it only costs 15p to waste them?'

'Yeah.'

'I can see some people voting for it.'

'And I know what you're going to say next. Win the war, lose the peace, right? How do we win the minds and hearts beforehand?'

'Something like that,' Luke conceded again.

'OK. The thing that's always missing. Fairness. Give everyone a chance.'

'What? Arm the smokers so they can shoot back?'

'Now you're being ridiculous.'

'Oh, sorry.' Luke slid back into the hide. Nothing would happen until tonight. He reached for the boiled sweets in one of the ration packs. 'Go on then. Win my heart and mind.'

'We set up on top of a high building. OK? Good angles.

All-round vision. We spot a smoker. Red dot them. Bit of a jiggle until they see it. They get thirty seconds to stub out. Or be taken out. Their choice, isn't it?'

'If they know what the red dot is.'

'Labels on all ciggy packs. Red dots can kill. Something like that.'

'Education. Always the key. But, that's it? One chance? What about, I dunno, someone who's short-sighted or colour-blind? Or am I just being a woolly liberal?'

'No, it's a perfectly valid democratic argument. Which is where we nick the three strikes rule from the Yanks.'

'"We" do, do "we"?'

'Yeah. So they just get a warning for the first offence, right? Blam. Fleshy bits around the armpit. You know the way smokers hold their arms when they light up.' He had put the Barrett's scope on one such target about to light up, watching him raise his arms slightly to shield the lighter from the wind. 'They get that fixed and, here's the clever bit . . .'

'It all sounds very clever to me so far.'

But Matt was winding up to his really clever bit, so missed the sarcasm. 'During the patch-up, the medics stick in an RFID implant. Use radio scopes that get a return path from the implant, right? Second-time offender. Blam. Opposing upper body shot.'

'And we fix that. And put in another implant?' Luke asked and saw Matt nod with a grin of delight. He knew he was being drawn in, but when Matt started on one of his theoreticals, it was like approaching a black hole. Once over the event horizon there was no turning back. 'So the next time they get tagged. Two return signals. Third offence. Kill shot?'

'But don't forget the thirty-second warning. It's their choice to stub out, or –'

'– be taken out,' Luke finished it off for him.

'Three shots. 45p.' Matt beamed.

'Er . . . what about the cost of the operations to patch up their armpits?'

'Less than five grand, on average, apparently. For a straightforward in and exit repair. We'd be using balls, remember. So, on average, three at five is fifteen plus the 45p for the ammo, right? Couple of grand for us and overall it'll save the NHS between ten to twenty grand. And don't forget, that's only for the right stubborn so-and-sos. I reckon most would jack it in after the first shot.'

'Or before. With enough publicity. We could get that Ross Kemp to do a show about it.'

'Right. As you pointed out. Education. Always about educating people. And multiply it all up by the millions of smokers we'd take out of the system. Money that can be better spent on roads and education and other health problems.' He held out his hands. 'Simple, yeah? But the best bit is that it gives people like us something to do with the skills the government has spent years giving us, but then doesn't know what to do with when we've finished killing on their behalf. So. We just carry on doing it for them. In a new way, with a renewed sense of purpose, while saving the taxpayer a fortune in the long run.'

'I get it. Stub out or be taken out. It's catchy. And you have thought it through, haven't you?

Matt nodded, as he slid back from the Barrett, while adding, 'And I've got the perfect name for it.'

'Go on.'

'Surgical Strikes.'

Luke couldn't suppress a laugh. It was so daft. So macabre. But made so much sense. As much as it did them lying in a hide waiting to take a shot at a fat bloke in a chippy.

'Never happen though, would it?' Matt grinned as he reached across for a granary bar.

'Something tells me not,' Luke replied.

'We'll just have to go back and work for the Yanks. Be the ones that the locals whinge about. They come over here. Take our sniper jobs. Kill our enemies. Kill our friends. Should be local killing by local people. That's what they'll mutter into their beards. And exactly what everyone's muttering here, isn't it?'

Luke looked across at Matt, now rummaging in the ration box for another granary bar. Sometimes he was never quite sure. The line between genius and madness.

'What you looking so glum about?' Benno suddenly asked as he wriggled out from a service duct dragging the 110 V cable behind him. No one else was small enough to fit.

'Oh, usual. Why life has to be so complicated.'

Benno just cackled. 'Keep telling you, Joey, lad. It ain't. Do unto others and all that. If everyone's OK, it's fine. But if they're not, then you have the right to slap back.' He held up one end of the cable. 'You figured this out yet?'

'Nearly. Get the return to behind that worktop.'

Benno nodded and started to pull the cable from its reel, as Joey mulled over Benno's words. It seemed like such a simple code. Much simpler than the turning the other cheek line. It was that simple but markedly different interpretation of the Christian ethic that had got him into so much trouble during his life. Especially the bit about not taking matters into his own hands but letting others like the school or the law do it for him. Problem was, they never did, really.

'It's probably the reason that mate you were telling me about can't settle after leaving the forces,' Benno offered. 'A lot of them can't. If someone sticks a gun in your hand and the authority to use it, must be a bit hard having to deal with the jobsworths you meet back home.'

Joey had been telling Benno a bit about Luke. You got to know someone very well when you slept in a sleeping bag side by side. Luke may have been on some mountainside with Matt, but Joey had spent many a cold draughty night with Benno, kipping down on site to save spending money on digs.

Joey had also told Benno that life seemed to be falling

into place for Luke when he met and married Janey. He had only a year left on his term before they would buy one of the small cottages on Top Road that, as its name suggested, looked down over Highbridge, and then start a family. How Luke then went to Afghanistan and while scraping the remnants of his colleague from the remains of a Snatch Land Rover he got the call to say Janey was dead. A relay of transport legs got him back for the funeral but 48 hours later he was back hunting the Taliban with a renewed vigour his commanders were concerned about but couldn't fault.

But, Joey explained to Benno, they had offered him all the usual psychobabble counselling, as he referred to it, but fell back on his own self-diagnosis. He had had only two things in his life and one of them was now dead, killed for no purpose other than becoming another statistic. It was not long before the disillusionment mounted alongside the body bags.

While the cause was worthy, Luke had repeatedly told Joey, the resources and political will were, as usual, lacking. Politicians always seemed to want to fight a civilised war. But, Luke kept asking, what the hell was that? The locals never appeared to mind blowing up their own, whether kids, women or passers-by. So why not let our lads get down in the gutter with them and rip 'em up?

They all knew it was about politics and opinion polls. And risk aversion. Just the system. But Joey also knew that, like Luke, Benno understood the real cause of disillusionment. Being screwed by that system. Just as Benno had become a victim of Health and Safety, so Luke became a victim of austerity cuts. Having decided to re-enlist he discovered that, despite his past service, he was, like so many others, no longer required. So he joined one of the American companies that provided what was euphemistically called 'additional security'. Luke knew he was following one of the oldest traditions of warfare, from the Roman legions through the Crusades and into Afghanistan. History's hired guns. Of course he was never allowed to use the term 'mercenary', but as Natasha had said, that was exactly what he was. And whatever he did, he made sure he was paid. Handsomely.

'So why'd he come home?' Benno had asked, going straight to the point.

'Dunno, Benno. Just dunno,' Joey had responded after deciding that despite how close they were, he wasn't going to say it was because after a late-night chat at the cottage, the obvious conclusion they had reached was to use the skills Luke had been given. And shoot the sort of people who had caused the death of Janey.

It was all this and the sense of camaraderie Joey shared with Benno that was going through his mind when Benno asked him why he looked so glum. To help one friend he would have to let down another.

Sean had been speaking for about ten minutes on the theme of how most people have strong opinions on what needs to be done but feel powerless to influence anything. A feeling that no one in authority listens or is in touch with them. Looking round the room he noticed how this just bounced off the seemingly impervious skin of officialdom. A sign that he was right? Or simply that they'd heard it all before?

He decided to ramp it up a bit.

'But, well,' Sean continued. 'We lost another of our young people at the weekend. Another senseless death. We probably all have our own individual opinions on what we should and shouldn't do. But that is always tempered, perhaps restrained, and constrained, by what we can do. I mean, what we are allowed to do.'

He turned and looked deliberately at the County and Council Chairmen and then towards Hilary, the major power brokers in the room. The Chairs remained impassive. Did they really have an opinion, Sean wondered, or was this just something they had to do as part of the role? But from Hilary there was a slight nod, although that, Sean knew, could simply illustrate either an understanding that people will take things into their own hands if frustrated enough, or her own desire to be let off the leash. To hang 'em and flog 'em. It did, however, give Sean his next line.

'But does that mean more draconian action? Zero tolerance? Round 'em up?' He looked at Hilary, then to Arthur Young who was now taking advantage of Glynnis heading off to the kitchen to work his way through a plate of mini chocolate éclairs. 'Hang 'em and flog 'em? Or, as we've tried that for years, decades, perhaps centuries, do we look for a new strategy?'

'And when that fails, yet again, is it any wonder that people are looking to fringe politics? If they think those in the traditional parties – those in power – don't listen or seem powerless to act, is it any surprise they start to look for answers elsewhere?'

He hesitated for a moment. Wondering how far he should push his own ideas today. Or should he just play the polite host? He noticed Arthur was now being joined by a few other grazers who had spotted the cakes. Sod it, Sean thought, I am paying for this. Taking a deeper breath, he raised his voice above the growing gabble.

'But do you know what I really think? We should stop messing about with all this.' He waved his hand in the direction of the CAD pop-up displays. 'All this partnership stuff is great, but what is the point?' He saw Gill's teeth immediately retract behind stiffening lips. A smile of apprehension. This could be bad.

'I don't mean the partnership bit. That's fine.' The lips remained tight. 'But what are we really working towards? Teaching people what cannabis plants look like? For what? So they can spy on their neighbours? Or worse, as someone has already pointed out to me, they turn informant on the local drug gangs and then get knee-capped, or worse, for doing it?'

Gill was slowly moving towards the County Chairman.

He might need some support, but Sean noticed he had a smile on his face. Did that mean he agreed? Or that he enjoyed someone making an idiot of himself? But the smile didn't match the one that now spread across Hilary's face, although Sean noticed her eyes were not on him but on an almost panicky Gill heading towards her main funder. Even the newshound was grinning as he put down his plate and reached for his iPhone.

'I don't mean to be controversial,' Sean continued, 'but surely the answer is in education.' He looked over to find the Head of the Comp, who had frozen, chocolate éclair almost in her mouth. He saw the expression on her face. Oh God, she was thinking. What's he going to blame me for now?

'Not in school,' Sean quickly added. 'As the kids probably know as much, if not more than any of us about the "drugs bad" philosophy, but real education about what drugs – any drugs – do to you.'

The éclair disappeared into a relieved and grateful mouth.

'We spend time teaching our children the dangers of things like bleach under the sink, don't we? We practically educate them on how to handle two other major killers: alcohol and nicotine. But on other things we remain silent. We don't even try to find out, if we are honest, because we feel it isn't, well, it doesn't feel right. Is that simply because we think that if something is illegal we shouldn't? Somehow we feel we are not allowed to learn more about it.' He emphasised it again. 'Or, is it because we are not encouraged, perhaps allowed, to discuss these things openly?'

Despite the now almost tolerant smiles from the Chairman and Hilary and the look of glee from the newshound, Sean could almost feel the temperature in the room drop. Vicar Dilby's lips were pursed. Almost as tight as Gill's. This isn't what they came for. It should have been a nice pleasant lunch. Not a seminar. Or a debate.

'I know that's not what I was supposed to say.' Sean was now almost apologetic. 'But, well, you are eating my sandwiches and what do they say: there's no such thing as a free lunch?'

It got a few weak smiles. But a lot more nervous glances towards Hilary and the Chairman, both having regained their impassive public personas.

'You calling for legalisation, then, Sean?' It was Arthur the newshound, now sensing if not a possible front page, then a definite spark for the letters page.

Sean glanced across at Gill. Eyes wide, head shaking slowly, lips forming the word noo-o-o. There was no grant funding in legalisation. His eyes flicked to Hilary. Her face rigid but her eyes smiling. Go on, you dug the hole. The Head was trying not to catch anyone's eye, while Winnie Garstang was beaming. Another man making an idiot of himself?

'No, Arthur,' Sean replied. 'But what about regulation? We do it with cigarettes and alcohol. Why not other drugs, like cannabis?'

'So you're saying cannabis is no worse than booze and fags?'

'Nice try,' Sean countered. 'But that's one for the medical professionals to answer, actually. There's a debate going on about whether terminally ill people should be prescribed cannabis as part of the end of life palliative care.'

'All cancer patients should be encouraged to smoke, then?'

'Now I know you are being provocative.'

'It's what I get paid for.'

'OK. One last thing, then I'll let everyone get on with the cakes, tea and learning how to spot the pot.'

There were a few relieved faces as Sean paused to try and put things simply and quickly. 'As a society, we have learned how to control alcohol and tobacco. No one really thinks of injecting pure alcohol or nicotine, as they would die. We have learned how to use those drugs by diluting them: 3–4 per cent alcohol. Dangers of tobacco. And so on. We teach our children these things. Why shouldn't we do it with other things? And, Mr Chairman, we have also learned to tax the use of those drugs. Taxes that pay for a lot of the services your authority delivers.' He turned to Hilary. 'I know we still have crime attached to their use, but at least the money that taxes raise helps provide the resources to fight it.'

As both the Chairman and Hilary gave a nod of concession Sean decided to quit while he was, if not ahead, then at least climbing out of the hole he had dug. 'OK. That's it for me. Except to remind you of the first public consultation up at Treetops tonight at . . . er . . . 7.30?' He looked across to Gill, who had a smile ready. Confirmatory. Supportive.

'So, sorry if I went off on one, but please support CAD whenever and wherever you can . . . And . . . have a browse round while you are here and spend a bit to help me pay for the sandwiches . . . And . . . everyone can have a 10 per cent discount for being so polite. Thank you.'

The last bit at least got the applause going and Sean headed off to get a cup of tea trying not to look at either Glynnis or Byron, who was now clearly in Glynnis's camp. Ten per cent discount?

Luke was alone in the hide. Matt had gone on the Costa run, leaving Luke mulling over the point that local people should kill local people. Another bit of perverse logic. But one that avoids the bit everyone forgets. Not the people doing the killing, but the ones who see the horror. He had no qualms or doubt that Fatchops deserved what was coming. Like his suppliers. If a half-inch piece of steel blew your head apart you wouldn't know it, but everyone standing around you would never forget it. Did they deserve that? Did everyone else deserve what happened to Janey?

He looked at his watch. 17.55. Then panned the Barrett along the street. The guy with the silver Transit would be arriving any minute. Silver was the new white van around Highbridge, Luke had noticed. Then the old boy from No. 78, who always struggled to get his wheelie bin out through the front of the house, would hobble along and wave to Silver Van Man. Then the kid on his mountain bike. The woman in the hi-viz jacket on her way home from the Community Centre. And all the other regulars would come and go. Habit. Routine. POLO.

Eventually the scope came back on to its intended target, now finishing off his nightly cleaning routine and, yes, putting out his box of special forks, just below the counter, below the one already open on the countertop. No one was going to help themselves to the specials. Another hour and the banker would arrive to stand in the alley with the stack of marked notes and the users would start arriving to convert their hard-earned or easily stolen cash. Luke put Fatchops's head in the cross hairs. It would blow apart like a ripe melon. If the bullet hit him. The problem was that it was going to have to be a cold snatch shot. No chance to readjust. When they had those five seconds they needed to make sure he was stationary and no one else would walk into the shot. He moved the scope down to Fatchops's torso, then grinned. That's too big to miss. Just as he did, the hi-viz jacket of the woman from the Community Centre appeared in the scope. Exactly what they wanted to avoid.

If he had squeezed the trigger then, the woman in the hi-viz jacket would have arrived just in time to see

Fatchops's head blow apart. She might even have ended up with some of his brains mixed in with her nightly cod and chips. And be traumatised for the rest of her life. Luke had long since been desensitised. He'd actually been trained, perhaps indoctrinated, to accept it as simply a natural outcome. They all had. And in the age of the Internet he couldn't understand how some still arrived in the so-called theatre of war and were shocked at what they saw. It was all over the web. If YouTube didn't let you see it there were plenty of other ex-military, soldiers of fortune or wannabe sites that had all the graphic detail, including, because of smartphones, the soundtracks.

That was the real difference, Luke remembered. The sound. They had all gone through the live fire drills with instructors yelling their lungs out, but unfortunately the targets and their families had not been on the induction courses. A dickhead pretending to be a bad guy was nothing like the wailing grief and eyes of pure hatred that came at you when things got really hot. Like the first time you get whacked in the school playground. It isn't play fighting. It hurts. And it's a big shock. And the bigger the whacking, the bigger the trauma. No, Luke thought, while Fatty deserved everything he had coming, that woman in the hi-viz vest didn't. And neither did her family, who would be left having to cope with her, perhaps for the rest of her life.

A low whistle brought his attention back to the hide entrance. It was Matt warning him he was on the way in.

'Whoa, you look like you've been brooding,' Matt said without any greeting but handing Luke his latte and panini.

'Yeah, I was just . . . You know . . .'

Matt was expecting another round of counselling about Janey, but was surprised to hear Luke say, 'I'm not sure we should slot Fatty.'

'You want to cut and run?' Matt asked. 'I'll do it if you don't feel—'

But Luke cut across him. 'No, it's not that. It's just . . . Do you think Joey could handle it?'

'Ah. I thought you'd been there and got past it.'

'So did I, but . . . They don't really know, do they? Ulster was the worst for me. Young, keen, thinking I was going there to help. And they were just like us, weren't they? Until you were told to kick in their doors and drag their men away. And raised on folklore that romanticised the struggle, they then came into direct contact with a size ten boot or rubber bullet. I hated that. I never believed in what we were doing.'

'Never our job, Luke. It was a civilian issue that they should have sorted politically before putting us on the streets. Last resort, we are, remember. Like now, probably. Why don't the cops just go and take this fat bastard out?'

'Why indeed?'

'So, do you want to scrub it?'

Luke hesitated for a moment. Matt already knew the

answer and waited for the shake of the head. 'Just change the scenario.'

'Nice one, Sean,' Arthur Young said as he shook Sean's hand on the way out. 'Great when someone stirs it up a bit.'

'Sells papers, does it?' Sean replied, with a laugh.

'Yeah. And you won't mind if we splash you over the front page? Local Boss Blasts Bureaucrats?' But he grinned as he saw Sean become anxious. 'No worries, Sean. You're one of the good guys. Who else would give this lot a free scoff?'

'That include you?'

'Of course. And much appreciated. Nah, you won't be on the front page. Not up to me anyway. The editor sent me here to get something on the dynamic duo there, wasting our money.' He nodded across to where the Chairs of County and Town had colonised a table and took out his phone to take a shot, just as the Town Chair was stuffing another custard slice into his mouth. 'Let them eat cake, eh? Yeah, it'll be those two. Something about fat cats and cream. Put money on it. It's that and good local celeb stories that sell the paper, Sean. So who've you got opening your grotto?'

'Well, I hadn't really thought of—'

But Arthur was already conjuring up a story. 'Have you tried Craig Harlow? My mum knows his mum, Wendy.'

Sean laughed. 'Your mum seems to know everyone.'

'Why do you think I came into this game? Long line of nosey parkers. Straight, though. He's often back on the quiet to see his mum and I bet he'd pop in one day and play Santa. Great front page that would be. Anyway, got to go. Apparently someone saw a ghost up at the war memorial last night. Always gets the letter pages going, that one. I'll send you Craig's details. Stay sharp.'

And with that he was off, leaving Sean to ponder on Craig Harlow. Local celeb. One-time boy-band member now Hollywood A-list actor. Would he actually do it?

'This is really about your girl, isn't it?' Joey heard Benno ask as he dropped to the floor to started fishing the 110-V cable behind the worktops. Once more going to the point. Joey had told him about the skirmish Tanya had found herself in a few weeks ago.

'Yeah, suppose so,' Joey responded, hoping not to have to go any further. Some chance with Benno.

'You have to do it, Joe.'

'What?'

'Go back.' Benno said, as he reappeared above the worktop. 'You have to.'

Joey knew Benno was trying to make it easier for him. Although he wasn't expecting the next bit.

'Besides,' Benno said, 'I'm off tomorrow anyway. Before Uncle Gus comes back.'

'What? Where?'

'Remember that job up in Borehamwood we knocked back for this? Still got a spot for me.'

'How? When did you fix this?' Joey asked.

'It's been brewing for a while now, hasn't it. Not letting me get to sleep having to listen to all your troubles.'

Joey laughed. That was a good one. But he appreciated what Benno was doing. Leaving him no excuse to stay.

'So, no point you hanging about fretting down here,' Benno continued, then fixed Joey with a hard stare. 'Or fretting about me. I can look after meself. You do what you have to do, lad.'

With that he disappeared into the service duct again, leaving Joey to finally make the decision. He bent to the service duct. 'OK, oh wise one. But I'll stay until the end of the week while we clear out the lock-up.'

'So you make sure you get your proper share?' came a cackling reply.

'There is that.' Joey grinned. But at least now he had something concrete to tell Natasha later.

'What's wrong with your face?' Natasha asked her daughter, as she stacked the dishwasher following the evening food fest. No matter how much she used the mantra, 'straight in please', somehow everyone always seemed too busy to bend down and open the door.

'Just got another message from Carol. Becky's gone missing again,' Tanya replied as she retrieved her jacket from the couch. Roscoe immediately saw it as a cue that he might be going for a walk, but was soon deflated. 'Not now, Roscoe. Mum'll take you later.'

Roscoe doubted that as he slumped back into his basket. He'd be lucky if he got a quick round of the garden, when he'd be under pressure to perform before being sent to bed for the night. At least though, he knew he'd get a Dentastick from the older female.

'And where are you going at this time?' Tasha asked.

'It's only nine, Mum. I'm just going to meet Cags and see if Becky is hanging out with Hus.'

'I'm not sure I like the sound of all this.'

'That's why I'm going. Don't worry, I won't get involved if she's with him. I'll text you later.'

'Be back by ten, young lady.'

But the door had been slammed. Natasha looked at the clock. That's when she was going to speak to Joey. She'd been worrying all day about what might be going on in his head.

At 21.30 Luke and Matt lay prone, watching the tide of customers starting to ebb. The earlier teatime rush had slowed and Fatchops was now getting everything ready for the late-night snackers. Luke had him framed in the scope as he was again meticulously cleaning the counter-tops to remove any traces that might have fallen from his box of special forks. Matt was slowly sweeping the street through the spotting scope. It was time.

'Still clear.'

Luke widened the scope to take in the whole shop. It was empty except for Fatchops and one of the two spotty helpers placing a bucket of chips beneath the mushy peas and curry table at the back, ready for the next incoming tide. As soon as Spotty went back to chipping more spuds, Luke would take the shot. If he still kept getting Matt's all-clear reports.

'All clear bottom end.'

Luke put the Barrett onto Fatchops. Slight refocus. He began to settle and steady his breathing. He just wanted those five clear seconds.

'All clear top end,' came from Matt.

Luke flicked off the safety and moved his finger to the trigger. He was just about to start the squeeze when Matt spoke again.

'Hold. That Merc SL is back.'

Luke flicked the safety back on and slid round to pan the Barrett, almost at the edge of its sweep on the tripod, and picked up the driver as he got out of the car, chattering away into the Bluetooth link in his ear. He walked round to the passenger side and opened the door, gesturing for someone inside to get out. Luke wasn't so much worried that they would arrive after the shot as that they would see the muzzle flash.

They had decided that the risk of anyone seeing the flash was small, as most of the residents of Highbridge would neither be expecting it nor recognise it for what it was. If anyone did see it they would probably assume it was kids messing with fireworks. Unless, of course, they saw it and then walked in to find their mate or relative spread all over the back wall. Unless, of course, they were up to no good. With no-good people who carried guns. Then they might put it all together.

However, the driver's demeanour caught Luke's attention. Suddenly his cocky swagger dropped as he spun round to focus on something further down the street. Through the scope it looked as if someone had called to him, as he seemed to wave, but hesitantly. Behind him, a mane of teenage hair appeared out of the Mercedes, followed closely by another.

'Amazing what a nice car will do for you,' Matt said as he turned his scope back down the street to see what the driver was waving at, and picked up another girl walking up towards him. 'And looks like he's ready to party.'

'If he is, we'll see the children's entertainer arrive next, judging by the age of those two.'

Matt panned the scope back to the Mercedes trio and let out a low growl. Luke could feel the tension. But Matt had spotted something else. 'Hey up,' he said. 'Isn't that Joey's girl, Tanya?'

Luke moved the Barrett. 'Yes. What's she doing here?'

He shifted slightly to pick up the girl as she was about to pass the alley beside the chippy. But she seemed to hesitate when she saw the other girls getting out of the car. Matt and Luke watched this silent movie play out in their scopes, watching Becky spin round as Tanya and Carol crossed towards her, obviously angry and agitated as they started dragging her away, shouting back up the street at the driver now holding out his hands in a form of protest. What could he possibly have done?

'Kiddy fiddling, that's what you've done, mate,' Matt muttered as he watched Tanya and Carol drag Becky away. He then went back to the driver and the girls who, now out of the car, looked in their early teens trying to look in their late twenties and curious about what was going on. The driver waved a dismissive hand in the direction of the retreating Tanya, Becky and Carol and then put his arms round the girls' shoulders and guided them towards the alley.

'Might be his sisters or cousins?' Luke suggested.

'Like the ones we saw being let out the back the other night? And if they are, why don't they go through the shop?'

Luke agreed as he watched the driver escort the girls down the alley to the rear fortress door, where he banged on the door, all the while talking into his phone. He could hear Matt's breathing deepen. Troubled. He knew why. And why he didn't want to go there right now.

'Let's stay on mission. Someone else can sort that one.' He moved back on to Fatchops and zeroed the scope once again. 'Shop's still clear. How's the street?' There was a hesitation as Matt was still brooding on what he'd just seen. 'Matt?' Luke hissed.

'Top clear. Bottom clear,' came the response.

Luke settled himself. Matt pulled the spotting scope back to cover the area outside the chippy. A five-second kill zone. Luke slowed his breathing. Moved his finger back to the trigger and put the cross hairs exactly where he wanted them. Cold shot or not, the target was big enough to make the mess he wanted. Breath. Hold. Squeeze.

'Hold,' Matt suddenly said. 'Tanya and her mates are heading back.'

Too late. The ball was in flight.

5

Changed Scenario

'Oh, and what? You've been one day away and now you're sure are you?' Natasha asked. It had that tone. The one that warned him she was not the little woman. The one who could be told what to do.

'I'm not saying my mind's made up, Nat,' Joey said, as he took a quick glance back through the window. He was out on the scaffolding. Above the skips that filled the yard below where he and Benno had colonised as their sleeping quarters. Builders' squatters in billionaires' bunkers. It was where he could be out of earshot. Although he needn't have worried as Benno was already cocooned in his sleeping bag and snoring for Great Britain.

Natasha, though, was going up a gear. 'Will we be able to manage?'

He held back. He was about to remind her that it was she who said life was not all about money, but he didn't want to enter the maze of female logic just yet. Especially long distance. He wouldn't stand a chance. So, instead, he tried a softer, more diplomatic line. 'All I'm saying is that I want to talk to you about it properly and I'm telling you now so you can think about it over the week. That's all.'

It seemed to calm her down. 'Oh . . . OK. I suppose we can . . .' But then her tone changed again. Concerned. 'Oh . . . Oh my God. I'll call you back.'

Joey was left staring at his disconnected phone. Natasha sounded really distressed. Which she was, as she rushed towards her daughter, who was helping a sobbing Becky and extremely distressed looking Carol through the door.

'What, what has happened?' Natasha's maternal eyes went straight to the cut and rapidly swelling bruise around her daughter's right eye, before darting to Becky then Carol and back again, as her brain ran rapidly through the index of potential parental horrors.

Tanya saw the worry in her mother's eyes. 'No . . . no . . . It's nothing like that. But oh my God, Mum. It's mad . . .'

'What? What's happened?'

The identical thought was going through a very nervous Mercedes driver who had rushed through from the back with two other men, shouting and gesticulating for them to secure the door and get the young counter servers out of the shop to the back. The one at the door was now shoving a couple of surprised Bingo goers outside before locking up. The other was scampering and squealing back and forth behind the counter, trying to scoop something out of the boiling oil in between yelps of pain. It was the special forks box.

Mercedes was still shouting for him to stop shouting so that he could make himself clear as he shouted for the one by the door to lock up and kill the lights. As some form of control returned, Mercedes stepped towards the counter. The soft drinks cabinet was wrecked, its door hanging open and the floor covered in sticky liquid, which he assumed must be from the shattered bottles. The fork box and wrapping paper had fallen from the counter but nothing else appeared to be damaged. He looked over the counter to see the prone legs of Fatchops. Lifeless. What had happened here?

Up on the hill only Matt and Luke knew as they watched through their scopes, their breathing slow with relief after witnessing the nightmare scenario almost play out in front of them. Fortunately the Barrett's 50 cal bullet had slammed into the chippy drinks cabinet seconds before Tanya and her posse arrived at the door.

Luke had automatically chambered another round ready, as he would later tell Joey, to take a shot if he felt Tanya was in any real danger. As it was, he had calmly watched as she was backhanded and brutally shoved out of the door just before the Bingo couple. It was only when Carol had pulled both her and Becky away and down the street that Luke had taken his finger off the trigger. She'd survive.

*

Natasha's phone was vibrating on the table. Joey was trying to get an answer. As was Natasha herself, now forcing a sandwich bag of ice on to her daughter's forehead above her swelling right eye. 'Slowly. Tell me slowly.'

'It was mad, Mum. Wasn't it, Cags?'

'Yeah,' Carol confirmed. 'We were just going back to see if Hus was there, and—'

'Going back where?'

'He was parked up the street. With two other girls, right, Becks?' Carol looked to Becky, trying to make the point, but all Becky could do was nod and reach for another tissue. Then hug Roscoe as he came over to offer support.

'The chippy,' Tanya said, beginning to regain her composure, taking over the sandwich bag as she stood up and went to the sink to get a drink of water for Becky. 'We were just about to go in and there was this, well, sort of huge bang. Right, Cags?'

'Yeah. Just really loud and then they all came rushing out the back shouting and screaming.'

'At each other. And then us,' Tanya added as she gave Becky the water then wrapped a piece of kitchen roll round the sandwich bag. 'They just shoved us into the street.'

'What do I want this for?' Becky asked.

Tanya looked at the glass. Good question. It must have been something she'd seen on the telly, but she added with a hint of her old sarcastic self, 'To replace the fluids you've lost on the way home?'

'That one with the beard really hurt my arm.' Carol was pulling off her jacket to examine it.

'Er, hello?' Tanya snarled, pointing at her eye. 'He did this to me.'

'Who? Why? What was it about?' Natasha asked, more in hope than anything else as she could see the teenage fright was now being pushed aside by exuberance, as they realised they were safe. Even Roscoe thought it safe to leave Becky and return to his bed.

Back in the now quiet chippy, the one with the beard had been the one at the door, who had backhanded Tanya, but was now switching off some of the lights, while the one without a beard was nervously guarding the rear door, nursing his burnt hands inside a dirty tea towel, as Mercedes slowly rounded the counter to approach the prone lump that was Fatchops. He was still not moving and his head was covered with the pile of wrapping paper he must have pulled down on himself as he fell. That was probably how the forks had ended up in the fryer. Mercedes stepped forward and delicately, nervously, kicked the life-less legs. Nothing. He took another look around. At the counter. The drinks cabinet. The floor. What had happened? Beard and Beardless shrugged. Both still apprehensive. They were all tense. They all knew what the real trade was that went across the counter. They all knew they could come under attack. At any time. But was this it? There'd been nothing on the CCTV monitors.

Mercedes looked back at the lump. Was he dead? How did you tell? He'd seen the movies where they touched a place just below the ears. But did that really work or was it just a Hollywood thing? He stooped down, being careful to keep his Prada jeans dry, then reached out and shoved Fatchops's back. It wobbled. But was he breathing or was that just fat sloshing around? He shuffled closer, carefully, still trying to avoid the liquid. Was it blood? He reached down and wet his fingers. Smelt it. But what did blood smell like? Cherries? He hesitated but then tasted it. Sugary, sweet? He'd heard that somewhere. But decided it was more likely to be from the soft drinks bottles. He did another duck shuffle to keep his Pradas dry and was just about to try and find Fatchops's neck when the lump moved, and as it did Mercedes fell back in fright and felt the sugary liquid soaking through his Pradas. He swore. Then kicked out at the prone body. Fat idiot!

'It's not marketing, Sean, it's throwing money away,' said Sandra.

'Bigging myself up, as you put it, must by definition fall into the category of letting people know about the business.' Sean was trying, but even though the VAT Goddess had turned out to be a mumsy size 18, he knew he had lost the argument as soon as he'd mentioned the 10 per cent discount offer to Sandra.

'Marketing is supposed to be about getting real people

in to spend real money. Not a bunch of freeloaders who then end up getting a discount.'

When she put it like that, as she always had the knack of doing, Sean knew it was time to retreat.

'How'd the rest of your day go, anyway?' He gestured to the TK Maxx hooded top and ruched leggings that had displaced the Armani.

'Mum and Dad are well, thanks. But I assume you want to change the subject because you've realised how daft you are?' He didn't answer, but went across to the boiling water dispenser.

'Do you want tea?' It might be taken as a peace offering. It wasn't.

'I'll do it. You might waste two teabags as we'll probably have to start economising soon if you keep throwing money away.'

He went across to the table, knowing he would have to take what was coming to him.

'And do you think it made any difference?'

'And that's what I'm trying to say about it being like marketing or advertising,' said Sandra. 'You never quite know what works, do you, except it does. You can tell by seeing the results.'

'What results?' She put the tea on the table and sat down opposite him. 'Go on, how will you be able to judge?'

But Sandra didn't get to answer. A third voice entered the debate.

'Hear you want to teach kids how to use drugs, Dad.'

'What?' Sandra turned to face Noah, who was coming into the kitchen dangling his car keys from his finger while treading his usual path to the fridge.

'Yeah, Dad ripped into the chatterati or something. Said we teach kids how to use tobacco and alcohol so we should do it with drugs. The Head was all over it this afternoon.'

Noah re-emerged with what appeared to be a piece of ham wrapped round a chunk of cheese. Then grinned at his mother's obvious discomfort. 'She asked me if I had "any worries" at home.' He then turned to Sean. 'Good one, Dad.'

'So now you know which part of your so-called marketing worked,' Sandra shot at Sean. Then back to Noah. 'She wasn't serious, was she?'

'As serious as any retard can be.'

'Don't use that word.'

'It's OK, Mum. You'll still be able to walk down the High Street without people pointing at you. They think it's Dad sniffing the plants in the greenhouses. And everyone knows the Head's a trembler. First sign of any controversy and she panics. Anyway, I'm just going to Josh's for a bit. See you later.'

'We should have put you on that curfew insurance scheme. I don't like you driving at night.'

'Except when you two have been on the drugs, you mean?'

'What?'

'Dad'll explain. Socially acceptable, but still a drug, isn't it, Dad? Alcohol?' With that he threw a sarcastic smile at Sean, received one back and left. His job there was done.

Sean started to smile. Pleased. Imagining the whittering that must have gone on after his speech.

'See,' he said to Sandra. 'That's a result.'

'It's not funny, Sean. The Head of the kids' school thinks you're some kind of druggie?' But she noticed he was drifting on to something else.

'Remember that motorhome we had? And we ended up travelling because you were always asking that sort of question. Well, it was more "who are they to judge"?'

She finally grinned as she accepted her own words thrown back at her. He had that impish, mischievous glint in his eye that she had fallen for all those years ago. Mr Goody Two-Shoes who was desperate to be a rebel like his little brother Joey. The Mr Perfect who loved being top of the form but hated being called a spod. Who loved being deputy head boy but hated not being able to kick a ball straight like little brother Joey. Who could talk for Britain with every girl in the school but was always too shy to ask for a date. The Mr Clean who never traded in cash and hated drugs. How could anyone think he was some form of closet druggie? Not her Mr Softie.

'Wish we'd just kept going sometimes,' she smiled.

'Nah, there was never enough room for the kids.'

'Is it that, then? All this, throwing our money at commu-nity causes because you worry what they think of you?'

'Bigging myself up, you mean?'

'Go on, how much did it cost us?'

'Sean spotted the emphasis on "us". He let out a sigh of surrender. 'Probably around five hundred for the food and lost business.'

'And the discount.'

'Yeah. But that lot wouldn't have spent much anyway. They wouldn't have been there in the first place, so what-ever they spent we made.'

'You're too soft a touch. Do you know that?'

'Better than bigging myself up?'

'Probably. At that price though I wish I had come now. I'd have loved to have seen Julia Erskine's face. And that prat Harold Peagram.'

'You could always come to the CAD consultation tonight. I'm, er, we're not paying for that.'

She shook her head. 'Same old, same old. Having Rupert Bronks staring at my breasts all night?'

Sean grinned. 'I had noticed, but I can't really blame him. Even in that top.'

She ignored the comment as she stood to go. 'But you know what, Sean. If you really want to do something, do it. Don't mess about. If you're going to waste our money on good causes, pick something that will really make a difference locally.' She headed for the door, but stopped and turned back. 'Or go into politics for yourself. I'd also love to see Peagram's face if you announced you were standing in the election. I'm going to see how Megan's getting on with her homework.'

Sean stared at the door. Was she really serious? Go into politics? After everything they had both said about politicians in the past? What everyone seemed to think about them at the moment? He had toyed with the idea before but always wondered if he could do any good as an individual councillor. He quite liked the whole networking scene, but getting anything done would mean he'd have to work his way in and then up one of the main political parties that seemed to dominate everything. More and more their idea of a good local candidate was a good national party member, which made it all feel close to the sort of nationalist totalitarian state parties that democracies were supposed to counter. Sean knew he would not be seen as one of the club so had always pushed the thought away.

He picked up his mug and went across to put it on the drainer, but then decided he didn't want another ear-bashing about why he couldn't put it actually in the dishwasher. He put it on the top rack and let the door swing up. Yes, he grinned, he might not make a difference outside the political clique, but, like her, he'd love to see Harold Peagram's face.

'No, they're all fine, Joe.'

Natasha was on the house phone as Joey had got

frustrated trying to get through on the mobiles. But his frustration was nothing against Natasha's.

'It's those swines down at the chippy, Joe,' she said.

Joey had already processed that Luke and Matt had done something. But as Tanya was safe he wasn't concerned about that. It was the vehemence that took him completely by surprise, as did the speed at which Natasha was winding herself up.

'You may have been away, Joe, but you must know what's going on down there. Those guys. The drugs. The girls. Something's got to be done. Someone's got to do—'

'Hold on. Wait. Hang on.' Joey was scrambling to catch up. Was this just mother's talk or was she winding up to telling him she knew what he and Luke were up to? 'Nat, Nat. Slow down. Talk to me. What guys? What drugs? And what girls?'

'Everyone knows, Joe. The so-called parties. Getting young girls off their heads with—'

'What?' This was something new to Joey. 'Are you saying Tan was—'

'No. No. She was just there looking for Becky's boyfriend and—'

'Is she involved?'

'Joe, look, accept that you're not here. You don't know. And you're not going to catch up over the phone. God only knows what happened down there tonight.'

Joey had some idea, but couldn't share it with her.

'OK. Yeah. But. You sure Tan's OK? Definitely?' He

heard himself still trying to sound calm while his mind was in overdrive wondering what the hell Luke was thinking, doing something when Tanya was around.

'Yes. Yes,' Natasha replied, causing Joey to relax slightly, but not for long. 'She's got a bit of a bruise . . .'

This additional bit of news immediately heightened Joey's anxiety about what Luke might have done. And what might have happened to his daughter. Again. But Natasha immediately sensed his anxiety coming down the line and knowing she was stepping into an area she'd prefer to keep from Tanya, she said, 'I'll call you back on my mobile.'

With that she hung up the house phone and looked across at Tanya, who, still holding the improvised ice pack to her eye had moved on from water to making hot chocolate, while Carol was at the toaster and Becky was scrolling her phone. They seemed to be getting back to normal.

Natasha was already pressing Joe's icon as she stepped out on to the patio, quickly closing the sliding door and not realising she nearly decapitated Roscoe who was on her way to join her. He pulled back just in time, then sat wondering what was so secret even he wasn't allowed to hear.

'She's OK, Joe. Honestly. Sounds like they walked into some kind of aggro going on inside the chippy.' She stopped talking and listened to his breathing. It was slow but hard. She knew he was trying to keep himself in check. Just as she knew he was probably rerunning what he had been saying to her over the weekend.

'You couldn't have done anything, Joe,' she quickly added. He didn't respond. She sensed he was fighting a similar thought. 'You can't follow her round all the time.'

'But,' he finally replied. Now calm. Cold and determined. She could imagine his back stiffening, hands clenching and unclenching. 'I could be down that chippy now, though, couldn't I?'

'And back in the cop shop again. What good would that do us?'

She could hear the breathing getting lighter. He was trying hard to control his frustration. 'Why are you so calm, anyway?' he asked.

'I'm not,' she replied. Making a greater effort to calm her own breathing. 'I'd like to go down there myself right now . . .'

'Nat, don't you even—' But he heard her voice go up a pitch as she cut across him.

'I'm just telling you how I feel. How everyone feels, probably.'

'About what?' Joey asked. Now cautious.

'Haven't you been listening to what your Sean and Sandra have been banging on about all these months? Or their Noah's campaign to clean up the park?'

'I try not to.'

'Don't be flippant, Joe.' She paused, realising she was getting wound up again, before adding, 'Something does need to be done. Somebody needs to sort them out, Joe. If the police won't do it. Someone has to.'

This took him completely by surprise. This was not like her. She usually dismissed Sean's rants as naïve do-gooder ramblings. 'Er, what exactly are you saying, Nat?'

'I'm saying, Joe –' Natasha explained. Slowly, deliberately – 'that you're not the only one who has time to think when we're apart. I know you, Nolan. And I know Luke Carlton.'

She let it hang in the air. Waiting for his response. He stood staring at the occasional electrical flashes that came from the overground electric rails. She always used his surname when she was making the point of where he had come from. Who and what she had married. Did she really know? Was she fishing? Or was this just something she'd dreamed up herself?

Before he could decide which one to bet on, he heard her voice again. She had turned to see Tanya and the others getting up as though they were getting ready to go out again. Damn.

'Look, I'll have to call you back.'

'Why?'

'Because I'm freezing. I'm outside on the patio.'

'That's why they're called mobiles, Nat. You can keep talking as you change locations and—'

But she was in a hurry to stop Tanya from leaving. 'Yeah, I know, but I need a sweater too. Call you back.'

Joey was left hanging in cyberspace. Not even a quick luvya. What's she keeping from me, he wondered. What did she mean about girls and partying? He stood looking at the urban skyline, thinking it through. Had Luke taken the shot? If he had, surely Tanya would have seen something? But would Luke really do that if Tanya was around? No, not if anyone was around. He'd told Joey about waiting for that clear five seconds. No witnesses. So, what had Tanya walked into? Whatever it was, it was a reminder that within a couple of weeks the apple of his eye had twice come close to being badly hurt.

He tapped the messages icon and scrolled to Luke's number. But he knew he couldn't text. He'd just have to wait. Which only lasted about five more electrical flashes on the horizon before he climbed back through the window, threw his stuff in his bag and was out the door. He'd call Benno in the morning.

Everything in the chippy was now calm, relatively. Fatchops, far from being splattered all over the walls, was leaning against the counter wheezing as the bearded one held a few pieces of crumpled wrapping paper against a cut on his forehead. The beardless one still appeared agitated by the rear door, while Mercedes was calming down as he twisted and turned, trying to gauge how bad his sticky Pradas were. He then went to examine the drinks cabinet but feeling the stickiness seeping between his legs he turned and aimed another kick at Fatchops.

Kicking 'must be a family thing,' Matt said, with a chuckle as, up on the hill, he pulled away from the spotting scope and prepared to pull out. Luke waited another second or two then slid back himself with a sigh of relief. He and Matt had remained motionless as they waited for the bullet's impact, thankful that at 900 metres per second it easily outpaced Tanya's run. She had arrived after its kinetic energy tore through the glass door of the drinks cabinet and blew six 2-litre Coke bottles apart with enough explosive force to set off a chain reaction of bursting cans as they flew off the shelves. The bullet had then passed through the cabinet, coming to rest embedded in the damp plasterwork behind. It was the impact noise that had caused Fatchops to turn, startled, and then slip on the cascade of Coke foam erupting from the shattered cabinet. He started to slide sideways, tried to stop himself by grabbing at the counter but only managed to spin so that he cracked his head on the way down, clutching and clawing at the wrapping paper. That was the moment Tanya had arrived, closely followed by Becky and Carol, only to be met by Mercedes and his associates rushing from the back of the shop. It had got a bit rough and heavy handed, but at least the bearded one had shoved them out of harm's way. That might help him later. But for Luke and Matt, it was time to move on.

They slid out of the hide, with the broken-down Barrett split between Matt's guitar case and Luke's backpack. They would have preferred to just go. With the collectors coming later. That way no one is connected. The shooters have no weapons and the collectors can claim they stumbled across it all. Using women and kids was even safer, as every rebel force in history had learned. Democracy's greatest weakness was its most valued principle: civil liberties.

Still, no one should be looking, but to help cover their activities they tipped out the contents of a bin bag. Their own ration pack boxes were replaced with a mixture of crushed soft drinks, lager cans, a collection of sweets, fast food and tobacco packaging. They wanted it to look like a temporary kids' hangout.

While they were clearing up, so too were Mercedes and Fatchops who were in the back of the shop trying to figure out what had happened. The counter servers had been sent home, as had the guy in the alley who acted as banker, along with a few disgruntled customers hoping for either their special forks or sausage curry.

After fifteen minutes or so of going over and over the fact that there was no one else in the shop, no one else in the street except for those stupid girls looking for Husani, and no other damage anywhere, they had all concluded that perhaps it was just a bottle exploding. Especially as they had retrieved one of the soggy labels to discover it was from the fake batch they had bought in from India.

Any further investigation was abandoned when the bearded one came through from the house with one of the young girls who was obviously wondering what Mercedes was doing. Immediately he lost interest in Fatchops's sensory powers or where the drinks came from, and went back to the real reason he had turned up tonight, but not before he reached over and picked up a few special forks that had avoided being deep-fat fried. He then waved for the bearded one to help Fatchops clear up, as he led the young girl back inside. Maybe she could help him out of his sticky Pradas.

All this was still being watched by Matt through a small night-spotting monocular as Luke finally gathered everything together.

'Looks like they bought it,' Matt said as he set up a huge commercial firework rocket and tube. 'We could have done with a few of these when we got caught in that goat market ambush.'

'They're probably banned under some goat protection convention,' Luke responded as he started off down the hill. After a moment or two to allow him to get a safe distance away, Matt did one last 360 with the night scope. All seemed clear so he lit the long fuse of the rocket and a couple of other ground-based fireworks before, as the instructions said, retreating to a safe distance, going the opposite way to Luke. Up the hill. By the time the rocket roared and soared skyward to explode with a sonic boom and brilliant starburst that would be heard and seen all over Highbridge, Luke was on his way down the hill, silhouetted against the Golden Rain that was spewing out behind him.

Now, if anyone had seen the Barrett's muzzle flash and bothered to climb up to investigate they would leave thinking it was 'just kids' messing about with fireworks. Like the initial reaction in the chippy. They would assume what they were already expecting. Job done. Get gone.

'Quiet, Roscoe,' Natasha soothed as she stroked his head, stepping out once again on to the patio. 'It's only a firework.'

She waited, as did Roscoe, head up, ears primed, but after a few minutes both assumed that was it. They then turned and looked back into the kitchen, now a scene of typical teenage occupation. Natasha had managed to talk Tanya's friends into staying put, so Tanya was handing out the hot chocolate. Carol was fighting someone in a distant multi-room, probably Ross, for control of the Sky EPG while Becky was thumbing her way through her phone menus. Natasha and Roscoe exchanged looks. Neither really wanted to go back but both thought they should.

'So, excitement over for the night then, boy?' Natasha asked as she stepped back inside and went to make herself a cup of tea, while Roscoe headed for the treats cupboard. He had, after all, warned them of the firework. However, as no one was paying attention he went and flopped back into his basket. Natasha realised she was unlikely to get much more out of her daughter as she was now preoccupied, reconnected to her digital universe, so she turned her attention to Carol, still trying to get control of the Sky Box. She stepped across, took the remote and pressed 204. There was no counter entry. 'If they see that, they know I am looking for something to watch.'

'I can't wait to be a mother,' Carol said as she went across to the table to join the others.

Natasha smiled as she collected her tea, not sure control of the Sky Box was worth going through childbirth for but it could be classed as an unforeseen benefit. She decided to try again, quickly, as she saw Carol picking up her phone, heading for the digital exit. 'So what do you think was going on down at the chippy, Carol?'

'Dunno. They were really freaked out by something, though.'

'Fridge exploded,' Tanya announced without looking up from her phone. 'According to Henry.'

'And Nisha's just tweeted: Dad's got me behind counter. Big Bingo rush. Chippy closed. He owes me,' Becky chipped in.

Carol had by now also gone digital. 'Holly's saying: Fatman Flops on Fridge.' She scrolled down the thread. 'Mia reckons Fatty fell over and smashed into the fridge and shattered all the bottles.'

'Wouldn't want him falling on me,' Tanya added. 'And that firework came off the hill, according to Zolly. Reckons it'll be someone off the Riverbeck estate.'

Natasha looked at the Sky remote and then back at the digital news service around her kitchen table. Who needed the TV news? She passed the control over to Carol and headed for the door with her tea. 'Wait about five minutes as I'll tell him he should be asleep.' Then, to Tanya, 'You all OK now?'

Tanya stood up and hugged her mother, then sat down, without taking her eyes off her phone. Natasha smiled again. And was that worth going through childbirth for? But seeing they were now all relaxed. And safe. Yeah, she thought, it was. And she'd get the full story from Tanya in the morning.

'But that's not the full story, Rupert and you know it.' Sean was on his way out of the public consultation, pleased with the number of nodding heads he had noticed while repeating almost word for word the speech he had given at lunchtime. He was now speaking to Rupert Bronks, local Golf Club owner, part-time scrap merchant and full-time cleavage gazer.

'It was a good speech, though. Really. And I liked that answer you gave about "if politicians can't find jobs for people they should find something else to keep them occupied". That makes sense.'

'And I believe it. Redefine our values so that what we consider "work" is also about what we do with our time, rather than just working for money.'

'That's where you lost me,' Rupert replied, nearly losing Sean as his gaze wandered towards the ladies' toilet where another cleavage had just appeared, but he didn't lose his thread.

'Seems to me,' he continued, as he turned to watch the cleavage head back to the function room. 'That the trouble is too many of them do that already. They want someone else to give them the money so they can have a good time without working for it. But no doubt that's too simplistic again, is it?'

'No. Not really,' Sean responded, waiting for Rupert to turn back. Which didn't look like happening. So he prompted. 'It's about balance, Rupert.'

This seemed to do the trick. 'Ah, balance,' Rupert commented as he turned with a smile on his face. 'Must be some sort of politically incorrect joke about balance and breasts, eh?'

'Or perhaps not?' Sean offered, wanting to neither agree nor subscribe to this male-bonding line.

Rupert just snorted. 'Being PC, are you?' But he didn't wait for a response. 'That's like balance. I hate that almost as much as I do "impartiality". I don't want to be impartial. I don't want to be balanced. And I don't want to be a reconstructed metrosexual, whatever that is. I want to do and think what I believe in. And that's not buying someone a new suit to go for an interview who could get a job digging ditches and save up for a suit. And they're only a few quid down the charity shop. Plenty of my old things in there, I can tell you.'

'I'm not really asking you to buy them a suit, Rupert.'

'I know, Sean. I know you're not that daft. Just as I'm not as daft as I make myself sound. You want me to look at the reasons they're like they are. Why they take to drugs? Why they become homeless? Become unemployable?' Sean nodded. Rupert leaned forward and prodded him on the shoulder. 'Then you'll have to adopt them all at birth. Think Sandra would go for that?'

'I know, I know.' Sean accepted this, but started to guide Rupert towards the door as he saw another group of women heading for the Ladies. 'But I'm trying to talk about what we do right now.' He continued: 'about helping the ones already caught up in it all. Give them a hand to try and do something else with their lives. Give them an option other than the street corner dealer.'

'And how many addicts do you have working your tills down at the garden centre?'

Sean gave a nod of defeat. He knew that simplistic truth was the killer point. If he didn't want to take the risk, why should others.

'Exactly. The approximate number I have at the Golf Club. Might have them among the membership, mind, but I'm after their cash, not letting them get at mine. Sorry, Sean. I never had anything when I was growing up. And I never turned to drugs.'

Rupert headed off for his car but stopped to shout back, 'Probably because I was too pissed to find them. But, er, not tonight of course.' He nodded over Sean's shoulder to where Hilary Jardine was heading towards them. Out of uniform but appropriately dressed by John Lewis. No cleavage. 'And give my regards to Mrs Nolan. Tell her I missed her. 'Night, Inspector.'

Hilary smiled a goodnight as Rupert headed off and she crossed to Sean. 'We'll have to stop meeting like this, or something like that?' She continued walking towards the car park.

Sean followed. 'Do you think you can get addicted to anti-drug get-togethers?'

'I get paid for it. Although,' she hesitated, before saying, 'And don't fly off the handle at me . . .'

'You're still wondering why I bother?' Sean finished the question for her. 'You and Sandra,' he added, waving to Rupert as he drove away in his old Jaguar XJR. 'Someone's got to try and do something. And if only it was as easy as getting a job digging ditches. Been there and done that. It's got to be how we think about work, hasn't it. In an area like this. Where so many people work for the state in some form or other.'

'Like me?'

'Yeah. And most of them at lunch. And here tonight. All getting cash from the state, just like people on benefit. I mean, you're a job creation scheme really, aren't you?'

'Never saw myself as that, I have to admit.' Hilary started fishing for her keys as they had reached her very sensible Skoda Fabia.

'No, because your job was created a hundred years or so back. When "we", society, decided we'd rather pay other people to keep the law than have to worry about it ourselves. But, if you think about it, you lot, and nurses, doctors, teachers, the fire service, are all there because we, society, or communities, decided to create those jobs. We didn't decide to create the job of shoemaker or baker or banker or blacksmith. Or people like me selling plants. They all came because individuals saw a demand and wanted to make a living out of it.'

'You're going to end up in politics if you're not careful,' she replied, but now with a real smile on her face.

'You are sounding like Sandra now.'

'Bet she's not encouraging you.'

'And you are?'

'Well,' Hilary hesitated, before adding, 'We could do worse. We probably are doing. And although you'd probably make our life a bit more difficult, we could do with a few more like you.'

'That sounds like some form of backhanded compliment.'

'You care, Sean. And that could get us all into trouble.'

Sean smiled. 'Think you're mistaking me for my son. Or my brother?' He saw the smile stiffen again. 'You don't seriously think Joe's up to something, do you?'

He was relieved to see the smile relax again.

'No. He's not trouble. Never was, really. Thinks he's Jack the Lad, but he's only a statistic. I get paid to sort out the likes of your Joe every now and then. But . . .' she let it hang, not sure whether to go on or whether she was adding two and two to get five.

'But?' Sean prompted. Then took a guess. 'Luke is from a different set of statistics?'

Hilary nodded. 'I know his history. Even before. And

although Joe has told me he has been a calming influence
. . .' She let that thought hang with a shrug as she changed
tack. 'Just ask Joey to make sure neither of them becomes
another statistic I have to deal with. Which also applies to
Noah. Goodnight. Love to Sandra.'

With that she drove off. Leaving Sean to ponder the
female hive question. How did all the women in his life
seem to say the same things? Was it that intuition thing
– or did they really converse telepathically?

By the time Luke arrived back at the cottage, Matt had
showered, changed and was taking the clothes he had been
wearing earlier out of the washing machine. As the clothes
were the only real chance of anyone tying them to the
vicinity of the hide, they were now destined for the charity
shop. If they burnt the clothes and the cops did happen
to come knocking, then they would find that suspicious,
but it was highly unlikely they would go rummaging
through the charity shop just on the off-chance of finding
a particular colour of jumper that matched a witness
description.

Luke immediately started stripping off and loading the
washing machine as Matt was searching the fridge.

'You should have popped in the chippy on the way back,'
Luke said with a grin.

'Funny that,' Matt replied. 'It was closed for some
reason. Get the Barrett stowed?'

Luke nodded. 'I'll have scrambled.'

'You'll get, as my old mum used to say, what you are given.'

That would be one of the one-pan meals Matt had mastered on their global excursions. Whether Palau or Risotto. Or Paella or Ragù. Or Scouse or Cawl. Matt started to slice and dice. 'You reckon it's safe under that bridge?'

Luke nodded and reached over for a bottle of water, then nicked a tomato from Matt's ingredients pile, just dodging a flick from his Blackhawk folding and barely legal Hornet knife. Another souvenir from his time as a US contractor.

'There's a local gun club not far down the track. If anything gets found the cops'll waste a day or two making two and two equal six and harass the law-abiding membership while they hunt for some imaginary gun freak.' He bit into the tomato. 'But they'd have to know where to look. We used to hang out up there. It's a small gap where the bridge supports meet the bridge itself. Some kind of bearing or shock absorber that cushions the load. You'd only know it was there if you worked on building the bridge. Or were bored out of your teenage brain and looking for things to do.'

'Boldly going where no one else in their right mind would go?'

'Probably. But then Joe and I did a lot of things out of sheer boredom.'

'Which explains a lot. And why Fatty and his gang have

them queuing down that alley. We going to hit him again tomorrow?'

'See how bright he is. Whether he figures it out and calls in the troops.'

'Let's hope he's brighter than he looks, then. How'd you want your eggs?'

'Just as they come?'

'Good answer.'

Which was something Fatchops hadn't found. He was still searching for an answer while throwing his clothes into a washing machine: it was part of his POLO as he was actually more concerned about his own forensic residue than that of Luke and the others, as it was more durable than that left by firing a weapon. For this reason he always appeared to wear the same clothes, having a cupboard capable of providing three changes a day. For the lunch, dinner and chucking-out time waves. He walked back into the now spotlessly clean shop and stood looking at the damaged drinks cabinet once more, not quite convinced that a bottle of fake cola could do so much damage. His head was still pounding from the fall. He'd take an over-the-counter drug, not one of his own, and figure it out in the morning.

6

Build-Up

By the time Fatchops began his search for the real answer to what had happened the previous night, Joey had visited Luton, Birmingham, Stoke-on-Trent and Crewe, reinforcing his twin beliefs that modern transport enabled people to make journeys undreamt of in his grandparents' age and that they were designed to make Londoners feel safe in their beds, certain that no provincial hordes could descend on them overnight in an orderly manner. Similarly, it was virtually impossible for anyone to escape the outer reaches of the capital beyond 23.30, when all long-distance trains were suspended, unless they already had an escape plan in place. Joey had three. He always had. Ever since starting the weekly commute he had wanted to know how fast he could get back to Natasha and the kids if wanted to. Like now.

The full-on emergency option was taking Benno's ambulance, but that would mean returning it. And right now Joey didn't think he would be coming back. By the time he left Benno going after a new world record for snoring, his options had been reduced to one of the other two. The 23.30 overnight bus to Liverpool had gone. That left the half-past midnight service to Manchester, but looking at his phone he knew it would be touch and go whether he could get to Victoria Coach Station in time. Its second stop at Golders Green was also on the edge. He could, however, get to its third stop at Luton Airport by 01.40 by taking a direct train from Blackfriars. After that he'd have to change buses at Birmingham, then drop off at Stoke and catch a train to Crewe, then home. It was part of his weekly routine to check the timetables in the hope of finding a more direct route, but there never was. At least this one allowed plenty of time at each changing point for delays. And pondering. On what he would be walking into when he got home.

Once at Stoke he knew Natasha could collect him within forty minutes, but that would mean her getting up early, not being able to do the school run, and that would escalate her anxiety. Better, he thought, to jump on another local train to Crewe and be home before she got back from the school run. Then he would be able to calm her down face-to-face. So at 07.00, just after purchasing his ticket to Crewe, he sent a holding text.

HOPE THINGS BETTER THIS MORNING. TRAVELLING. TALK LATER. LXXJ.
He then tapped his favourites and found Benno's number.
Time to tell him what he was up to.

Neither Mercedes nor Fatchops were in the best of moods
as they came through from the back of the chippy.
Fatchops was fiddling with a large crêpe bandage that
was now wrapped round his head. Mercedes was fiddling
with the drawstring on a pair of definitely non-designer
baggy, and chequered, catering trousers. Their depression
was deepened by the knowledge that no matter what had
happened last night, they had lost most of their product
to the deep-fat fryer and while that had had to be cleaned
out, the money for the product would still have to be
accounted for.

Waste was a term with only one meaning in their
business and if they didn't pay up it would be applied to
them. While a grumpy Fatchops moved to start getting
things ready for the day, a sullen Mercedes unlocked the
external door then threw both the keys and a killer look
back at the counter. Giving a last irritated look at the
baggy trousers, he opened the door and stepped out,
pulling his coat around him against the wind as he hurried
to his car, grateful for the keyless entry that would allow
a quick exit before anyone with any fashion sense could
see him.

Whether Matt had any real views on the subject was
open to question and if he did they were probably directed

more towards Joey's sartorial companion Benno, but the sight of Mercedes scurrying up the road made him laugh.

'He doesn't look like a happy bunny this morning,' Matt's voice announced in Luke's ear. They were now using Motorola MT352 walkie-talkies with voice-activated headsets held securely in place with surgical tape as they were wary of using the pay-and-throws for extended periods, or of relying on the vagaries of the mobile networks for instant communication. The Motorolas had an advertised potential range of 35 miles across 22 channels, each with 121 privacy codes. The 35 miles claim was always followed by an asterix, of course, meaning don't rely on it, but they would cope with a few miles round Highbridge. And they might not survive being dropped out of a helo or Warrior, like their usual comms kits, but they came with a few other advantages. They were really cheap, licence free and could be bought for cash. And while their expensive encrypted kit was designed so no one could eavesdrop, that always assumed someone was trying to listen. The other great advantage of the MT352s was that their frequencies were illegal in the UK, so the chances of someone else having one and stumbling across which of the 2,662 potential channels they chose to use was remote.

While Matt was back on the hill, Luke was sitting in an old Transit van just down the street from the chippy.

It was parked so he would have a clear line of sight from its side door, although at the moment it was closed and he was sitting watching the Mercedes start to move away on a small colour monitor he had taped to his thigh. It may not have been as sophisticated as the chippy's CCTV, but the small inspection camera at the end of the flexible optic tube they had wedged into the door seal gave a clear view of the whole street.

'It's not bad, this. How much was it?'

'Seventy quid in a sale from Maplin. Got it for sixty-five for cash,' Matt replied. 'Says it'll do night vision too. But only at 1.5 metres.'

'Useful to see who you've tripped over, then?' Luke asked as he slid back behind the Barrett.

'Think they had inspecting your drains or hidden wiring, rather than target spotting, actually, Carlton. And something you might find in a crappy builder's van.'

Luke had the Barrett on a tripod so he could shoot from a sitting position. He was wedged between side racks of chaotically stacked trays filled with electrical fittings and plumbing pipework, along with all the screws, nails and general bits and bobs that make up the organised chaos of any typical builder's van. To the casual eye. To the more experienced viewer it would look exactly what it was. A collection of junk and scrap. For two weeks, alongside scoping the chippy, they had been scavenging skips, taking full advantage of the throwaway society.

After running a vehicle check paid for with a prepaid

credit card, they had bought the van on eBay for £300, complete with eight months' MOT and one month's tax by phoning the buyer direct. They had turned up, paid cash and given the address of a Domino's pizza outlet in Birmingham. Neither should have done that under eBay's terms, but then again, neither should people be selling illegal drugs. Nor other people planning to shoot them. By the time the DVLA V5C form had worked its way through the system, Fatchops and the Transit would be history, someone at Domino's would probably return the V5C to the DVLA and the seller would be an innocent victim of who knew what. All in all, eBay would probably never find out. Especially that its one-time listing was now parked up in a northern town as a sniper hide posing as just another builder's white van. To the casual eye.

And it was casual eyes they were depending on, as they had agreed that, although it was a long time to sit and wait for the spudman to make his delivery, parking up early was the best option. Most people are half asleep on their way to work or school, so they wouldn't notice Matt park up and leave a white van with a tool bag. Just another builder doing a job somewhere. But a guy sitting in a van for three or more hours would attract attention. Even to a casual eye.

As a result, Matt was now halfway up the hill watching through a pair of birdwatching binoculars. Just another middle-aged bloke filling his unemployed time, but he could be back at the van within minutes. As soon as he saw the spudman approaching.

'They do make me laugh, these characters,' Matt continued. 'They live among the world's filth but are always so flash – no, fastidious, about their appearance.'

'Playing the part,' Luke responded. It's like the footballer's manual. Tattoos. 4x4. Big headphones. These guys think it's designer clothes and cars.'

Matt chuckled again. 'He's probably got a gold-plated phoney AK under his bed too.'

'Is anybody likely to walk past and see you talking to yourself?' Luke replied.

'That Lukey for shut up and wait?'

'It is.'

'OK.'

It was also Luke's way of keeping everything as normal as possible. Ordinary. It's often not what's in front of people that matters but what they pick up or sense. Even if a passer-by saw Matt chuntering away to himself they would probably just think he was talking on his handsfree. But perhaps not if he was animated while looking through his binoculars. Joining dots that are sometimes not obvious. Like peripheral vision and the reason they kept their eyes moving, from point to point, as it's the peripheral vision that picks up movement. Or like the lines they had sprayed on the road the week before. There for everyone to see. White, like the ones councils spray round holes instead of fixing them. One circle with an arrow pointing to the kerb. Another arrow on the kerb pointing into the road. Few would even notice, never mind wonder what they were, but when the Transit parked with the arrows lining up with the two mud splashes below each door window, Matt and Luke knew that when the side door cracked open a few inches it would present a perfect shot. Like the previous night. Straight through Fatchops's front door. It's all in the prep.

'Tell me what really happened last night before the beasts come down,' Natasha asked, as she leaned across to examine Tanya's now badly bruised eye. 'You'll need to cover that a bit more.'

'Why?' Tanya asked, defiantly. 'If anyone asks I'll tell them what happened.'

Natasha sighed. Knowing she had already lost the argument about not provoking more trouble. But she had a maternal duty to probe. 'Well, you could start by telling me?' she asked. More in hope.

Now it was Tanya's turn to let out a long sigh. She had a teenager's duty to evade. 'Just Becky still not getting it.'

'What?' Natasha couldn't follow the logic jump. 'Last night it was all about things exploding and guys pushing you about?'

'We were only there because Becky can't get what that guy's after.'

'Which is?'

Tanya just looked. 'Er. . . Where've you been for the last few years? White girls are easy?' With the faintest shake of her head she took her tea and headed for the door.

'Is that it?' Natasha called, but got no answer. Obviously it was no longer a trending tropic, but at least Tanya appeared to have her head screwed on about sexual predators. That just left Joey to update. She headed across to the patio doors to let Roscoe in after his morning patrol and pulled her phone from the pocket of the fleece Joey really hated. One of the advantages of him not being around in the week. She could grab whatever was still on the bedroom chair, like every other school run mum. She saw his holding text then replied. WHAT TIME TALK? LX2T The text went the three miles to the nearest phone mast, then the ten miles to the nearest exchange, 200 miles to the central server then back, to be delivered to Joey's phone half a mile away, as the cab that was ferrying him from the station turned off the High Street towards home. By the time he got there, there was only Roscoe waiting with a happy but confused look on his face. It couldn't be the weekend already!

'Aye, lad,' Joey said as he grabbed Roscoe's nose and gave him a playful to-and-fro. 'New routine.'

Roscoe just stood. Waiting. As a puppy he used to like this game that would end up in a fun fight round the kitchen, but as he got older he had adopted a resigned tolerance, knowing that it wouldn't last long. He was right. Joey gave him a head rub, then went to the coffee machine as he texted Natasha. AFTER SCHOOL RUN? LMOREXXXJ Natasha looked at the text from Joe, but was too preoccupied trying to keep up with her mother's spiralling conversation.

'I'll follow you, then.'

'Mum, you gave up driving five years ago.'

'Did I?'

'Yes,' Natasha confirmed, trying to keep the frustration out of her voice. It only made matters worse. 'Remember, you had that funny turn when you ended up nearly driving into the canal?' How could anyone forget that, she thought, but the mind is a mysterious thing, especially when it starts to fail.

'Not really. You sure that was me and not . . . er . . . not . . . ?'

'Who?' It was an automatic response, but Natasha was still coming to terms with her mother, Grace's, early signs of dementia. Or perhaps not coming to terms with it, as Joe was beginning to say.

'You know. Oh, what's her name . . . ? You know. She's always at the doctor's. Practically lives there.'

'I wouldn't ask if I didn't . . .' But she bit her tongue. Go with the flow. That was the advice. She drew breath. 'Give me a clue?' she smiled and squeezed her mum's hand.

'Oh, I am getting forgetful these days. I know it must be difficult. I was only telling Pamela yesterday that I can't remember from one minute to the next at times.' She stopped and squeezed Natasha's hand harder. 'I do have a friend called Pamela, don't I? She's still alive and living close . . .'

Natasha couldn't help but laugh as she interrupted the flow. More out of relief than the dark humour of trying to keep up with the short-circuiting that was starting to happen in her mother's brain. Sometimes she felt like she was carrying on three separate conversations at once. 'Oh, Mum. Yes. Auntie Pam, as we all grew up calling her. And you were at the baking club with her yesterday.'

'I knew that bit. Just had to check whether it was real or not. I'm getting confused more regularly these days, aren't I?'

Natasha just nodded. It was true. Even if it was difficult to admit. Like this morning. She still hadn't found out why her mother had called to ask her to come round straight away.

'Bound to happen. Seen so many of them down at the hospice,' Grace continued. 'Can't remember their own names, some of them. Remember the one who used to live next to the garage off Market Street? Had a snake tattoo. On her arm. Oh, what was her name? Began with the same letter as the shop over the road. You know, from where the vet used to take the horses.'

Natasha just stared. Trying not to look concerned. Go with the flow. But now totally lost. 'I er. . . I don't remember anyone with a tattoo, sorry Mum.'

'I'm not surprised,' her mother said. Then started to laugh and point at Natasha. 'Your face. Had you there, didn't I?'

'Mother! It's bad enough without—'

'It's all right, love. If I can't laugh at it, who can? And at least I still can. Anyway, it was Betty I was thinking about.'

'Betty?'

'Who drove into the canal? Remember?'

'Are you still winding me up?' Natasha asked warily.

'No, I meant before. When I was trying to remember who I thought had driven into a canal. I was thinking of your sister-in-law, mother. Betty. The doctor's receptionist. But she reversed into a paddling pool, didn't she? At Joey's brother Sean's lad's birthday party. Noah. And it wasn't his paddling pool but the younger one's. Megan. She did that around the time I went through that fence and nearly . . .' she emphasised it again, 'when I nearly, went into the canal. So, I just got the two things mixed up, didn't I? But, you see, I can still remember things.' She gave Natasha a broad smile, then sighed. 'Just not every now and then. Or in the right order.'

To stop the tears welling, Natasha squeezed her mum's hand again, then started to gather the teacups. 'Well, while you're remembering, you stopped driving after that.'

'I remember it was you who stopped me,' her mum shot back. 'And leave those. I can still manage.'

'It was actually Joe. And it was the right decision.'

'I know,' her mum conceded. 'He's usually right, your Joe. I've always listened to him.'

It took all Natasha's strength to resist asking, since when? Just as it was fortunate her mother stood up and started gathering the teacups. Otherwise she would have seen Natasha's jaw hanging with incredulity. Her mother never listened to anyone, never mind her son-in-law. She was still telling anyone who would listen how Natasha had wasted her life on him. Go with the flow, she told herself. 'So you still can't remember why you asked me to call round. Urgently?'

Grace slowly shook her head. 'But you did say to dial Star 6 if I needed you. Perhaps I should write things down first. So I won't forget.'

'Yes, perhaps,' Natasha agreed, thinking how long it had taken to get her to remember the speed dial function on her phone. 'Was it something to do with lunch over the weekend?' It was a wild guess, but she had learned that Grace was entering that stage when food became the focus of life.

'Yes. Yes, that was it. Was it? What time will we be eating, do you think?'

'The usual time. As always. And we'll pick you up and take you to the restaurant.' She stood up and tried again to take the cups from her mother. But Grace held on. Slightly defiant.

'I'd better go,' Natasha said, to avoid the confrontation. 'I left Roscoe in the house.'

Grace nodded, put the teacups back on the occasional table and walked her to the door. 'Give my love to er. . . er. . .' But seeing her daughter's expression, not amused, she smiled. 'That bloke you've been married to for seventeen years. Text him my love or whatever you do these days.'

'I will. Bye, Mum.' She gave her mother a last hug and left, sending the text to Joe straight away. MUM SENDS LUV. GETTING WORSE, MAKES ME MISS YOU MORE. SPEAK LATER LXXT No sooner had she pressed send when a text from Tanya arrived. GOING BECK'S AFTER SCHOOL HOME 9ISH.XX THAT WOULD MEAN LESS ARGUING AT HOME. OK XXX It would also give her a quiet hour to speak to Joe, as although he said he wanted to talk, she knew he found it difficult while at work.

What she didn't know was that he was beginning to pace the kitchen wondering where she was. What he didn't imagine was that she was cursing her long-gone dad, as she always did when she had to ease the Q7 round the walled flower bed he had hand-built right opposite the front door, but smiling at the memory of how proud he was of it. He had no idea at the time that his daughter would at some point be driving a civilian troop carrier. Once clear of the wall and pointing towards the gate she turned to wave back at her mother who was, as always, standing in the window waving.

Time and age, Natasha thought as she gunned the Q7 down the road, it gets us all in the end. Something similar was going through Grace's mind as she watched her daughter drive off, too fast, as always. She turned away from the window and felt in her cardigan pocket for the card she had folded inside. Typed in bold were three words. Time. Clock. List. Beneath them Grace herself had written Betty – Sean's mum. Sandra – wife. Noah – oldest. Megan. She sighed, looked across at the clock on the mantel. What should she be doing now? She headed off towards the kitchen to look at her list, leaving the teacups where they were.

'If you want to change anything, Sean, you should run for mayor or something. At least get it out of your system.' It was another of Glynnis's throwaway lines as she manoeuvred a Christmas tree through the entrance of the café. Stopping when she had another idea. 'You could get your sister-in-law to design your electioneering pamphlets. People'd like that. Local jobs for local people.'

She then left him with that thought and he was more convinced than ever about the female hive. Or that Glynnis and Sandra either talked every day or were separated at birth. It was almost word for word what Sandra had said to him the night before when he had tried to recount his after dinner chat with Hilary Jardine. Followed quickly and emphatically with a reminder that they had put their time in building the business and all she now wanted was to enjoy the last few years they'd have with the kids before they all flew the nest.

His phone chirped as a text arrived. It was Arthur Young passing on Craig Harlow's contact number. He chuckled at the thought of a global rock star turning up to play Santa. But stranger things happen, he thought. And if Craig could win a Grammy, then why couldn't he himself win an election? Then he chuckled again as he wondered what Sandra would make of her soulmate Glynnis's idea of him running for mayor, even though Highbridge was too small a town to have an elected mayor.

Yet, he wanted to do something and as he liberated the Santas with a last slash of his retractable knife, he looked at his watch. Just time to get the Santas deployed before lunch. He grinned. Perhaps he could start his own party and take over the whole process. Local politics for local people. His grin morphed into a laugh. The idea of revolutionising local politics was probably not what Sandra would consider a way of enjoying the last few years with the kids. His laugh then developed into a chuckle. If he became some sort of party leader, though, it would be a good excuse for her to renew her wardrobe

Joey walked along the landing to the spare room, now changed and his hair wet after a quick shower. He looked in to see their weekend sanctuary, away from Tanya and her friends, was now doubling as Natasha's work space. Printed copies of inspirational quotes she would sell on Etsy were strewn across the bed and what looked like a half-finished design was still drying on the printer. He was now beginning to feel a sense of anticlimax. The hero's overnight odyssey battling the creatures of the night to be by the side of his princess was rapidly feeling like a sad over-reaction.

Where could she be? Joey wondered as he made another coffee. Anywhere, he concluded. Another reminder of how they led separate lives during the week, and while he imagined what lay behind the weekly headlines he never quite knew. Another side effect of mobile phones. You never had a clue where anyone was these days. Should he text again? But that would probably get her going. Then again, he'd said he'd call after the school run. She'd expect him to call around now. 'What do you reckon, Rosk? I travel all night to get back and support her, and she's nowhere to be seen. Any clues?'

But as usual Roscoe opted to not get involved and went to the patio door to be let out. As he closed the door behind him, Joey reached for his phone. CAN YOU TALK? But no sooner had he pressed send than he heard Natasha's phone chirp, accompanied by a loud OMG of surprise. He turned to find her in the kitchen doorway holding both phone and hand to her chest.

'What the hell are you doing here?'

Not quite the heroic welcome he had expected. 'Yeah. Sorry. Didn't want to worry you last night, so I—'

But she cut him off as she crossed over to hug him, causing her hair to nearly suffocate him once again. 'You scared the . . . Jesus, Joe.'

At the end of his lung capacity he eased her back and

kissed her. This was a bit better. 'Sorry for giving you a shock but I thought . . .'

She hugged him again and then stepped back. 'No need. It's why I love you. You always know when I need you.'

As she took off her fleece Joey watched her closely. His attention on the frown across her forehead. He guessed his instinct had been right. Something was going on here that she'd been trying to keep from him. But she was recovering.

'What . . . What about the work?' she asked.

'Not important. Benno's sorted it. Just jumped the overnight bus.' It was all she needed to know at the moment. He'd tell her about the wino at Birmingham and psycho at Stoke some other time. 'So. Go on. I'm here. What's going on?'

'Don't know where to start, really.'

'How about something typical? Cup of tea and begin at the beginning. Just ramble.'

And so she did. For the next hour.

'Cracklin' cocaine,' Luke suddenly heard in his headset. He didn't respond, just waited. He knew one of Matt's philosophical ramblings was on its way. 'There's Crack Cocaine, isn't there? Fatty's just invented another variety. Deep-fried? Crack-ling? Cracklin' Cocaine.'

Luke managed a smile as Matt chuckled at his own joke. Then carried on.' I mean, it's priceless isn't it. Why put the stuff so near to the fryer in the first place?'

'Because he's at the bottom of the food chain?'

'Yeah,' Matt agreed. 'And looks like he's working out all his inner tensions on that countertop this morning.' His tone changed as something in his binoculars caught his attention. 'Now then, what's Fatty doing now?'

Luke couldn't make out the detail on the monitor but Matt relayed how Fatchops was struggling to drag an old fridge from the back room towards the damaged cold drinks cabinet. He then started to pull the cabinet away from the wall to make space for the fridge. And as he did he noticed the damage the 50 cal round had made in the plasterwork.

'He's found the impact point.'

Luke leaned on the Barrett but kept an eye on the monitor while listening to Matt's commentary as Fatchops eased the cabinet forward, to see the hole in its back lined up perfectly with the damage to the wall. They both waited. Tense. It was too early for him to discover what was going on. After a moment or two of fingering the damage, perplexed, wondering whether an exploding bottle of cola could do such damage, he backed away. They relaxed. His body language said it all. What else could it be? Even if he knew what he was looking for he wouldn't be used to seeing – never mind expect to find – the damage from a 50 Cal. Luke heard the relief in Matt's voice as he described Fatchops giving the damaged drinks cabinet one last shove to make space for the old fridge.

'Do you think he's wondering if that's a design fault and it's still under warranty?' Matt asked.

Luke smiled as he checked the Barrett one more time. It would be another cold shot, but from this distance he could probably just point and shoot. Still, they had already laser-ranged the distance so he was ready. The closer distance reduced the margin. No flight time for people to accidentally step into the shot. This time, almost as soon as Luke squeezed the trigger the target would be destroyed. In one way it was easier. But in another way much more dangerous, as they would be in close proximity. Even with a suppressor the noise would be noticeable.

Again they were relying on the unfamiliar and unknown. And that there would not be many folk around at the time. However, there was always the chance of a passing smartphone and the chance of getting on the evening news. Unlike the previous night, this time they would have to get the job done and get gone, sharpish. Luke glanced at his watch. 30 minutes.

'We've only got half an hour before we have to be back for that stupid enrichment lecture,' Carol shouted from behind the toilet cubicle door.

'He said he would wait for me until lunchtime,' Becky countered as she continued her pleading to get Tanya and Carol to go to the chippy.

'Listen to yourself,' Tanya counter-countered, while

looking at her bruised eye in the mirror. 'If you did you'd realise how pathetic you sound.'

'I only want to find out where he is.'

'God, Becky. How many times. Look at this!' Tanya pointed to her bruised eye, as Carol emerged from the cubicle. 'And he was with two other girls last night.'

'He said he was only giving them a lift. But you wouldn't wait to find out, would you?'

Tanya turned to Carol. Help me out here.

Carol tried. 'But why was he giving them a lift to some greasy chippy?'

'I don't know. You'd have to ask them.'

'Don't want to know, you mean,' Carol fired back. 'You've read Lizzie Peterson's feed about the parties,' she made the quotation marks gesture to emphasise the point. 'The parties where they all get off their heads. He was probably rounding them up for his mates.'

'Lizzie Peterson's a skank,' Becky tried to protest. Lamely.

'And?' Carol asked incredulously. 'I don't think it's her social standing they're after. They don't even want her standing.'

'Look,' Becky was becoming tetchy again. 'I know you hate him. But you don't know what he was up to any more than I do. So he might have given a couple of girls a lift to help out his friends. It's their choice and . . .' she turned to Tanya as she saw her about to come back in. 'They go to that chippy because their parents don't approve of, well, you know.'

'What? Him salivating over white girls?' Tanya asked, her exasperation getting the better of her. 'And he's probably already engaged to some fat cousin he's never seen in some village he's never heard of back home.'

'Don't be so racist.'

Carol pushed between them. Sensing Tanya's impatience would cause Becky to stomp off by herself. 'C'mon Becks, he's twenty-five or something, isn't he? And still worrying about what his parents will say about who he dates?'

'It's . . . It's some kind of religious thing. He doesn't want to upset them.'

'So who's being racist, then?' Carol asked.

'It's not racism. It's religion,' Becky responded as she headed out of the door.

'Oh, so that's OK then? Selective prejudice,' Carol called as they followed her out.

'And like religion hasn't led to people killing each other all over the world?' Tanya chipped in again.

'All right, all right. I get it,' Becky fired back. Now getting angry herself. 'It's not just because you don't like him. You don't understand his culture.' She strode away from them. But towards the Sixth Form Centre.

Carol turned to Tanya. 'Well, at least that stopped her going out.'

'Why can't she see it, Cags?'

'Now listen to yourself!'

Carol headed off after Becky, leaving Tanya chewing her lip. She had spent most of her life sidestepping predators, but for Becky this was the first big thing. Why couldn't it have been that moron in her geography group who kept buying her cupcakes?

It took a moment for the motor to get going, but it wasn't long before Byron had to jump aside to avoid the spray of artificial snow heading his way.

'Careful, Sean!' Byron called as he took a long arc to come up behind the snow machine Sean was trying to position it so that the artificial snow would fall directly in front of the entrance doors. 'Are you sure it wouldn't be better over the exit?'

'Byron, the whole point is to get people in the Christmas spirit on the way in. So they will spend more inside.'

'Well who's going to clean it all up when people traipse it inside?'

'It dissolves, like rain. And most people are like you. They'll dash through it. But hopefully it will make them smile. Especially if they've got kids and are coming to see Santa's Garden.'

Byron didn't look too impressed. He didn't have kids. 'If, and it's a big if, they actually know it's here. I don't care what young Ben says about social media, it's only like being in the pub. If you're there you can join in the conversation. But if you don't even know where the pub is, how can you? We need to spend money advertising. Telling the real people. The old people—'

'Older people,' Sean interrupted.

'The people who can come in here on a wet Tuesday afternoon.'

'They those wet people who traipse in, in their wet and muddy wellies?'

'Touché. And I know it's one of Sandra's ideas so it will probably work, but you can tell the staff they will need to clean up.'

'Do you really think so,' Sean replied with a huge grin, as he nodded over Byron's shoulder.

Byron turned and let his shoulders sag as several of the staff were already running in and out of the snow, scooping up handfuls and throwing them at each other.

'I think it's a primeval thing. And . . .' Sean said and then indicated a young lad standing under the snow shower taking pictures on his phone and then putting his thumbs to work, 'I think Ben's already got the digital gossiping going.'

He began to walk away as Byron fired one last shot about doubting that Ben had their customer database in his favourites list before going over to remind everyone that they still had work to do. Which Sean also had to do. He pulled out his own phone and pressed redial.

'Hi. It's Sean Nolan for Craig, again. Any chance?

OK. Yeah, understand. Fine, no problem.' He then went on hold and listened to Craig's latest single, wondering exactly what were the chances of getting Craig Harlow to open Santa's Garden. Probably two. Slim and fat. But just as he was starting to tap along with the music, he was back on with Craig's PA. And his mood soared.

'Really? He's considering it? Great. Yeah, I'll be here all afternoon. Thanks.' He was about to ask what the hold music track was but the line clicked off. His face started to beam in a broad smile. Their local pop star was considering opening Santa's Garden. However, he didn't get much time to dwell on it as his phone sounded the klaxon alert that meant one of the kids was calling. It was Noah. Speaking at light speed as Sean put the phone to his ear.

'Noah, Noah. Slow down. You're going too fast.' Sean was standing surrounded by Singing Santas, once again speaking into his phone, knowing that Noah was extremely upset not just by his voice but by the fact that he had actually called. This was way beyond the power of text. 'Tell me again, from the beginning.'

By the time Natasha had talked Joey through everything that had been happening with Tanya and Becky over the past few months, he had gone from thinking they had just wandered into something outside the chippy by accident to worrying that his own daughter was slowly being pulled into another modern horror story of drugs and sex abuse. To be fair to Natasha, she had got it all out in about five minutes but he had kept asking her to go over and over the details, trying to make sure he wasn't simply reacting to media perceptions and local prejudices. He was not alone in regretting the way Highbridge had changed through an influx of outsiders, or offcomers, as the old locals called them, but he had always parked that as a natural resistance to change. Until it came close to his own. Then it became nothing more and nothing less than a threat.

'So, you reckon Becky's being groomed by this Egyptian bloke?' he asked again.

'Tanya certainly does. And as usual she is getting herself involved too much.'

'Wonder where she gets that from?' he smiled.

She returned the smile, appreciating that he meant them both, but then it hardened. 'So, as you came back, you obviously feel something needs to be done too?'

'What? Like asking Luke to go and sort them out?' He said it facetiously, expecting her to treat it as a throwaway, but was completely caught by her response.

'Well, it wouldn't be anything he's not used to. And what's he doing here? He's never hung around this long before.'

Joey now decided to deflect. Worried by where this was going. 'Do you think he might just want to take a break?' He then tried to use the same line he had with Hilary Jardine. 'Spend some time at home? On the anniversary of Janey's death?'

Natasha considered this, but shook her head. She knew Luke almost as well as Joey. Not just from personal experience, but from all the tales Joey had told her. And since he had married her sister-in-law. 'He's been running ever since Janey. So I don't see why he'd suddenly decide to settle down. Here.'

'He might,' Joey offered, still trying to steer her away from where he thought this conversation would inevitably end up.

'Yeah. Like getting you into a fight down the Lion?'

'OK,' Joey conceded. 'He might still be a bit messed up, but what I'm more concerned about is why you are suddenly wanting to go to war.'

'I . . . I dunno, really. Last night. God, if you'd seen them when they first got back. In fact when you see the bruise on Tanya's face. If you'd been here then, as I said, I'd probably be still trying to bail you out.'

He got up and squatted next to her, hooking his arm round her shoulders. 'So? I'm here. As you said. When you need me. But . . .' he hesitated before posing the question that would take them over a line. 'What do you really want me to do?'

She held his stare for a moment. His eyes had gone cold. She knew he wouldn't have come back if he wasn't really concerned. Which meant that no matter what he said, he knew more than he was admitting. Which meant he was ready to do something. He was really asking her permission.

Her own eyes hardened. 'You're already up to something, aren't you? You and Luke?'

Joey hesitated. He wasn't sure how she would react. But she had asked. 'You don't need to know.'

Suddenly she felt cold. Perhaps the shiver people often spoke about going down the spine. Although she had asked the question, she hadn't really expected that answer. She'd always known who and what Joey was. How he'd changed or, more correctly, held himself in check. For her. So she should have expected something like this. But hearing the words brought it home. It was too easy to constantly say something needed to be done about this, that or the other, but only a few people would have the nerve to actually do anything. She knew he had. But was that what she really wanted? She stood up and walked across to the patio doors to let Roscoe back in, partly to give herself a moment or two to think.

Joey stood and leaned against the table. Waiting. Watching. As she stood looking out across the garden where the kids had grown up. Where they had had many a BBQ. A happy lifestyle perhaps about to be put in jeopardy.

'How risky will it be?'

'You don't need to know that either,' came the matter-of-fact response. In fact, too matter-of-fact.'

'Christ, Joe. It's not some game or street corner brawl we're talking about.'

'And what are we talking about, Nat?'

He was pushing. She knew. He was pushing to get that permission. He didn't want her involved in the details but he wanted her to be aware of what he might get involved in.

'I . . . I don't know, Joe.' She turned back to face him. 'Perhaps it's all . . . Last night. The way my mum is. That's where I was before.'

'Is she really getting worse?'

She nodded. 'And something else to deal with.' But then she brought them back to the point. 'Perhaps all I want is what you've just given me. To be back here. With me. Sharing the load?'

'OK. You've got that. But . . .' He hesitated again. Not sure how far to go. But, as always, he needed to go the extra step. 'That wasn't how it sounded on the phone last night. Or before.'

'I wanted them dead last night,' she admitted. 'Which is probably why it is best to sleep on these things.'

'And having done that . . . what do you want to do?'

Natasha could only chew her lip. The line was right in front of her. Did she really want to cross it?

Forty-five minutes after taking the call from Noah, Sean was in the Custody Suite standing in front of a custody sergeant who looked younger than Noah and wondering why life did this. One minute he's on the phone ecstatic because Craig Harlow is considering opening Santa's Garden, yet without giving him any time to really savour the moment that same phone is informing him that his son has been arrested for public disorder. Fifteen minutes later they were in the garden centre Land Rover heading home with Noah trying to explain to his father why they should sue the police for wrongful arrest, harassment, entrapment and brutality while disrupting a perfectly peaceful protest in the park.

By the time they reached home, Sean was trying to explain to Noah that the police were not victimising him and his friends but trying to act on behalf of the whole community by preventing him and his co-protesters from coming to any harm.

It was met with a typical teenage 'as if' look. Followed by, 'And I don't need the Mark Twain quote about how much I'll realise how wise you are by the time I leave university.'

'The point, Noah –' Sean toughened up as he brought the car to a stop outside the house – 'is that it stays with you for the rest of your life. On a file somewhere. Never mind all this stuff about spent convictions and sealed files. They never delete anything. And you don't know where you will want to be in the future. And how it might count against you.'

'Oh right. "Teenage kid arrested for trying to save a children's playground." Definitely be on the US Homeland watch list with that one.' With that parting shot Noah went to get out of the car, but Sean put his hand on his arm. Just enough to stop him.

'No, but "organising protests against the state" might. It depends who writes the report.'

'Yeah, and history is written by the victors, Dad. But our democracy is about controlling the report writers, isn't it? And the only way we can do that is to make them and everyone else aware of what is going on. Evil prospers when good men remain silent and all that?' He gathered his stuff ready to bail out, but turned back to face Sean. 'Er, I think someone in this car once told me that.'

With that verbal dig he was out and on his way into the house, ignoring the Singing Santa trying to wish him a Merry Christmas, as Sean sat reflecting on hearing his own words thrown back at him. Hire a teenager, he concluded. While they know everything.

As he got out of the Land Rover, Sandra's Mercedes SLR 300 swung into the drive and she emerged, still in her tennis gear.

'Have you heard what he's been up to?' Sean called, hoping for some support.

'The whole town has,' she replied, holding up her phone as she swept past to find Noah, which she did at the fridge. 'I had to leave when we were 5–3 up in the final set for this.'

'Sor-ree. But I didn't organise the timings. And that's another thing.' Noah turned back to his father. 'Invasion of privacy.'

'What?'

'They must have hacked into our accounts or something to get there that fast. We were only there five minutes before the riot squad turned up.'

'You mean this account?' Sandra offered her phone and then did what everyone does in times of crisis: put the kettle on. 'I suppose you'll want to eat now you're here.'

As neither responded she took that as consent and started to drag the necessary components out of the fridge.

Noah had looked at the phone, passed it to his father and flopped on to the bench that wrapped round the kitchen table wall. Deflated. Sean was now looking at the phone and grinning.

'Who needs Big Brother's surveillance society when we've got social media?' he asked as he waved the phone at Sandra. She nodded towards her handbag and Sean dropped it in.

'Who came up with the Kids for Kiddies Facebook page?' Sandra asked.

'Does it matter?' Noah sighed. 'Just one of the group. And I told them not to post until we were actually there and established.'

'And . . . Dump the Druggies?' Sandra asked.

'That was me. It's the way to beat them. Name and shame. Drive them out. Social media is the new public protest.'

'Or village mob?' Sean asked.

'Or posting a target on your back?' Sandra asked, the scathing edge slightly softened by a mother's concern.

'Don't you think your druggies will be online too? As well as the police? And who would you have rather got to you first?'

Noah glared at her. Wanting to fight, but caught by her logic.

Sean couldn't suppress the wide grin on his face. Nor resist saying, 'That could be Mark Twain's missus, that.'

'You can be such a dick sometimes, Dad.' And with that he got up and went out. No doubt to reconnect with the group.

'Language,' Sandra called, more from habit than anger. That was directed at Sean. 'Did you have to?'

'No. But I don't really appreciate being dragged away from work to collect him from the police station.'

'Well you can't say your family hasn't had experience of that in the past. So let's hope he hasn't inherited the wrong Nolan genes.'

Sean took the barb. This might be rites of passage stuff, but he too hoped his son hadn't inherited any of the more aggressive Nolan genes. Like his Uncle Joe.

'Ten minutes,' Matt announced from his position halfway up the hill.

Luke glanced down at the monitor again. The street was quiet. As expected.

'You can record on that monitor as well you know,' Matt added, assuming Luke was watching.

'You know where that can end up,' Luke replied as he

arranged the black weed matting he had got from Sean. It was supposed to be for the cottage garden, but before that it had been commandeered to act as blackout inside the van. Even when he slid the door back to take the shot, anyone who happened to be looking in the direction of the van would find it difficult to make him out. 'Bad enough when we had to do it. Ended up collecting evidence on ourselves.'

'Yeah. Perhaps not the best of ideas. Hey up. Spuds on the horizon.'

Luke watched the monitor as the delivery guy's van came down the road towards the chippy. He then settled back down behind the Barrett. It was already chambered and ready to fire. He pushed a foam earplug into his right ear. Even with the suppressor the muzzle blast inside the van would be enough to cause temporary deafness. He tugged on a cord attached to a pulley system rigged to the side door. Just enough ease it back a few inches. They had taped and wedged the door lock to make it easier, and quieter, to slide open and if they had lined up the van properly with the marks on the road, then pointing the Barrett at the scratch mark on the inside of the door would line it up exactly on the open chippy door. And zero it in on where they had expected Fatchops to drag in a replacement fridge. It was. Spot on. Luke flicked off the safety.

'How close?'

'Twenty seconds,' Matt replied. 'Take the shot.'

Luke pushed the other earplug into his left ear and started to steady his breathing. Clear shot. Squeeze.

The old fridge exploded before the trigger finished travelling. Fatchops was once again diving for cover. Even before he hit the ground Luke had panned left a few degrees, sliding the bolt to reload, then steadied and the back wall turned green under a fountain spray of mushy peas. Luke came back right, now lined up on the delivery van.

A second later the driver discovered what the anti-material weapon was really designed for when he was thrown forward into his windscreen as a shattered engine block brought the van to a juddering halt. At such close range, without armour there was no need for luck. The 50 cal round had probably pierced the aluminium block, to smash a connecting or push rod, immediately causing the engine to seize.

Luke had already slid the door closed and was looking for the discharged cartridge casings as he felt the Transit rock, then start to move. Matt had arrived, as planned, just after the second shot, to drive them away, past Spudman, who was getting out, nursing his head, to inspect the steam, water and oil pooling beneath his now immobilised vehicle. As Matt turned the corner he could see Spudman was recovering the usual box of forks from the front and heading for the chippy, with an occasional glance back, wondering what had happened.

Inside the chippy, Fatchops was now getting to his feet and making his way to the old fridge. This time he could see the entry hole in the buckled door and, not having had the time to fill it, he could also see the exit hole at the back. He pulled the fridge out and saw the damage to the wall. Not too far from and not too dissimilar to the damage caused the night before. It took another second for it to register and another one for him to drop to the floor again. Now he got it. Someone was sending a message.

7

Follow-Up

'When was the last time we did this?' Joey asked, pouring water into two glasses as Natasha put the reheated chicken casserole meals on the table.

'What? Have lunch together in the week? Or plan on attacking someone?'

'Well, I do that bit quite regularly.'

'Don't, Joe. It's not something to joke about.'

He nodded to accept the rebuke. And acknowledge that what Luke termed a proportional response did not come naturally to her. After a moment of guiding the chicken pieces round her plate she pushed it away and sat back in her chair. She had no appetite. For food.

'Go on then. Tell me.'

'Really?'

'Just what or how you are involved.'

Joey still hesitated. He didn't want her to know much, just in case it blew back. He wanted her to be ignorant. So ignorant the cops couldn't charge her with anything. Just as Luke kept telling him to keep out of the details. The operational logistics, as he put it. He'd given Joey the talk about the law of conspiracy. Just talking about doing something illegal was enough in itself, without actually committing the crime. For murder the sentence was mandatory life. As it was for conspiracy to murder. So, how far was he involved? And how far could he allow Natasha to go?

'OK. I'm going to try and pick my words here,' he began. 'I don't know what Luke is up to. He won't tell me because he doesn't want me involved. Because I can't be involved. OK?'

She nodded and waited. She had had the conspiracy chat too.

'All I'm doing is helping a mate working on his cottage. And lending him a few quid here and there. OK?'

'Bankrolling him?'

'Helping a mate with his cashflow.'

'How much?'

'About five grand so far.'

'What? And where's that coming from?'

'Stuff Benno scavenges from the skips every weekend. Stuff that rich Russian fella keeps throwing away.'

'But . . . But that's supposed to be going to set you . . . set us up back here.'

'I know, I know. And Luke is going to pay me back when he gets his next job sorted. It's just that he hasn't got it at the moment, to pay for – well, whatever he needs to do.'

Natasha was silent, her brain trying to process how Joey seemed to be using their cash to bankroll a couple of mercenaries. 'How?' she finally asked.

'How what?'

'How did you get involved?'

'I'm not involved.'

'How did you start lending your mate money, then?' She tried hard to take the edge off the sarcasm. But the irritation remained.

Joey now sat back in his chair. 'The night that prick took a knife to Tanya.'

'What? You just went to Luke and said, "Someone's just threatened my little girl, will you sort them out please?" Really sounds like you, Joe.' No effort to hide the sarcasm this time.

It brought an ironic smile to Joey's face. 'He's already told me it's nothing to do with me any more. 'He's just found a way to get some sort of payback for Janey. The bloke who killed her is probably long dead. But he, well, he just wants to take this lot out so they won't kill anyone else.'

'And he actually believes that?'

'No. 'Course not. Just wants the excuse.'

'Why? He must know the police will come after him.'

'Doesn't care. Said he's screwed up mentally anyway. Walking dead.'

Natasha took a moment to digest this. She could believe it. 'He always was off his head. That's why Janey was so good for him.'

Joey reached over and squeezed her hand. 'Like you and me. You pulled me back. And that is the real issue. If he was on the edge before. She pulled him back. So where do we think his head is now?'

'God, Joe. You seem to be so, I don't know . . . matter-of-fact about it all. He's your best friend. You can't just give him a few quid every now and then and wait for him to do God only knows what.'

Joey was trying to remain calm, but was becoming exasperated. This was his world. Even if it was one he tried to keep from her. 'Nat, look. Do you trust me?'

'What kind of stupid question is that?'

'No, it's not. I mean. You do, don't you?'

Natasha nodded but didn't comment. She did trust him. She trusted that all of this would have been thought through long and hard. And she wanted to know where it was going.

'So you'll know that whatever Luke is up to,' Joey continued, 'I know it's not something he suddenly decided last weekend. It's not something he decided after that fight in the Lion. Up to that point it was him who was holding me back.'

'What?'

'No, listen. We've both wanted to rip the town up ever since Janey's funeral. But . . . we held each other back.

By telling each other that I'd already lost a sister. He'd lost a wife. And the kids had lost their aunty. I didn't want them to lose their uncle. Just as I didn't want to lose my best mate. So by holding me back he was also, actually, holding himself back. Yeah?'

'So far,' Natasha said.

'And it was working, Nat. I kept feeding back what he had always told me about how random shit like that happens. Random shit. That was always his phrase. His stock in trade, he told me. So I fed it back. Over and over. But every now and then it would boil over. Like in Luke's head when that idiot desecrated where Janey died. Then later on started mouthing off about us only having jihadists running amok because of what guys like Luke were doing in Iraq and Afghanistan. I could have punched him myself, I tell you. If—'

'So,' Natasha finally cut in. 'So what happened to this great pact of self-control?'

Joey emptied his lungs with one huge sigh. This was the bit he didn't really want to get to. 'Me. That's what happened,' he said but held up his hand so she wouldn't ask anything else while he pulled the words together. 'I lost it.'

She gave him a look that asked what else was new, but he slowly shook his head to signify that this was a bit more than usual.

*

'Human beings, that's why. After all we've seen and done, does anyone have to ask why there are bad guys. Adam and Eve. The serpent and temptation. Sin. All that.'

'You fantasising about Sister Frances, again?' Luke turned to Matt as they settled back into the No. 2 position overlooking the chippy. Halfway along the Hilltop Walk, from where they could still look down on the chippy.

They had not long visited the fifth skip they had used to dump the last of the stuff out of the van. Each one at the back of a factory or industrial unit where guys dumping building waste from a Transit would be too common to notice. Now it was in the car park of the Hilltop Walk, stripped and cleaned. In case someone had said they'd seen a builder's van outside the chippy. It was now just another white van.

They held on to the Motorolas as with no data records anywhere they were just tools of their offshore trade. Another piece of typical British logic. Ownership in itself was not illegal, but using them was. The Barrett was left under the railway bridge, from where it would be retrieved by Billy Higham, once they told him what weapons they would like next.

'Now Sister Frances was sent by the devil. Defo,' Matt continued as he trained his birdwatchers on the chippy. 'Did I tell you she used to stroke my backside?'

'Once or twice. And, if I remember, you only made that

up after Joey told us about getting his leg over the woman next door.'

'Er, I think you mean I felt safe enough to confide in you.' He drifted off into some real or imaginary memory. 'Pity I was too young to realise what was going on.'

Matt let out a long, regretful sigh at the distant memory and opportunity, in his mind, lost, while Luke had a more immediate thought in mind as he started to dig out a ration pack from the rucksack. Fatchops too was over-seeing the lunchtime trade, but also staring at the piece of plastic that had just cost him a sausage dinner. He had been given it by the guy who had come in ranting about reporting him to the Trading Standards people after finding it in his mushy peas. Normally Fatchops would've argued, too used to people trying to get anything free, but the last thing he wanted was to have anybody official poking around inside the shop. Especially as the shard of plastic looked like a piece of the shattered drinks cabinet. He went across to the peas and gravy counter tubs and started fishing. It only took one swirl before he was reaching for his phone.

'No, Nat. When I heard about Tan being threatened with a knife I just . . . After Janey. I went hunting. Down the Riverbeck estate.'

Now Natasha became alarmed, but Joey was staring hard at the table, avoiding eye contact. Which worried her more.

'It wasn't hard, tracking him down. I got enough out of Tanya to get the rest out of one of the street corner gangs. He had one of those daft tidal wave style haircuts. He'd be in the park. Behind the precinct or up on the old bridge across the railway. Third time lucky.'

He then fell into a reflective silence and used the arrival of Roscoe, who plonked his head on Joey's thigh, to avoid looking at Natasha again. Perhaps Roscoe had sensed the need for moral support, but it gave Joey an extra moment or two before having to answer the next obvious question.

'And?' The anxiety was equally obvious.

Joey carried on ruffling Roscoe's head for a moment until the question came again. More insistent. And in a tone that made Roscoe decide it was time to slope back to his basket. Out of harm's way.

'And? What happened, Joe? Or is this something else I shouldn't know? Or something you can't trust me with?'

Joey looked across at her. A slowly brewing and volcanic mixture of concern, anxiety, irritation and anger. Trust her? With his life. But admit his failings? Face up to his own imperfections? He couldn't hold her stare.

'For Christ's sake, Joe. Cut the macho numb act. Just tell me what you did. Or what you shouldn't have done. I've worked that bit out.'

'I didn't finish the thing,' he responded, his own sense of frustrated anger erupting. 'I had him hanging off the railway bridge ready to drop him in front of the next train.'

Tanya physically recoiled. Whatever she was expecting, it was not this image he was conjuring up.

'All I had to do,' Joey continued, 'was wait. Wait for a train to come through and . . .' He tailed off again.

Tanya waited. Hoping for the 'but'. It didn't come. Nothing did.

'He's moving,' Matt announced. The food was forgotten and five minutes later the Transit was slowly cruising behind Fatchops, who was scuttling down the High Street.

'Absolutely classic,' Matt said as he watched Fatchops turn into the park and head for the playground area. 'He's heading for smack alley.'

'Double bluff, so he thinks,' Luke replied. 'If the users think it's safe, so will he.'

'What do you reckon, then? Don't want to be sitting in this thing for too long looking at the kiddies' play-ground.'

Luke nodded. No one would think they were planning to shoot someone, but plenty would immediately identify them as potential paedophiles. He started to edge the Transit away, watching Fatchops flop on to a bench on the far side of the park. Away from the playground, but right next to another entrance. 'Let's go round the other side. They'll probably come down Waters Street.'

Which they did. A BMW X5 came to a stop outside the park entrance and three guys got out and headed towards Fatchops. Just as Luke and Matt arrived to watch. One was white, undercut and windswept top hair, wearing a heavy leather duffle-style coat and leather ankle-strap boots. Expensive. From that, and the way the other two – one Caribbean, one Asian – had shaved heads in mid-market designer sweat pants and puffas, obviously not yet earning real money. They let Leather Jacket go out in front suggesting he was Fatchops's next link in the chain, and confirmed by the way he greeted a now nervous but grateful-looking Fatchops. A quick head butt, punch to the side of his head and a push back on to the bench. The sweats and puffas took up positions at either end.

'Another classic. Don't look at us folks, whatever you do,' Matt chuckled. 'Easto, like Fatty, you reckon? Looks like he grew up where the hard men wore leather. Stasi. KGB.'

'Russian Mafia chic?' suggested Luke. Then added with a grin, 'Or subscribes to Bobby McBain's counterfeights catalogue.'

Matt nodded. 'Interesting thought. Although the other two probably nicked a box set of *The Wire*.'

They sat watching as Fatchops appeared to be talking eighteen to the dozen, finally showing them the piece of shrapnel he had fished from the mushy peas. Leather Jacket took it and turned it over in his hands. Eventually he nodded, but then leaned in to Fatchops with a pointing finger to emphasise some form of motivational message along the lines of, if this happens again you're dead. It seemed to work, as when he flicked a dismissive hand Fatchops was up and scuttling away, once more at a speed no one would have thought possible.

Leather sat for a moment, leaning forward, examining the piece of plastic. That, the fridge and hearing about the Spudman's engine meant someone was sending them a message. But who? And why? He stood up and headed back to the BMW, with the other two hurrying to get there first. One to open the door for him, the other to get into the driver's seat.

'Follow?' Matt asked. Luke just nodded. Matt started the Transit and followed the BMW as it pulled away and headed back out of town along the expressway.

'Until?' Natasha finally asked, still hoping. 'For God's sake, Joe. Who? What?'

'Someone grabbed me from behind.'

He finally looked across at her and saw the fear as she was running through all the possible scenarios. Joe dropping the boy. A train hitting him. His friends gabbing. The police? What? What? What?

Quickly he reached across and grabbed her hand. Reassurance. 'It was Luke. He pulled me and the kid back.'

'So . . . So you didn't . . . ?'

Joey shook his head. 'Luke had tracked me. Pushed me to one side and got hold of the kid himself. Pulled him back up. Calmed him down. Then asked him, really calm, did he understand why I was after his skin? The kid was terrified but nodded. Luke then asked him if he would tell anyone about it. Kid naturally said he wouldn't. He'd have said anything to get away.

'How . . . how old was this "kid"?' Natasha suddenly asked.

'Younger than Tan, not much older than Alex. And I know what you're thinking. He had a mum and dad. Perhaps even together. Probably. Brothers. Sisters. I dunno.'

'Christ Joe, and you . . .'

'Yeah, I know. I know. I was only going to smack him about a bit but he was such an arrogant . . . He'd told me whatever I did to him he'd do to Tanya . . . Which is why I lost it. He wouldn't be able to do anything if he was dead, would he? So right then, right there, when he was screaming for his life, I didn't care if someone, somewhere loved him.'

He elapsed into numb macho mode again, until Natasha prompted him.

'And would you? Really?'

'I've gone over and over it . . . And honestly. I'm just glad Luke turned up. Then turned it all back on me. Fed everything I'd been feeding him. How it would be you and the kids, and Sean and his lot, who would lose if I got put away.'

While Joey continued to unburden himself, Tanya started to realise how close all this was coming to her family. Her sister-in-law. Her daughter. Her nephew. Now Joey getting involved. How pervasive it was becoming. No wonder people talk about it as some form of virus-borne disease. Or even cancer. And Joey and Luke were trying to cut it out.

'Jesus, Joe,' she interrupted. 'You can't take this on. Shouldn't it be the job of the police?'

Joey couldn't help but give a derisory snort, then leaned forward in his seat. Challenging. 'Hang on. Last night you wanted them dead. That's why I travelled all night.'

'What? Who will rid me of this meddlesome priest?'

'Er, that from one of those period dramas you watch without me?'

'History GSCE,' she corrected. 'Henry II said something like that about Thomas Becket, which led to him being killed. It's more about being careful what you wish for. And that was last night. In the, I don't know, heat of the emotion, I suppose.'

'And that's what it takes to deal with these people. When they attack you. You fight back. There and then.' He was vehement. Driven by emotion. But seeing the worry and anxiety still on her face, he softened again. 'And I took it that you obviously needed me here.'

She reached forward to him and clasped his hands. 'I do, but not running round on some vigilante mission.'

'At least it's in a language they understand.' He sat back again, his impotent frustration still dominating.

'Oh, like what?' she threw back, equally frustrated. 'Asking some stupid teenage kid to promise to play nice in future?'

'Making him aware what will happen if he does it. Sean craps on about making people aware of the consequences of doing drugs. But what about the consequences of selling them?'

'I know, I know. But isn't that what the laws, and the police, are for?'

She knew she said it more in hope than conviction as she was wrestling with her own position as much as Joey's, so was not surprised when he gave another snort of derision. But then he added, 'It used to be. But now we have a so-called justice system where everyone has rights. Including the right to feed off other people.' His mind was back on his confrontation with Gustav on the London site the day before. 'They're everywhere, Nat. Lowlife. Parasites.'

'So your response would be to just let Luke kill them all?' she kept pushing. While still fishing.

'They're killing people!' But he immediately held up his hands in apology, realising they were starting to go round in circles. He had also noticed the slight flicker of suspicion pass across her eyes, which was quickly followed up when she asked him about Luke and Tanya's attacker.

'You talked about consequences. What did he do?' she asked.

Joey broke eye contact. Which told her there was more. 'What did he do, Joe?'

Joey let out a resigned sigh. 'He told him he wanted to give him something to remember us by.' He hesitated. She waited. He finally continued. 'Then he held out a folded hand. You know, the way you give something to someone. Kid holds out his hand. Luke just grabs his thumb . . . and breaks it. Crack.'

Natasha winced at both the thought and this further image.

'He just did it. To a kid. So he is right. He is screwed up. He used to be . . . He used to be a real laugh. Do anything for you.'

'For you, you mean. And your Janey,' said Nat.

'Yeah, but . . . Anyway, we know all this, but . . . he also made me aware of what he'd been going on about. About his tradecraft. What he did, still does, for a living. And from that moment everything turned over. He was no longer holding back but, well, protecting me. He'd found what he had been looking for. The excuse. To do some hunting of his own.'

'And where's that going to lead?' she asked, still horrified.

'I honestly don't know, Nat, but, remember how you felt last night? With your daughter injured in front of you? Keep that right there.' He tapped the front of his forehead. 'Don't let go of that. Otherwise, they win.'

Before Natasha could even assimilate that thought,

never mind respond to it, her phone rang. She looked. Then stood up, alarmed.

'It's Mr Bryce. He lives next door to Mum,' she quickly told Joey as she answered, listened and then let her shoulders sag in relief as she thanked Mr Bryce. She ended the call and turned towards the door. 'C'mon, she's locked herself out again.'

'Up and over?' Luke asked. Matt nodded. They waited until the BMW X5 passed the exit lane before they pulled off and Luke accelerated up to the junction roundabout that flew over the expressway. He timed the gap in the oncoming traffic to slot in, drive across and go straight back on to the expressway, now several more cars behind the BMW X5. If they were watching they would probably have seen the white Transit go off and then relaxed, or if they weren't watching, another white Transit joining the expressway wouldn't register. Probably. But just in case, Luke kept a five-car separation.

It was not long before they saw the X5 indicate and turn off, heading down what looked like an old country lane that had probably, at one time, been the main link between the outlying villages but now, a mile or so along, it became a back route into a sprawling post-war housing estate. The X5 stopped outside what appeared to be the original old farmhouse, now sitting on the edge of what was officially called Downside, although it had become known locally as Downer-side until some 1980s regeneration plan had renewed the street lights and pavements and renamed it Orchard View. Everyone now knew it as The Spew.

The farmhouse had been upgraded and sold off privately, but the social housing came right up to one side of it. The back and other side still sat in a field, but the front looked on to the road, probably widened to allow access to the estate.

'Good 3G signal,' Matt announced, checking his phone as they cruised past. 'Very nice property too. Shame about the neighbours.'

'Probably more customers,' Luke added as he looked in the nearside wing mirror to see Leather Jacket get out of the X5 and head into the house. The X5 then carried on, now following them, until Luke spotted a cul-de-sac sign on his left and indicated to turn in. The X5 drove past. With an exaggerated gesture of having made the mistake of turning into a dead end, just in case anyone was watching, Luke turned the Transit and went off after the X5 once again, just in time to see it pull off into a pub car park.

As they approached they could see that, like the old farmhouse, the pub had been chosen for its prime location. One way in. One way out. And nothing else around but cleared sites where houses used to stand. And nothing but clear sightlines. No one could approach without being seen. No one should be there who wasn't welcome. These were the situations Luke dreaded most. He'd rather run across a moonlit fire zone than walk a hostile urban landscape where the only people watching his back would be the ones getting ready to kill him.

The pub was called the Spotted Greyhound. No one knew why. No one cared. The locals called it the Fast Dog. The two shaved-headed minders were out of the X5 and exchanging fist greetings with two other guys sitting astride quad bikes. All eyes turned to watch the Transit go past and, while being a white van man provided a certain degree of invisibility, Luke and Matt decided this was not the time for surveillance. They would come back later.

'This happen often?' Joey asked as Natasha got back into the Q7, having retrieved her mother and got her safely home.

'Not that often. But more and more, recently.'

'Do you think it's time for a care home?'

'I think we've got a bit more on our plates at the moment, Joe,' she snapped back and sank into silence as Joey eased the Q7 round her dad's raised flower bed, waving to Grace now standing in the window.

'What did she say about me being back?'

'I told her you were the taxi driver.'

'What? Why?'

'Because she's losing it. Which I think I am at the moment.'

Joey knew he'd get a more coherent answer later, just as he knew now was the time to leave Natasha to let her work out what was in her head. She turned and watched the countryside go by, still struggling for a real answer. Struggling with the images Joey had planted at the front of her head. She knew she could easily repeat the mantra. Leave it to the police. But she was feeling uncomfortable. No matter how unpalatable it was she knew she was facing another moment when she had to reaffirm both the reality and the strength of her relationship with Joey. As it often did. As it always had.

She had always prided herself on having been the one to get him from the wrong side of the tracks. Back on the rails. Defying everyone. Her parents. Friends. Defending him against everyone. You don't know him. He's changed, she would say. Then, later, what a great dad he was. And all the rest. And when it came to her own lioness moment, seeing her cub under threat, she felt she was capable of doing what many always said should be done but never had the bottle to do themselves. Perhaps when it came to the crunch, she wouldn't actually be capable. But she knew Joey would. Just as she knew that was why she loved him. He made her safe. He had bottle. To defend his own. No matter what the risks. And that was why she wanted to remain strong. Play her own role in their relationship. Protect him from himself.

At home she got out of the car and went straight inside. Joey sat for a moment wondering where she was up to. He knew he had pushed their relationship a few times in the past, but she had always been there. Right behind him.

Or dragging him back. But this was different. How would this one go, he wondered, but decided that the only way to find out was to go after her and force the issue. She was starting to clear the table when he reached the kitchen and asked the question.

'I'm not sure what I'm thinking,' she began. 'Part of me, I don't know whether it's the maternal thing, whether it's right or wrong, wants to just tell you to get on with whatever you and Luke are up to. Another part is saying I'm losing my mum, so sod it. Who cares about those scum? Another, probably the sensible grown-up part, is with your Sean about trying to sort it out through some form of community action or . . .'

She saw him react negatively at the mention of this huggy-feely stuff, as he always called it, but she palm-punched his shoulder and hardened her eyes. 'You are going to listen. Especially if you are home for good,' she continued.

'I am,' Joey immediately replied, holding her shoulders, gently. For reassurance.

'Then perhaps you will have more of an influence on Tanya, like you've been saying. Getting her to be more careful.' She cradled his face in her hands. This time asking for reassurance. But it wasn't coming.

'And what happens when the boys get older? It's touched us twice. I don't want a third time.' And to emphasise the point he took her hands and intertwined them with his own. 'It is like some form of cancer, Nat. And someone's got to cut it out.'

There. He'd said it again. The line to be crossed. It was now up to her whether she wanted to take that step. They both stood holding hands. Silent. Natasha still assimilating the journey Joey had just taken her on, while he waited for the decision. Eventually, it came. As she pulled away and went to the table to collect their now congealing dishes. Wanting to start retrieving some sense of normality.

'You're right. I don't want to know any details. Except one. You are only helping a mate with a bit of cash? That's it? Nothing else?'

Joey nodded. Then put his arms round her as she placed the dishes on the worktop above the dishwasher. 'It's the only thing I'm allowed to do. Deniability, I think they call it.'

He felt her body relax slightly as she turned to face him, smothering his face with her hair again and mumbling something into his chest. He pulled away and asked her what she had said.

'We should be careful what we wish for.'

Immediately, Joey thought that if he was still of the faith he'd probably say Amen to that.

'Thanks for coming back, Joe,' she said.

'Well,' Joey grinned. 'I knew you'd never ask.'

Joey grinned as he felt her smile against his chest. Then, as she hugged him more tightly the pheromones flowed and his second thought was about whether he could get away with suggesting something else he often wished for.

But he decided against it. He didn't want to lose this moment. The hero's real return.

Matt had taken delivery of a Ford Focus hire car when he had handed over the Transit to be kept out of sight. In a lock-up they had been using for the duration. One that they could just walk away from. No connection. Just as they could from the Ford Focus, hired in the name of Elsie Jordan, a resident of the Pines Care Home who, despite being bedridden, still held a clean driving licence and a Gold credit card. Her son, Terrence, was down as a registered driver so if stopped, Matt would have seven days to produce his documents, while Terrence could prove he was in Amsterdam at the time.

Even before he had slowed to a stop at the traffic lights, Matt could see it coming towards him. The window wash hustle. One window washer. One flower seller. He had pulled up in the outside lane as instructed. The flower seller came to the driver's window to block the view while negotiating, while the window washer stood by the passenger door and covered one side of the windscreen with suds, totally blocking any view from that direction. By the time the window washer had moved round to the driver's side the flower seller had gone, leaving a fairly large bouquet. Matt handed over a £20 note and got a theatrical protest in return, along with two £5 notes. The same trick Fatchops was using. Each note had the not uncommon random numbers scribbled on it. Different colours. Different writing. A legacy of someone's petty-cash counting system.

On one, the writing was in purple ink and circled. 3–24. He glanced down at the bouquet now on the passenger seat to see the top of a set of registration plates at the centre of the bunch. They would be from another Ford Focus matching the one he was driving but, like the Transit, now sitting in a lock-up somewhere, off the road. Out of sight. The cloned plates would pass unchallenged through the number-plate recognition system that was on all major roads. The numbers on the £5 note meant they had it for three days.

Pulling away he marvelled once again at the way Billy and many like him around the world could deliver. On both sides of the line. Operating in the twilight world often referred to as Black Ops by the media, without which many covert things could not be done in the name of democracy. Don't ask: don't tell. But it didn't stop Matt wondering how Billy and his team knew the registration number was safe for three days. Was it stolen to order? In a garage for repair? Sitting in a long-term car park? Or did it come from a black database at the DVLC?

Whatever it was he never dwelt on it, just accepted that it was what they did. He always wondered more about when someone would finally wake up and recognise two things. One was that the bad guys didn't play by the rules. So things like ID cards and number-plate recognition systems only worked if no one cheated. The other was that formal education had no link to intelligence. If entrepreneurship thrived on opportunity, then opportunity wasn't restricted to purely legal activities. At one time getaway cars and drivers commanded a premium. Just as safecrackers were like gold dust. Now it was all cyberwarfare. All about computer hackers and cloning.

For the next three days Elsie's car would not be tracked. Everything would be logged against the one sitting out of sight somewhere, and provided they didn't go through any speed cameras no one would be the wiser. With that in mind, Matt headed back to Highbridge. With their new 72-hour cloak of invisibility.

'So, what do you reckon? Got time before the school run?' Joey asked, hopefully as he held her round the waist and nuzzled her neck.

'Oh yeah. Let's decide to bankroll a bunch of mercenaries to run amok round the town and then jump into bed. Great turn-on, that is.'

'Power's supposed to be an aphrodisiac, isn't it?'

'Power is. Losing your mind isn't. Ask my mother.'

Joey relaxed his grip and arched back to examine her eyes. Anxiety. Second thoughts? She saw his concern. 'I'm OK. Really. But I meant it. All we are doing is helping a friend with some cash. Nothing more. Clear?'

He nodded.

'Say it, Joe.'

'I'm clear. Nothing more. No details.'

She then sank back into his chest, giving him just enough time to find a breath hole.

'Promise?' she asked again.

'Promise,' he reaffirmed.

'And I can feel where your mind is going,' Natasha said, as she pressed her groin against his, then pulled away. 'But I do have to go, as I want to look in on Mum before picking the kids up. So calm down.'

'What about tonight, then?'

'You'll be out.'

'What? Where? I'm not supposed to be here.'

'But you are. And now you're here, you can do the taxi run tonight.'

'Where to?'

'Oh, Tanya's off on one because I've said we won't let her go on holiday with this new boyfriend of hers.'

All thoughts of a romantic night evaporated. 'What new boyfriend?'

'Exactly.'

'But . . .'

She started gathering her handbag, phone and car keys. 'The compromise is that she can go to the student night at some new club they've been badgering me about for ages. Provided that I – well, you now – can drop her off and pick her up. And that she stays with the girls.'

She gave him a quick kiss as she headed for the door.

'Hang on. Why's she going out on a school night? And where is this club?'

She finally smiled. 'Warrington.'

'What? That's an hour each way. And how were you going to do this if I wasn't here?'

'Er. . . Alex is fourteen.'

'You leave them on their own?'

'Joyce pops in from next door. Welcome to the world of shared parenting, Joe.'

With that she left, leaving Joey realising how much she had kept from him while he was away. What else did they all get up to when he was trying to stay awake listening to Benno's stories? But then his phone vibrated on the worktop ALWAYS 2MORO. GET SLEEP. I'LL WARN KIDS YOU HOME. LXXT Joey grinned. Tanya's going to love me being here to hound her, he thought, but his mind soon went back to his main concern. Who is this boyfriend?

'Oh My God, you're trending,' Megan announced to Noah, scrolling through the Twitter feeds as they walked in from school.

Sandra had insisted Noah came straight home. And stayed home.

Noah instantly snatched Megan's phone to look. Which she instantly snatched back. And then had it instantly snatched by Sandra.

'Mum!'

Sandra then handed the phone back. It wasn't her daughter she was getting angry about. 'Look. The pair of you.' But she focused on Noah. 'Today was not your

Mandela moment. No matter what your father said about peaceful protest. OK?'

'So how many dead kids does it take, Mum? Someone's got to do something,' Noah shot back, obviously liking the Mandela reference no matter how pejoratively Sandra meant it.

'But not you, Noah. It's bad enough having your father banging on, without you getting yourself arrested for fighting with the police.'

'I wasn't arrested . . .' Noah countered. 'We were just protesting. Remember?'

The sarcasm could not be missed. It just bounced off Sandra, who was straight in Noah's face. 'Did you get permission?'

'Permission to protest? That's an oxymoron.' But he stepped back a little as he said it. Just in case.

'The only moron around here is you.'

'I'll go with that. I'll tweet it,' Megan offered unhelpfully.

'Don't you dare, young lady . . .'

The tone was enough to cause Megan to put her phone down and move to the kettle. 'Tea, anyone?' she asked. Sweetly. Proto-teen sarcasm. Also not missed, and she turned away sharply to sit at the kitchen table in response to her mother's glare.

'Well?' Sandra demanded.

Noah flopped into a seat opposite Megan. 'I told Dad. I told the plod. We were talking about next Saturday's match and how we're fed up with having to get there early to help clear up all the mess the druggies leave behind on Friday nights.'

'What sort of mess?' Sandra asked, deciding to follow the logic chain. 'Syringes and things?'

Noah exchanged a quick glance with Megan. Eyes and ears wide open. 'It's not *Trainspotting* or whatever movie you grew up with, Mum.'

'Like sex, is it?' Sandra asked.

'What?'

'Drugs are something else your generation discovered?'

'I didn't mean it like—'

'Your look to your sister did,' Sandra shot back, which was a reminder that thirteen-year-old Megan was at the table. 'Megan. This has nothing to do with you.' Sandra pointed to the door.

Megan thought about making a symbolic protest but knew that's all it would be, so huffily stood up, grabbed her stuff and headed for her room, stopping just outside the kitchen door to try and listen. Until.

'All the way. Go. Now.'

She gave an exaggerated eye roll and headed off. She'd find out all about it later. Online.

Sandra refocused on Noah. 'Continue with my education.'

'There's an occasional syringe.' Noah started. 'But it's mostly wraps. Bottles, cans.' Then, with a glance over his shoulder to make sure Megan wasn't still lurking,

'Condoms. Tampons. Although finding a dead body was a first.'

Sandra gave him a disapproving glare. Enough. But her revulsion remained.

'And you have to clear all this . . . mess up before you can play football?' Sandra asked.

Noah nodded. 'For some reason they always use the goalmouths,' he added.

'That's because the trees shelter them from the wind.' Sandra said. Authoritatively. Which was not missed by Noah.

'Oh yes. And, how do you know that?' he asked. Grinning. Intrigued.

Sandra couldn't help but grin herself. 'I told you. Your generation didn't invent everything.'

'Moth-er!' Noah said. Surprised.

'Anyway,' Sandra said. Realising it was a detail too far. Wanting to get back to the point. 'What's any of that got to do with being arrested?'

'Well, why should we be forced to do the clearing up? The teachers used to do it while we were too young to see life's dirty little secrets. But now we are apparently old enough, we can help share the burden of protecting our young.'

'So you decided to organise a protest?'

'Er . . . yeah. I think that kid's death took it to a whole new level. We only wanted to highlight the point that it's getting worse. It was supposed to be peaceful. Until the robocops arrived.'

Now having a bit better understanding, Sandra tried to offer some support. 'Everyone's a bit sensitive about that area at the moment. Not just the drugs but whether they're going to sell the playground. So I suppose the Council and police are getting a hard time about anything that goes on down there.'

'So they end up giving us a hard time?' Noah asked. The irritation returning.

Irritated by his irritation, Sandra toughened up again. 'And you end up giving us a hard time by making a show of yourself.'

Noah stood up to gather his stuff. Obviously he'd had enough. 'Oh, what? All the gossip in the hairdresser's, is it?'

Sandra rose to meet him. Enough was definitely enough. 'It's more the way you went about it. And yes, you do have to have permission to protest, Mastermind.'

Noah tried to end the lecture with a dismissive shrug and turned towards the door. Until—

'Stay.' He stopped. Recognising the rising but controlled maternal anger. Sandra continued. 'Since our generation invented not only sex, drugs and rock'n'roll, but raving. They passed laws making it illegal for any more than half a dozen people to gather in one place outside.' She paused to increase the emphasis. 'Without a licence. It was to stop people turning up spontaneously and taking over fields for rave parties. And, yes, that means we invented flash mobbing too.'

'So what, Mum? So you were all teenage rebels. Great. But so what?'

'The "so what" is because . . .' She was trying to hold on to herself as well as her son. 'Because some people acted irresponsibly, laws were rushed through that in the end caused people to fret about whether they needed a licence to have a barbecue in their own gardens. Imagine how that would have affected the business.'

'But that's a stupid law,' Noah responded. Voice rising.

'A lot of laws are,' Sandra shot back. Increasing the decibels to match. 'Because some people act stupidly . . .' she said as she tapped the side of his head, invading his personal space as only a mother can. 'And then so-called intelligent people try to be too clever trying to stop them. Instead of everyone talking to each other first.'

'So, we're supposed to go to the cops and ask permission to protest against them not doing their job?' His frustration was building again.

'In a nutshell, yes,' Sandra said. 'It's what's called democracy.'

'Then it's wrong.'

There it was again. Teenage perception. Black. White. No greys.

'Yes,' Sandra replied. 'And you can do the bull elephant thing with your father, but don't try it on with me.'

Noah held her eyes, but not for too long. Even if it wasn't fair, he knew she was right. He could have a real fight with his dad but that mother thing . . . A lifetime of obedience and gratitude for the pain of childbirth. He reached for his only defence.

'Can I go now?'

She nodded, accepting the capitulation, but couldn't resist her maternal right to dispense advice. Although she softened her tone once more. 'What I'm really annoyed about, Noah, is that you didn't think it through.' She tried to take his hand, but he pulled it away.

'You can do the wise oracle thing, Mum. But don't patronise me. OK? I don't need anything kissed better.'

She gave another nod. This time accepting the point. He took it as a concession. A small step in acknowledging that he was growing up. She took it as a need to defuse the situation.

'You don't have to ask permission to protest about the police not doing their jobs. But they'll have all the excuses lined up for that. You should protest about politicians not giving them the resources to do their jobs. Then they'll see you as being on their side. Not as the enemy. Then they'll help you. Not arrest you.'

'That it? That the end of today's life lecture?' But as her face tightened and eyes flared, he grinned. 'I get it. I do.'

Instinctively she reached out to stroke his forearm in maternal acknowledgement. This time he accepted it, as it was also a sign that he could go. At the door, he stopped. Unable to resist a final shot.

'It's bullshit though, Mum. Someone's got to do something. And not sitting around chatting like Dad.'

'Go,' Sandra snarled. A verbal flash of the claws.

He did. And she was left recalling that Sean had told her to try and go easy on him. He was a good kid at heart and all that proud dad stuff. But it's always the good kids who can't spot where the real trouble can come from.

Six hours into their 72-hour window, Luke was heading for the Fast Dog, having just dropped Matt in the lane about 200 metres from Leather Jacket's farmhouse. Matt was now working his way along the field, behind a hedge that kept him screened from the road. He was in full blacks: boots, coverall, turned-up beanie, Motorola in place, and carrying a backpack. When he reached the corner of the field that touched the front of the farmhouse fence, he swung the backpack off and settled down. Listening. Apart from a passing car, there was nothing. All quiet on the other side of the fence. Satisfied that no one had seen him approach he took out his phone and rechecked the 3G signal. Still strong. He squawked the Motorola to advise Luke, then opened the backpack and started setting up the drone.

Outside the pub, Luke had never felt so exposed. As Matt's squawk came it faded. He had tried re-squawking but had no response. He was out of range and he'd just been marked. One of the quad bikes they had seen on the recce had followed him into the car park. With the

Motorola useless he reached for his pay-and-throw. No signal. No backup. He was on his own. With only his good looks and smooth tongue, as his mother had often said.

While Leather Jacket had demonstrated his desire to remain below radar, Luke knew from the lack of helmets and registration plates that law enforcement, never mind Health and Safety, was not something the two young bucks riding the quad were concerned about. They only had one thing on their minds. Him.

'Oh, I love him. You will bring him in here for a cup of tea won't you?'

Sean had just told Glynnis that he'd had another call from Craig Harlow's PA. He would come along on Saturday and take a look at what Sean wanted, when he visited his mother. Her surprise at this was beaten only by Sean's over her excitement.

'It is still up for discussion, Glynnis.'

'If he's coming here because his mum says so, it's a dead cert.'

'Perhaps, but . . . it's supposed to be a quiet, private visit, Glynnis. He, er, we don't want too many people to know just yet so we can make a big splash in the paper later.'

'Have to put a bag over his head then. Cos as soon as he steps through that door, word'll be round town like wildfire.' The surprises then kept coming. 'Hey, if he's not coming into the café, will you introduce me? Do you think he'd sign a menu for me? Or have one of those pictures I can put up on the wall? I might even get a mobile phone so I can get a selfie.' Without waiting for an answer she then went off, with an excited grin across her face that Sean had never seen before. 'Can't wait to tell our Hilda.'

That was something else new. He had never heard Glynnis refer to anyone in her life before. No family. No friends. So who was Hilda?

'No idea,' Byron replied when Sean asked him later. Nor did he have any idea who Craig Harlow was, but he still agreed to be sworn to secrecy.

Luke sat slowly tapping the steering wheel. Fight or flight? He knew they couldn't match him for speed, just as he knew that if he pulled away it would confirm whatever was in their heads and from that moment he would be a target. The quad had shot past and spun to a stop right in front of him. Headlight to headlight. Luke wondered what, or who, might come next. That came in the form of a small van, speeding into the car park and stopping within six inches of his rear. Blocking any thought of reversing.

No one moved. Luke knew this game. They were waiting to see what he would do. The driver had a retro skinhead and parka look. The rider looked more Ragged Priest with long, lank hair. They were probably a bit older than he was when he first signed up. Still just kids. Playing at cops and druggies. If they had weapons they would have showed them by now, so Luke assumed they were in the van. Out of sight but ready. He looked in the mirror but could only see two heads against the panel obscuring the back. The same reason they had chosen to shoot from a van. How many more could be inside? He knew that in the car he had a chance. Out of the car he had none. They would have to come to him. So he sat and waited. And waited. His cold stare matching those of the quad riders.

After a three-minute staring contest, the Ragged Priest slowly dismounted and walked up to Luke's window. He lowered it. Only partly. Waiting for the challenge.

'You lost, then?' The global question. The same neutral non-aggressive tone. The one he had heard the world over, no matter the dialect or language. It wasn't an offer of help, but a probe. To get a response. In many places, from Belfast to Helmand, a response in the wrong accent would have meant a death sentence, but at least here he wasn't already tagged as an enemy combatant. Or at least he hoped. Just someone who had strayed where he shouldn't. He looked in the mirror again. No movement, but also no way back. Only forward. So forward it had to be.

He slid the Motorola under the seat out of view and ran through the cover once more. He was looking for the David Lloyd Sports Centre. He'd clocked it on the way in. Part of the routine. Keep logging. A nearby location. Close enough to be easily missed. Stay as close to the truth as possible. The rev of the quad engine informed him their patience was running out. Time to play. Luke got out of the car, a move that made the Ragged Priest step back. He wanted the swing space but looked nervously at the van, confirming Luke's early assessment. If it kicked off that was where help would come from.

As he straightened, Luke held up the pay and throw with a useless shrug. 'David Lloyd Centre? Satnav's useless.'

'Signal's crap round here,' the Ragged Priest responded.

'Right. Do you know where it is?'

'Yeah.' But nothing more.

Luke held his stare, knowing it was part of the anxiety test. 'And?'

'You passed it on the way here.'

This was the all-important moment. The one when the van men would decide whether he was a potential threat or just some random idiot.

Luke tried for the idiot badge. And idiot's ramble. 'Oh, really? Damn. Must have been looking at this and not the road. Then it, well, the Maps app just seemed to stop and I couldn't figure out where I was, so I decided to pull in and ask. And then you . . .'

It seemed to do the trick as the Ragged Priest let out a sigh of frustration, while distracted by a commotion near the recycling bins. Three men were dragging another, followed by one more, that Luke immediately recognised. Leather Jacket. The Priest was obviously as curious as Luke and wanted to go and see what was happening.

270

'OK. It's back that way,' he quickly announced. 'At the end turn right.' Then, with heavy irony, 'You can't miss it.'

'OK. Thanks. Thanks for that,' Luke responded.

The Priest waved to the van. All OK. Then started to walk towards the action over by the recycling bins. But stopped as Luke made a show of locking his car and heading for the main pub door. The Priest's acolyte jumped off the quad and stood in front of him.

'Where you going?'

'Er, been on the road a bit. Just thought I'd er . . . use the er . . .'

The Priest felt he should tell him to wait until he got to David Lloyd's but knew that might get the idiot, whoever he was, either too curious or so irritated that he might start something at what was supposed to be an ordinary pub. The sort of ordinary pub to be found in many inner cities where men dragged other men around the car park. So he nodded to the acolyte to let Luke pass. He was also too curious about what was going on over by the recycling bins.

As the van headed back to its watch position and the quaddies headed over to the action, Luke went into the pub, gave a quick résumé of his story to a barmaid and was pointed in the direction of the toilets. Once there he checked the pay-and-throw again. Still no signal. He took out his real phone. No signal. He tried to make a call. No network. Then it dawned on him. They were jamming. Anyone unlucky enough to be categorised as suspect, enemy or traitor wouldn't be able to dial a friend. They would find themselves dragged out to that recycling bin. Not a black spot. A black hole.

8

Let's Chat

nside the black hole, Luke had managed to get the toilet window open slightly, just enough to use his phone camera to watch Leather Jacket overseeing some form of kangaroo court around the recycling bins. From what he could see and hear, or figure out, the guy they had dragged out was pleading that they'd got it wrong. What he had or hadn't done Luke couldn't determine, but it amounted to the same thing: insubordination. And as with every armed militia everywhere, the code was the same. Zero tolerance. The outcome inevitable. And like every legally constituted judicial system it relied on precedent. Broken code. Broken bones. Summary justice.

What Luke hadn't expected was the form of summary justice, although it was clear that the transgressor had, as the wet stain that appeared on the front of his trousers indicated when he heard the deep roar and burble of a heavy diesel engine start up. From where he was, Luke couldn't see the source, but turning the camera to follow the terrified look of the transgressor he saw a crane hook descending above him. The guy made an attempt to run but was soon caught and pinned over the recycling bin. A flexible bike lock was then wrapped round his ankles and in what looked like a well practised drill, an extender cable was looped through, hung on to the crane hook and the still screaming and protesting guy was yanked into the air, swinging wildly to and fro.

As the assembled group separated and stood back, more to get a better view than to keep out of the way, they looked across at Leather Jacket, now leaning on the front of a Porsche Cayenne Hybrid. That caught Luke by surprise. But then he checked himself. Why not? Drug lords can have an interest in saving the planet. If only for themselves. From his display in the park with Fatchops, and now the cold detachment he was showing here, it was clear that this was no mere link in a chain. Here was someone who controlled the summary justice system. He was the kangaroo judge, jury and executioner.

The signal came as the judge looked up at the now dangling and slowly rotating figure rapidly running out of energy even to plead for his own life. After savouring this for a moment, Leather waved his arm towards where the crane must be parked. The hoist brake was released and the jib given a slight nudge so that the figure was flicked to one side as it crashed to the ground. Another well practised move so that the hook itself would not hit whoever had been unfortunate enough to be dangling from it. That way the injuries were consistent with a fall from height. Not being crushed by a heavy metal object. Falls are common. Being crushed by a crane hook isn't.

'I like this lot,' Matt said, as he reviewed the recording on Luke's pay-and-throw before deleting it in the car on the way back to Highbridge. 'In a certain way, right?'

Luke knew what he meant. They were efficient. Down to the guys waiting with a hose and gardener's pressure spray knapsack ready to cover the impact point with bleach before they hosed it down. Kill the guy. Kill the DNA.

'Wonder if they dumped him in one of the recycling bins?' Matt asked. 'But what do you do with a dead druggie? Compost heap would be better.'

'I didn't wait for that bit. How'd you get on?'

Matt nodded. 'Good. Should have plenty. If that night vision camera worked.'

The drone had been on Billy Higham's shopping list. Along with full blacks and the weapons. Aware that Joey's budget probably wouldn't stretch to a full spec Reaper with Hellfire or Sidewinder missiles, Matt had asked for a DJI Phantom so he could rejig the provided camera. You could run a small war with an Amazon account. Except for the weapons. That was the bit Billy did. Don't ask, don't tell. Just use and return in good order.

As they came off the expressway, Matt was still mulling over Leather Jacket's style of execution. 'Probably got the crane idea from that *Homeland* series.'

'Or YouTube?' Luke offered, being careful to slow down for a speed camera. Even if they had cloned plates, it didn't seem fair to leave someone else to pick up the bill. Apart from the risk that the camera might be linked to a live control room and a mobile police patrol might decide to ease their boredom by running a spot check. 'Plenty of footage from Iran or Saudi.'

'Or,' Matt said, 'the tale of Mary the Tennessee Elephant.'

Luke emptied his lungs in an exaggerated sigh. But knew it was unavoidable. 'Go on.'

'She was hanged by a crane,' Matt continued. 'But I'll keep that for another day when you are in a more appreciative mood.'

'I am now.'

'No, you're not. I know that sigh. You're only doing it to humour me.'

'You could be right.'

Matt nodded. As they reached the swing bridge into Highbridge, he switched back to the mission. 'You want to hit them here?'

Luke nodded. 'Yeah. Main route in and out of town. Choke point.'

Matt nodded. It was. He was looking forward to it.

*

An hour later Joey was not looking forward to his dad taxi night as he cleared the choke point and directed the Q7 towards the expressway. Joey could never persuade Tanya and her posse – unlike the boys – to go out in the Jag.

'So, you sure you don't need ID to get into this club?' It had been his last hope of opting out of a five-hour drop, wait and return evening.

'One of the guys knows the owner.'

'Which guy?'

'You don't know him.' And the bit about not needing to know him was implicit in the tone, reinforced as Tanya spun in the passenger seat to share some latest digital headline with Becky and Carol.

It was also the signal for him to adopt the learned routine of going deaf and just driving, but as he did he glanced in the rear-view mirror to see them all suited and booted and excited at their first, he assumed, big night out, remembering how he, Luke and the others had always been on the hunt for such conquests. The thought immediately put him back into dad mode as he glanced across to the apple of his eye, thinking again how stupid, yet apt the phrase was. Another relic from the nuns. The apple being the eye and the eyelid being God protecting such a precious thing. Or so they said. Anyway, Tanya was precious to Joey and the thought of the sort of thing happening to her that had happened to Janey was what had driven him to agree to fund Luke's plan.

He was not naïve enough to think that Luke was doing it out of pure altruism. He knew it was all wrapped up with looking for some form of revenge, or closure about Janey, but he was also not blind enough to think that Sean and his windbag mates would ever find a political solution. Better people had tried and failed in the past, just as equally arrogant folk would try and fail in the future. At least this way, Joey thought, guiding the Q7 on to the motorway for the short leg to Warrington, we can chase them off for a while and give Sean's cronies a chance to get their act together.

He took another quick look at Tanya. Although the skirt was shorter than any dad would really like, she was, at least, fully covered on top. A bit of her mother there, he thought as his mind was dragged back by a shriek.

'He's coming! Oh My God! He's coming!' It was Becky. Now even more excited.

'Tell me it's not true.' That was Tanya.

'Afraid so.' Carol confirming.

'I didn't. I didn't think he would,' Becky said as her thumbs battered her screen to reply.

'Why did you tell him where we were going, Becks?' Tanya again. Not pleased.

Joey was trying to stick to the rules and not get involved in the conversation, but he guessed this must be the mysterious Egyptian Natasha had told him about.

'We were supposed to be having a night out away from

278

him,' Carol moaned. 'I don't want to be spending my night watching you making an idiot of yourself.'

'You don't have to.' Becky. Defiant.

Joey was fighting hard to remain in role, something obviously sensed by his daughter as she put her hand on his arm. 'It's OK, Dad. Just teen stuff. We're cool, really.'

'I hope so,' Joey replied, trying to make it light but with the perceived fatherly warning.

She flashed him a smile. 'And you'll be in the getaway car outside, won't you?' She patted his arm again and went back to the backseat conversation.

'You're your mother's daughter all right, my girl.' Joey laughed as he checked the satnav against his own, probably out of date, local knowledge and a short while later pulled the Q7 in to a bus stop opposite the old supermarket that had been converted into the latest techno music palace. Almost before the car stopped Tanya was leaning over to kiss him on the cheek before getting out to join the others.

'Park down the road, or something.'

'Well I can't stay here. Text me just before midnight.'

'What?'

'The time you're leaving.'

'Yeah, right.' And with that she was out, flicking her hair back over her head as she linked Carol's arm for mutual support as they guided their seven-inches across the road.

Joey waited to watch them get across safely, only to find

a 4x4 pull up next to him and block his view. Who's this clown, Joey thought as he started to move the Q7 forward, but turning to try and see Tanya he saw the leather parka behind the wheel and realised the 4x4 was Bobby McBain's Range Rover out of which was pouring a male posse. As the lads headed across the road to join the girls in the queue, Bobby eased forward and lowered the passenger window.

'Hey up, Joey lad? One of yours going in there?'

'Aye. Tanya and her posse.'

Bobby nodded. 'Hold up.' He turned and whistled out of his window. One of the lads looked round and Bobby waved for him to come back. He then parked in front of Joey, got out and put his arm round the lad to say something in his ear. The lad nodded as Bobby pointed over to the club. At Tanya.

Joey's heart sank. It couldn't, could it? he thought as he watched Bobby nod and then point to Joey, pull the lad closer and speak to him before giving him a hug and a small shove off towards the club. He then walked across to the Q7 with a huge grin on his face.

'What you doing here? Thought you lived with your other family mid-week. Lots of cock and knees and all that?'

'Don't give up your day job for the comedy club circuit, Bob,' Joey flashed back, but took the proffered high five hand-clamp.

'Never had a day job, mate. Fancy a quick coffee?'

*

Luke was also preparing a coffee as Matt loaded up the video from the drone's SD Card. They were back at Luke's cottage.

'Nice old farmhouse. Plenty of outbuildings. Got himself a pool out back. Away from the road. Overall. Not flash. Not run down. No one would take much notice. Unless you look here. And here.'

He pointed to the screen as the video showed them an aerial view of the house and grounds, before homing in on the CCTV cameras. Then the solid fence. And re-inforced back door.

'Looks very quiet,' Luke commented.

'It was. Watch.' Matt pointed back at the screen and the video image widened to hover over the farmhouse. After a few seconds all the security lights came on to give a much cleaner picture.

'I threw a piece of wood over the fence to see if there were any movement detectors.' He nodded at the screen. 'Obviously. But no action. No one home.'

'Unless they were watching the cameras.'

'True,' Matt conceded. 'But no cars.'

Luke conceded that one with a grunt. He knew exactly where Leather Jacket had been.

'What about kids? Any signs?'

'Unlikely.' Again he gestured at the screen. 'After getting no reaction to the lights I took the drone lower. No bikes, swings or trampolines. But. A big doggy bowl.' He pointed to something on screen. 'I mean big.'

Luke grunted again. But it wasn't anything they hadn't tackled before. Matt paused the video and switched to a Google satellite view.

'We can come across this field. Right to the back fence. We can access down this road here, to what looks like another pub or restaurant.' He zoomed the image.

'We leave the car in the car park. Go behind this shed or whatever it is, through this bit of a wood and cut straight across. Five minutes. Ten, tops.'

Luke leaned forward to study the satellite image, wondering how old it was. Anything could have been put in their way since it was taken. Nothing beats a live feed. Sensing his friend's concern, Matt switched back to the drone video. From hovering over the farmhouse it turned away and swept across the field, took in the pub car park and then made its way back across the route Matt had mapped. It was clear. Luke turned and grinned.

'No more than 300 metres. Or the drone would have done a GPS auto return.' His grin matched Luke's. 'So all we need now is: go or no go. And when?'

'Usual knockin' hour,' Luke replied immediately. 'Tomorrow. Keep the pressure on. Billy do the exchange?'

Matt nodded. 'Checked when I picked up the B-Kits. Two H&K MP5s. SD3s with suppressors and red dots. And a dozen mags.'

While the MP5 was one of the most widely used law enforcement submachine guns, the B-Kit was a term they had coined for a full blackout kit of boots, coveralls, gloves, balaclava and body armour. It wasn't meant to completely obscure their identities, just provide a temporary disguise in low to medium risk situations. For anything higher they went for an A-Kit: A for anonymous. Head to toe covering. Nothing in, nothing out except what was filtered through their face masks.

'We'll use one MP5 for the stand-off,' Luke said. 'Pick it up on the way.'

'Going live?' Matt asked, already suspecting he knew the answer.

Luke just shook his head. 'Poke and provoke tonight.'

'You sure? They're likely to be.'

Luke shook his head again, thinking back to his encounter at the Fast Dog. 'They keep the guns mobile.'

Matt was still a bit apprehensive, but at the same time relieved that Luke was calm enough to stick to the plan. And it was his call. Bring them back to the choke point. 'OK. Natural charm it is then. Tonight.'

He then woke up the laptop and pointed at the farm-house fence on the satellite image. 'Any clues as to how we get over that?'

'Improvise. And hope he's at home when we come calling?' Luke responded, but Matt was ahead of him again as he tapped away at the keyboard. A new window opened with a live stream from the farmhouse parking area.

'Someone is,' he said as he pointed to the screen where a Mini Cooper convertible sat parked. 'Must have come home while we were on our way back.'

They were watching a feed that was coming direct from a battery operated 3G camera. Matt had hooked it over the fence, right next to one of Leather Jacket's own, so the risk of detection was small. Just as peripheral vision catches sudden movement, familiarity overlooks small changes. Things hidden in plain sight. Especially in the dark. The battery would last around ten hours and provide a constant stream that could be accessed from any phone with the app. It would also detect any new movement and send a text alert.

Another grunt from Luke. 'He's got a Porsche Hybrid.'

'Bit of a tree hugger then?' Matt asked with the same level of interested surprise Luke had checked himself on earlier. 'What do you reckon? WAG? Boyfriend? Cleaner? Cook?'

'Don't say bottle washer,' Luke quickly cut in.

Matt ejected the drone's SD Card and put it in the microwave, ready to nuke just in case they got a call during the knockin' hour. The usual pre-dawn raid when no matter what social habits people have they are likely to be at home, having been out and returned to the nest, or getting ready to leave it for the day. Since the dawn of warfare, the time when people were still slightly groggy.

'Time for a nap, I think,' Luke said as he looked at the time on the computer screen. 'We'll go at 0430 regardless of what we see there. If he's not in, we'll let him know we have been.'

Matt smiled broadly as he headed for the fridge to crack some eggs. At last. If he wanted to be a spook he'd have joined MI6, but this was what he signed up for. Cracking heads.

'What's worth more, Joe? What you know or who you know?'

'Which is why she didn't need ID,' Joey replied as he offered a Costa latte to Bobby, busy on his phone.

Bobby took the mug and gave a deep gravelly chuckle, but never deviated from his phone as he replied, 'Pal of mine owns it. I've told him to keep an eye on them. There'll be no funny stuff inside. And, as I can see that dad look in your eye, I've told my lad there's two things I'll kick the shit out of him for. Hitting a woman and getting one pregnant.'

It was some comfort. But not enough. 'There's a lot more in between, Bobby.'

Bobby laughed, the pockmarked pebble-dashed face cracking as he glanced up from his phone.

'He's a good lad, my Max, Joe. Really. Sometimes I think he might be a bit of a shirt-lifter, but . . .' he shrugged.

Joey couldn't help but smile as the irony of Bobby wearing Alexander McQueen struck him, but Bobby didn't notice as he swept on.

'At least he's not a tranny, like that bloke in the optician's. Suppose he thinks folk won't notice his five o'clock if they need specs.' He went back to the phone. 'I'd have to love him though, wouldn't I, even if he was. And I'll tell you what. These kids aren't as rampant as we used to be.' Then the gravel rattled again. 'No one is.' He put his phone down for a moment. 'I mean. Would you have ever imagined, when we were out marauding . . . that we'd be ferrying our kids about and then sitting having a coffee, while waiting for them to whistle?'

Bobby shook his head as he sipped the froth from his latte, at both the realisation of what he'd said and the memory of what his dad would have said if he'd even asked for a lift anywhere. His phone vibrated. He picked it up, looked at the message but this time didn't respond.

Joey grinned at his own memories of his youth and how he never even had the option of asking for a lift. 'I guess not.' He raised the latte in a mock toast. 'But er, how long have they been . . . ?'

Bobby just held out his hands and shrugged. 'That's one thing that hasn't changed. Did we tell our parents anything? Christ, I don't even tell them what I do now.'

'I think they might have guessed, Bobby.'

Again the deep gravelly chuckle that developed into a gurgling laugh. 'I guess you're right. At least about some of it. But they're all Facetwitters anyway, aren't they?' He waggled his phone. 'Not that hard to guess what they're up to. Unlike those that don't put it all out there. Like you?'

Joey felt this wasn't a casual question. It was leading somewhere.

'And how do you know that, Bobby?' He nodded at Bobby's phone. 'You posting now?'

The gravel rattled in his throat again. 'Weekly sales reports. Can get anything you want through these, can't you.' He leaned back in his chair. 'Except what Lukey Carlton and merry Matthew are up to?'

That was where he'd been heading. Joey tried not to react, but could see Bobby was reading his body language. A predator hunting.

'Go on. You must know,' Bobby pushed.

'Know what?'

'You're doing some work up at his ghost house, aren't you?'

'Don't call it that.'

'It's what it is, isn't it? A shrine to his dead missus?' Then added, to emphasise the family connection, 'And your sister, of course.'

Joey didn't rise to the bait. 'The only thing he's shared with me is where he wants the sockets and switches.'

'Bollocks.' Bobby crossed his fingers. 'You and him were like that. If he'd tell anyone it'd be you.'

'And why do you think he's got some big secret?'

'He might come back every now and then to keep the flame burning, but what's he brought his Matty for?' Bobby asked, fastening his predator's eyes on Joey. Probing. Joey decided to leave the question hanging in the air. He wasn't going to become the prey. He matched the predator's stare. After a moment it was Bobby who blinked. Perhaps aided by another vibration from his phone.

Bobby leaned across to pick it up. 'You know what I reckon?'

But this time Joey didn't need to think about a response. That moment had passed and Bobby was off on his own track. 'He's always wanted to find the smacko who did his missus. He's always come back hoping to stumble across him. And if he has Tonto with him, I reckon he's found out who it was. Am I right?'

He then made a quick response on the phone.

Joey smiled. He knew his body language couldn't possibly betray him now. 'I really don't know that, Bobby. Honest. You'll have to ask him.'

The predator sniffed. But seemed satisfied. 'He won't tell me. But you can tell him something for me. If he wants a hand with anything. He's only got to ask. And I mean anything, Joe. Right?'

'That be one of those fifty quid contracts you can organise? Or, what was it, five hundred for a proper job?'

The pebble-dashing cracked again. 'Daft, isn't it. But true. And if you ever want anything, Joe . . .' The crack widened even further. 'As we may be father-in-laws soon.'

'God, I hope not.'

'Thanks.'

Joey laughed. 'That came out wrong. I meant, she's too young.'

'She'll always be too young, Joe.' Bobby's phone

buzzed. A call. 'But I mean it,' he continued. 'If you ever need anything.' He looked at his phone and stood up. 'Have to take this one. Suppliers. Want another?' He pointed at the latte cup as he started to walk away.

Joey nodded and started to ponder why Tanya had to go for Max McBain. She could have the pick of the town, even if that was, like Bobby, only proud dad thinking. So why the town gangster's son? Brought her up too well, perhaps. Too much telling her to take no bullshit and take people as she found them. All that stuff about people having to live with what fate gave them. Good and bad in everyone. Why didn't he just tell her to be more picky?

'Because she wants someone with a bit of edge, Joe. Like I did with you,' Natasha said on the other end of the phone.

Joey had called her as soon as Bobby moved away. 'I get that. But why didn't you tell me it was Bobby's lad?'

'Er . . . perhaps because I didn't know. Exactly.'

'And what does that mean?'

'She only said it was someone you'd throw a strop over.'

'Me?' He felt offended. More that his daughter could so easily read him.

'What you doing now?'

'Confiding my concern?'

'Could be a strop. Anyway, it'll blow over soon enough. She's too young for anything serious.'

'You're not exactly,' he emphasised the word, '*comforting* me here.' But all he got back was the sound of her giggling.

'Oh, Joe, you're so funny when you get like this. She'll be fine. Just think how safe she will be with no one daring to try anything. Not even the poor lad himself, if what you said Bobby said is true. So . . .' she giggled again. 'Enjoy your dads' night out with Bobby.'

At least she was a lot lighter than when he left her, Joey thought. 'I'm sure I will. Now that you've comforted me. As if.' Then instinctively he lowered his voice. 'But er . . . You still OK with what we talked about?'

There was only a slight hesitation before she replied. 'Yes. You know I'll back you. Always.'

'Yeah. And . . .' Now he hesitated as he felt his eyes mist slightly as an emotive mix of gratitude, admiration, pride and appreciation swept over him. He was unable to put it into words. It was at times like this that he wished he'd stayed at St Bede's longer. No matter what he said about surviving the Comp being the best education anyone could want. All that now came out was 'I really love you, you know.' He might always be ready to take on the world, but it was a lot easier knowing his soulmate would always be there. Right behind him. No matter what. 'I really do,' he added. Unnecessarily.

'I know,' Natasha replied, referring more to Joey's typical macho male inability to vocalise his emotions. 'As I love you.' Then came the quick caveat. 'But . . . just like we said. Yeah?'

'Yeah. Yeah. Promise.' And he had to say it again. 'I do really love you. And thanks.'

'Love you too. But stay safe,' Natasha replied. He could hear the emotion in her own voice even though she was doing her best to sound matter-of-fact. It was one of those calls when neither side knows how to end. Mainly because the one thing you couldn't send over the phone was the very thing they both needed. A hug. Time to end the call.

He looked across to see Bobby, still on his phone, dropping some money on the counter with a keep the change gesture, and heading back across to Joey. 'Anyway, he's on his way back,' Joey said. 'I'll see you later, eh?'

'You may see me but I'll probably be asleep when you get back. But look forward to tomorrow, eh?'

'Absolutely. Love you.'

'Love you too' came the automatic response. But this time held for that extra second or two, before Natasha added, 'No matter what. 'Bye.'

As Joey watched the call end on his screen he knew that, despite the reassurance, they would, no doubt, revisit everything in the morning. He looked back at Bobby and wondered what sort of sales figures he was receiving now. But whatever they were, Bobby's body language suddenly changed. He ended the call, turned and waved to the girl behind the counter, pointed over at Joey and received a nod.

'Sorry.' He waved his phone. 'Got to go. But I've ordered you a raspberry slice as well.'

'No problem,' Joey replied as Bobby turned away, but then stopped. 'You coming to watch the game tomorrow? Now you're back.'

'What game?'

'God you are out of touch, mate. School match. Your Alex plays for the Under-15s, doesn't he? Used to do them on Saturdays in our day but . . .' He shrugged. 'They either won't pay the overtime, or they're all too busy getting excees for the community teams. So they miss Maths and English instead. No wonder the BRIC economies are racing ahead, eh, and buying up all them London mansions you make your cash out of.' His grin broadened. 'Give my love to Anastasia. And my future daughter-in-law. See you at the footie tomorrow?'

Joey refused to rise to the Tanya crack but nodded agreement on the football. But then asked, 'What about Max? I could give him a lift back.'

'What? And watch the two of them snogging in your back seat? Er, awkward. As they say.' Then he let out another deep, gurgling laugh at Joey's obvious discomfort thinking about it. 'Honest, Joe. You've got a real dad's face on you tonight.'

Joey shrugged to acknowledge that he had, as Bobby swept on.

'But thanks. Although there's no need. The only benefit

of still having the ex on the scene is that he stays with her midweek. I don't mind dropping him, but she'll have to turn out later. Give him a lift home on her broomstick. But I best be gone.'

The phone back at his ear, he waved to remind the counter staff not to forget Joey's latte and raspberry slice. Joey watched Bobby's rapidly departing back, thinking there was more to this parenting than he remembered. He checked the time and wondered whether to call Nat back, but decided that might kick them both off again. He then checked his texts. One from Benno. ALL GOOD. LOCK-UP STUFF TOP PRICE. ON NEW JOB. OLD MATE. CATCH UP WHEN. That sounded good. Joey had told him to sell everything from the lock-up after moving on. Without him Benno would soon become another target for the bully boys. You always needed someone watching your back.

There was nothing from Luke. Joey wondered what he and Tonto, as Bobby had called Matt, were up to at that moment, but knew he wouldn't let him know. Then something else caught his eye. Outside. Bobby was walking rapidly towards an old boy who was sitting on what was some public artiste's interpretation of a bench. As he finished his call, Bobby pulled out what looked like a £20 note, wrapped it round the phone then neatly dropped it into a shopping trolley by the side of the bench. Nothing more than a faint grin passed between the two as Bobby headed off to find his Range Rover.

Now Joey had something else to wonder about. The mysterious world of pay-and-throw phones.

Sean had just entered the code for the alarm and picked up the plant tray Sandra had selected and asked him to bring home in the Land Rover, when his phone went. He hadn't bothered putting in his Bluetooth earpiece for the short walk to the car so thought about ignoring it, but then wondered if it might be Craig Harlow calling back. Or worse: Noah in trouble again. He put down the box, fished out the phone and saw it was Joey. Yo, bro, he heard, as he tried to wedge the phone into the crick of his neck and pick the box up again so he could talk and carry the box, but as usual found it wouldn't stay in position. So he put the box down again.

'Don't you wish these so-called smartphones had rubber grips or something round the edges?' he asked Joey.

'Er, not something I spend that much time on, to be honest.'

'You can't wedge them into your neck, like the old ones with buttons.'

'That's true but, er, have you tried those little things that go in your ear and connect . . .'

Sean sighed. He'd asked for it. 'What's up?'

'Where you now?'

'Where do you think I am?'

'Either at some charity do annoying Sandra or locking

up. But . . .' Joey let it hang, to egg Sean on. 'Guess where I am?'

'How many guesses do I get? Seeing as London is such a big—'

'Warrington,' Joey cut across.

'Why?'

'Because I love my wife and kids. And want to be near them in their hour of need.'

'OK,' Sean said, getting the gist. 'But when . . . ?'

'Last night. Well, this morning. You heard what happened to Tanya outside the chippy?'

'Had Sandra in my ear all morning. She's my personal social networker. Then had Noah all afternoon.'

Sean brought Joey up to speed on that, trying to keep his temper under control as he relived the trauma before eventually asking him what he was doing in Warrington.

'Taxi duty,' Joey responded. 'No point going home. By the time I got there I'd be on my way back. So been hangin' with Bobby McBain.'

'What'd he try and sell you?'

'Reassurance. About Tanya and his lad Max.'

'What about them?' Sean asked, surprised. And intrigued.

'Boy/girl stuff. I've been told not to fret about it.'

'I would.'

'I'm not you, though.'

'True,' Sean responded. Recalling his earlier thoughts about hoping Noah wouldn't turn out like Joey.

'So what else should I know about Bobby?' Joey asked.

'Oh, he's winding everyone up with a makeshift car park off the High Street.'

'When you say winding people up do you mean real people or—'

'Or my do-goody council mates, you mean?' Sean felt the spike of annoyance he always did on hearing his little brother's dismissive tone.

Joey felt the resentment. He'd done it again. Pressed the insecurity button. He tried to row back. 'I didn't mean . . . But, well, it's the same with his counterfeit stuff, isn't it. Everyone says it's disgraceful. But everyone's got one. He'll say it himself, Sean. He just offers what people want.'

He had a point. As did Bobby, but right then was not the time to get into a semantic argument about market forces and social policy. 'Can we argue this over dinner or something? I've got to get home.'

'Things to do, you mean. Instead of chatting to your brother who is trying to while away a few hours waiting for his daughter?' But it was light. Banter.

'How about I call you back when I'm in the car. And bluetoothed?'

'Great. You struggling with something?'

'Yeah. Box of winter greens to spruce up Janey's grave.'

'Ah yeah . . . and er . . . as usual, big bro. Thanks for doing that sort of thing.'

'No worries. It's Sandra actually. But part of what we do. So what you after?'

'Feel a bit crap now, but was going to ask if you had the trailer hooked up?'

Sean hesitated. He knew it was a hook for something. But in the end he had to fill the silence. 'Go on. Yes, so what?'

'The one you could sling on those fence panels you promised me?'

Sean let out another sigh of frustration and glanced back at the now bolted and alarmed compound. 'How about we sort that tomorrow, now you're home?'

He could hear Joey laughing at the other end.

By the time Sean drove home, Joey had driven back to park outside the club, using the travel time like he did on the train, to catch up on things so he could thoroughly impress his big brother by knowing who Craig Harlow was. Being Joey, he had crossed paths with nearly everyone from Highbridge during his own rites of passage years, but he'd duly agreed to be sworn to secrecy about Santa's Garden. Due to his own history he was also able to calm Sean down over thinking Noah was going off the rails, then arranged for Sean to drop the panels the following day, confirmed arrangements for a family lunch at the weekend and explained why he was back. Fed up with London. Missing the kids' growing up. Eventually getting to the part about realising that, although she would never admit it, perhaps everything might be putting too much stress on Natasha, especially with her mother deteriorating. And how he was grateful their own parents still seemed fit and well. He decided not to mention the bit about bankrolling Luke to sort out the chippy crew.

Instead he switched the conversation to whether Sean knew anyone who needed work doing. Now he was back, he'd have to start building up his business.

'Well, there is one thing you could do for me, actually,' Sean replied. 'Santa's illuminations?'

'Will I be able to tell anyone about it?' Joey laughed.

'If they work. Catch you tomorrow.'

'You will.' But before ending the call, Joey fired another question. 'Hey, Sean. Bobby told me there's a guy in the optician's who's a tranny.'

Sean immediately brightened. At last something Joey didn't already know. 'Everyone knows that, Joe. Well, those who live here.' He couldn't resist the barb. Nor the follow-up. 'But that's a double hit.'

'What is?'

'Well, Martin or Marian as he, or she calls herself must be the only thing in a dress you haven't tried to bed.'

'Oh, nice one, Bro.'

'Tomorrow,' was all Sean said before ending the call. But Joey heard him laughing at his own joke. That made him chuckle, wondering how early the optician had started and, if he was even half decent, whether he might have tried to pull him at some stage. He decided not to go too far down that memory lane as he swiped the phone to check his messages just in case there was anything from Luke. There wasn't. But he was getting a visual message from the two piles of muscle outside the club. Being suspicious was part of a bouncer's job description. He might be just another dad waiting to pick up the kids. But he could be an illegal taxi driver who would kick off a fight with the licensed guys. Or he could just be a perv on the prowl. No matter, they now had him on their threat assessment list.

As he washed the dishes after their meal, Luke was also thinking about tomorrow. Going through the operational plan, such as it was. Get in. Poke the nest. Get out. Matt had already lost himself on his laptop, alternating between cookery, military forums, property, cars and porn, noting wryly to himself how his preferences had changed over the years. A few years back, porn would have been first on the list, but there was only so many times you could get excited about some MILF flashing her bits.

Luke took the opportunity to reflect on whether it was time to sell up and move on. He knew everyone else had their own theories as to why he kept the cottage, and most had some validity. It was unfinished business. A reminder, like the nodding Buddha, of happier times. Or tragedy. It was a foothold back home. But above all, for him, it was a safe bolthole. Somewhere to aim for when things got too hot elsewhere. Where he could find a friend like Joey. And, as he had told him, what else would he do with his cash?

It was the same reason Matt was constantly trawling

estate agent websites, searching for somewhere to buy. Matt's trouble, though, was that since splitting from his wife before any kids came along, then losing his parents, he didn't have any roots from which to grow. Luke had thought of selling up and buying something closer to his own parents, but the idea of an apartment on the Costa del Pensions didn't exactly do it for him.

He picked up the nodding Buddha and gave it a tap. How long was it since he had felt real happiness? He rolled on his bed to look at the picture of himself and Janey on the bedside cabinet. It had been taken on the Thailand trip after she flew out to meet him on that 72. To stop his mind going down the blind alleys he had explored too often he rolled away from the picture and got up. He'd go over the plan one last time. The plan for payback. And that, he knew, was the real reason he kept coming back.

Joey was scrolling through the radio station list, another reminder of the lack of choice once outside the capital, when a text message popped up on his phone. HELP. It was Tanya. A microsecond later Joey was out of the car and heading for the two suits on the door, more High and Mighty than Jacamo and who, rightly, didn't know what this potential madman had on his mind. Until he held up the phone and pointed to the door, where Tanya was rushing out frantically looking for her dad. The bouncers hardly reacted at this all too familiar scene. Just another kid discovering reality is different from expectation and comes running for Daddy to sort it out. Still, before any of them had to do something they might later regret, Tanya, relieved at seeing Joey, pointed to the door and ran back to help Carol, who was struggling with a drunken Becky while trying to fend off the ever pursuing Husani, who'd swapped his Prada for a D&G look.

'Let go. I'll take her home,' Husani was saying. 'She's safe with me.'

'Oh yeah. She looks it,' Carol shot back.

'Here,' he tried to pull Becky away from Carol. 'I will take her.'

Which was when Tanya flew into the fray. Shoving Husani backwards. 'We're doing it, Hus!' she shouted.

The bouncers exchanged looks, then stood back and flicked their heads for Joey to pass. They had seen all this before too and knew it was best to let the domestics sort themselves out. Apart from which, they knew what might come next. As it did. As Becky attempted to empty the contents of her stomach on to the pavement between them all. While Joey was not quick enough, it had the effect of disentangling Husani's arm from between Carol's and Becky's. Joey looked down at his sick-splattered trainers then, fighting to control his irritation, gestured for Tanya to get Becky over to the Q7, while he turned to Husani.

'Who you?' came straight at him.

'I'm the guy who's taking them home.'

'No need. I do it. I'm with Becky.'

'Not any more. Tonight.'

Husani just grinned and went to step past Joey, but Joey leaned sideways, jamming him against the wall. He reacted by shoving Joey away. The bouncers took a step forward but Joey held up his hand. No trouble. Then leaned back in to Husani.

'Now, what you lot do tomorrow is between you and them, but I think it's best if I take my daughter . . .' Joey hesitated to make the point. Which Husani took. Hell's fury over a scorned woman had nothing on a protective dad. He stood back. Slightly.

It was enough for Joey to continue. 'So I'll take her and her friends home and you can go and finish your night. Somewhere else. Yeah?'

Husani held Joey's eye for a moment, then looked across to where Tanya was pushing and Carol pulling Becky into the Q7. He didn't seem to want to let her go and stepped forward once again. Joey blocked his way. The bouncers went on alert again, but this further flash-point was defused as another well-cut suit came out of the club. Joey's age. Very smooth manner but the fresh scar across his forehead suggested he had recently seen the sharp end of life. The bouncers nodded deferentially and made sure he avoided the souvenir from Becky. A man of influence.

'Er, anything I can help you gentlemen with?'

Both Joey and Husani turned to the new arrival. He

immediately sized them up, turned to Joey and then nodded at the girls. 'That your daughter?'

'The one pushing, yeah.'

Husani immediately realised that his age and the numbers were against him. 'I text you, Becky!' he shouted and started to back off towards the club.

The bouncers looked to the man in the suit. He shook his head, so they indicated that Husani should carry on walking, which he did, towards his Mercedes SLG, throwing a dismissive wave over his shoulder.

As the bouncers watched him go the suit turned back to Joey. 'Sorry. Bobby McBain . . . ?' He searched Joey's eyes for recognition. Then continued when Joey nodded. 'Bobby asked me to keep an eye on them.'

'You own this place?'

'And a few others. We did watch them. Even checked when he showed up, but they said they knew him.' He glanced at Husani and shrugged. What could they do? 'But then they started to look a bit uncomfortable,' he continued. 'Which was when your girl probably decided to call for Dad's army.'

Joey grinned but it faded quickly as he turned to see Tanya suddenly leap backwards, as Becky vomited out of the side of the Q7.

'And er . . . I'll leave you with that, shall I?' the club owner asked.

'Er . . . Yep. No problem,' he replied as he started towards the car.

'Oh,' the club owner called after him. 'You will tell Bobby we looked out for them?' His voice was edged with concern.

'Oh yeah. I'll give you a five-star rating.'

The club owner hesitated. Was that good or bad? Still, as he couldn't influence anything he continued to be as good as his word. And left Joey to deal with the vomit. Which he had to do again ten minutes into the return journey.

'Stop. Stop. Stop!' Tanya screamed from the back seat and started hauling a retching Becky over her lap to the door in the hope of escaping potential contamination. It was a good move. Joey brought the Q7 to a stop, but not in time to get Becky far enough across to miss the door. He just sat, eyes fixed ahead. He didn't have to look. He'd been through the scenario before. Already he could hear Natasha having a go at him for letting it happen. In her car.

Joey waited until they were fifteen minutes down the motorway before glancing into the rear-view mirror and saw the now mopped and wiped Becky across Tanya's lap, asleep. Carol was snoring as good as anything Benno could manage, while Tanya was staring out of the window, pre-occupied about something.

'You OK?' Joey offered.

'Yeah. Sorry about . . .'

'It's OK. It's your mum we have to worry about.' He saw that at least that made her smile.

'Didn't turn out like you expected?'

'It did, actually. She's such a retard.' Her voice was laced with venom, but she stroked Becky's forehead at the same time.

'Who was the bloke?' He tried to make it sound causal, but she knew he was fishing.

'A bigger retard.' It was accompanied by a huge sigh that signalled the subject was probably off-limits to parents.

Joey decided he'd make one last attempt.

'No sign of Bobby's lad, though?'

'If you mean why wasn't he looking after us' – the sexist implication was clear – 'he had to go home early when Mummy came to get him. OK?'

Joey understood. Just drive. And then took another glance in the mirror. Tanya was still stroking Becky's forehead, but had gone back to sharing her thoughts with the window. Joey smiled. Bobby had been right. His ex must be a right dragon.

A few hours after Joey had delivered the girls home and cleaned up the Q7 as best he could, Luke and Matt were once again on the expressway. Matt had got the text alert on the way. At 04.47 and on checking the feed, saw that Leather's Porsche Cayenne was now parked outside the house. They'd had nearly six hours' sleep. It was time to go knockin'.

Matt was monitoring the live 3G feed on his personal smartphone, accepting that this was the most dangerous bit. Transporting weapons. Overseas they slept with them. But back home, no amount of blarney, Irish or other, would get them off a firearms charge. If they were walking down Highbridge Hill they could claim to have found it and were on their way to hand it in. But driving down the expressway or in a pub car park there could only be one conclusion. They were up to no good.

To create some form of alternative script Billy had delivered the weapons, as usual, unassembled, wrapped and bagged as replacement parts. Matt had taken one of the MP5s and further separated the components into different bin bags, ready to be discarded if they thought they were about to be pulled. If they couldn't dump the bags they would argue that they were only carrying spare parts. Not a weapon. No ammo. And hope for an importation offence. Back from overseas. A bit of black market on the side. Add a dash of remorse and naïvety and with the right lawyer that was probably a fine or six months inside. Perhaps both. But that was better than the potential seven years for possession of a firearm. And six months in a British nick was not as daunting as a few of the tours they had been through.

It was all probably academic though, as they knew the chances of being pulled were low at this time of day, when austerity cuts had trimmed police numbers. But they were prepared. As always. To improvise. Which they did by commandeering two metal rubbish bins from the side of the pub across the field from Leather's farmhouse. Matt pulled on his gloves and reassembled the MP5. If they were caught exposed he would ditch the gun. Nothing on him. Nothing on the gun.

They then checked the feed from the 3G camera. All quiet. Leather's Porsche Cayenne was still parked up. Time to go. They calmly walked the 200 metres to huddle against the farmhouse fence. From this viewpoint it looked exactly like what it was. A fenced compound.

Luke lifted his phone to the top of the fence, once again using its camera to scan the other side. All quiet. One last look at the feed. No change. He then set off round to the front of the property. Down the side where Matt had fixed the camera earlier. Matt followed.

Two-thirds of the way down the fence, when they were just in front of the farmhouse, they upended the rubbish bins but Matt carried on to the corner of the field where he had been earlier, loosening his backpack as he went. He reached up, unhooked the camera, dropped it in his backpack and went back to Luke. He dropped the back-pack as Luke made a hand step to boost him on to one of the bins. Matt in turn held out a hand to help Luke up on to his bin.

They then checked every angle and listened to the sounds of the night. Background traffic hum. A far-off blue light siren. A couple of animals talking to each other or shouting at perceived threats. Luke turned to Matt. Go? A confirmatory nod came back, so he finger-counted down from five and went over the fence. The movement detectors immediately picked up his presence and the security lighting illuminated the entire area inside the fencing, accompanied by the instant sound of a large dog barking inside the house. Luke grinned. All as predicted. So far.

Leather Jacket wouldn't want to attract too much attention from the outside, but would want to be in complete control inside. Luke looked across to the parked Cayenne and Cooper convertible. Knowing that anyone now up and watching the CCTV screens would see him clearly, Luke deliberately ducked low as he hurried across to the Cayenne and tried the doors. Then moved towards the Cooper. He wanted to appear as, hopefully, perhaps, just another opportunistic car thief. Even better, a stupid car thief. The only type who would have a go at the local drug lord's car.

They had reasoned that the house would be another typical drug fortress, so without resorting to the standard entry procedure – of blowing a hole in the wall quickly followed by a few flash bangs – their best bet was the same as the choke-point plan. Get anyone inside to come out. Right now, Luke hoped, Leather Jacket would be looking at the CCTV monitors, outraged that some idiot was trying to snatch his car. The more outraged he became, the more careless he would become.

Luke was right. After a moment or two the front door flew open and the dog that belonged to the bark rushed out. A German shepherd. Followed by Leather Jacket, but now in sweatpants and hoodie. It looked like he had hurriedly pulled it on, as it was unzipped, exposing the kaleidoscope of body art across his chest. He looked like he worked out a lot. It also looked like Matt had been right. There was now a Beretta Over-Under shotgun pointing directly at Luke. This could get a bit tricky.

9

Go Or No Go

Matt was now ruing his decision to go along with Luke. He had been tempted to slip one magazine into his backpack, just in case, but accepted the associated risks of being found in possession. They agreed they would use live ammunition only when they knew they were on their final exit plan. Which included fighting their way out. Right now, he thought, it wasn't going to be down to natural charm or blarney, but sheer bottle. And spotting an opportunity.

That came in the form of the dog doing what he had obviously been trained to do: attack. In its rush to get at Luke it brushed against Leather's legs, causing him to sidestep and take his eye and shotgun off Luke for a moment. Which was just enough time for Luke to turn and use the Cooper's bonnet as a step towards the Cayenne's roof. The dog tried to follow but slipped off the Cooper, went to try again but was stopped by a whistle from the front door. Luke looked across to see what must be the WAG, also in sweatpants and hoodie, but in pink and designed to show more the results of working out than the working out itself.

'He's goanna' scratch me car, soft lad!' she shouted at Leather in pure Scouse. But stopped dead in her tracks as a flash of red went across her eyes and a red dot bobbed across her breasts.

Immediately the dog turned its attention to this latest intruder but before he could even attempt a lunge up at Matt, now leaning on the fence behind the MP5, he was halted by another whistle from Leather, who had the Beretta back on Luke. The dog looked confused. What was the point of being trained to attack people if they kept stopping you? It sloped over to the WAG and sat beside her, obviously knowing who was its real best friend.

As Luke had earlier, Leather decided to buy time while he figured out was what going on. The all blacks. The red dot site on what looked like an automatic with a silencer. This was no random carjacking. This was an organised team and he was caught in a stand-off, out in the open with a useless dog and his equally useless WAG, now a bargaining chip. But a bargain can only be concluded if both sides play. It was a game he needed to control.

He shouted over his shoulder at Matt. 'You hurt her and—' He didn't finish. A jab of the shotgun towards Luke made the threat clear. The accent was thick, but to

Matt and Luke's surprise it was more East Manchester than Eastern European. A mixed marriage.

'And you,' he jabbed at Luke again. 'Tell your mate to back off. Or we start a shooting war. And this is legal – his isn't.'

'Yeah, but you'll be dead before the cops even get here.'

Luke saw the flicker. Leather now knew they weren't cops. Just as Luke intended. But it did little to dent the bravado.

'And you won't be?'

'Maybe,' Luke said, making a play of holding his hands up as he sat down, crossed-legged on the car. Leather might have thought he was capitulating, but he was actively reducing his size as a target while putting more flesh between the Barrett and his genitals.

'But,' Luke continued, 'you that accurate? You're going to have to hope you hit me here' – he framed his face with his hands, making it look like a small target. 'His will go where that red dot is. You might make a bit of a mess of me, but I'll live. She'll be burying you.'

It was the tone. The calm detachment. The way Luke spoke, rather than what he said, that put the doubt in Leather's mind. He looked across to Matt. These guys looked and sounded like pros. Or total headcases. Which was worse. What was he up against? He needed more time. Needed an opportunity.

'Nice cozzies,' he said. 'What is it? A Terrorist-a-gram? Trick or treat for Halloween, or something?'

'Not bad, that,' Luke chuckled. 'But let's not turn it into a Halloween movie, eh?'

'So what is it you want? Before I tell you what you can expect.'

Luke pointed first at the shotgun. Put it down. Then at the dog. Send it inside. Leather held his ground. Luke then directed Leather's attention by pointing to the WAG. Matt moved the red dot across her eyes and steadied it in the middle of her forehead.

'For Christ's sake, just give them what they want.' She was terrified.

Leather sighed. He could have done with a little more resilience, but he laid the shotgun down. Carefully. It was expensive. He then turned to the dog. 'Inside. Go.'

The dog looked totally perplexed. This game was supposed to end with him ragging someone's arm then being thrown a steak, or at least a sausage. Not this. He hesitated for a moment. Just in case. Until—

'Go!' It was harsher. Temper being controlled. Not to be ignored. The dog slowly skulked across to the front door.

'Now, back up and close the door,' Luke said to the WAG. 'Arm's length. Don't step too close or it'll be the last step you take.'

Meekly she did as she was told, all the time looking at the red dot that was now back on her cleavage. As she reached back and pulled the door closed it immediately deadlocked. The dog wouldn't be coming out again.

'Well trained,' Luke said to Leather, not differentiating between WAG and dog.

'As you are, by the looks . . .' Leather snarled back. As Luke had witnessed earlier, he was used to being in control so was struggling to contain his anger. 'So what the frig do you want?'

'Not a lot,' Luke answered as he slid off the Cayenne's roof to stand square on to Leather, side-kicking the shotgun out of reach. 'Just you out of Highbridge.'

Leather half smiled. This was now becoming more than irritating. It was becoming ridiculous. Who did these guys think they were? Or were dealing with?

'Really?' he asked. It said it all. No way.

Luke returned the half-smile. 'You may think you own the town, but you don't. The people we work for do. And they want you out. No matter what it takes.'

Leather once again looked Luke up and down. Deliberately. Then back to Matt holding the red dot on his woman. Still trying to buy time. Trying to think of a way out.

'Tell them who you are, Peter!' the WAG screamed, desperately hoping his reputation would frighten them off.

'I think they might already know,' he replied. Calmly. This was, he now thought, strictly business. 'You do Fatty's place the other night?'

'I heard about it,' Luke replied. Equally calm. 'Town's getting dangerous for those who shouldn't be there.'

'And what if I tell you to go and f—' Leather started again, winding himself up, but stopped as a red glare caught his eye. Then he noticed the red dot dancing on Luke's chest. Then move down on to the ground and across to him. Up his legs, circle his crotch and settle in the centre of his chest. His anger was simmering at his own impotence. Luke nodded towards Matt, then tapped Leather on the chest. Twice. The double tap of death.

Luke noticed Leather's fists clenching and unclenching. Just like Joey did when he was either winding up for a fight, or keeping himself under control to avoid one. It meant Leather was now on a very short fuse and could kick off at any moment. He was probably also trying to decide whether he could dodge the red dot long enough to grab Luke as a human shield, so Luke took a step away, towards the shotgun, but the meaning was obvious to Leather. He'd never make it.

'You can have this week. But after that . . .' Luke paused, leaving the thought in the air, before adding, with heavy emphasis, 'Pete.'

Although he returned a caustic glare, Leather took the point. They did indeed know who he was, and didn't seem to care.

Luke picked up the shotgun. 'Nice gun,' he said, as he broke it slowly and took out the two cartridges while backing away towards the perimeter fence. 'After this week, Highbridge is off limits to you and yours.'

There was neither humour nor threat. The neutral tone

was enough for Leather to conclude that this was, as he thought, strictly business. There was no further attempt to argue. He just wanted to get the situation over so he could regroup. And get back in control. To do that he had to stand and watch Luke drag his patio table and a chair to the fence, then watch as he placed the Beretta on the table, stepped up and over. Improvising.

The woman immediately hurried over to join Leather as the red dot danced between their chests. The warning was obvious. But just as Matt turned away and was about to drop out of sight, Leather called out. 'Oi. You do know what to expect, don't you?'

He took Matt's slight hesitation as acknowledgement of the threat. He couldn't see the smile beneath the bala-clava as he dropped from view. The bait had been taken.

Joey was also up early as usual to let Roscoe out on his morning patrol, and when he'd made sure that the boys were up and ready for school he had gone out to check on the Q7 after its emergency clean-up from the previous night. But he knew human vomit was second only to spilt milk to make a car uninhabitable. He'd take it in to Glass & Shine and see if they would do a valet while he waited.

He was just taking his morning Colombian from beneath the coffee dispenser when Becky came into the kitchen, hunting for her stuff, still in the clothes she had been wearing the night before. Like many, she had suffered the nightclub exchange rate. Going in looking a million dollars: coming out a million lire. It might even be drachmas these days, Joey was thinking, as he heard the kitchen door open.

'Oh, sorry, Mr Nolan. I er . . . I wanted to be gone before anyone . . .'

'It's OK, Becky. You're not going into school with—'

But she hurriedly interrupted. 'My mum's in the car outside.'

'OK. But remember, it happens to us all every now and then, you know.'

'Yeah. But not, like, spewing over someone else's car.' She had gathered up the abandoned shoes and bag from the stagger-in, so headed for the door. It was only when the front door banged that Tanya came hurrying into the kitchen, pulling on a thick tartan dressing gown.

'Was that Becks?'

'Think she was off to find a hole to crawl into.'

'Why? What did you say? You didn't have a go at her for—'

'No.' Joey cut across her. 'I know it's part of my job description to take the blame for everything, but this time: no. Think it might have had something to do with leaving her scent on your mother's car?'

This seemed to calm the lion cub, for she walked over to the table, dropped into a chair and took her phone from her pocket. Her thumbs got to work as she spoke. 'God, Mum doesn't know, does she?'

Joey shook his head and sat down opposite his daughter. Every week he noticed a change. Each week losing a bit of his little girl, as the woman emerged. Nat was right. He had been missing the kids growing up. Not that such things were on Tanya's mind.

'She is such a retard.'

'Are we still on your mother now, or—'

'Becks. That bloke, right. God, what was she like?' She put her phone down and leaned forward. There was still a bit of his little girl wanting to share a secret with her dad. 'He's the one that keeps stalking her. He's really creepy, Dad. I'm sure he spiked her drink.'

'That's some accusation, Tan.'

'Then why'd she start behaving the way she did?'

'And I don't suppose they gave out any discounted shots?' He was, after all, still the dad trying to guide his daughter towards the realities of life.

She considered it for a moment. 'Well, yeah, but we all did the same.' She saw his eyebrow move. Even if involuntarily. 'But I suppose we're, well, Cags and I, are more used to it.' She saw his eyes harden. The little girl retreated, to be replaced by the cub. 'And don't look like that. I'm nearly seventeen.'

'You're supposed to be eighteen to drink.' But Joey knew he had slipped too far into protective dad mode and was losing the moment.

'Yeah, right.' Her phone lit up. She looked. 'She's going

home to clean up. Why didn't she do that here? You sure you didn't say something?'

'No. But what I should have said to her, and I'm now saying to you, is that you are all still too young to be hanging around in clubs owned by the likes of Bobby McBain. Or going out with his son.'

'God, you're so hypocritical. It was OK for you to hang out with his dad when you were our age, but I'm not supposed to see Max? He's really sweet.'

'Sweet?'

'Yes, he is, actually. Just because his dad's some big gangster, doesn't make him one.'

'It's not him. It's where he'll end up taking you.'

'And where's that?'

'I don't know.' Joey instantly knew that was a stupid thing to say. To anyone, never mind a teenager.

'Oh, right,' Tanya said as she stood up. The moment was definitely moving away from Joey. 'You haven't got a clue what you're talking about but you want me not to see Max, just in case there might be something, but you don't know what?'

Joey tried to recover. 'OK, put like that it sounds daft. But—'

'It doesn't sound daft, Dad. It is.'

'I can always ground you, you know.'

'Oh, great. You haven't been around for God knows how long and now you come swanning in thinking it's all going back to walks in the park and teddy bears, or something. I don't think so.'

With that she was gone. His little girl had definitely morphed. That was the real killer. He had missed that happening.

'They're all trying to get in on the act now,' Glynnis said, as she delivered Sean's Full Welsh to his corner table in the café. Sean glanced up from his Google search. He thought he had better know a few of Craig's chart hits before he met him. He saw Glynnis standing, tight lipped, arms folded, glaring out at Santa's Garden where there was a small army of little helpers tidying and primping. Sean smiled, but couldn't keep the quizzical look from his face.

'Don't look at me,' Glynnis quickly said. 'There's where you want to look.' She nodded out to the hive of activity, where Byron was directing operations with all the aplomb of a concert conductor. 'He's probably been and goggled or boggled or whatever you do on those things –' she pointed to Sean's iPad. 'And now he knows what a big cheese is coming. He'll be trying to be first in line, you know.'

She used it as her departure line, but the meaning was more obvious. *She* wanted to be first in line. Sean chuckled as he dissected the egg to start creating the glue for the egg and bacon sauce, as a text message popped up on the iPad screen. Sandra. WHAT TIME CRAIG DUE? Sean nearly choked on the first piece of bacon, sausage and black pudding. They were all trying to get in on the act.

Luke and Matt were now naked. They were going through the drill of loading their mud-splattered blacks into the washing machine to clean them up and get rid of any superficial dirt that could link them back to Leather's farmhouse. Not that they expected Leather to call it in. The concern was always dog walkers. Or joggers. See something suspicious. Call the police. The nation had been inculcated in this mantra. A couple of guys in black coveralls and balaclavas carrying bins across a field might fall into that category. The idea that it would be Leather who pressed charges was a fallacy imported from American crime shows. In Britain it was the cops who decided whether you needed lifting.

Having set the washing machine going they went upstairs for a shower. If they had just got back from a firefight they would have changed, burnt their gear and wiped down not far from the scene, so they could travel home relatively clean. They knew that forensics might always find something, but that was when they were looking and after they'd picked up any superficial clues. Matt had switched the car registration plates as soon as they got back, feeding the cloned car set into the incinerator Luke had installed as part of the eco-heating system. It burnt all household and garden refuse to provide the hot water that was now running over their backs.

They had talked through the likely scenarios on the way back. About how Leather would probably assume it was a land grab. So he'd come looking for who was likely to gain, not some old school chums out for revenge. That would go one of two ways. He looked the type who would want to react quickly to stamp his authority – yet, the execution by crane suggested a man of detail and planning. Who needed to be in control. That suggested he would wait until he felt the time was right.

Either way, they agreed that he would come after dark. More creatures of the night. They might be brazen enough to act in daylight on their own patch, but not in Highbridge. Yet. That was why they had to be stopped. Before they did.

The plan was to stop them at the choke point. The swing bridge into town. If the bridge opened at the right moment they would have to stop. And once stopped, they would be fixed targets. There for the taking.

'We going to be ready at the swing bridge every night from now on, then?' Matt asked, as Luke came into the kitchen still pulling on a sweatshirt.

Matt was now showered and throwing together another one-pot dish. Paella.

Luke nodded. 'You sure you can get all the cameras to work?'

'Don't see why not. Four cameras. Four IP addresses. Four feeds,' Matt responded, but then added, 'You sure Billy couldn't just swing a drone for us? A proper one.'

Luke laughed. 'I'm sure if the price was right. Although someone in Nevada might query the idea of targeting that chippy.'

Matt shrugged, accepting that was probably a fair observation, which was why they were going with Plan B. Supplementing the 3G camera they had used at Leather's farmhouse with three more, each positioned on the expected route to Highbridge. Each of the four cameras would be mounted inside what looked like a standard bird nest and feeder box, the sort that often have a camera rigged inside so enthusiasts can watch the birds feeding and nesting, and the chicks growing. However, with Matt's boxes the camera was pointing outward. Each had a small power pack with a long trailing power cable. Each was painted in British road sign grey. They also had large zip ties attached so they could easily be strapped tightly to any one of the many road signs that cluttered roadside landscapes. They would look just like any another piece of kit some jobsworth somewhere had put up to monitor only they knew what.

'How long will it take to rig everything?' Luke asked.

'Couple of minutes each, tops. Travel out. Back. I can set up the laptops on the way back. Couple of hours, say three tops?'

'We'd better get them rigged this morning, then. Rest up this afternoon.'

'OK,' Matt replied, reaching over for two plates. 'Get the water. And did you find out about the bridge?'

Luke nodded, putting two water bottles on the table. 'Found out that it only opens on demand, though.'

'How's it work? Can we rig it?'

'It's electric. Operated from a control room overlooking the canal.'

'So,' Matt concluded, as he scooped out the paella on to two waiting plates. 'All we have to do is hot wire it?'

Another nod from Luke. 'And if we can't, I think we know a man who can.'

Matt grinned. 'I think we do. But er . . .' He stopped for a moment. Not sure whether he really wanted to bring up the subject. 'But er . . . We – or you – sure about Joey? I know you had another word, but . . . Is he still up for it all? I mean, frightening Fatty's one thing, but we know where this is going, don't we?'

Luke acknowledged the point with a nod. 'And that's something else I'm going to ask him. Go or No Go.'

'And what happens if it's a No Go? If he can't live with it?'

Luke pondered for a moment. The same issue. Easy to say people should be shot. Different doing it. And different living with the trauma of feeling responsible. 'Let's see what our man says first.'

That man was now walking down the High Street looking for Bobby McBain's controversial car parking scheme. Joey was curious and had time to kill while the guys at Glass & Shine removed the stench of Becky's stomach from the rear door side panel of the Q7. With a bit of luck they'd all get away with Natasha thinking he had had the car cleaned as a surprise.

It didn't take him long. He just followed a convoy of cars that turned off the High Street into Saddlers Street. As he rounded the corner he saw they were then turning into a wide open space, that once housed the junior school. On one corner was a small shed, outside which a young lad with a shock of red hair was collecting money. Joey walked over and asked the lad if he knew where Bobby was. A phone came out and within five minutes Bobby's Range Rover arrived.

'You trying to scrounge another coffee, Nolan?' the gravel voice called as the driver's window slid down.

'If you're buying.'

'Get in.'

Another five minutes and they were walking into Costa. Again. And for once, Bobby had turned off his phone.

'Politicians are like ex-wives, Joe,' Bobby said. 'Never know what they want and when they get it they're never satisfied.'

'What you on about now?'

'You asked me about the car park. They carp on about wanting inward investment and businesses to invest in the community. When you do, they start harassing you.'

Joey laughed. 'I don't think they had you squatting on their land in mind, Bob.'

'Er, careful, Joe. It's not theirs. It's ours. The people's. That's what they don't get. And that carrot head manning the car park? Slung out of school because of his "anti-social" behaviour. His dad's inside. His mum's got something missing upstairs and he's number nine out of, er, twelve I think. That's conjugal visits for you. So no wonder he's anti-social, eh? But he's a brilliant lad. Hard worker. Because I give him what he wants. A bit of love and respect.'

'So you're Uncle Bob, are you?'

'I am more than the Council lot, but . . . That's all I wanted, you know. Bit of encouragement. Want to grab a seat? I'll sort out the order.'

Bobby then walked to the front of the queue to give the order to the young lad on the till. Joey looked round. Every seat seemed to be occupied. Until Bobby noticed him, still hovering. He walked over and gave an exaggerated sigh of disappointment, which was immediately picked up by a group by the window and one near the toilets. Both stood up and offered Bobby their seats. He pointed Joey towards the window group then, with an appreciative wave, he went back to collect the coffees. Joey, slightly embarrassed, eased himself into the still warm chairs.

There was no such embarrassment from Bobby as he came back with napkins and cutlery. Still in full flow about the Council.

'They're supposed to be there for us, aren't they. Not themselves.' The pebble-dash cracked again. 'That's our job, isn't it. Looking out for us and ours.'

Joey gave a nod of agreement. He couldn't fault Bobby's logic.

'Anyway,' Bobby continued. 'They knocked down the junior school, right? Guffing out some tosh about falling school rolls while the population's actually increasing. How'd they get away with it, eh? But they did, and created that big open site. So, I moved a few lads in there and we charge a quid an hour or a fiver for all-day parking. And on market day. Coining it, mate. Coining it.'

'Haven't they tried to move you off?'

'Oh yeah.' The gravel laugh again. 'They hate me. Hate me. I'm even worse than the travellers, aren't I? I'm never going to move on, am I? But in terms of investing in the community I may be trespassing, but I'm not asking for water and 'lecky, and I'm providing a much needed service: cheap parking and a little haven from the traffic wardens. Everyone wins.'

'Except the Council.'

Bobby just gave a dismissive shrug. And then surprised Joey by adding, 'Doing it for my own lad, actually.'

Bobby saw Joey's curious look. 'Got a few legit things building up to pass on to him. That's why I sent him to Hazelhurst like your Sean's kids. Give him a better education than the one we didn't get.'

'We learned a lot more on the streets,' Joey agreed. 'And at night school.'

The gravelly laugh. 'Didn't we just. But it wouldn't be

so romantic in that park these days, having to step over dead smackheads.'

'How'd it get to that stage, Bob?'

'Life doesn't change, Joe. Just the illegal highs. In our day it was send someone into the offie to get the booze, and then back to the swings to split it up before coming down the cut and through the fence at the back. We learned a few things in those goalmouths, didn't we?'

We did indeed, Joey thought back, as the lad from the till brought the coffees over. Bobby gave him two £20 notes.

'Keep a fiver and put the rest towards what they had,' he said as he nodded over to the previous window group now standing near the toilets finishing their drinks.

'So now it's drugs instead of drink?' Joey asked as the lad left.

'Both. It's never either–or, Joe. People want it all.' Abruptly Bobby switched tack. 'They'll have to find a new playground, though. When they turn that old one into houses.'

'Er, how's that go?'

'Everyone knows what's going on. Council. Cops. They can't stop it. So they reckon that if they get rid of the playground there'd be one less place to hide.'

'Just move the problem somewhere else?'

'But it might stop my Max and your Alex discovering they've got a dead druggie in goal.'

'When do you reckon that'll all happen?' Joey asked, completely surprised by the news.

'Soon as the Council can fiddle the planning. The real reason they demolished the old junior school, and the reason they really hate me, is that it's right behind the playground. One big plot to sell off. And I'm the poison pill in the middle.'

'How do you know all this stuff?' Joey asked. But didn't get an immediate response as one of the previous window group came over and thanked Bobby for covering their drinks. Joey smiled. Amazing. He walks in, throws them out of their seats and they end up thanking him. Did people respect or fear him? He remembered him always being in trouble. And saying that if they treated him like a gangster, then he was going to be the best Highbridge had ever seen. No doubts on that score.

'Go on,' Joey continued. 'I keep up with the local paper while I'm away. So how'd you know more?'

'This stuff's never in the papers, Joe. Cops are a good source of stories and the Council's a big spender on ads. Why would the paper really want to upset them by asking awkward questions? Like why the Council is demolishing stuff so they can sell off the playground for houses? You should check it out. Someone will want a sparky if the house deal goes through.'

'And will it? As you seem to know everything.'

Bobby just cracked the pebble-dash. 'My business to know, Joseph. Talking of which. How's your girl's mate today? Sounded like a right slimeball trying to get in her drawers last night. Want us to give him a seeing to?'

Joey felt his back stiffen. A reminder. He was, after all, supping with the devil. And his daughter was going out with the devil's son. No matter what Joey wanted, the devil would protect what he thought was his own.

Joey just grinned and shook his head, no need. He also wanted to steer the conversation back to Bobby.

'Anyway, did you talk to them beforehand?' Joey asked what he thought was a perfectly obvious question. 'They might have let you do it?'

Bobby shook his head. 'Trouble is, Joe, it's like being back in school. They never let you stand up, do they? Never let you get back on your feet. Always waiting to knock you down because of what they think you are.'

'I remember,' Joey said, thinking back to the way he'd been treated differently to Sean. He was the swot. Joey was the scally.

'I'm branded so can't change, even if I wanted to. So they won't even talk, never mind listen to me. Which is OK, because I can play them. Like the travellers. I'm forcing them to go through proper processes and all that bollocks. That'll drag on so long and get so heavy-handed that local support'll force them to let me keep the site. Or find me another one. That'll make it legit. The lad'll then have a car park business to keep going. Just have to keep one step ahead of the buggers. And, I don't know why I'm telling you all this.'

'Because you're leading up to the real point?' Joey asked.

'Rather than distracting me with some tosh about worrying about your kid's inheritance.'

He knew Bobby too well.

Matt was nearly right. It had taken only two hours to recover the Transit, travel to Leather's and set up three of the four cameras on the way back. At each location, Matt had jumped out the side door, rigged and positioned each camera, then set up a cheap but clean laptop on the way back with a 3G dongle. Like the cameras, it too was disposable. They had already placed the camera outside Leather's gates and two on the speed limit signs without any trouble. Apparently two council workmen rigging monitoring equipment. Hiding in plain sight. Invisible.

Unfortunately, when they got to the preferred location of the fourth, the lamppost next to the Welcome to Highbridge sign, they discovered real Council workmen. Not hiding. Actually in plain sight. The lamppost was undergoing routine maintenance. That was ninety minutes ago and there were only so many times they could drive past to see how things were going. The cloak of invisibility would only last so long. Especially since Billy had told them that their new cloned registration plates only had a life of six hours as the donor was in having an MOT.

'Let's hide the van, then come back to this one,' he suggested to Luke, who then pointed the Transit in the direction of the swing bridge.

*

'Fantastic. No. Saturday's great. Thank you. Please tell Craig how delighted we all are,' Sean said as he ended the call and allowed himself a smile. A more demonstrative gesture would have been to punch the air, or go into a semi-crouched position while thrusting his clenched fist forward. However, with young Ben and Deborah on the tills he felt the need to maintain a certain managerial decorum. Nevertheless, he was pleased.

'He's still coming then,' Glynnis asked. She had been hovering while he was on the phone.

'Yes, Glynnis,' Sean replied, his smile broadening. 'Saturday morning to take a look round.'

'Brilliant. I knew he would. Once his mum asked him,' Glynnis responded, a smile also spreading across her face. 'Oh, it's exciting, isn't it?' This was aimed more at Ben and Deborah.

'My mum will be excited,' was all Deborah said.

'Can I tweet it yet, Mr Nolan?' It was Ben, the resident social networking expert.

'Er . . . No, not yet, Ben,' Sean replied. 'Let's wait until he confirms the real thing on Saturday.'

'But you'd better have your thumbs on standby then,' cautioned Glyniss. Cos as soon as he walks in it'll be all over town. I'm telling you.'

Sean shared a knowing smile with Ben. Typical Glynnis – until she turned her attention to him.

'And here's something that might wipe the smile off your face. Remember that 10 per cent discount you gave away to that druggie lot. Well, a couple of your councillor mates are coming in to use it later.'

Glynnis was right. The smile had disappeared, as she continued. 'You know, the ones that are married and claiming two sets of expenses. They phoned up to ask if it applied to lunch as well.' Glynnis's distaste was obvious.

'Oh, what did you tell them?'

'I said, you're a man of your word. And if you're daft enough to offer it in the first place, then you'd be daft enough to give it on lunch as well.'

And with that she headed back to the café.

'Can I tweet that, Mr Nolan?' Ben asked. 'About the councillors coming in?'

'No. I'm giving them enough without the publicity.' He tried to make it sound light. But he was already wondering how much it would cost him in the end.

'Probably scare off people as well,' Deborah suddenly chipped in, before turning to help a woman unload her trolley.

But if they do come in, Sean thought as he headed for his office, at least I can tell them about the business with Noah. And ask what they are doing about it all. That should be worth 10 per cent.

'There, that's it,' Bobby said, sitting back in his chair. 'It's just a, what do they call it, a hypothetical.'

Joey knew it was more than that. If Bobby did, as he claimed, know everything that went on in town, then he was now fishing. The devil was after the detail. And the last thing Joey wanted to do was help him get it.

'So, your plan—'

'Hypothetical,' Bobby corrected.

'Your idea is to round up a few of us and sort out the fat get in the chippy?'

Bobby nodded. Casually. 'Like we used to.' But then it came. Casually again but as Joey knew, fishing. 'Or would you use Carlton and his oppo for that?'

As he'd been expecting it, Joey was able to look surprised. 'Go on, then. What's that mean?'

Bobby leaned forward in his seat. This was not for everyone's ears. 'Just that they like a bit of aggro those boys, don't they. Sign up for it. Get used to it. Must be hard holding back when they know they could sort out stuff like this with a well-timed knock on the door in the middle of the night. Bag over the head. Off the viaduct and into the river. Who'd know?'

'You. As you apparently know everything,' Joey replied and leaned in closer. 'And the police, perhaps?'

The pebbles rattled in Bobby's throat again. 'Now you're winding me up. Or getting confused about policing and justice, Joe. The cops know. Well, most things. Trouble for them is that that isn't their job. Their job is to prove things. Knowing isn't enough.'

'But good enough for you?'

'Natural justice. The only justice people like you and

me believe in. The way they did things in the old days. With strangers' fields.'

'Which was?' Joey asked, intrigued.

Bobby edged even further forward. 'In the old days, villagers sorted things out themselves. Any stranger giving aggro would be taken down to a field. The strangers' field. And sorted out. One by one, each villager would land a blow. Weapon or fist. Didn't matter. Then everyone took a turn in digging the grave. Everyone had to take part. Everyone culpable. Everyone knew everything, so nobody spoke. Mutual responsibility. Mutual respect. That's how we should handle things. People like me and you, Joe.'

Joey was about to protest, but Bobby came back with a quick jab. 'And don't try and give me some old bollocks. I know . . .' he emphasised it. 'I know. You'd soon give someone a good smack if they came near you and yours. Like you would have done last night at the club? Eh? Your trouble, Nolan, as it's always been, is that you can't just walk away. Damsel in distress. Someone getting a hard time. Get yourself involved in things when you don't have to. Max tells me your Tanya's the same.'

The comment stung. Unintentionally. And ironically. That was exactly the opposite to the way Joey was feeling at the moment. He shook his head. He was thinking that he hadn't been doing much getting involved lately when they were interrupted by a voice from behind.

'You two look like you're up to no good.'

They both turned to find Luke standing behind them, a coffee to go in his hand.

'That a bit of the old SAS training? Creeping up on people?' Bobby asked.

Luke shook his head as he joined them. 'Not necessary when people get locked in to their own little worlds.' He indicated how close they were sitting, then pulled a chair round to join them.

Joey noticed he was now, like himself, in a more light-weight jacket and jeans, obviously not having come straight down from the hill.

'So what you doing?' Bobby asked, with a glance to Joey. 'Still hanging round?'

'Just needed a chat with Joe about some electrical work I want doing.'

'Up at your ghost house?'

Luke just grinned. Refusing to be baited. 'Where else?'

It was enough for Joey. There was something else. Otherwise he would have just agreed. The devil also picked up the detail. It was a probe. What did he know? So he fired one back himself.

'Thought your services would be much in demand in this troubled world we live in?' he asked.

Luke followed Bobby's quick glance to Joey, as he also reached to pick up his phone. Luke's arrival had served as a reminder to Bobby that he had been out of touch for too long.

'You going to record this bit, Bob?' Luke asked. It was

a deflection, but a grin showed he was joking. Bobby's counter-sneer showed he wasn't impressed.

'Bobby reckons you and Matt could solve the town's drug problem by throwing people off the viaduct,' Joey said, trying to sound casually incredulous.

It didn't go unnoticed by the devil. It was a heads up on the conversation.

'Ah. How much?' Luke asked Bobby, believing the best form of defence is always attack.

'Where's your community spirit?' Bobby asked with a throaty laugh.

'Expended on some far-flung foreign battleground. Go on, how much?'

'Bobby told me last week he could get it done for fifty quid,' Joey said. 'Or, five hundred for a proper job?'

Bobby took a quick look round in case the wrong sort of ears were within range. Too much detail even for the devil. It was Luke's turn to laugh.

'And how many of these proper jobs end up with the executioner in jail?'

Bobby just shrugged. Like Joey, no matter how tough he felt, there was something cold and measured about Luke that made him feel, if not inadequate, then slightly out of his depth.

'Enough to make it not worthwhile. There's three kinds of crime the cops take seriously. Multiple rape. Serious fraud. And murder. They'll verbal a lot about everything else, as we all do, but when it comes down to it it's those three that frighten the powers that be. Those three that get everyone agitated. Worrying that it could happen to them. Or get people asking questions about why they should keep paying taxes and keeping them in jobs. Why? Because people do a lot to protect their lifestyles.'

He focused on Joey. 'How long you been going up and down the country for a decent job?'

Joey conceded the point, as Luke pressed on. 'And Hilary and her gang aren't really interested in your fake knock-offs, Bob. Or clocking someone doing thirty-five in a thirty. They want to be doing the serious stuff. And so long as they do a good job we put up with all the pettiness that comes with it.' He grinned at Bobby. 'So, five hundred quid? For ten to fifteen years inside?' Shook his head. 'Need to multiply it by a thousand to make it worthwhile.' He then grinned. 'To do a really proper job.'

This time Bobby appeared to miss the look that went between Luke and Joey as he was now scrolling through his accumulated text messages. The look that reminded Joey what he was getting for his money. Something more than community spirit. Revenge for Janey.

'Well, that takes me out of the frame,' Bobby said with another throaty chuckle, as he stood up and waved the phone. He had to go. 'But if you drop your rates, I might have a list you could work your way through.'

With that he headed for the door, then across the street to where his Range Rover was parked half on and half off the pavement.

'Do you really have a job for me?' Joey asked Luke.

'I'm thinking of adding a steam generator to the shower. If anyone asks. But I'm also interested in learning more about the way electricity works. Like you told me how you can always get power from street lights.'

'Go on.'

'Just wondered how, for instance, someone could rig the swing bridge to open. For a prank, say?'

Joey shook his head. 'That'd be a bit of work. You'd have to, I'm guessing, be working with any number of combinations from 11,000 Volt multi-poles, 415 Volt AC, 240-Volt three-phase down to 12-Volt DC control systems. That's why I've got certificates.'

Luke looked deflated. Until Joey grinned. 'But there's an easier way.' Then added, in answer to Luke's curious look, 'Remember Gary McClintock? The guy who used to come to school on his trail bike?'

Luke nodded. 'Got expelled for tearing up the running track doing wheelies or something?'

'Doughnuts. Anyway. He's got the keys to the castle.'

'What?'

'He lives in the old cottage on the towpath. Just along from the control box. Where he . . . ?' He let it hang for Luke to pick up.

'Operates the swing bridge?' Luke asked. Intrigued.

Joey nodded, but noticed that as Luke took this in he seemed a bit more preoccupied with something else. 'And?' he asked.

'One last question from me.' He leaned forward and brought the coffee cup up to his mouth, obscuring his lips, just in case. 'Go or no go?'

'What's that mean?'

'We're trained for point and shoot. In, out, job done, get gone. Someone else always has to consider the consequences. It's always someone else who has to make the final decision.' He left it at that. For Joey to think about. To think through the consequences.

Joey did. For him, Natasha and the kids. Of him getting caught. He had thought of little else since his chat with Natasha. But he'd also thought a lot about Janey. About what had happened and nearly happened to Tanya. And about the young lad found dead on a sports field named after another young lad who'd died tragically from a heart condition. That was a waste. But how much greater waste was it for someone to be killed by drugs?

'If you mean can I live with the consequences of . . . what? Whatever you want to do with your body warmer? Then, yeah. I can.'

The two old friends held each other's eyes for a moment. Understanding. It was go. Before their attention was drawn to the window by the sound of the horn on Bobby's Range Rover, as he roared off.

'Hilary was right. Can't help himself,' Joey laughed. But then turned back to Luke. More serious. 'Do you think he knows anything? Or just guessing?'

Luke remained unfazed. 'Even if he does, he's not going

to talk. The real question is, why is he letting this bunch from out of town operate on his patch?'

It was a good point. And one Joey had completely overlooked. If Bobby did know everything that was going on in Highbridge then he'd know exactly what was really being sold at the chippy. And, much more to the point, was he in on it? Was the devil really fishing to protect his own?

Over by the gas heaters Sean was in deep discussion with Mr and Mrs Councillor.

'Yes, we heard all about the demo. But that is not the way to go about things. There are procedures.' It was Mr Councillor, Malcolm Sawyer, Chair of Education.

'And as for the playground itself, Sean, it's been debated and agreed. It's for the good of the town.' Mrs Councillor, Sarah Sawyer, Chair of Planning, declared in a tone that she expected would bring the conversation to an end.

'Who by?' Sean replied with an incredulous edge that seemed, to the Chair of Planning, to be challenging the very principles of democratic government.

'By the elected members of the Town Council, Sean,' Mr Councillor, Chair of Education, replied on behalf of both himself and his spouse and fellow Chair.

'And did they consult anyone who might be vaguely interested? Like the public they are supposed to represent?'

'We are elected to do the job on their behalf,' Education

responded. 'You know how it works. If you don't like it, you can easily vote us out.'

'Oh come off it, Malcolm,' Sean responded. 'All I'm asking is whether it's true, or not, that you lot are flogging off the kids' playground.'

'It's your tone we are finding objectionable, Sean,' Mrs Councillor, Chair of Planning, replied. Firmly.

Sean decided to take a breath. Count to ten and continue. But he only got to three before Education had had enough of this intrusive invasion of their shopping trip.

'Look, Sean, we are out trying to enjoy ourselves by spending money here, with you. If you feel so strongly about this matter, then write to us formally.' The Chair of Education then took the elbow of Planning to guide her away. Obviously the meeting had been declared over. But Sean stepped in front of them. With Any Other Business.

'Hang on,' he said. 'All right, I might have been a bit harsh, but what is that political saying? If you can't stand the heat, get out of the kitchen?' He glanced round, and smiled, hoping it would defuse the obvious tension. 'Or greenhouse, perhaps?'

'Your apology is accepted, Sean,' Planning responded. 'But Malcolm is right. If you feel . . .'

It hadn't worked. 'I didn't apologise, Sarah. I've . . .' He emphasised the point. 'I've done nothing to apologise for.'

'Are you implying that we have?' Education suddenly blustered.

'Well,' Sean commented, slightly surprised by the vehemence of the reaction. 'What's that other saying about he who protesteth too much? Have you Malcolm? Is there something going on that we, the electorate, should know?'

'How about this, Sean? We won't tell you how to grow plants if you don't tell us how to run the Council. Now, are we still welcome to buy a spot of lunch?'

'Look Malcolm, I know you see yourself as part of some sort of local political dynasty, following on from your dad and granddad, but you are there to represent everyone, remember, not just the ones who voted for you.'

'Well if more people bothered to turn out and vote . . .'

But Mrs Councillor recognised that this was drifting towards a typically male, locked-antlers confrontation so demonstrated why she had become Chair of Planning, and intervened.

'Sean, if what you are asking is, are there any plans under consideration for redeveloping the playground area, then the answer is yes. We have a preferred developer, but all is being done above board and under the EU Procurement Rules. Which we have to abide by, of course, whether we like it or not.'

She succeeded in making the two stags back off, but only long enough to allow Sean to draw breath and come back with another question. 'If that's the case, then how come the public and local media don't know anything about it?'

'Sometimes we have to act, on behalf of the people if you like, under a cloak of commercial confidentiality.'

'And what does that mean?'

'You know as well as we do about all the problems attached to that playground.'

'Yes. Including the young lad who was killed there the other night,' Sean countered.

'We don't know if he was killed,' the Chair of Planning shot back. No doubt as a Point of Information. 'Only that he died. Tragically, perhaps, but we mustn't jump to conclusions. About anything.' It was her turn to emphasise a point.

'Sarah, look . . .' Sean was trying to remain calm in the face of this political stonewalling. 'He died of a drugs overdose. Those who sold him the drugs killed him, in my book. And those who allow that to happen should be . . .' He hesitated as he could see her lips beginning to purse and the Chair of Education's complexion changing to a ruddy hue as his blood pressure was obviously creeping up. 'Should be challenged.'

'Through the proper procedures,' the Chair of Education replied, clearly thinking he needed to educate Sean on the workings of the Council. 'As I said at the outset. And if you have any trouble with that, I suggest you take it up with the Chair of the Council, Councillor Peagram.'

'The Chair of the Council? Why are you being so formal,

Malcolm? What happened to the spirit of public–private partnership?'

'Because, Sean, that only goes so far.'

'As far as a free lunch, perhaps?' Sean regretted it as soon as he said it. He had thrown them a way of getting off the hook. Dignified outrage. Something they appeared well used to deploying.

'Is that really the way you see public service, Sean? Scratching backs and feathering nests?' Education enquired. Loftily.

'None of us enter public service expecting gratitude or favour,' Planning added. For information.

Sean now appreciated how good and formidable a pair they were as he tried to recover. 'I didn't mean . . . That came out wrong. I'm just trying to find out what's happening.'

'Then I suggest that the first thing you find out is how the formal procedures should be followed. But if it suits you better, if you don't like what we say, then, by all means, talk directly to Harold. Now, may we go for lunch?'

Sean knew when he was being stonewalled, or ignored, but tried to smile graciously as he stepped to one side and offered a guiding arm towards the café.

The Chair of Education headed off gruffly, without another word, but the Chair of Planning, the real politician of the pairing, leaned closer to Sean. He thought she might be going to offer some word of political advice. He should have known better.

'I hear Craig Harlow's going to open your Christmas attraction. How thrilling. And we'll be here to support you. I'm a big fan.' She almost sounded guilty, as she gave a hunched-up smile and headed off.

Perhaps he should listen to Glynnis and Sandra more. Especially about running for the Council himself. If he had had any doubts before, he didn't now. Even if it was just to see the look on their faces as they discovered that, in the end, there was no such thing as a free lunch. But, right now, he thought, if word is creeping out I'd better make sure everything works properly for when Craig arrives. And I can throw a bit of work Joey's way at the same time.

Joey had just finished replacing the wattle hurdle fence when the call came from Sean. Could he come over the following day and check the wiring for Santa's Garden as a celebrity was visiting on Saturday?

'That'll be Craig Harlow,' Natasha said when he asked her if she knew anything.

'How'd you know that? Sean just said it's a secret.'

She gave him a look. 'But not from Sandra?'

Joey nodded, then added, 'As you know everything. Is there a tranny working in the optician's?'

'You mean Marian?'

'If I knew I wouldn't be asking, would I?'

'Everyone knows that. He's a bit weird but seems very efficient. So everyone says.'

Joey was about to ask whether he wore a dress to work or not, but noticed the number of plates Natasha handed him.

'What are all these for?'

'It's pizza night. All the kids bring friends over.'

He had no need to say anything. His face said it all. Another of life's rituals he had missed but would have to start getting used to.

'How much else have you not told me about while I've been away?'

She leaned over and kissed him on the cheek. 'Only the stuff you didn't need to worry about. I just set the plates and cutlery. They do the rest online. And I settle down to my spinach and apple salad in front of *Eastenders* and stare at my phone, hoping you will call.'

'Oh yeah? Like the good little wifey?' he teased.

'But I've got you here tonight, haven't I?' Then, with a mischievous seductive laugh, 'In the flesh.' She pulled down her cowl-necked sweater to reveal the Elle Macpherson bra he had bought her for, as she kept reminding him, his last Christmas present. It took him by surprise. Something else his face gave away.

'What's wrong?' she asked.

'Nothing,' he said quickly. Instinctively. Then corrected himself. 'Didn't think you'd be, well, in the mood, after . . . You Know.'

'What? After you confirming what I'd been suspecting for the past month or so? C'mon, Joe. So long as you promise me you won't get directly involved. And it doesn't affect the kids. I don't care . . .' But she hesitated. Correcting herself. That wasn't exactly the way she felt. She did care. About Luke as her brother-in-law. But not for the ones who didn't care about her kids. They were due anything that was coming to them. 'I don't care what happens to the people Luke is after. So long as you keep your promise.'

He reached out to pull her closer, but she resisted the full engulfment. She wanted to look him directly in the eye. Knowing that she would see any nanosecond of doubt. There wasn't any. So she let herself be engulfed. They were, as always, locked together.

Matt and Luke were, if not enjoying, then finishing off another ration pack. Italian Tuna Pasta. Matt had opted for the cherry flavoured isotonic drink while Luke had gone for the lemon. Matt was looking at the empty sachet.

'How come we get Italian pasta from a company in Denmark that has it made in Thailand? Shouldn't they be making Thai curried chicken or something?'

'Italians probably doing that,' Luke responded.

They were sitting in the Transit watching the four camera feeds on the four cheap laptops. Matt had got back to the Highbridge sign and fitted the last camera as soon as the maintenance team moved on for lunch. Thanks to Joey's earlier seminar on tapping into a lamppost's power supply, each camera would be permanently on, even though they expected Leather and his gang to appear mid- to late evening when there would be people around to squeeze. They would use the same global drill. What have you seen? What do you know? Any strangers in town? Who's been here you didn't know? What did they look like? A robust mix of coaxing, cajoling and outright torture, if necessary. The aim was twofold. Gather information. Spread fear.

The laptop was cable-tied to the loading rack just by the side door, and had its power pack connected to a power inverter linked to a deep charge 12-Volt car battery. It would run for the hours they needed it and be rotated with a replacement battery each day, if required. They didn't need a seminar from Joey on that one.

'So Gazza lives down in the old towpath cottage now, does he? Come with the job?' Matt asked.

'Don't think so. But he was mad on fishing, wasn't he?'

Matt nodded. 'And he gets to walk two minutes to work. How'd we contact him?'

'Three rings on his Emergency line. No pick-up. And he'll pop down and open the bridge. According to Joe, he reckons if it's after midnight and we can be in and out within a few minutes no one will kick off. Between about half nine and midnight it'll be fifty-fifty. Any earlier we'll have to break into his cottage, drag him out and make him do it.'

Matt spluttered out half a pack of a fruit and nut mix.

Luke just shrugged. 'That's what Joe said.'

'Does this sound like he's done it before?' Matt asked. 'Or am I being paranoid?'

'Stag do's, apparently! I didn't want any more details,' Luke responded. It was all Matt needed to know.

They sat for a moment dividing up what remained of the ration pack, while going over what each had to do when Leather's crew arrived. They both knew that this time it was not going to be about front. Or bottle. It was going to be win or lose. Nothing else.

'One thing,' Matt suddenly said. 'When this is done . . .' He didn't finish the sentence. He didn't need to. The reflective sadness in his voice was enough.

'OK,' Luke said. 'I know.'

Matt held out a wide five. Luke clasped it. The pact was sealed.

A few hours later they were both asleep. Matt had checked the feed from Leather's house as soon as they got back to the cottage, but there was nothing in the log. No activity. So they had done the only thing they could do. Recharge their own batteries. The old maxim. Sleep when you can. It was something many took to the ultimate level, even sleeping on the helos on their way into a hot zone. Matt was never that relaxed. With the pact agreed, he couldn't wait to get into the fray.

10

Consequences

lthough having to sit through *EastEnders* was not what Joey had in mind for a regular regime, sharing a settee with Natasha was a lot better than a boil in the bag supper with Benno. As the drum fill sounded on the theme music he took advantage of the cowl neck to slide his hand inside to cup her breast. She took it out. She wanted to return to the conversation they had been having before she'd shushed him so she could focus on that night's hook.

'The biggest surprise in all this, Joe, is actually you wanting to be involved with Bobby McBain.'

'Oh, the family's good enough for your daughter is it, Nat, but not for me?' Joey protested, tongue very firmly in cheek.

'There's not much we can do about who Tanya fancies,

although from the picture she showed me he does look quite cute.'

'Well he didn't get that from his dad, did he?' Joey said as he continued to tell Natasha about the conversation with Bobby. How he was trying to set up a few legit businesses to, if not leave his own past behind, then at least give Max a better chance. How it was something all parents wanted and who were they to pre-judge him like everyone else did? And how, once branded, it was difficult to shake off the reputation.

'And what makes you think people still don't ask me why I ended up with you?' she asked, but was smiling.

'He's going to send me a copy of the Council's confidential briefing for potential developers.'

It worked. She was immediately intrigued. 'And how'd he get that?'

'Apparently . . . He knows everything that goes on in town.'

'Which is exactly why you shouldn't get involved. He'll only be getting that briefing through some dodgy dealing.'

'But it would keep me home more.' He slid his hand across to cup her breast again.

'If you don't end up in jail.' But she didn't remove his hand this time. Which was when Tanya came in, just in time to see her father's hand rapidly retreat from inside her mother's top.

'Oh, sorry. I forgot, you didn't get any last night.'

'Tanya!' Joey spat out. In instinctive father mode. As

was his look to Natasha. 'Is this what she's like when I'm not here? As well as out clubbing on a school night?'

'Oh don't start again. Tell him, Mum.'

'I think you're quite capable of telling him yourself,' Natasha replied, not wanting to get involved. It would help Joey catch up if she left him to fend for himself. She stood up and collected the plates. 'Tea, darling?'

Joey nodded, noting the grin. As did Roscoe, who probably decided Joey could cope as he followed the carbonara plates out. Joey turned back to Tanya. 'Look—'

'Don't be so patronising,' the return came back, with power.

'What?'

'People who start by saying "look" are like teachers or politicians who think they obviously know better than the lowlife they are deigning to talk to.'

'OK. I get that. All I was . . . am trying to say is that Bobby and I go back a long way. So, I know what he's like.'

'I'm not seeing him. How gross would that be?'

'I know, but—'

'Dad, look—'

'Deigning to talk to me, are you?'

She gave him the lip curl, folded her arms and bit her lip. The point was obvious. Was there any point talking to him?

'All I'm trying to do is advise you. OK? And you were right, I can't ground you if I'm not here. And I'm not up here because I spent too much time on street corners with the likes of Bobby, and so I am now trying to catch up, to give you all a better choice. A better choice than hanging round street corners and getting up to mischief and . . . you know.'

'What? Get pregnant to get a council house or something?'

'No, of course not. I'm just nervous that Max might end up like his dad.'

Tanya couldn't contain her anger any longer. 'And I get all that. But for God's sake, I've been out with him a couple of times and one of those he had to go home early because Mummy said. You've already done your job, Dad. I can tell the difference between a lad who thinks and one who thinks it's all about what's between his legs.'

He was about to try and recover, when Tanya's friend Carol came bursting into the room.

'Tan, Tan. Oh sorry, Mr Nolan. She's gone.'

Tanya started towards the door. 'What? When?'

'She got a text and then just went,' Carol explained, as she followed, smiling apologetically at Joey, just as Natasha came in with two teas.

'What? What's happening?' she asked, as they heard the front door slam.

Joey shrugged. 'Sounded like the other one's gone AWOL, or something.'

Outside, Tanya and Carol were hurrying to try and catch up with Becky. They ran to the end of the cul-de-sac, but by the time they reached the corner by the main road Becky was climbing into a parked and familiar Mercedes. Too late. Becky was gone.

'And, apart from having a free house tonight, where did that come from?' Sean asked, stroking Sandra's hair as she lay across his chest.

'Dunno, really. That business with Noah. The young lad in the park. The greenery for Janey's grave?' She looked up at him – then kissed his chest. 'Just made me think how lucky we are, really.'

Sean squeezed her closer. 'True. But saying Janey was run over is a bit of a euphemism. Bloody psycho off his head on drugs.'

'That's what made me think about it, I suppose. And, how I like how you get so concerned about things. No matter how daft, or sad, you get about them.'

'I'll take that as a compliment,' Sean responded.

'You can. Just this once. But is Craig Harlow definitely coming tomorrow?'

'So his manager said.'

'Believe it when I see it.'

'Don't think he has a choice. His mum is a big mate of the local paper's editor's mum, apparently. Make a great front page, apparently. So Glynnis tells me.'

'Ah, now I'm beginning to believe,' Sandra commented. It's a powerful thing this mums' mafia,' Sean added, with a smile.

'We do have our uses.'

'So I just witnessed.' Sean laughed, until he saw a maternal flash of admonishment. 'Or was that me being useful for you?'

'Good recovery,' Sandra grinned.

'And Craig on the front page will be better than "local businessman says legalise drugs".'

'Indeed.'

Sean kissed the top of her head and wondered how long he could lie there before she would let him go.

'You can go if you like. Now you've had your wicked way with me.'

'Er . . . who was being wicked with who?'

'I know you want to go and do something else. I can hear your breathing.'

'What's my breathing got to do with anything?'

'You're not relaxed.'

'That was very relaxing, actually.'

'But you want to go and phone Harold Peagram.'

'Who said anything—'

'Sean. How long have we been together?' She pushed herself up and kissed him. 'And why did I say I loved you before?' She then rolled over on her back. 'You can either take me as I am, or make me a cup of tea.'

'Cup of tea?' He'd been with her the same length of time.

'Good choice. As I know you're incapable of anything else.'

He thought of trying to respond but knew he'd lose. So he leaned over, kissed each breast, then her lips, and got up and started to dress.

'I might just see if Harold is in. As you mentioned it. You coming down?'

'Think I'll stay here. Catch up on my Sky box.'

He nodded and headed for the door. 'I'll bring it up in a minute but er . . . what about that snow machine? I think it should be in Santa's Garden.'

'Anywhere you want it, babe.' She was now flicking through her planner. 'And I wouldn't mind a bit of toast.'

'Now that you've burnt off a few calories?'

She hit play and the voice of Benedict Cumberbatch as Sherlock Holmes filled the room. Time to go.

'Are you sure?' Luke asked. One final time. 'Point of no return?'

Matt just nodded. 'I knew where this was likely to end up when I signed on. And if I'm going down, this time I don't want to be caught with nothing more than an expensive club in my hand while some clown is pointing a loaded shotgun at me.'

They were in the back of the Transit, assembling the MP5s. This time with live magazines. There was now no point of separation or ambiguity. No legal eagle on the planet would talk them out of this. Especially with six body bags in the back. They were definitely going out equipped to do serious harm. It was win or lose all round. But they had no intention of losing. Anywhere.

Although they had prepped and were ready to come back night after night, they had read Leather as a man of action. It was shortly after ten, when Gazza had predicted they'd have a fifty-fifty chance of no one complaining about the bridge, when a text alert told Matt there was movement outside Leather's house. Sure enough, on the 3G live feed they saw the gates open and a figure come out, just as the BMW X5 they had followed came into frame. It stopped momentarily to pick him up, then sped off. Several minutes later they saw it come up on camera 2, and a short while later on camera 3. They were on their way. Time to call Gazza.

By the time the X5 passed the Welcome to Highbridge sign, Gazza was in place, Matt was standing at the field entrance, his hi-viz jacket slung over his shoulders to mask both his body armour and the hanging MP5. His task was to walk out into the road in front of the X5, so Gazza could see him and start opening the bridge. At the same time Luke backed out the Transit. At speed. Causing the X5 to slide abruptly to a stop. The internal hand gestures at odds with the politely waved apology from Matt as he guided the van back into the field, then followed with another apologetic arm raise.

Leather and his crew were still gesticulating as they attempted to carry on, only to find the red traffic lights flashing, the barrier dropping and the bridge slowly opening and in doing so masking them from anyone stopping on the other side. There was, as yet, no traffic coming up behind, not that they noticed, as they were too busy trying to top each other's cracks about country yokels. Nor did they notice Matt fling the hi-viz jacket into the field, pull down his balaclava and follow Luke out of the field.

There were four occupants, but none of them noticed Luke slide round the back of the X5, to come up on the rear passenger door. They didn't notice because at the same time Matt was tapping the X5's passenger window with the MP5's suppressor. They all turned to see the red dot dance around the car as the muzzle of the suppressor steadied then gestured for the passenger door window to slide down. All the city-slicker street bravado dissipated. There was the expected moment of hesitation as they tried to figure out what was going on. That was a serious piece of kit pointing at them. Leather said something over his shoulder to the back seat and made a play of putting up his hands as he got out.

As he did, the rear offside passenger door opened quietly, slowly, and a Skorpion machine pistol emerged slightly ahead of its handler, who yelped in pain as the stock of Luke's MP5 hit him hard on his wrist and his hoodie was yanked backwards, fast, down, to the tarmac. Hard. A kick to his side forced the remaining air out of his lungs.

Luke side-footed the Skorpion under the car and

towards the kerb. He then stepped back, put his red dot on the driver's head and gestured for him to get out. It was one of the shaved heads that helped terrorise Fatchops in the park. But now the swagger was gone. Glancing nervously at the writhing figure still gasping desperately for breath, he meekly followed Luke's gesture to pick up the other guy and take him round the back of the car. Luke followed while doing a quick 360 check. Nothing else on the road. Yet.

On the passenger side, both Leather and the fourth occupant had taken in the full blacks, military stance, and the rapidness with which the others had been neutralised. Whatever, or whoever, these guys were, they were serious players. Leather's next assumption, on taking in the MP5s close up, was that it was some form of police SWAT team. An occupational hazard, but at least they would have to play by the rules.

'What the . . . ? We haven't done . . .' was about all he managed to say before Matt's left hand chopped his throat, causing him to gag, gasp and be unable to resist being propelled towards the back of the car where Luke had the other two at the end of his MP5, but with an angle ready to cover Matt. This didn't feel like part of the rules. The fourth occupant, the biggest of them all, obviously the muscle, remained defiant until Luke put his red dot on his chest, with a slight slant of his head. Do you really want this?

Normally, they would be barking commands, using the

most disorientating weapon they carried: their voices. Like all animals, humans are programmed to fear loud noise. Loud voices startle. But not tonight. Tonight was do not attract attention night. Gestures were enough. The guy turned and followed the others towards the field. Once inside and out of sight of the road, Mr Muscle's legs buckled under the force of Luke's boot. As he went down, everything went black as a hood came over his head. He then felt the weight of Luke's knee in his back as his hands were pulled back harshly and zip-tied. The other three soon joined him in a line, on their knees facing the hedge. Tagged and bagged. Out of sight. All now starting to feel real fear. No, this was definitely not part of the rules.

Luke gestured for Matt to go along the line to make sure they were not carrying anything else. And collect their mobile phones. With a nod to Luke to say they were clear, he then went back to check the X5, scooping up the Skorpion as he did, wondering if that too came into the country as parts. Opening the tailgate he found a holdall. By the weight he suspected it was the weapons bag. He hoisted that on to his shoulder then headed back to the field, noticing that the swing bridge was already closing and a car was approaching. He glanced at his watch. Three minutes. Hopefully still on the good side of Gazza's fifty-fifty bet.

Luke had already bundled the driver and the now whimpering Skorpion handler round to the open back doors of the van. Matt put the holdall on the passenger seat and then grabbed Mr Muscle, immediately feeling resistance – he was primed, ready to fight. As was Matt. He spread his legs slightly, so if the guy lunged back he wouldn't be knocked off balance. He then leaned forward.

'Do it,' he said. The challenge unambiguous. Goading.

Immediately Luke sensed the danger. From Matt. Win or lose.

'Problem?' he asked.

Whether it was the proximity of Matt, with his hot, adrenalin-pumped breathing, or Luke's warning tone, the guy unwound and allowed himself to be dragged up and pushed to join the others by the van doors. Matt slowed his breathing and gave a nod to Luke. No problem. Luke returned the nod, but was not fully convinced, as he tugged at Leather's collar to get up.

'You're dead,' Leather hissed at Luke as he begrudgingly allowed himself to be forced towards the van.

'You got that one wrong. I died a long time ago,' Luke replied. Then added. 'Peter.'

At the sound of his name Leather spun back. Now he knew what this was. The guys who had tried to warn him off. But he was roughly turned back to face the van. Then the hoods came off. Suddenly Leather felt weak. In front of him on the floor of the van were the body bags. He realised that was the point. They wanted them all to see the bags before the hoods went back on and they felt themselves being pushed into the van, the doors slammed and the engine started. Leather now felt more than weak. He felt vulnerable. As it sank in. He was inside a steel box. An execution chamber.

'I understand all that, Harold. Yes . . . I do . . . But all I'm saying is that if we, the community, don't do anything then some hothead is going to take it into their own hands. And none of us want that, do we?'

Sean was sitting at the kitchen table, in the Paul Smith black dressing gown Sandra had bought him for his birthday, still talking to Harold Peagram, but was beginning to lose his thread. Sandra was taking advantage of the free house and, having paused Benedict Cumberbatch in mid-sentence, she came gliding in, wearing the Jane Woolrich negligee set he had bought for their last anniversary. She was also looking for the promised cup of tea. Sean mouthed sorry and pointed to the phone.

She pointed to the Jane Woolrich. Which is more important? He knew it was no contest, but had to finish listening to Harold repeating the proper procedures line as he watched Sandra seeming to float around the kitchen, the long silk train appearing to act like a hovercraft skirt. Or a Dalek, he thought. Good job she was anal about keeping the floor clean. But Harold broke through again.

'Well, yes,' Sean switched his attention back to the phone. 'I might. I might even consider running for election myself. I am that serious. Yes.'

He managed to carry on the conversation with Harold

even when she came over and mischievously nuzzled his neck, but with tea made, she playfully scooped up the negligee and let it glide across his head as she left the kitchen. The sensuality of the silk combined with a waft of her perfume was too much.

'Er, Harold, I'll have to call you back.' He was tempted to say that something had come up, but decided against it. 'Yes, I'm free for lunch on Tuesday. Great.' He put the phone down and headed after Sandra. The Council could wait.

Whether it was the sight of the young girls being spit roasted, or the dog attacking the young boy, or the guy being dropped from the crane that sent Matt's pulse and anxiety level off the scale, Luke couldn't be sure. Matt would later say it was the sound. The cries of those being tortured against the sound of Leather laughing, that acted as the tripwire. Whatever it was, they were now looking down at Leather crumpled in a heap in front of them. Put there by several wild strikes of a baseball bat.

It had only taken a few minutes to reach the old chemical quarry. The name was a historical reference. It was in fact a toxic lake. The quarry had originally been used to extract stone but the chemical industry had appropriated it as a convenient and unregulated waste dump. The result was that after a century of dumping no one now knew exactly what was in there. And no one wanted to carry the cost of finding out. Building was prohibited anywhere near it and, although slowly rusting away, the signs on the fence made it clear that you were risking your life by venturing beyond the perimeter. It was a conveniently overlooked legacy of the industrial revolution and, as every local scally knew, the perfect place to get rid of evidence.

It was highly unlikely they would be disturbed while interrogating their guests. They had dragged them out one by one, into the old weighing-in station, to be stripped naked and forced to stand in the stress position. Legs back and spread to put all their weight on their fingertips. Luke and Matt stuck to the drill. Keeping their balaclavas on at all times.

By the time they had brought the last one in, the Skorpion handler, the other three were starting to shiver, while Skorpion was sobbing almost uncontrollably. Mainly through fear but also the stench of his own embarrassment. He had made such a mess of his jeans that Matt doubted any amount of washing would get them fit enough for a charity shop. When he was told to strip, Luke and Matt exchanged surprised looks. They could see this was a young body, still forming, but the back and sides were covered in slowly healing knife slashes. Despite the smell, Matt stepped closer, made him turn round to get a better look, then angled the guy towards Luke. Someone had carved 'For Pete's Sake' on his back. That was the first trigger point.

Matt slammed the stock of his MP5 into Leather's

lower back. Not enough to put him down, but enough to arch his back in pain. Yet, it was the lad that protested.

'Don't. Please. Don't.'

Matt couldn't believe it. He whipped round and yanked the hood off the lad's face, so he could eyeball him. 'You what? You pleading for this . . . this . . .'

But Luke stepped across and physically pulled Matt away. He knew what would now be running through Matt's adrenalin-fuelled mind. The brutalisation of the innocents. But he didn't want that to take control right now. Because he also recognised the lad. It was the Ragged Priest from the quad bikes. Now, with tears running down his face, and legs covered in his own excreta, he looked about twelve but was probably in his mid-teens. And far less threatening than he'd seemed before.

Always the same, Luke thought. Always the kids. He was the only one actually carrying a weapon. The others would try the same line of fiction he and Matt had off pat. Been away. Just back. Not knowing what was in their mate's car. But the naïve, impressionable kid would get a juvenile sentence and be back with the troops in a year or two. Same the world over. The so-called hard men hide behind the kids.

'Please don't hurt him because of me.'

'Why? Got brothers, have you? Said he'd do the same? Or a sister he'd do worse to?'

Even though Leather was still winded, facing away from him with his hood on, the lad was terrified. Luke had been there before. He knew it was hopeless trying to break through a lifetime of conditioning. No matter how short that lifetime had been. He just gave the lad a tap on the shoulder, put the hood back on and put him in the stress position. He was already in his own hell. A bit more suffering wouldn't matter. And it was safer all round.

He then backed away, taking up the watch position. Matt, now calmer, stooped to open the holdall from the X5, into which he had tossed the mobile phones and wallets he had taken off the drug crew. He lifted out three aluminium baseball bats, two cut-down shotguns, the traditional close-quarter weapon of choice, another Skorpion, and a Glock 21 .45 – The higher-calibre handgun of choice for many of the world's more macho law enforcement organisations. Very nice, thought Matt, as he removed the clip and lifted it to show Luke.

'Like your guns, then?' Luke directed at Leather. But received no reply.

'Our guys get banged up for bringing souvenirs like this home. Did you know that?' Matt shouted across to the four naked shiverers. 'Criminal that, I'd say. What do you say?'

Again, no one answered. No one knew how or whether they should risk it.

Luke was also watching Matt. Looking for any more signs of volatility. He still looked calm as he lined up all the six mobile phones the drugs team had had between them. Two – the Samsung Galaxy and iPhone 5 – would probably be their legit domestics. The others a collection of throwaways. He then noticed Luke watching him.

'I'm, OK. OK?' he said.

Luke nodded and watched as Matt stood, made sure his MP5 was on safety and at his back so couldn't be easily grabbed, before going down the line.

'Now,' he started. 'I'm guessing we've all seen the box sets of *The Sopranos* or *The Wire* or *24*. And what Jack Bauer can do to people he doesn't like. We don't want to do that. Well,' he leaned closer to Leather. 'In your case we do, to be honest, but we won't if . . .' he paused for the emphasis. 'If . . . If you just tell us, first, the unlock codes and then, for bonus points, everything else we want to know. OK?'

The two foot soldiers agreed immediately, as they probably only had the throwaways. Mr Muscle told Matt what he could do with the phone, which didn't sound too comfortable, so he edged his feet further from the wall.

Matt then moved back to Leather. 'Well?'

Once again. No response. Which was when Matt took out his Blackhawk folding knife and quickly rammed it into Leather's hand, catching Luke as much by surprise as it did Leather, who let out a squeal as Matt twisted the knife, before yelling out his unlock codes. He was obviously a Jack Bauer fan. Matt looked across to Luke. Did it work?

Luke held his stare for a moment. What was that? Matt

shrugged. He didn't care. Did it work? He nodded towards the phones. Do the codes work?

Luke thought back to seeing Leather drop the guy from the crane. Matt was right. He didn't actually care either. He tried the codes. Then nodded. Leather's phones opened. With pictures of the dog on both. Snarling. So much for Leather's Scouse Spouse. He then disabled the lock codes so they would stay open.

Matt smiled, pleased his tactic had worked, and backed over to Luke who was now scrolling through the Samsung's heavily populated address book. A gold mine, if they knew what they were looking for. He then opened the photo library and among all the usual family, dog, holiday shots he found a video folder named Stuff. He opened it and started looking through the content, his face hardening. Matt leaned over to take a look. And that was the second trigger. When it had really kicked off. What put Leather into a heap on the floor. It didn't explain why they were now searching for him, and the Ragged Priest, in the dark.

Since watching Husani's brake lights slide round the corner at the end of her road, Tanya had not heard or seen a thing from Becky. She was now sitting in Becky's parents' kitchen trying to calm them down while wondering if she should really be doing this role reversal thing. She was even more suspicious of Husani than they were, but here she was with Carol trying to reassure two parents that their daughter was probably safe and just infatuated by some rich guy in a flash car.

When they asked her whether they should call the police she wanted to scream, yes, do it, but when she glanced at Carol she could see her wide eyes were expressing exactly what was going on in her own head. No-o-o. How embarrassing could that be? She'd go crazy if her own mum and dad called the cops if she went off with a new guy. But that's if they knew, she thought as she looked back at Becky's mum now desperately chewing her lip and looking to her husband for support as she was replaying all manner of horror news stories in her head.

'And you think this lad's been stalking her?' she asked.

Another look to Carol who was also beginning to pick up the anxiety and focus her attention on Becky's dad, himself trying to erase the media images from his mind. They had to call the police. It was seeping from every pore. They couldn't just sit and hope, could they? It was conveyed in a look towards Tanya. This isn't fair, she thought. I am just a kid. Really.

And in that moment she decided to do what kids often do. Phone the ones they often ridicule. Their mums.

It had only taken Luke a moment to get across and grab the baseball bat, to stop Matt cracking open Leather's skull. It wasn't that he was fussed one way or the other about what happened to him. The images on his phone had already condemned him. What he was fussed about was having traceable DNA splattered all over the place. It had only taken a moment, but that was all it ever took. One lapse. And from then on you're on the back foot trying to catch up. Like now, out in the dark, without night vision. He never envisaged they would need it and they were, after all, operating on someone else's budget.

After pulling Matt off, Luke had put his fingers on Leather's neck. He had found the pulse. At least he was still alive.

'You should have let me finish him,' Matt whispered as they peered into the darkness. 'While I was in the grip of the beast.'

It was a phrase Matt had adopted to explain the surges of rage. It was part of the post-traumatic stress litany. Matt knew that. As he knew that it was never a problem in normal civvie life. At least not in the parts where people didn't go round terrorising others. Especially kids. That was always the trigger. He knew that too. As did Luke. Ever since the snatch and grab just outside Basra. Going house to house to find the target, they had come across a group gang-banging a small girl. It was outside their rules of engagement so they were backing away, until the rapists sent an eleven-year-old boy old after them with a suicide vest. The boy died, as did the rapists. They'd made a mistake. And given due cause.

Matt had then carried the young girl ten miles to

the field hospital with a shrapnel wound to his thigh. They were both treated, but she later died of her injuries. There's always one moment that does it. Imprints a memory impossible to dislodge. For Luke it was Janey's death. Nothing could dislodge that. And looking across at Matt, now squatting against the opposite wall, working to keep himself under control, Luke knew those memories were why they were both here. Wondering what to do next.

Originally the idea was to snatch them, slap them around, and terrify them to the point that they would agree to move on. But it didn't seem to be going down that route. As soon as he had seen Leather order the crane execution he knew these weren't just street corner dealers. They had, he thought, not missing the irony, stepped into a war without proper intelligence and without a plan for its execution and aftermath. If that is the case, his thoughts continued, we will have to do what we have always done in such circumstances. As they had done at Leather's farmhouse. Improvise.

It was why he was surprised, but not shocked, when Matt stuck the knife into Leather's hand. After how they'd seen him treat the young kid he could have ignored anything Matt wanted to do to him. The next stage of the improvisation was to see what deal could be struck.

'OK,' he had suddenly announced, as much for Matt's benefit as for the drugs crew. 'Let's see where we're up to? I told you to stay away. You didn't. Now, we have you bollock naked. We have your phones. On which are all your contacts and photos. We have your weapons. All of which constitutes enough evidence to put you all away for a very long time. We also have body bags. So, we have a few choices.'

He looked across to Matt who seemed to be in agreement, if curious as to where Luke was going.

'We could leave you all here and call the blue lights,' Luke continued, but saw that didn't particularly appeal to Matt. 'We could simply slot the lot of you and leave you in the body bags.' That got a more considered nod.

'Or,' he continued, looking at Matt, expecting a reaction. 'We could call it a truce and all get to go home.' Matt didn't disappoint. His eyes flared. No way. But Luke held up his hand. 'And never come back.'

Matt was shaking his head. Why was Luke offering a way out? Not only had they seen what Leather was capable of but he would be running the same scenario as Matt was in his head. Say yes. Get home. Recover. Come back better prepared.

But it was Mr Muscle who broke the silence. 'Tell him to go piss—' But it was all he got to say, as Matt placed the muzzle of the MP5 on his back. Shut up.

The driver tried next. 'Say, yes, Pete.' He didn't have to add the begging please.

Eventually. It came. 'OK. OK. Deal.'

Luke turned to Matt. Matt shook his head again. You

can't. Luke nodded. He wasn't. 'Not you,' he then said to Leather. 'But the rest of you can go home tonight.'

He stepped across to Mr Muscle. 'Even you.'

But that was the moment.

Perhaps it was because he was deliberately goading Mr Muscle into action, Luke had just got careless, but the result was the same. Mr Muscle answered as he had all night. With defiance. A pure attack dog. Even though still hooded he pushed himself back from the wall and swung out, just catching Luke a glancing blow. It wasn't enough to knock him down, but it pushed him across Matt's line of vision. By the time it cleared, Mr Muscle had his hood off and was grabbing the driver and pushing him towards Matt. He then turned and ran for the door, but Matt had sidestepped, grabbed another of the baseball bats and cut him off at the knees. He then dropped his weight on to Muscle's back, yanked his hands round and zip-tied them again. This time attaching him to the remnants of the old cast iron heating system. After putting the hood back on he looked across to see Luke doing the same to the driver. But Leather had gone. Along with the young kid.

A moment. That's all it takes.

'There's coppers all over the place, Joe.'

It was Gazza. Calling Joey. Telling him what had happened at the bridge.

'Do they know the bridge was open?'

'No, don't think so. Just saw them talking to a couple of wrinklies who got stuck behind a car.'

'OK, then go home. And Gaz . . .'

'Yeah?'

'Thanks. But don't call me again on this number. OK?'

'Er . . . yeah. OK, Joe. And er . . . We quits now, yeah?'

'No problem.' Joey ended the call and turned back to the house, only to find Natasha leaning on the open patio door.

'Who was that?'

He just looked at her. She nodded. Remembering. She didn't want to know. 'Although,' she then said, 'I would like to know what's going on with Tanya.' She turned back to the house, but stopped. 'Is that a new phone?'

'Er . . . yeah. Something I picked up from Bobby.'

She turned as her own phone rang inside. Going to answer it she shouted back, 'I hope it wasn't one of his knock-offs.'

Joey followed with a wry grin. He hadn't been referring to the phone itself. Only its disposability.

'There,' Matt hissed. Directing his hand and Luke's eyeline to a small weed-covered mound about 30 yards to their right.

Luke nodded when he saw the small movement. A sniper's target. A geometric shape in amongst nature's chaos of weeds. A head. Trying to determine where they were. Despite having neither night vision headsets nor sights on the MP5s, they did have one small advantage. The pasty white skin of the young kid. While their blacks would make them hard to see, even in a half-moon naked flesh would jump out. Matt had rolled off to his right to try and work his way round to their left side, while Luke moved to the left, to come up on their right. At least they didn't have any weapons. Luke had checked they were all still in the holdall and that was now locked in the van.

Coming level with the mound, Luke could see Leather and the kid had run out of places to go. They were on the edge of the quarry.

Luke waited until Matt's red dot danced across the crouching figures. He then stood up and flicked on his own, so that it was clear they were now caught in a cross-fire. Slowly Leather stood up. Again the hands were up in surrender. He was still hoping to deal his way out. Slightly more nervous, the young lad looked up at Leather, who flicked his head to tell him to give up. He too started to rise slowly, until he was quickly grabbed by Leather, who twisted his arm behind his back and held his throat, to use him as a human shield.

'What's the point?' Luke called. 'You're not going anywhere.'

But Leather thought he had a bargaining chip. Their emotions. He had noted their reactions to seeing the cuts on the kid. He'd use that as a way out. He tightened his grip on the lad's throat, causing his eyes to widen in pain and confusion.

'That deal you offered. I'm up for it.'

'It's not on the table any more,' Matt said, as he moved closer, maintaining an arc of separation so that Leather had to keep glancing from side to side.

'I'll toss in the kid.' He then laughed at what was coming. 'Either in the deal. You lay down your weapons, let me walk away . . . Or . . . I'll toss him over the edge.'

'What sort of daft offer is that?' Matt asked. 'You'll be dead then.'

The young lad was sobbing again. 'Please. Please,' he kept repeating.

'I was dead inside there, wasn't I? But I'm here now. And . . . I'm guessing – but I don't think you want this fella to die, do you?'

Luke glanced at Matt. He was fifty-fifty. But Luke could see the beast emerging.

'Go on,' Leather continued. 'You'll get what you want. I won't come back. I can't, can I? You've got all that evidence. Like you said. And the kid lives.'

He squeezed again. The lad gagged.

'OK. OK,' Luke called and lowered his weapon, gesturing for Matt to do likewise. 'OK, Deal. Let the kid go . . .'

Leather, more suspicious of Matt, turned to take a quick look at what he was doing. It was all Luke needed. To quickly bring the MP5 back up. Just a moment when enough of Leather's head came into Luke's reticle. Just enough for the kill. Two quick *phludffers* and it was done.

377

The force of the double-tap took Leather back towards the edge of the quarry, but to Luke and Matt's horror the young lad went with him. He hadn't been hit. Leather had died instantly so was no longer holding him. The horror was that the young lad had lunged and grabbed him, to try and save him going over the edge, but his weight had pulled the lad over as well. By the time Luke and Matt got to the quarry top, all they could see were the ripples spreading across the moonlit caustic pool.

Natasha had only been on the phone 30 seconds when Joey heard her tell someone to stay where they were. She was on her way. He was then designated babysitter as she scooped up her handbag and keys to the Q7. Before long she was at Becky's house, where, having been brought quickly up to date by Tanya, she had turned to Becky's mum. 'I wouldn't risk Becky's safety because we all feel embarrassed.'

This was all Becky's dad needed, and he went to the phone. 'But you are sure she went off with this Husachi, fella?' he asked. It was directed at Tanya.

She nodded, but corrected the name. 'Husani.'

'Jesus Christ,' Matt said as he and Luke watched the ripples starting to fade away. 'I thought I'd seen it all . . . But what was that about?'

Luke didn't have any immediate answer. He could say they'd seen tortured hostages trying to protect their tormentors before. But that was usually in fear of the future. This one had none. He'd also told Joey that he and Matt were damaged. The things they'd seen. The things they'd done. To survive. But there always seemed to be something else. He'd learned not to dwell. That way only took him to deeper pits. And lost focus. They still had to clear up. He turned away and went back to gather up the holdall.

Matt dropped down on his haunches. Staring down at the now calm quarry lake below until Luke came back.

'If you didn't know what was in it,' Matt said, 'you could say it looks quite picturesque, couldn't you?'

'Every picture hides a story?' Luke asked, as he unpacked the guns.

Matt nodded. But was asking himself the question he knew had no answer. Why does it always have to be like this? People in terror of psychos. Who always weaponise the kids. He knew the tactical reason. Because of what had just happened. The good guys always baulked at harming kids. That gave an advantage. A weakness to exploit. And that thought alone, he reflected, proved how screwed up it all was. Calling it a weakness? Caring about kids?

His attention was caught by three splashes as Luke tossed the cut-down shotguns over the edge. Then the Skorpions.

'Shame about the Glock,' Luke commented as he

followed its trajectory to see the splash. But, on top of everything else, they didn't want to get caught with weapons that might be traced back to whatever Leather and his crew had been up to. The bloodied baseball bat and its two companions went next. It would be a long time before anyone ventured into that chemical stew. And even if they did, the odds were that the guns would be traced back and the assumption made that it was all part of some drugs war.

Luke then turned to Matt. 'You OK?'

Matt nodded and stood up. 'You mean can I hold it together?' There was more than a slight edge to the question. But it was controlled.

'Well?' Luke asked again. Adding his own edge. 'Nothing new.'

'Except it's on our own friggin' doorstep?' More edgy.

'Which is why we agreed to do this. Yeah?' Luke spat back. 'That kid . . . Those like him. No matter what we think. Or feel. About where and how they got like they do. You know. They'd still kill us if told to.'

Matt hesitated. He did know. But that didn't make witnessing it any easier. But after a moment he nodded. 'Just . . . I get it when we're away. Foreign. But it shouldn't be . . . Not back home.'

'And I should be happily married now?' Luke asked, the irony weighing heavy.

This brought Matt back. What Luke had been through. Why they were doing this. He finally touched his friend on the shoulder. 'Sorry. Didn't think anything could get to me any more. Perhaps my PTSD is wearing off.'

'Do you want a hug?' Luke asked, adding a grin.

Matt gave a sardonic smile. 'Now who's engaging in displacement therapy?' He bent, picked up the holdall and tossed it into the lake. The moment had come and gone. 'What now? We still on for the other?' he asked.

Luke nodded and held out another wide five. The pact was solid. 'Just need to sort the other two out first.'

Matt took a last look down at the lake. Still once again. It was anyone's guess what's down there, he thought as he turned to follow Luke back into the weighing-in shed.

'Got away did he?' Mr Muscle asked, sneering, as he heard Luke and Matt enter.

Luke went over, checked he was still cable-tied to the pipe, then pulled the hood off. He was still in his balaclava but wanted to see Mr Muscle's eyes. Wide, glaring, hard. Hate. 'Let's just say he's not with us any more. OK?'

Mr Muscle stared back, trying to process this information, until Matt helped him out. Lifted the muzzle of the MP5 and pushed it against his nostrils. He didn't have to phone a friend. He could smell it. And, finally, the eyes narrowed. Fear.

Matt moved across to the driver and repeated the process. 'What about you? Want to follow your leader?'

'No. No. I said . . . Before . . . I said . . . I'll take the deal back. I swear.'

Matt turned to Luke. What do you think?

Luke looked at the two remaining captives. Even Mr Muscle now looked subdued. But Luke kicked him to test his reaction. He didn't get one.

Matt took over. 'C'mon. You go along with it?'

Mr Muscle nodded. But it wasn't enough.

'I'd like to hear it,' Matt prompted, putting the Blackhawk knife against his face.

'OK. I'll take the deal back, too,' he shouted. The eyes back wide and full of hate. 'We won't come over here. But, if I ever see you anywhere near our territory . . .'

'Yeah, yeah,' Matt said as he pulled the hood back over his head. He then went to do the same to the driver. Who immediately tried to pull away.

'I'll . . . I'll do . . . I'll do anything you want. Or say. I will,' he gabbled quickly. Still petrified.

'All right. Chill. We have a deal, don't we? Someone will come and get you.'

The driver flopped backward. Relief. Exhaustion. But found himself being pulled forward as Matt tugged the hood off again.

'One last thing. That kid. After what your mate seemed to have done to him . . . Why? Why'd he . . .' he glanced in the direction of the lake, thinking of the way the young lad had tried to stop Leather from falling. 'Why was he so protective?'

The driver looked away. He didn't want to go there. But Matt yanked his head round. 'What?'

The driver hesitated again. 'What?' Matt asked again. More forceful.

'Pete was his dad.'

Matt almost stumbled backwards. But Luke was already right on his shoulder, thankful that bit of news hadn't come out earlier.

At the swing bridge Hilary was talking to her officers who had responded to a call about an abandoned car blocking the bridge. She was off duty, having stopped on her way back from visiting her parents. She learned that no one seemed to have seen anything. The occupants of the car had just disappeared. Already there was talk of an alien abduction. While Hilary considered they might be alien to Highbridge, she was sure they were of this world. Regional Crime had flagged the car as registered to one of the regional drug lords. And the APNR had it logged as coming in and out of town a few days ago. It was enough for Hilary. Two and two were not only making five. But six, seven and eight.

'It should make you feel better, shouldn't it?' Matt asked, as they tossed their bags into the hire car outside the cottage. 'Knowing you've dug out a parasite. But . . .' He shook his head and went back to contemplating the question with no answer.

Luke set the cottage alarm, locked up and headed for the driver's seat. He was not going to let Matt get them pulled over for speeding. Before he dropped into the car he took a long look at the cottage, then across the roof of the car to Matt. 'It makes me feel better, if that's any help.'

'That'll do, for now. But . . .' he carried on, as he got into the car, 'another one'll pop up. They always do.'

'But it'll buy time. That's what we always do. C'mon, let's get it finished and get gone.'

He had already texted Joey on the pay and throw, which he had then dropped into the bag along with the others, the Motorolas and the drone, which they would leave for Billy Higham under the railway bridge. They were still in their blacks. The balaclavas and body armour were on the back seat. With the MP5s. Within reach.

Having served its purpose, the Transit van had been collected and was now being driven down the track that led down to the old salt quay, long abandoned since canal barges had been displaced by trucks. The only people who went down there now were hard-core dog walkers and the occasional teenage taboo breaker. And the summer kayakers who usually generated a bit of interest in trying to restore the quay as a tourist attraction, reminding everyone that it was the Romans who originally built it. No one took any notice.

Nor was there anyone around to notice the driver get out and go to the engine compartment. Nor would anyone have noticed him remove a spark plug and squirt in a bit of water. They might have noticed the clanking clunk as the engine fired, then seized solid as piston, water and cylinder head all met with the explosive impact of ignited diesel. As water cannot be compressed it was the steel that gave way. The engine was now useless so the van could not be driven away. Soon it would be an easy target for teenage curiosity and spares vultures. A stripped carcass to the passing onlooker, but a cornucopia of mixed DNA to a forensic examiner.

In all this, the only thing anyone might have noticed was the shock of red hair as Bobby McBain's car park manager jogged away into the night, tossing his biodegradable rubber gloves into the canal.

Joey had received the text from Luke and deleted it straight away. It took him a moment or two to gather his thoughts, then his tool kit. With Natasha off fetching Tanya, it was an easy win getting the boys to stay put by saying he had to pop out. In the Jag. If Natasha left them alone while he'd been away, he was sure they'd be OK for half an hour.

Twenty minutes later Joey had pulled the ancient fuse that still controlled the street supply. Everywhere went dark, including the chippy's CCTV system. But not Joey's phone. It vibrated. It was Luke again. On his real phone. TA MEET COTTAGE 20. A few seconds later he heard the jangling crash of the chippy's front door being smashed. He headed off up the street, not looking back. Just as he was told.

Inside the chippy, Fatchops had shown another turn of speed as he came out of the back to see what the commotion was, only to find himself grabbed, spun, slammed into the tiled wall and dazed, as his arms were pulled back and zipped together. He was then shoved through back into the rear. The biggest human shield Luke and Matt had encountered to date.

They passed though the neatly tidied workspace, everything cleaned and stored. Just so. Everything as Fatchops's Mr Sheen POLO. It smelt of disinfectant. Unlike the smell that greeted them when them went through the door to the living space. Tobacco. Alcohol. Cannabis.

The bearded one was there. Sprawled on a settee watching *Newsnight*, with two young girls leaning either side, neither of them appearing too interested in current affairs. One looked asleep, drunk or drugged, while the other was stripped down to her underwear and undergoing a slow breast massage.

It was a moment for the bearded one to realise that Fatchops was walking rather oddly. Like some form of giant, obese penguin. With two smaller penguins following. Too late his vision cleared and the penguins were upon him. He tried to react but even without the weight of the girls he found himself trapped under the falling mass of Fatchops. Luke stayed with them as Matt went on through the house, MP5 raised and ready.

It took him seconds to check the ground floor and go up the stairs two at a time, opting for speed and surprise rather than stealth. Four doors off a small landing. He went into the first. Bathroom. Nothing. Second door. Messy bedroom. But nothing. He crossed the landing. Third room. This was it. On the bed was a man having sex with a girl young enough to be his granddaughter. He was overweight. White. To one side were two others, more like uncles, one black, recording it on his phone while the other, Asian, was stripping off. Obviously next.

The girl was crying and asking for the old guy to stop which, unfortunately, seemed to be what he was after, as he turned and played up to the phone. His gurning face turned to shock as he saw Matt, but the phone-holder didn't, until he was flipped round and felt the full force of a head butt. He fell next to the other one, now trying to dance away with his jeans round his ankles, who then felt his legs kicked sideways, his head hit the floor and then his chest crushed as Grandpa was yanked backwards off the girl and dumped on top of him. As Matt's boot came down on Grandpa's genitals, the girl rolled off the bed and curled up in a corner.

While zipping all their hands, Matt tried to make reassuring noises and gestures to the girl until she calmed down, finally appreciating that he might be a good guy. He then indicated that she should stay put, while he went to check out the remaining room. When he got there, his stomach turned. Curled up on the bed was Joey's girl's mate. The one he had seen being dragged away the other night. Damn.

Downstairs. Luke had other problems. Crunching glass. Someone was in the chippy. Having secured the bearded one Luke knew he wouldn't be going anywhere, especially as he had tethered him to Fatchops. He gestured for the girls to be quiet. They nodded. Too frightened to do otherwise. He then slowly made his way back through the food preparation area and took a quick look from the darkened space into the chippy, lit by the sodium glow from the street lights. It was Hilary Jardine.

11

Resolution

Joey had made a critical mistake. He had let his heart rule his head. Despite being told not to stop, not to look back, for anything, he couldn't walk past the old boy struggling to get his wheelie bin out the front door. In the dark. The darkness he was responsible for. He stopped to help, but then found himself inevitably turning and glancing down the road – to see Hilary Jardine stepping into the chippy. Could he just walk away now? Not look back? Knowing what Luke had told him about fighting his way out?

No matter what. Luke had repeated it. Over and over again No matter what. You can't get involved. Walk away, Joey told himself. Walk away. But he couldn't. Not when two of his oldest friends were about to confront each other. It would only end badly for one of them. And Joey knew that would be Hilary. No matter what came after, right there on that street, he knew Luke would do anything to get away. And if anything did happen to Hilary, it would be his fault.

Luke was also running through the scenario. She's sussed it. But she was alone. Out of uniform. No blue lights. What's that mean? Trying to prevent something? Old times' sake? Only one way to find out. He took another quick look. She had her back to him, examining the smashed door. He pulled off his balaclava and unclipped the MP5 as he quietly stepped out into the shop, putting the gun just behind the counter, out of her sight.

'What you doing here?'

She spun round to face him. The confirmation clear. 'Should I be asking you the same?'

'Just saying goodbye, actually.'

She started to walk across but he held his hand up, with a quick glance sideways to the MP5. 'Don't.'

'Why?'

'There's something here you shouldn't see.'

'Really?' It was a challenge. He was questioning her authority. She pointed at his body armour. 'And I suppose that is to protect you from the hot oil?'

He held her stare. Knowing this was the point. No going back. Win or lose. But one last try.

'Hilary, please, can you just take my word.' Then he hardened the edge. The language became clipped. Of command. 'You do not . . . Want to get involved in this. Right now.'

'Think I've seen enough already,' she responded. Her own crisp tone now that of the Superintendent, not the old friend. This was her jurisdiction. Her authority.

But he came back. Harder. One of them had to get the upper hand. 'Believe me. If you do get involved you'll have to act. And . . .' He paused. Another of those moments. No going back. 'And I'll have to respond.'

It was unemotional. Calm. Cold. A coldness that Hilary had not been expecting. Just as she had not expected to feel her pulse rate increasing in direct proportion to her anxiety, as the preconception of the hot-headed guy she used to know was forced out of her head. This was now nothing more than a threat standing in front of her. The past friendship might just allow her to back away, but nothing more. She had to let the training come though. Even though she was wearing a Per Una Quilted Stormwear overcoat instead of body armour, and armed with nothing more than her John Lewis Coney across body handbag.

So they stood. The head girl up against the playground vigilante. But a lot of time, water and trauma had flowed by. And, back then, neither of them carried weapons. She was sure that was what he had on the countertop. Just as she knew he was right. If she saw him with a weapon there was no choice. No going back. He was also right about one other thing. She didn't want that. Right now. Which is why she had come alone.

'OK,' she said. 'I'll blink first, if that's what you want.'

She moved to one side, deliberately allowing him to see

that she was obscuring any possible view of what he might have on the countertop. But she also wanted to let him know that she was working it out. She pointed at the single point sling hanging from his shoulder. 'And I don't suppose that is for attaching your ID to?'

'Among other things,' he replied. But he smiled. That moment had been defused.

But not for long. Luke suddenly caught something in his peripheral vision. A head taking a quick glance through the window. He stepped towards the counter – towards his weapon, Hilary thought, as she saw his eyes were now locked on the window. She turned to see a figure, silhouetted against the street lights, slowly making for the door.

'No, stop,' Hilary called, spinning back and forth between Luke and the approaching figure. 'Stop. Stay where you are. Both of you.'

She was relieved to see Luke step back from the counter, but surprised by the reason.

'What? What's going on?' Joey asked from the door.

Back in the house, Matt had corralled the gang-bangers downstairs and had them lined up, on their knees next to Fatchops and the bearded one. A motley multi-ethnic mix. He had the phone they'd been using upstairs, and was going along slowly, recording each of their faces. A bewildered Becky was helping the now dressed but still sobbing girl from upstairs into the room to sit next to the equally bewildered girls on the settee. They had come for a party and had ended up in a horror movie.

'What the hell you want?' Fatchops asked. Defiant. 'No money here.'

The beast within Matt was on him in a moment, back-handing his head. Not enough to put him down, just enough to shut him up.

'What I want, is for you to stop doing what you do out there.' He pointed to the chippy, then turned to the others, held up the phone. 'What I want, is for you lot to leave these kids alone. But you probably can't, can you. So I'll have to stop you, won't I?'

He raised the MP5 and put the red dot on Fatchops's head. Which was when he heard someone fumbling with the back door. Someone was trying to get in.

Out front, Luke and Hilary were still holding their ground, holding their stares, as Joey was babbling about having fancied some fish and chips, then saw the door smashed in, and then seeing them. Hilary knew this was all nonsense. She had seen the look that quickly went between Luke and Joey. She hadn't been able to read it but she knew it was connected to her earlier suspicions about Luke's return.

'Go on, then. What's going on?' Joey asked again. Carrying on the charade. Hoping to find a way out. For them all. But that wasn't likely to happen as the street outside started to strobe blue.

They turned to look in unison. Joey looked alarmed as Luke again moved towards the MP5. Hilary turned back and held out an arm for him to stop.

'It's nothing to do with me. This time, trust me, Luke. Let me check.' Then she turned to Joey. 'Stop him. Whatever he's planning.'

It was the old friend, now crunching across the glass towards the street.

Joey and Luke watched her pulling her warrant card from her handbag as she met the approaching patrol car. Ordinary markings. And ordinary beat bobbies getting out. This was not an armed response team.

'I told you not to—' Luke started to say, but Joey cut across him.

'I know, but what did you expect me to do, seeing her coming in here? But now's your chance. Take it.'

Luke took another look outside. Hilary was in deep conversation and pointing up and down the street. It didn't seem like she was summoning reinforcements. There was still time. He picked up the MP5, causing Joey to step back in surprise.

Luke grinned. 'What did you think we were going to do? Hand out Bibles and hope they found God?'

'Er . . . No . . . But I . . .' He was back to the gibbering schoolboy in front of the military pro.

'We're doing this because we want to, Joe. Remember. Our choice. Just as it's our choice not to be taken. Win or lose.'

394

'What? You'd really shoot . . . You'd shoot your way out?'

'That's what we do. And what you do, is forget this.' He tapped the MP5. 'And tell her –' he nodded out the window – 'you know nothing.'

'OK,' Joey said, turning to glance at Hilary outside. When he turned back, Luke had gone.

Matt, behind the rear door as it opened, stepped out and hit the new arrival square between the shoulder blades with the MP5. Even with live rounds it was still a very expensive, but effective, club. The new arrival hit the wall opposite and then sideways, his head going one way, his legs the other as Matt executed the well-practised move, letting the target's own body weight do most of the damage. Matt was just bringing in the prone figure to add to the line-up when Luke came through from the front of the shop, carrying his MP5 and saying they had to go, and Becky started screaming.

'Stop . . . Stop . . . You can't . . .'

She flung herself on the new arrival. It was Husani.

Luke pulled her away as Matt forced Husani down on to his knees. Was this more of what he'd witnessed up at the quarry? Victim dependency? But there was something else in her voice.

'Please . . . please . . . He's not one of them. He isn't.'

And then it echoed back. 'I'm not, I'm not,' Husani gabbled, realising the situation he had walked into. He then turned to Fatchops. Anger. Real. And rattled off something in what sounded to Matt like Serbian, but whatever it was the disgust and disdain was clear. As was the blaze of anger in Fatchops's eyes about something of which he'd just been accused.

Matt stepped forward and backhanded Husani across the head. 'English.' They had been in this one before, too.

Becky leapt up. 'Leave him alone. He's done nothing.'

Matt rounded on her. 'And you can understand English. So, sit down and keep quiet.'

She did so, but only after Husani nodded. Then turned to Matt. 'I said he had let me down. I asked him to watch over her.'

'And I did,' Fatchops replied angrily. In English. 'She was safe in another room. Until they came.' He glared at Luke and Matt.

Husani ignored him, still trying to make a connection with Matt. 'I asked him to do this, while I,' he threw another look of disdain at Fatchops. 'Until I went to get money.'

'What for?' Matt asked. Still suspicious.

Husani hesitated. And looked to Becky. She didn't hesitate.

'We're going away. To get married.'

She might as well have thrown a stun grenade.

Outside in the street, Hilary had discovered that the patrol car was just that. And had been asked to check out the chippy in case there was a young girl, Becky Hargreaves, hanging out there. Then they saw the street in darkness. Hilary had explained her presence by saying she had been passing and saw the chippy door broken. She was about to call for backup, but in the meantime they should check with the neighbours who were out trying to discover what had happened to the electricity.

She stood for a moment. Point of decision. Or no return. She looked up and down the street at the growing number of people drawn by the blue lights. Sometimes they attract more trouble than they solve, she thought, as she reached into the car and switched them off.

'That might give Luke some reassurance,' she said to Joey as he stepped out of the chippy, still trying to digest what Luke had just told him.

'He's gone anyway,' Joey said, hoping it would slow her down. It didn't. She pushed past him and went inside, making sure she was out of earshot of the street before calling Luke's name.

Joey decided, this time, to take Luke's advice and stayed outside.

After a moment, Hilary decided to go through to the back, but found her way blocked by Luke. That was the last thing he wanted her to do. Once again he left the MP5 out of her sight.

'They came looking for a young girl,' Hilary immediately offered.

It worked. He relaxed. Slightly. 'She's in the back,' he

told her, but then added quickly, seeing her concerned look, 'She's OK. With her fiancé, apparently.'

She looked a little surprised, but that wasn't her concern right then.

'I can't just let you walk away, Luke.' She glanced outside. 'Not now they are here. They know I've been in here.'

They held each other's eyes again briefly as Luke digested her words. The chain of command. 'OK,' he said. 'This time I'll do the blinking. We'll go out the back.'

'No, that's not what I meant.' Neither head girl nor old friend. Back to win or lose.

Luke considered. Then nodded slowly. 'I understand, but . . .' he paused again, trying to find the words. 'OK. I know you'll have figured out what this is all about. Who and what we've become. Just as you know what this is for.' He flicked the lanyard.

'I have my own weapons team,' she countered.

'You have. But you need to know that we will use ours to get out.'

That was it. The last step. No going back.

'That a threat?'

'Just a fact. And your call.' He stepped back. His voice became clipped again. 'I've always like you, Hilary. I respect what you have to do. But you must be clear. Right now. Don't follow.' He held her stare, before adding, 'Please.'

With that he stepped away and went through into the back.

She stood for a moment. Should she follow? Would he really harm her – or respect her authority? But the training came through. Don't be a hero. Call for backup. She turned and headed outside for the police radio.

On the pavement Joey was hovering. He followed her to the patrol car.

'What's going on?'

'It's an operational matter now, Joe. Keep out of it.'

'Are you sure you really want to do that?'

'I have no choice.'

'And neither does he. Did he tell you that?'

She rounded on him. What did he really know? 'Tell me what?'

Joey saw the look. The official look. The look that said he had to be very careful. 'What he's told me a thousand times in the past. That, after Janey, he just doesn't care what happens to him.'

She turned away, dismissing that as pub talk. Joey tried again.

'What about suicide by cop, Hilary? Have you thought of that?' Joey was making it up as he went along, trying to make sure he didn't say anything that could be tagged to a conspiracy charge later. Like Hilary, he knew the old relationship would only get him so far. But it got her to hesitate.

'And even if it's not that, are your guys really up to taking on those two psychos?'

'It's what they are trained for, Joe.'

'Are they? Really? I'm guessing here, but they might be good on the practice range or in training drills. Or taking down the odd psycho or schizo with superior numbers and weapons. Perhaps keeping the lid on something until someone like Luke turns up to clear it? But how good will your guys really be under a military-style attack? What's your acceptable body-bag count, Hilary?'

It hit home. Whether she liked it or not, it had elements of truth within it. She knew the firearms teams would do what was asked, but she also knew that part of their ethos was avoiding conflict. Containment was what they were trained for.

'What do you expect me to do, Joe? I can't just turn a blind eye.'

'It's what I don't want you to do, actually, Hilary. Like causing someone to write letters to the families of the guys you will lose. Explaining that they died needlessly. Or, just guessing again, will that come from some later investigation?'

She tried to respond, but couldn't immediately. Her mind was still sorting the cascade of images it was conjuring up from Joey's words and Luke's chilling response. Before she could get things sorted, Joey threw one more at her.

'Do you really want to put your team in harm's way?'

Fatchops now felt in harm's way as Luke had dragged him back into the food preparation area and told him to start the fire.

'I . . . I can not . . . They, they'll come. Worse than you.'

'I doubt that,' Luke replied. 'Get on with it. I want you to burn your own house down.'

'Why? Why you ruin my life?'

'Maybe because you've been doing that to the kids round here.'

'That not me. That just life.'

'And this is a life-changing moment. That's if . . .' Luke suggested, 'you want to keep your life. Your choice.'

It was decision time. For Luke and Matt it was only what they left behind. For Hilary it was everything. The final decision wouldn't be hers. She knew the chain of command as well as Luke. But her duty was to set things in motion. Refer up. If she didn't, her career, at the very least, would be over. If she did . . . well, she had spent enough time reading the post-trauma reports. Could she cope with that? To send in the tactical response team wouldn't be her decision, but she knew, ultimately, that she would shoulder the responsibility if it went as Luke had warned her. No matter. She knew what she had to do. She reached for her phone. At least Luke would have ten minutes. And she guessed he would know that too.

Having used some of those precious minutes on Fatchops, to Luke the smoke that was now billowing out of the chippy seemed to indicate that he had made the right choice. That same smoke now masked the departure of Becky, Husani, and the three young girls, shepherded by Luke and Matt, MP5s at the ready, but pulling off their balaclavas. Matt was carrying the girl from the bed. He put her down at the top of the alley.

'Take her to the health centre for a check,' he said. 'And tell them what happened to her. OK?'

But the girls hesitated, throwing worried looks down the alley at the smoke billowing out of the chippy.

Matt took out the phone he had taken from the Asian granddad. 'This is going to the local paper. So their families, friends, neighbours and assorted bigots and racists will know what they've been up to. I doubt they'll stay around for long. Now go. She needs help.'

They all nodded and walked away. Matt watched them go, still controlling the beast, as he knew this one would survive, before turning to Husani.

'How'd you get in? I could have blown your head off.'

'Borrowed the keys from my cousin. The one with the beard,' he explained.

Matt nodded. 'Sorry about back there. Occupational hazard.' Then added, 'But behave with her, OK?'

Husani didn't know whether this was meant as advice or a threat, or whether to say thanks or tell him to mind his own business. But looking at the guns he decided just to nod.

Luke turned to Becky. 'We're probably sounding like

bossy uncles or something, but phone home and tell your folks you're OK.'

She felt she didn't have to apologise or complain, but knew what she wanted to do: reach out and give him a hug. He held on to her for a moment longer. 'And good luck,' he nodded towards the waiting Husani.

She smiled, thinking he meant with the intended wedding. He didn't explain that he meant when she told her parents.

He turned to Matt. 'Time to get gone?'

Matt nodded and they walked away, stripping off their body armour as they did.

They had left the others face down in the back of the chippy, reasoning that after a while, as the fire got closer, they would risk defying the final order to stay put or be shot. One by one they'd come stumbling out into the alley and into the arriving armed response team.

Up at the cottage, Joey had stumbled into something he hadn't been expecting. With Natasha back home with Tanya, he had told her he needed to pop out. She hadn't asked why.

Outside the cottage was not Luke, but Bobby McBain, leaning against his Range Rover and offering Joey an envelope. Inside was £5,000 in cash.

'What's this?'

'Down payment on the rest of the job?' he said, and indicated the cottage. For once the gravelly voice was sombre as he tossed the cottage keys to Joey. 'Lukey, wants you to finish it. And get it ready to sell.'

'What? What you on about, Bob?'

'Reckons the memories have changed. Time to move on, he said. Also said you'd know what he meant.'

Joey just nodded, understanding the real meaning. And if Bobby was delivering this message, had he been involved all along? 'You been playing me, Bob?'

'How'd you mean?' It was genuine surprise.

'You had Luke sorting out the competition for you?'

But Bobby shook his head. 'No, Joseph. And if we didn't go back a ways, I'd be a bit offended now. I wanted those scumbags out, sure. But I wasn't in that game. Christ, you can make more out of smuggling tobacco than you can for selling your soul to those psychopaths.'

'Then what?' Joey asked.

'I'd like to say I was all public spirited and that but, well, Fatty and his clan were bad for business. Attracting too much attention from our Hilary and her merry men. And you couldn't get boys like Luke and his oppo for five hundred quid now, could you? So, bit of cash to help them out. Why not?' He just shrugged. Good business.

'You were paying?' Joey asked. Shocked.

''Course I was. That's what that envelope is really about. You couldn't have afforded some of the gear they were after. Or had the contacts for all the other stuff. Especially if it escalated.' The gravelly laugh returned. 'Clever bugger, though. Kept us apart until the end. Tradecraft. Need to know. Small cells. All that special ops stuff.'

Joey was struggling to take all this in. He'd thought he was the one helping Luke, but now it seemed he was just a pawn.

'So he played us both?' he finally asked.

'Played us all, mate, played us all. But we're all grown-ups, aren't we? Got what we wanted.'

'Did we?' Joey asked. Unconvinced. Remembering something Luke had said. Wherever they went, a military solution could only nullify the current threat. Buy time. Then it was up to people to find a political solution. 'He might have left us with a bigger problem.'

Bobby gave a nod of agreement. 'Got the same war and peace lecture. He wins the war and we have to win the peace? But that's down to the likes of your Sean, isn't it?'

Joey didn't look too convinced.

'Don't look so depressed, Joe.' The gravel started to rattle in his throat. 'Like the rest of them, he won't be able to create too much trouble. Without you behind him. Lukey might have pulled the trigger, but it was you and yours he was doing it for. Janey was just the excuse. Not the reason. And your Sean won't do much unless the likes of you are behind him. Pushing. Keeping him on track.'

'Do you reckon?'

'I do. But I was up at the old chemical quarry before. Bit of tidying up to do.'

Knowing its usefulness for the likes of Bobby, he didn't

ask for the details. As he'd told Natasha, it was best not
to know. He just waited, wondering where Bobby was
taking him next.

'Reminded me of you.'

This should be good, Joey thought. It was.

'A catalyst. That's what you are, Joe. Something that
makes other things happen.'

'I . . . I didn't do anything.' He waved the envelope.
'Not even this, it seems.'

'But you did, Joe. You stepped up. Crossed the line
because you knew no one else would. Takes real bottle,
that. To put, as our Lukey might say, yourself in the line
of fire. And you're over that line now, mate. No going
back. People will look to see what you do in future. People
like Gazza down on the bridge.'

Joey tried not to react to any of this, but the predator
opposite spotted the telltale eye flicker. And held up his
phone.

'Told you, I know everything. And if this knows,' he
tapped the phone, 'I also know that you are stuck with it
now. You're like the town conscience. We should call you
TC, for short.'

'Er . . . That's a bit much to lay on me, Bob?'

'Y'reckon?' he asked. Deliberately mimicking Joey's
earlier dismissive response. Then cracked the pebble-dash.
'You were born to it. People don't like cops or politicians.
But they'll follow real people. Real leaders.'

'Oh yeah. And what about you in all this? You seem to have it all figured out.'

'Joe, I'm a villain, aren't I? People like the cheap fags, fake designer gear or free parking. But "Vote for Bobby"? Nah. You're stuck with that role, TC. The power behind the throne. Our own *Game of Thrones*. But someone always needs to bankroll 'em. And your Sean will need it too.' He tapped his chest and then Joey's. The meaning clear. It was going to be them. Then he turned away and headed for the Range Rover.

'As you will,' he shouted back. 'And I'll always need a good sparky every now and then.'

With that double-edged sword placed at Joey's feet he sped off, this time without his customary bang on the horn.

Joey turned and looked at the cottage, then at the cash, and wondered where his friend was now.

It was something that rattled round his head as the week rolled on with no word from Luke. Not even when the local paper came out with its best front page to date. A big picture of Craig Harlow, with Sean and Sandra opening Santa's Garden. Out of focus behind their shoulders were, as promised, the Chairs of Planning and Education, but the main headline was: Craig Harlow to be Santa's Helper. Below which ran a second strap: Owner set to run for Council. In the sidebar next to it there were two teasers.

A picture of the burnt-out chippy with the caption: *Chippy Owner Sought In Child Sex Scandal, See page 5*; together with, on page 3, *No Clues In Alien Abduction Theory*.

'Plenty of news this week, then,' Natasha commented, coming up behind Joey and nuzzled his neck as he made his morning Colombian. But she felt the tension.

'What's wrong?' she asked. 'You're in the clear, aren't you?'

'Yeah. No worries,' he replied, trying to sound casual.

'C'mon, what is it? Your neck muscles are like steel.'

'My secret identity out, is it?'

'Joe?' she pulled him round and saw a sadness in his eyes she wasn't expecting. 'What? What's happened?'

'Nah, I'm just being daft. Having a moment,' he said as he tapped the newspaper. 'We might have saved the town. And I might have the town gangster as a future in-law thanks to Tanya's choice of boyfriend, but . . . I may have also lost my oldest friend.'

She put her arms round him and cuddled into his chest. 'He'll be back, Joe. When he needs you again. Just as we need you, and I'm so glad you're back.' Then she smiled. 'Especially for the lie-ins when you do the school run.' She finally felt him relax slightly, as she continued, 'And, anyway, I thought I was your best friend.'

'You are. My best . . . mate,' he said, emphasising the word mate, before adding, 'If you don't suffocate me with your hair.'

'Oh, I can find other ways to do that.' She pushed back

and opened her dressing gown, revealing the pink and black nightdress they had bought on a weekend in Dublin, the first time they had managed to get away alone after Lucy turned five.

'No point in you being back,' she continued with a wicked, grin, 'if we can't take advantage of the kids being at school, eh?'

'No point indeed,' he replied, starting to follow her to the door, just as the doorbell sounded and his phone vibrated. Typical, Joey thought as he went to the door while looking at the phone. A text from Benno. HOW'S LIFE? Joey smiled as he opened the door. A DHL courier offered him a package. Back in the kitchen he opened it to find a slate plaque with the words *Pro Bono Ad Populum* engraved on it. He opened the small card inside to find the translation printed: For the Good of the People. On the other side was: For Old Times' Sake, Conscience and a Better Future.

Joey knew it was from Luke. So he must be safe. Somewhere. As he heard the floorboards above creak, he went to finish the tea while looking at the sender's address on the packaging. Domino's Pizza in Birmingham. His face broke into a satisfied smile as he sent a reply back to Benno. LIFE? INTERESTING.

Acknowledgements

There are two things every producer dreads in television and film: agreeing the billing at the beginning and the credits at the end. In many cases, at the end of a difficult shoot, you sometimes feel that instead of a list of credits, it feels more like a list of who to blame. Fortunately, this particular endeavour has not been like that, but like any creative activity it has required a great number of people to bring it to fruition 'behind the scenes', many of who I simply do not know. But thanks to every one of you. I hope we can meet one day. Also, another wide acknowledgement to all those folk who have given me answers to questions they might not have fully understood at the time, I did it that way to keep them free from blame and protect their reputations. But I am also grateful to them all.

However, all writing is a collaborative activity that requires someone to write and someone to bounce the ideas off. Francesca Pathak at Century has coped brilliantly with being bounced off, while Susan Sandon at Penguin Random House has kept the faith and made sure I got this far.

And, finally, even if it is a bit corny or clichéd, but something learned the hard way about the power of the off switch in television, is that fiction is nothing without its readers and audiences. So, thank you to anyone reading this. At least you showed some interest.